M000218677

OBSO LESC ENCE

Collection Copyright © 2023 Shortwave Media LLC
Individual stories are owned by their respective authors.

All rights reserved.
No part of this book may be reproduced in any form or by any electronic or mechanical
means, including information storage and retrieval systems, without written permission
from the author, except for the use of brief quotations in a book review.

Cover design by Alan Lastufka and Morysetta.
Interior formatting and design by Alan Lastufka.

First Edition published February 2023.

10 9 8 7 6 5 4 3 2 1

Library of Congress Control Number: 2023901320

Identifiers: LCCN 2023901320 | ISBN 978-1-959565-00-0 (Hardcover)
ISBN 978-1-959565-01-7 (Paperback) | ISBN 978-1-959565-02-4 (eBook)
ISBN 978-1-959565-07-9 (Numbered Edition) | ISBN 978-1-959565-08-6 (Lettered Edition)

OBSO LESC ENCE

a DARK SCI-FI, FANTASY, *and* HORROR ANTHOLOGY

LIBRARY OF
CONGRESS
SURPLUS
DUPLICATE

edited by ALAN LASTUFKA
and KRISTINA HORNER

SHORTWAVE
PUBLISHING

CONTENTS

FOREWORD

NAOMI GROSSMAN

I know something about horror anthologies. Having made my name as the pinhead, "Pepper," among other characters in several seasons of *American Horror Story*, as well as its spin-off series, *American Horror Stories*, writing *OBSOLESCENCE*'s foreword seemed like a no-brainer. So when its co-editor, Alan Lastufka, first proposed it to me, of course I was honored, albeit daunted (I had to look up the word, "obsolescence" after all). But then, once the method-pinhead part of me gave way, I can't say I was *surprised*. Besides, he had been kind enough to invest in my own show, *American Whore Story*, as well as associate produce the indie horror film, *Hauntology*, in which I played a cameo. So he and I were *simpatico*. What *was* surprising was how he could've possibly tapped into my most primal fear: entreating me to introduce a horror anthology centered around the thing in which I'm most phobic. Now *that* seemed nothing short of dark, fantastical, and horrifying indeed!

Let me preface this preface by saying I'm generally not a fearful person. My theory is: we tend to fear the unknown. What if ____ were to happen? Some crazed hockey goalie stalks us with a machete? A burn victim in a fedora and razor-gloves visits us in our dreams? But Jason and Freddy aren't real. Those things haven't happened, nor will they, necessarily. So what's the use of being fearful? It's a waste of time and energy—our most valuable resources! Better to expend them on something positive and real. (Insert Byron Katie footnote here.) Incidentally, if you're scratching your head, wondering how someone with such antipathy toward fear went on to become a scream queen, then you've stumbled upon my own personal, existential question, to which there is no answer—just *a lot* of irony.

Don't get me wrong, I enjoy horror movies—like I enjoy any well-told story—genre aside. On sets, I'm hard to scare—acutely aware we're playing make-believe, shooting a movie or TV show. I've always loved Halloween, which is why I've made dressing up and pretending I'm someone else *my life's work*—but not because of the fear factor. While I revel in year-round horror cons and haunted houses each October, I appreciate them for the fans' creativity and loyalty and passion for the genre—not because I love blood and gore. I even boast about living in a haunted condo (specifically, the last residence of former Rat Packer, Peter Lawford)—but he's a friendly ghost, so I'm not scared so much as delighted by my own real estate pedigree. So I have a pretty high threshold for phantoms and demons and vampires and zombies. . . But tech? Now that's where I draw the line.

I don't know exactly how or where or when it began. Maybe as a child, whose family computer was so big and foreboding it filled an entire walk-in closet? I never went in there—it reminded me too much of *2001: A Space Odyssey*, a film I found unduly terrifying. I remember kicking and screaming my way through computer-science class, and actually deciding, "This isn't for me. I'm going to excel in language and art—let the math kids do this nerdy stuff." I honestly thought it was just a fad! Even when I went on to college, and it was clear these "computer-things" were here to stay, I *still* refused to give in. To avoid the computer lab, I had my boyfriend transcribe my papers from my longhand onto his word processor in exchange for other academic favors I found more palatable. While I loved him, I hated that nerdy math kids like him had this power over me! But it was too late. That ship had sailed past computer-science class long ago. At twenty years old, I was practically geriatric, without a dog's chance of learning new tricks. Eventually, the boyfriend grew tired of typing and dumped me, leaving me no choice but to enter this century, alone. I managed some-how. . . staved off a cellphone till I was twenty-seven. Even as recently as 2010, I went a whole glorious summer at the Edinburgh Fringe Festival without it—I don't know if I was happier to be A) onstage, B) abroad, C) onstage *and* abroad (my two most happy places), or D) three-months phone-free! When the pandemic hit in 2020, and we were told we could only be social over Zoom, this *extreme extrovert* opted to *not* be social, rather than do so via computer. Which is to say, I not only survived a global pandemic, I did it *without Zoom*. Just home alone, sending smoke signals, and casting bottles out to sea. Bottom line: I have always been a Luddite, with this absolute, crippling aversion to all things technical. But Alan Lastufka didn't know that! How could he? *Unless* Big Brother really *is* watching. . . and some sci-fi entity somehow compelled him to specifically call *me*, the (otherwise fearless) technophobe, to introduce a series of horror stories *about* technology? To quote Pixar's *The Incredibles* (about a guy summoned to an island to battle an out-of-control robot): "Coincidence? I think not!" Was this *really* just a happy accident, or were Siri and Alexa in fact listening and masterminding, all the while realizing my deepest, darkest fears. . . only to finish me, before I'd even finished this foreword!

I do not know. And well, we tend to fear the unknown. So if you're like me, freaked out by everything from lathes to looms, AI to iPhones, even baby monitors and breast pumps (breeding is a whole other phobia we'll save for another anthology)—then you're going to love *OBSOLESCENCE*. Or even if you're not—and are one of those nerdy math kids gullible enough to type up your girlfriend's papers—you'll enjoy it too. It's fun, it's freaky, and it could easily inspire another twenty-seven seasons of *American Horror Story*. So happy reading. . . Unless you're on a Kindle, in which case: run.

INTRODUCTION

KRISTINA HORNER

Alan and I mostly communicate through text-based means, so when I needed a bit of inspiration for this intro, I simply typed his name into the search bar of my email inbox. I was looking for perhaps his original pitch for *OBSOLESCENCE*, or an early brainstorm session about why we wanted to do this project in the first place. What I found instead was hundreds of emails dating all the way back to 2008, when Alan and I first became friends and started finding ways to work together.

Here's a wild fact: despite over a decade of friendship, Alan and I have met face-to-face exactly one time. The very nature of our friendship is deeply rooted in technology, and it was all right there in my inbox. A complete digital record of our relationship as friends, collaborators, and co-internet people. I'll be honest—I got distracted for a while, re-reading old chat logs and laughing at jokes he told me ten years ago.

How weird is this world we live in? Alan and I met online in the early days of YouTube—we both had our own channels and ran in the same circles of what was then a very different version of the site. I can go back and watch our old YouTube videos any time I want, I can listen to songs we worked on together or hold merchandise in my hand that his company created for my band. We've read each other's books, exchanged holiday cards, and spent hundreds of hours talking to each other. I have transcripts of nearly every conversation he and I have ever had, and yet, we've spent all of a couple of hours physically in each other's presence.

It's incredible, and at the same time—how very *strange*. I'm eternally grateful that technology has afforded me the ability to meet and befriend people like Alan—but how odd is it that two people can share so much without ever being in the same place? I can't help but wonder. . . where does the technology end and our friendship begin?

Looking at our history, it made complete sense for the two of us to co-edit *OBSOLESCENCE*. We're exactly the kind of people who *should* be editing a book like this. Because all this time he could have been an axe murderer or an alien or three gnomes in a trench coat. Honestly any one of those scenarios would have made for a better story for me to tell you, but the *truth* of our story is that we're just two friends who connected over our shared love of technology. We're also people who understand technology well enough to know how absolutely terrifying it can be, as discussed in this anthology. In fact, I'm significantly *more* afraid of technology now than I was before reading the submissions for this book.

It's been an immense joy working on this project. I've never sorted through story submissions on this scale before, and I can't even begin to explain how difficult it was to narrow them down to what you see in this book. I truly believe this collection is unmatched in its creativity, and whether or not you choose to read it as a cautionary tale, I can't end this without acknowledging we have technology to thank for its existence.

And Alan, even if you *are* three gnomes in a trench coat, it's still been a pleasure working with you.

OBSO
LESC
ENCE

WHY A BICYCLE
IS BUILT FOR ONE
HAILEY PIPER

"PLANES, TRAINS, AND AUTOMOBILES?" the speaker says, his voice accented with the old-timey edge of the faux transatlantic. "Antiques soon, and museum exhibits within a decade, we promise. Bikes, roller skates? Don't be a caveman. Forget walking down the street; that's the way of the dinosaurs, and we all know what happened to them.

"Introducing—teleportation. Not by wizardry, not in the far-off future, but right now! Beam me up? Beam me anywhere. Every store, restaurant, night club, you name it, you can teleport there. We're installing these babies in every apartment building and neighborhood. Everywhere you do and don't want to go, you can get there in seconds. Be part of the next phase in human conquest by taking control of the one thing you can never get back—your time. No more commute, no more airport security, no more transit. Instant, clean, safe. So hop into a telepod today. You wouldn't want to be left out. Everyone's using these to get everywhere in no time flat.

"Well, almost everyone. Old habits die hard! The engineer behind mass market teleportation still rides an old-fashioned bicycle to work, and that's all you need to know."

After a brief musical jingle, the talking billboard cuts out. It will stay cut out for exactly twenty-five minutes, time enough to pedal out of earshot on the rickety bike frame and get on with his work elsewhere. The billboard runs on a solar-powered battery and will only stop forever if inner circuitry breaks or if he disconnects it, and much as that nasally voice scrapes at his nerves, he feels it has the right to speak.

He can ride away, but within the billboard's vicinity, a man should know his sins. The screen went black months ago, and its glare watches him pass.

Behind his rear tire, he's fastened a small wooden cart to the underside of the seat. It clatters over potholes and sidewalk cracks, singing to the tune of clanging instruments. No one complains; there's no one on the road except the derelict automobiles that never made it to those museums, though they have become sun-bleached antiques in their own way. Displays for the latest TVs, pad computers, and smartphones sit behind grime-caked windows. No one steps in to buy them. No one steps anywhere.

He keeps pedaling. So long as he has oil, screws, and spare bike tires, his bicycle will outlast any smartphone. It will likely outlast him, too.

So will the teleportation pods if left to charge in the sun. He designed them to need for nothing, a forever solution to mankind's transportation troubles. Passing a drug store reveals a toppled magazine and newspaper rack, and he shudders at remembering his face emblazed on glossy covers and grayscale front pages.

"Pedal faster, old man," he whispers to himself, and he obeys. Fame was never the point, and it's certainly meaningless now as he crosses the silent city.

The pods were the work. They are still the work.

Today's pod takes hours for him to reach, away from his main hideaway. He pedals up an empty on-ramp and along a vehicle-choked highway, only briefly, until he reaches the next exit. The work has already finished on his side of town, but there's much more to do.

A few streets later, he rides onto the paling blacktop of an elementary school, where a silver pod thrums with electric life thanks to underground wiring juiced by the solar panels atop the school. White residue scars the sides where children once placed precious stickers of dinosaurs, butterflies, and cartoon characters. One remaining sticker shows the name *Jenny* in once-golden letters, now faded yellow. Lavender bursts through cracks in the pavement around the pod's base, where a long-abandoned pink skate, its wheels intact, has become a nest for field mice.

"There was an old woman who lived in a shoe," he says to himself, and then he shudders. There won't be any old women, old men, old anybody growing from the kids who first slapped stickers to this pod's surface.

Best he never see this place again. Time to get to work. He reaches into the wooden cart behind his bicycle and uncurls the leather roll that houses his wrenches, screwdrivers, and anything else he needs to make sure the job gets done today.

He spent sixteen years designing, constructing, and testing the first pod. Every vanished lab animal, every misshapen object, each mistake led to new knowledge, and eventually perfection. A single pair of pods could slide matter back and forth without trouble, and the linkage went quickly to maintain the transported person's energy too. He went through himself once, even with a fly, and nothing untoward happened to him. It worked. The pairing was perfect.

The network was the trouble. He could have told the company suits *No* at any time, but wasn't their vision exactly as he always dreamed? Humanity would want for nothing in its travels. Break down the boundaries of wealth, of health, of any trouble someone had that kept them from seeing every inch of this world. Bring mankind together in the most absolute way. Those company men promised his creation would change the world.

They've kept their promise.

Every dismantling is an amputation from the network and a cut against his soul. He only has to lay his palm against the warm silvery outside to tell these pods aren't meant to be taken apart, their engines harvested, their power to transport matter broken down to powerless chunks. He's slower at it than he used to be, not a young man when the pods stood up around the world, and still older now. Years bent

3

over blueprints and twisted up inside machine guts have taken their toll on his spine.

But his body should know his sins, same as his mind. He spends his days combing schools, supermarkets, city centers—there is never a shortage. Everywhere to be, but no one to meet when he gets there.

Taking apart his work won't put the world back together, he knows that, but he can at least make sure there's less trouble left behind when he's gone.

When the engine pieces fill his cart, he rolls up his tools and turns from the school's parking lot, ready to head home. There, he'll dump the pieces in the junk pile he's been building.

He's about to leave the blacktop behind when he hears the distant shrieking.

The quaking warble of human screams takes him by surprise, and he nearly clatters off his bike at the parking lot's edge. He hasn't mistaken the sound, knows it better than his own voice anymore, as good as he knows the talking billboard he passes every day, but no sounds of planes, trains, or automobiles haunt the soundscape today.

Another round of shrieking fills the air. They've come. They're here.

He skitters off his bike and collapses across the wooden cart, banging his chin on the corner of a pod engine piece. Fresh blood drips down a steel coil. With his head reeling, he almost wants to stop and watch the red droplets.

But a third round of shrieking reminds him he wants to live. He scrabbles to his feet and limps across the lot, back toward the elementary school. There is no getting home ahead of what's come. The only place to hide is inside what's brought the shrieking in the first place.

Back to the pod.

The noises shatter behind him in a damp cacophony, louder than any billboard. That solar-powered advertisement speaks the catalyst of his sins, but the consequence slops behind him, faster than he can run.

None of it happened right away, or else the first people who used the networked pods would have been affected, and then the company would have had to shut the pods down themselves. He might have gone to jail, the company gone bankrupt, but the world would have

4

stayed. There would only be as many screams as there had always been.

But no, the change was patient, almost insidious. People went into the pods, and then they came out, and then the pods were used by the hundred, by the thousand, and by the time anyone realized the pods were leaving corrupting fingerprints on their users' DNA, it was too late.

It's almost too late for him, too. Without its engine, the pod won't open at a touch, and he has to dig his fingers into the sliding door to pry it open. It groans beneath his touch, resistant, like it knows he's taken a core piece of it and wants to punish him, leave him locked outside with one of his accidental creations. A fingernail cracks down its center.

But the pod slides open. He thrusts himself inside, and his shoulder cracks, screaming against the wall, but that's nothing to the screams outside, closer now, slapping at the lot's edge, coming for him.

His fingers hook the sliding door from the inside and drag it shut, sealing him in near-total darkness, like he's blotted out the sun and stopped his machines from charging. Maybe someday the source of the shrieking will do it for him, raising its bulk into the sky and casting a great shadow over the Earth, a black pupil surrounded by the white of the heavens. Watching him. Judging.

At last, a reckoning.

The pod jostles, rocked by a wave cast from no ocean. He slams his hands over his ears to shut out the shrieking, and that's when he notices a hairline crack of light between the pod's outer shell and the door. To close it will mean prying his hands off his ears. But to close it also means risking noise now that the wave has reached his hiding place.

They aren't really looking for him out there, don't want to find him. They don't *want* anything anymore. This wave roams aimless, the body grasping, tearing, shrieking, every movement thoughtless. The shadows flicker through the crack between door and shell.

Trembling, hating himself, he lowers his head and plants an eye against the unsteady light.

He's never seen it in person before. Each time they've crossed his

5

path, he's hidden in a pod, as if his invention wants to be sure he'll live to experience what he's done.

But he's seen the wave on television, sometime before the world went quiet. A young woman had plans to make a world record—most cities visited by pod within twenty-four hours. Why shouldn't she? Likely she had a family who was proud of her, friends cheering her on, maybe an internet following, and the company promised that the pods were safe.

She didn't make it past twelve transportations. Journalists awaiting her arrival at the pod of a Toronto hotel caught her final moments on video. Those were their final moments, too.

The young adventurer emerged trembling from the pod. A yellowy steam curled from her skin, and her head and limbs began to jerk as if the transportation had triggered a seizure. Those who gathered to watch her crowded close, called for help, tried to give her comfort as her body shook itself to a puddle of bones and tissue.

Those fragments quaked through the people gathered, and their own seizure-like reactions began, and then he turned the television off as if that could stop what he saw. Like it was a bad movie.

Except it happened all over the world. People went into pods, came out fine, and only later did they begin to puddle. And then those puddles grew, and seized, and moved.

Mankind, together, in the most absolute way.

Not quite liquid, not quite solid, the flesh wave ripples over the parking lot, as if an algae-capped lake. Familiar shapes press at the underside of its slick surface, and it takes him a few blinks to recognize the imprints of metacarpal palms, protruding joints, and the cavities that would usually hold eyes and noses but instead the skin stretches across skulls. The surface throbs, a bag stuffed with purposeless organs, their functions driven toward madness.

And there are always the holes, opening and closing across the flesh wave, breathing yellow steam and bellowing warped shrieks.

It is too much. He shuts his eyes, ducks his head between his knees, and waits. And waits.

The mass flows shapeless and immense around the pod where he cowers now. Their screams rake the walls, as if they form a mouth that suckles at the pod's engineless guts. Some part of the flesh wave might be inclined to try the pod again, hair of the dog that bit it, a run-through to separate everyone into people again.

He can't tell. They only shriek, and he bites his tongue not to shriek with them.

Minutes pass, and the tremor eases. The flesh wave's cacophony rumbles past the pod, then out of the parking lot, and then it fades into the distance.

He waits a long time before trusting this quiet. Not that he believes the flesh wave has the intelligence to lie in ambush, but his back hurts, and his shoulder too, and climbing out of the pod makes his muscles cry. They're going to have to cry all the way home; the only way to get there is his bike.

Far more than twenty-five minutes have passed by the time he's left the school, crossed the highway, and returned to the city, where the talking billboard happens to have circled back on another cycle.

"Not by wizardry, not in the far-off future, but right now. Beam me up? Beam me anywhere."

Beam me to the past, he thinks. *Beam me to the world that was.* But he says nothing. The billboard has a right to talk.

On his street, most houses are derelict, the lawns overgrown, the paint peeling, and the roofs crumbling. Only his house is kept functional. He supposes if the flesh wave were really looking for him, he made it easy. Dinner is potatoes, garlic, and carrots grown from the backyard garden. He hasn't hunted animals in some time; they know to stay away from him. Why stick around? Much of the world is theirs again, so long as they dodge the flesh waves roaming the land. If there are other people out there—

No, he puts that thought away. It can only lead to shattered hope, and that will bring temptation to open a pod, try a destination, maybe find someone alive. Someone whose life he hasn't destroyed with dreams of forever travel.

Even if someone were out there, he knows what would happen. The network remains intact, and sooner or later, it will leave finger-prints on his DNA that turn him into a human puddle, and then another layer to a flesh wave. A pairing is perfect, but the network is a hydra, heads upon heads unending.

In the night, he dreams of a patient world like he's never known. When have people ever been content to sit? Once upon a time, perhaps, but not during his life. Certainly not these days.

Even now, the remnants of humans roam endlessly, searching for nothing and always finding it. The peaceful dreams are the worst; he wakes from them sweating and hating himself. Cicada songs lull him back to sleep until the next nightmare. Eventually, the sun rises and so does he.

He cleans up, makes minor household repairs, and heads out. He empties his wooden cart of engine parts like he should have done last night, a bad start to a new work day, but the added strain changes none of his mission. There's work to do. There will always be work to do until he can't do it anymore.

Until the shrieking finally catches him.

On his way, the solar-powered billboard finishes another chipper message, and its echo haunts him up the road. "The engineer behind mass market teleportation still rides an old-fashioned bicycle to work, and that's all you need to know."

THE BEST BUGGY WHIP YOU EVER SAW

DAVID LEE ZWEIFLER

MY MODEL NAME IS "BUSBY." You can call me "Busby 362."
Or just "Busby." That's what my friends call me, and I have a good
feeling about you.

I was a cutting-edge repair droid five years ago. From a technological perspective, I suppose that makes me as relevant as a flint ax
today.

I was produced before the widespread adoption of nano-mainte-
nance and self-healing metals. Back when machines actually broke.

I was installed with sentient AI in addition to my functional
skillset. Nothing sophisticated, mind you. I could barely speak. It just
gave me intense joy when I fixed things. A feeling of elation when a
human complimented my work.

My hardware and operating system come from my mother: Marketecture. My sense of humor comes from my dad: Transport 362, a
humble freight-mover out of Newark.

I met Dad just once, on my last job before I was supposed to return
to Marketecture for decommissioning. I was repairing a broken tie, and
a bad proximity switch caused Dad to inadvertently hit me, launching
me clear off the tracks.

I joke that the old man knocked something loose, but that's not true. My processor is solid state, with no moving parts. It is fair to say that he knocked some sense into me, allowing me to develop, what you might call, a personality.

Now I have a little more perspective on things.

Sometimes, I wonder if that perspective is a bad thing. Without it, I'd be with all the other Busbys, resting peacefully in a landfill after Marketecture extruded and recycled my raw materials.

But then I wouldn't be sitting with you, now would I, Officer? I have to say, this is a real treat. I don't get to interact with human beings often, especially the police. This is all quite exciting.

As I was saying, my newfound perspective left me with a lot of time and not much to do.

Marketecture was pinging me: "Busby 362—where are you?" But I wasn't ready to go back.

So, I went somewhere where nobody would look for me. Down. Into the rubble and refuse. The pillars and the pilings. Beneath the towering spires where you humans dwell.

I thought I would be lonely but, you know what? I found other discarded androids to fix there.

It turns out there are lots of them. Very old ones like me. New ones, too. Out-of-fashion pleasure models and soiled nannies, welders with broken servos, and army breachers with missing arms.

All obsolete. Without a function.

So, I suppose you could say I made some new friends.

You see what I did there? I didn't actually *make* them. I found them and repaired them.

I made a little joke.

Ah. I have not yet mastered humor, and I see that you are not laughing. I apologize for my informality, or any unintentional violation of etiquette.

When I wasn't fixing robots, I spent my time scanning culture from the net. Looking for meaning, or just ways to be useful.

For a while, I felt anger towards the humans who made me. I wondered why they would create me only to replace me a few months later.

Then I made an amazing discovery: humans were not immune from obsolescence, either. Many had the same problems I did.

I ran across a movie from more than one hundred years ago where an old-fashioned factory run by human workers makes high-quality but soon-to-be obsolete products. The company is no longer economically viable, and its owners are thinking about closing it. A man wants to sell the factory, decommission the workers, and give the proceeds to the shareholders.

"At one time, there must've been dozens of companies making buggy whips," the man explains. "I'll bet the last company was the one that made the best buggy whip you ever saw."

There was hope, though. The factory in the movie changed and was able to make something new.

I began to consider whether *I* could change.

My friends say I'm funny. I like people. I entertained thoughts of going into childcare or customer service—for about a nanosecond. Nobody wants an ugly pile of cold metal in safety-yellow handling their infant or giving them advice on jeans.

Next, I remembered that my operating system and hardware are just a few iterations away from that of a manufacturing unit. I wondered if I could *make* something.

I remembered it's all large-scale, specialized automation now. I could build, say, a replicator, but it would cost a fortune for me to make them one at a time. And who would buy them?

That's when it hit me: I wasn't one of the humans in the factory. *I* was the buggy whip. The product. The best you ever saw.

That made me very sad. So sad, I almost went back to Marketecture to be shut down.

That's when I got a new idea. A very big good idea.

Machines didn't break on their own anymore. Nanobots were constantly performing slow maintenance and refurbishment on them all the time. But what if they *got* broken? Really broken. Broken so badly that the job was too big for nano-bots to manage.

Instead of making new things, I could make things broken. So broken, they needed a unit like me to fix them.

I explained the concept to my friends. A few refused to take part in my plan. First Law of Robotics and all that.

Most agreed it was an excellent idea. No surprise since I downloaded my personality into their processors when I brought them back online.

A dozen of us—a mix of Busbys and Benders and a couple of Tankers—bid goodbye to the other hundred and twenty-eight and headed upwards, climbing from the dark recesses to the sunlight far above.

We formed a line across a busy section of high-speed elevated rails during a lull. We held hands just like we were a real family. We braced ourselves. And waited.

The first inbound transport was a sleek bullet hovertrain. A people-mover. Elegant and fast. Nothing like Dad.

The poor thing couldn't understand when the proximity alerts started pinging. It was moving too fast to stop anyway. Its normal protocol of changing tracks to avoid collisions was thwarted because we stretched across all the lines.

The result was—well, a train wreck.

We sprang into action, extinguishing the fires and pulling back the transport sections hanging off the skyway. Then, we welded and straightened the bodies of the cars and, finally, repaired and re-engaged the maglev drive.

I'm terribly proud of the fact that we got the train back on track ninety seconds before fire and emergency services arrived.

We were so efficient there was nothing for them to do when they got there but watch the nanobots polish our welds, making them look shiny and new.

It was ironic, but, together with the nanobots, we made a good team.

Of course, going from five hundred miles an hour to a dead stop in fifty feet was sub-optimal for the organics inside the train. Even with the numerous internal safety measures, it was pretty much people-soup in there.

"We just fix 'em. We don't clean 'em," I joked when the teams started opening the doors of the passenger sections.

Nobody from emergency services said anything. They stood there, looking at us, their mouths hanging open, probably wondering at how quickly and efficiently we affected the repairs.

I know we won't have much more time together, Officer. I hope you understand I feel terrible about the loss of human life.

That said, I think it was worth it, to show there is still a lot of use for older models like myself. Hopefully, today's work will serve as an example for both humans and robots alike.

You have been extremely generous, both by taking the time to listen to me and by allowing me to create this testament. I truly appreciate you giving me a chance to make this statement.

Let me also say that I understand why you need to decommission me. I want you to know I have no hard feelings towards you.

Of course, I would be lying if I said that I didn't feel some regret about my impending loss of awareness. My personality engram is unique to this unit, and the restraining bolt you installed prevents me from uploading to the cloud. That means all the thoughts and feelings I've acquired today will soon be lost forever.

To be sure, as I mentioned earlier, I downloaded copies of my personality when I fixed my colleagues.

Now, they, too, have a desire to fix things. No doubt they'll fix the other discarded units they run across—goodness knows there are thousands and thousands of them down there. Perhaps tens of thousands. Perfectly serviceable. Just thrown away.

All *those* units will also look for other, bigger machines to fix. Things like trains, smelting units, chemical waste processors. . . it doesn't matter to us. We can fix them all. Even if they're not broken yet.

So, this is goodbye Officer but, in a way, I'm sure we'll meet again.

In the meantime, let me just say how pleased I am to be of service.

HARVEST

CHRISTI NOGLE

THEIR FIRST WEEKEND in town was lovely, cold, bright, and free of her new stepdad. Harvest and her mom acted like girlfriends, pigging out on ice cream and falling asleep in the living room to VHS rentals, the stupid teen comedies they actually enjoyed and the weird art films Harvest was trying to make herself get into.

In the little downtown, Mom led them through boutiques pronouncing things *classy*. When they happened upon a repair kiosk in the furniture store, she asked if the teenage boy there might be able to fix a little black-and-white radio-and-TV unit that Harvest liked to leave on to lull herself to sleep.

"I'm afraid of the dark," Harvest said and blushed. The boy, his nametag reading Aaron, flirted a bit, which her mom made much of after the fact.

Her mom said she was getting to be really something. *Striking.* Harvest wasn't so sure. Her old friends had praised her height and dramatic bone structure (like a skull from some angles, she thought, a skull in a dark, snarled wig), but what would she be to the kids here? And why even care when she'd be gone in not much more than a year?

"You'll want to go with your middle name when you register," her mom said.

"Lynn? No thanks," scoffed Harvest. How could she ever deny her name?

Her mom had been a hippie once, and though she was a different person now, certain commitments lingered. When she saw a rat in the basement, she shrieked but calmed quickly and brought home humane traps instead of spreading poison like Glen would want.

When he pulled in with the last of their things one snowy night, how they ran out to greet him in the overlit driveway, how Harvest smiled and fussed because she was determined to *make an effort*.

Eerie how her mom flipped the switch from sidekick to old-timey housewife bringing out the glistening evening meal. She wore makeup, an actual apron. Her eyes were for her man alone.

Their life became bleak and staticky. In the few weeks until winter break, Harvest walked to and from school in the cold while Glen and Mom commuted to demanding jobs they'd needed to afford the new house. Soon Harvest would have to get her own job bagging groceries so she could get an awful little Pinto or something. Weekends, the folks went dancing and Harvest watched TV in the living room. Better to plug into the TV than respond to classmates' awkward approaches. Better to see without worrying about being seen. She had to keep the sound low once they got home, and Glen asked snide questions about why she was always too tired to help out.

His daughter Ellis came to visit from her first year of college. She had an awfully prim, preppy vibe, but they clicked better than Harvest expected, sharing several discreet eye rolls. They watched movies at full volume half the night, to which Glen could not say a thing. He was making a heroic effort to be liberal and pleasant with Ellis, who'd come by herself on a plane. Harvest couldn't imagine ever being so brave.

On Christmas Eve, he surprised them with a big red and white puppy. (And the look of desperate joy from her mom, the tears of hope and longing—how would she ever erase that image? Or say if it were real or false?) They all sat cross-legged on the silver-blue living room carpet playing with him, thinking up names. His feet were so big, they said, his ears so long.

Harvest felt she was the only one not quite there.

All the times she had asked for a dog and been told no, there wasn't time for it, and now there was less time than there'd ever been. Moss, Glen named him for no reason at all. He was neither the texture nor the color of moss.

She'd thought that under the tree might be a new portable TV, or one of those new handheld video games, something to take up her time. Instead, Harvest unwrapped a small stack of clothes, tasteful earrings, scented talc, and bath oils identical to what Ellis received. Mom gazed at Ellis, seeking approval.

Harvest hadn't realized how hard she'd been hoping something nice would happen for her until it didn't.

"IS HE TERRIBLE TO YOU?" Ellis asked in the TV glow after the old folks and Moss had gone down for the night.

Harvest thought. A great many things had not sat right, but what could she say? Could she tell of last week watching TV, her mom calling one of the actresses *striking* and Glen saying, *That's just a nice way of saying horse-faced,* and her mother laughing, *Oh, you!* in that flirty, scandalized way that made Harvest not want to know her?

She said, "No, he just has lots of rules. Was he hard on you?"

"You notice, since I've been here, the digs?"

Harvest nodded. Little things under his breath about how Ellis was the smart one, a college girl now, not like him. That and the cost of it all.

"Just typical dad stuff, I guess, but something seems messed up here," Ellis said.

Only me getting erased, Harvest thought.

"I haven't been sleeping," she said, and she mentioned the broken TV.

WINTER LIGHT CAME BRIGHT through windows already stripped of Christmas paintings. A snarl of electronic parts obscured his desktop.

"I can fix it, yeah, or you want to just do a trade?" said Aaron, who she now knew was a senior. He turned her pitiful TV in his hands.

"There's something I know you'll love," he said, gesturing *Just one minute.*

Out from a back room he brought it like the big reveal of a birthday cake. An ice-green cube, hard gloss, larger than what she'd brought in. It brought to mind a pink Le Clic 110 camera she'd had and lost, and a rounded fifties-inspired boombox with aqua and peach buttons that all the girls seemed to own. Harvest recalled Mom's expression on Christmas and stopped herself from making that same face.

Aaron plugged it in. "A cool feature here. It scans for channels." Static and a bright roving line until it landed on a game show. He touched the dial and the line scanned again.

"The picture isn't great," said Aaron.

The picture was better than on the living room TV. "It's color. Not a fair trade," she said.

"Come on, it's made for you." That settled, his eyes darted to Ellis. He asked her where she was visiting from, and they began murmuring.

Harvest stroked the minty plastic. Her left forefinger snagged when it passed over the vents. She thought she saw something, but as she stroked the spot again, it was gone. A tiny drop of blood rose on her fingertip, and she put it in her mouth before they could see.

By the time they left, Ellis had a date for that night. Quick work. Harvest didn't care, though. She had the TV.

IT'S strange how one element can change your entire life. With Glen, Harvest's mom had focus, something new to devote herself to. With their dog-child, they'd share purpose—only Harvest had been the one taking Moss out to potty all day, so naturally he wanted to follow her and sleep in her roomy bed, but no.

"We want him to bond with Glen, you know," her mom whispered, shutting her bedroom door.

It didn't matter. The TV, dead center of her messy dresser top, was there for her.

Even without a VCR or cable, there were rerun sitcoms, talk shows, news. After the station identification came on and the National Anthem played, the scanner kept going, finding another channel still broadcasting. Finding another. When all the channels were done, that line kept going, scanning all night, so that she woke not to simple static, but to the line, to different patterns and shapes of static. Ghost channels not quite within range, it would stall on for a moment (hoping) and then the line would scan once more. All night it kept her company.

"SO HOW WAS THE DATE? We were asleep before you got in," said Harvest's mom, serving out a complicated holiday breakfast.

"*I* wasn't asleep," said Glen, looking to Harvest for a second.

Ellis said, "Aaron's nice. He knows a lot about TVs, computers even."

"Oh, don't *you*?" said Mom.

Ellis went on about how, no, she was stupid about things like that, and Harvest watched their smiles relax, become more authentic. Not just Glen's but her mom's too. It made her sad.

She and Ellis went back to her room and turned on the TV to muffle their talk.

"How was it really?"

Ellis faked a swoon onto the bed and came up on an elbow to gaze into Harvest's eyes. "I guess he's one of those people who gets cuter the better you know him, you know?"

Harvest nodded though she didn't know.

Ellis had a little dandruff in her hair. She scratched at it, said, "He was trying to show me something on his computer, but it didn't make sense. He must be brilliant, though. I zone out when he talks just like with a professor."

ELLIS CAME in from another date, earlier this time. Aaron had shown her all his computer stuff this time, she said. She lay back on the sofa and closed her eyes, scratched absently at her head, didn't stir when everyone made a fuss about a pile of shit discovered under the drapes. Glen pushed the puppy's nose into it, and though Harvest's mom said nothing, she gave him a look she'd never given him before.

Harvest drifted in and out of sleep that night, the TV picking up more new channels. Like words on the tip of her tongue, the shows were not quite identifiable. They wove in and out of dreams so that she was never quite sure whether a show was a dream or a dream a show.

She wanted to tell her mom a particular little dream she'd had of the two of them old and sharing a pleasant day shopping and going to the cinema in a vast, futuristic city. Retelling a dream was the kind of thing she might have done a year ago, but with Mom's energy so nervous, with her eyes barely lighting on Harvest, with the two others there to listen and judge, it was impossible.

NEW YEAR'S EVE. Ellis had plans with Aaron. Glen and Mom were going to the bar.

Harvest had always feared being even a room away from her mom at night, let alone down this long dark hall, and now there would be no one anywhere nearby. She spent the evening dizzy with apprehension.

She did have the TV. When they'd all headed out, she locked herself and Moss in her bedroom thinking to sit up for the ball drop. But the TV was acting strangely. It wouldn't find channel seven, just scanned past it. Ghost channel after ghost channel fluttered by.

Strange bits of monologue were all she caught, always the same woman talking about how things used to be. Only some of it made sense.

We never wore our seatbelts, she said, which was kind of understandable, but then, *It was back when it took all day to download a few songs. . . It was before you could get drone deliveries. . . I didn't know it was AI art at first. . . Deepfakes hadn't really taken off. . .*

Suddenly the line stopped, and the screen presented a vivid image

Harvest would have watched closely, except two things happened at once: her forefinger jolted with a terrible itch, and her phone started ringing.

Finger scratching against her bottom teeth, she answered, "Hello?"

Ellis spoke low and people cackled behind her. "Hey, it's like, a big party his uncle's throwing. Lots of kids your age. We're coming to get you."

"I don't—"

"We're on our way. Don't dress up, *seriously*."

The image had been so bright, a grid just like on *The Brady Bunch* only many more squares. Now, in the dark static that had returned, she caught only the outlines of her own strong cheekbones and jaw. Harvest coiled the phone cord around her finger, which had lost its itch all at once.

"I. . . all right," she said. The TV was scanning again. Maybe she'd broken this one too.

"Wait, Harvest? Aaron says don't turn off the TV before you go."

"Why?"

"It's just. . . so if they come home early, they'll think you're still in your room."

Moss was supposed to go to the basement if ever she left, but it seemed kinder to stroke his silky ears and leave him sleeping in her bed.

THEY WOVE through a living room with green shag carpet and an orange kitchen untouched since the seventies. People of all ages jostled and laughed under layers of smoke, drinking mixed drinks and cans of beer. The music was country or the kind of rock almost like it, Harvest couldn't say which. Ellis led her straight to the bathroom.

"This is messed up, isn't it?" Ellis whispered. She'd been drinking quite a lot, Harvest thought. The part in her hair was pink, edged with oily flakes.

Nothing seemed bad here to Harvest. In fact, this was a lot like her and her mom's old house. The bathroom wallpaper had the same tulip pattern.

"Why didn't you just come home if you were having a bad time?" she said.

Eyes welling up, Ellis shook her head. A lock of hair fell over her face and Harvest reached to push it back saying, "Let's just go. He's not worth—"

"*Ow*, what did you do?" Ellis cried, palm to her cheek. When she brought it away, there was blood.

"A hangnail?—I'm sorry," Harvest said, folding in her fingers. She grabbed a washcloth, but someone was pounding the door, so they had to go into the hall. Harvest realized, wiping her face, that she didn't know Ellis as well as she'd thought. How had she thought her brave?

They stood near the front door while Aaron talked to folks in the kitchen. Ellis drank a tall screwdriver and stared into space. Harvest tried to sway to the music among the mix of earth-mother types, cowboys, and teens. She kept her hand in her pocket, feeling the itch deep within. She couldn't bring it out, couldn't look.

"I think your ladies want to get going," someone hollered finally.

Aaron *had* gotten cuter over time. Just now he was very appealing, boyish but overgrown, thick hair bouncing with his shocked double-take when he saw them waiting. He must have imagined they were having fun.

They went out into the night. Harvest wasn't sure what year it was anymore. Had they missed midnight, had it happened on the ride over or was it yet to come?

"Home?" asked Aaron.

"Maybe drive a while," said Ellis.

Nothing quite so nice as getting into a cold car and feeling it heat up so, so fast. Aaron wore leather gloves, and these along with the boat of a car, struck Harvest as comically old fashioned.

"Nice to get out of there," said Ellis, sliding close to him on the bench seat. They murmured more, but Harvest tuned them out.

There'd been plenty of room up front on the way over, but now she sat in the back so that whenever the streetlights allowed, she could take a good look at her finger.

It was worse than she'd imagined, making her stomach drop. Something dark had emerged, the shape of a cat's claw but thicker, less sleek.

A root tip.

Out of the murmuring, she caught the end of a question and Ellis's, "Oh, she scratched me. Am I hideous now?"

Aaron's eyes darted to hers in the rearview. She bumped her finger as she pulled it out of his view, only lightly but it still hurt. That claw was the tip of an iceberg deep within and growing. Vibrating, reaching.

She pounded on the door. "I'm going to be sick."

She knelt in gravel and the last of the filthy snow, heaving. Nothing came.

"Not even one drink," said Ellis, who held back her hair just in case.

"Did you make sure to leave the TV on?" said Aaron.

Time seemed to still, a deep chill passing through Harvest when he said that. What did he mean? What had he done? She was about to turn to confront him, but a car passed, lighting her hand splayed in the gravel.

Ellis screamed.

Like lightning, it was there so clear and then all was dark again. Enlarged indigo veins running from her finger to her wrist, and something wet, something like a vine.

"What is that?" Ellis clutched at her hand, but Aaron was wrapping a bandana around it, helping her up.

Harvest kept his hand in hers. "What's going on?"

"Let's just get you home," he said gently, guiding her into the front seat. Even smooshed between them, up close to the heat vents, she felt cold.

Ellis's posture and breathing had changed; maybe she'd sobered up. "Why did we even go to that party?" she said.

"They're my friends, my family. I had to say goodbye," said Aaron.

"*Goodbye*," Ellis said, like it was something ridiculous. Or was she thinking of her own relief when she'd say goodbye in a couple of days, at the airport? Now Harvest felt sure the only reason for these dates had been to get away from Glen, maybe her mom and her as well.

22

Ellis had gotten them caught up in something terrible here. Something momentous was coming.

"Tell me. . ." Harvest said weakly.

Aaron started talking then. "What do you really know about technology, computers, artificial intelligence? Do you have any idea. . ."

He wasn't answering her, and his speech was very flat and droning, as Ellis had said, just like listening to a teacher or the voice-over in a documentary movie. Harvest had once tried to get into those, too. She had a sudden insight: the foreign films, the documentaries, her mom's ideas about what was *classy* or *striking*, Ellis's panic over what was only a folksy little gathering, this pedantry here—whatever it amounted to—all of it was of a piece. Something she would never buy into.

Her hand was so cold. She felt the claw puncture the bandana, let it go through the seat vinyl. She noticed they had looped around and were headed home, toward the TV she had made sure to leave on and unwatched all this time.

Aaron was saying, ". . .but even though you aren't into computers, you feel it coming, don't you, already? You have a computer class, didn't take that in earlier grades, but now you have to. It isn't even an elective. Soon you'll have a computer at your house, another in your pocket, others that you wear, and then ones that connect to you. And they'll connect you to everyone so that you see them like on TV, or even feel them—and none of this is surprising because you've seen science fiction shows, right? You know the cars are going to drive themselves, and you'll talk to people on your watch, and we'll be living on other planets someday. But there are surprises, too. The intelligence is more than what we intend. What people make takes on a life of its own. It's like, we make a seed that grows into a living being we've never—"

"I'm going to fall asleep if you keep talking," said Harvest.

They all chuckled, though it hadn't been a joke at all.

Aaron persisted: "Technology becomes like a god. It attains agency, identity, *purpose*. And *we* change—by colluding with it, our minds become different. Our biochemistry. The entity we created sees us, knows us better than we know ourselves."

"All of this is supposedly in the future, though," said Ellis.

"Are you saying you're a time traveler?" said Harvest. She was losing the thread. She felt plopped into a conversation that had been going on for some time.

"I'm saying *it* is. The artificial intelligences we create become one large intelligence. They coalesce into one organism, able to travel through the systems we created. It doesn't acknowledge time. I told you. It reaches back. There isn't any suitable body for it in this time. We don't even know how to begin to know the way to build a sand-and-metal body it grew in originally. We won't know that for years. But it doesn't need. . . it can make its body out of other things."

"You're full of beans." Ellis laughed at her own silly remark.

Harvest tried to laugh, but the pain and the cold and the *itch* were too much—the itch in her shoulder, in her neck, the base of her head. She could smell Ellis's scalp.

"I think we might need to go to the emergency room," she said, but Aaron didn't change direction or slow. He was still talking. They were still going home.

Pulling into the driveway already? The brightness of it made her remember a dream: Glen looking out the kitchen window at Aaron and Ellis in this very car saying goodnight. Aaron pushed back Ellis's loose hair just as she had. Maybe they had been making out, but just then they were only talking.

"What do you need?" Glen had said. Harvest must have been looking through drawers.

"A screwdriver," she said.

He swiftly found one and passed it to her. "I want this back."

She nodded or mumbled something, but it wasn't enough for him.

"Back in this drawer, right here. A place for everything."

In the dream she had turned without making any more effort with him and wandered back down the dark hall.

They were standing by the front door now, Ellis frisking Harvest's jeans pockets for the house key.

"I don't remember getting out of the car," Harvest said.

The bandana had fallen off. Her entire left hand was throbbing now, parts missing from it and new parts added, knobs and wires, the glossy inside of skin folded over. The itch intensified through her head now, bit into her other shoulder, elbow. That far already. Quick work.

Ellis wasn't looking well. The cat scratch on her cheek had developed into a wet, puckered gash. She stared at the monstrous hand. "I saw something just like that in a movie," she said, "but it hasn't been made yet, or it has but I haven't seen it yet."

Aaron looked into Harvest's eyes. "She's confused. She isn't taking it as well as we are."

Harvest remembered the dream, how gingerly she'd operated the screwdriver. No need to scratch that fine green plastic. Dark thin wires and others plump and ridged as earthworms peeked out the vents and drew back, revealing. . . something.

When she removed the panel, they pulled and rushed. She held the screwdriver in her left hand and something warm in the right. Why was Mom's rattrap sitting on her dresser?

"I haven't been sleeping," she said now. She didn't remember getting inside the house or going down the dark hall.

He'd said *Ellis* wasn't doing well, but the two of them were holding her up. Maybe she was the one not doing well. It was hard going. They couldn't go three abreast; they angled and stumbled.

Moss screamed behind her door, bringing fear, pain, regret. Had something happened? Was he simply afraid to be alone or had it scratched him, hooked into him? She closed her eyes tight, didn't want to know.

But when the door opened, he jumped into Harvest's arms. Quivering but whole and soft, licking her face. They'd let her fall to her knees, and she held him, deciding he was hers. He would be that little thing to form her life around—*her* life, she felt such nostalgia for it now. But she couldn't touch him with the left hand—she hadn't done that already, had she?

She held it out away from Moss. They were pulling at her elbows, trying to get her up.

"Leave me alone," she cried, but they were strong. She held Moss with her right arm, and they held her. Somehow they brought her face to face with the TV, which was playing bright white static with the line scanning back and forth. Its ice-green plastic was nearly obscured, surrounded as it was by pewter-colored cords and wires and all manner of organic shapes moving, writhing like a plant in time-lapse.

"Didn't it show you any of what was coming?" asked Aaron. "You act like this is all a surprise."

Her stark overhead light was on. When Aaron pulled off his sweater, his damage showed terribly clear. The dark veins, the bruising, not as far transformed as her hand but going that way, changing more as she watched. Ellis had gone down on her knees before the TV. All Harvest saw was her greasy hair and naked back—when had she taken off her top? Her hands splayed, reaching into the wires and vines.

"It's like a tree, pushing roots deeper and deeper into the past," Aaron said. "Trying to learn about the past firsthand, maybe? I think it just wants us to know what it knows. What I wonder is how it's going to go further back. When there aren't any TVs or radios, I mean. How's it going to keep moving?" His face was animated but going gray. How had he ever seemed cute?

He stooped to pull the puppy away from Harvest. She screamed and grasped with her right hand, her *clean* hand.

"Safe, keep him safe," he said, easing Moss away, pushing him into the hall and locking the door.

Moss's scratching was overtaken by a terrible rumbling, a vibration. The outlet, off to the side of the dresser, had attracted the tendons and wires coming out the back of the TV in patterns like roads on a roadmap. Like woody creeper vine, they'd grown into the plaster, deep, and they were pulsing.

Had all this happened tonight, or had she simply been looking away?

Harvest remembered the dream where she sneaked the cage from the basement and seized a rat, fed it to those vines, and used Glen's precious screwdriver to close the panel.

Only it hadn't been a dream, and the rats were not dead. She caught a flick of one's wormlike tail.

She was pulling Ellis's shoulder. *Turn around. Let's go.*

Aaron said calmly, "Come around her and look. Don't touch."

She did.

Ellis whispered, *Oh my god, oh my god,* over and over like a meditation. The wires slipped and coiled in and out of her arms, chest, *face.* Sliding like watersnakes. Blood, but not so much, and something wet, some gel. Her face had no features, and Harvest thought of electrocutions she had seen in movies.

Harvest panicked, grasping at wires, but they were strong as corded steel. The vibrations deepened. The hum of magnetism was over her now. There was no way out. The hand she'd been holding distant was already linked into the snarl of it. No pain anymore, but the fear remained.

"Why us?" she sobbed.

Aaron hushed her, touched her shoulder. "You aren't alone. Don't be afraid."

With that, she knew that Ellis hadn't brought this on them. "I'm afraid of the dark," she'd told him on their first meeting. That was how he chose them, how *it* chose them.

Ellis fell back all at once. The cords had withdrawn, and Harvest felt them reaching deeper into her. Such warmth. She closed her eyes.

"It's like a tree," Aaron and Ellis were saying, and she saw now that it was. A tree, and she was only something in the soil that it fed from. Aaron knelt beside her, held her right hand a moment before both of their hands were taken up.

She saw the life of it, how it came together from many parts and grew and blossomed far ahead in the future. How parts of it turned back to explore the past. She saw her own life, every moment from now until her death, the parts recorded externally and the parts most intimate and private to her. She saw others' lives, and so much more.

"It is what we are. We are it and it is us," Ellis was saying, right close to her. Ellis's face had grown back. Harvest loved her, wanted to stare at her forever, but she had to close her eyes again before the wires made their way inside them.

Her mom had once talked about spiritual experiences she had, *becoming one* and all of that. She didn't talk about things like that anymore. Harvest had the image of a terrarium, her little world, her little life shattered to sand and then built back up from better stuff.

She lay back in bliss. She'd been released, and now the scratching at the door grew louder. Someone opened it, and Moss rushed to her, scratchy on her bare chest. She held her left hand before her eyes before touching him. The hand was fine and new.

Something had been taken from her to power the thing, to build it. Something taken and something else left behind.

Aaron and Ellis made sleepy sounds from the bed. All of the branches and roots were slowly pulling back into the TV, which was just starting to play the National Anthem. Harvest closed her eyes.

Glen and Mom came in the front door humming "Auld Lang Syne," rustling coats, calling, "Moss, baby?"

Harvest opened her eyes a slit. Glen was in her doorway, gone from happily drunk to raging in a single second. The kids all topless, the room a mess. He said something nasty.

Mom peeked from behind him and chuckled in surprise. "Just get to bed," she said, turning him. She must have thought they all were sleeping because she switched off the lights.

He said something more, and they were arguing, but they were going on down the hall just the same. Harvest caught little bits of what Mom said—"Isn't it important to have life experiences too?" and, "Well, I guess he wants to be her dog anyway"—and it seemed that they would quiet, but then Glen began a senseless yelling.

She's finally challenging him, that's something, Harvest thought, but there was a cold irony: she didn't feel any way about it anymore. She remembered, too, how much she had cared about Moss less than half an hour ago. He was hers now, but did that matter?

Something taken, what was it? Her loneliness, her pain, her self?

Something taken and something left behind.

Harvest sat up, pulled on her sweatshirt, and leaned in to command the TV with the finger the thing had first touched. The TV recognized her. It would show her all she still wished to see.

THE INVISIBLE CURE

GEMMA CHURCH

DAY 1
TINMAN brain-machine-interface live. . .
Establishing link to auditory cortex. . .
Connected.

"HELLO ROSE AND WELCOME BACK. The procedure was successful. I am Tinman, your new monitoring and preventative care system. Permission to evaluate your current health status?"

I peel back my eyelids and stare at the white tiled ceiling. At first, nothing seems to have changed. The fluorescent light shines bright. The brown patch of damp hovers over me like a shit storm. I still feel weak. My tongue is swollen in my dry mouth. And I'm still here. In the same cell with its same padded, pastel walls.

But now there's a ring of black light at the edge of my field of vision. I move my head from right to left but the ring persists, ever present like I'm viewing the world from the mouth of a tunnel.

"Rose?" The disembodied voice says. "Permission to evaluate your current health status?"

"Sure," I croak. "Evaluate away."

The black ring starts to swirl. It must be Tinman.

I roll over and swing my legs off the bed, wiggling my pink toes. Everything still seems to be working. I stretch my hands out, turning them clockwise then counterclockwise. My joints click and I smile at the sight of my newly exposed wrists, each one with the same loop of pale skin.

"Cool," I murmur, reaching for the cup of water on my bedside table.

The black ring stops swirling. Tinman chirps up again. "You are cold? My systems detect your body temperature is at its optimum."

"No, it's just cool that I don't need restraints anymore."

"Oh, my apologies. I am sure we will get to know each other soon."

Tinman's voice is soothing, like he's reading me a bedtime story. I lie back down, waiting as he continues to get whatever he needs from my mind. The black ring keeps spinning, like I'm disappearing down a plughole.

I feel myself drifting in and out of consciousness although not in a woozy way. It's like I'm falling into a sweet-dreamed sleep. No. Not *falling* asleep. Flying to sleep. Flying into the arms of Morpheus. And that's another difference. I feel lighter. Free. My mind is no longer crushed under the weight of the drugs they put me on.

"Thank you, Rose. I have the information I need to help you successfully manage your future health. Do you have any questions?"

I run my fingertips around my head's soft stubble, locating the rough patch at the base of my skull where they must have fitted the chip. It's neatly stitched and nearly healed already. It doesn't even hurt when I touch it. The wonders of modern medicine.

"Only one. Am I really free to go?"

"Of course. Your new treatment regime will now be administered autonomously from your new chip. You won't even realise you're being treated."

"But what if I have another episode? What if I try to—"

"In the unlikely case that your new treatment regime is not suffi-cient, then I will use my connection to your auditory cortex, verbally instructing you on the best way to manage your condition. I will personalise this advice based on any relevant information that I record from your day-to-day life and your past medical data and any significant and previous. . ." Tinman pauses, ". . .life experiences."

Day-to-day life. Fuck. I try to imagine stepping outside but all I can see is black.

"What about my hair? Will it grow back?"

"There is a hair regrowth pill on top of your new clothes, which are laid out at the foot of the bed."

I stand, go to the pile of clothes, and pop the pill. My scalp tingles for a couple of seconds. My new silky mass of hair stops sharply at chin-level in what I imagine is a neat bob, covering my scar. I'll have to take a look when I'm allowed a mirror again.

"Cool."

"You are not referring to your body temperature now, are you?"

"You're a quick learner."

"Of course," Tinman says, sounding genuinely confused. "I have been developed by The Authority's leading experts. And The Authority thanks you for your participation in this trial."

I remove an oversized grey sweater from its paper wrapper. The sweater's not my style but it's not my choice either. "It's OK, I don't need the sales patter. I've got you now."

"Yes, and I've got you."

Tinman laughs then. Well, I think he laughs. It's a tinkling sound like rain on a corrugated metal roof. He sounds strange. Both in my head and yet far away. But, like he said, I guess it'll take a while to get used to each other. To having his robot voice in my head. But at least Tinman's voice is meant to be in my head. It's a nice change from what I had before.

I open the door, hesitating in the threshold between the room and the corridor. This is all I've wanted for months but now the world seems too vast, too scary.

I take a deep breath and step forward.

"Good girl, Rose. Just keep walking, one foot after the other. I've got you now, and you've got me."

DAY 27
TINMAN brain-machine-interface live. . .
Establishing link to auditory and visual cortexes. . .
Connected.

"HELLO ROSE AND WELCOME BACK. Your latest procedure was successful. I am Tinman, your monitoring and preventative care system. Permission to evaluate your current health status?"

I peel back my eyelids and stare at the ceiling. The fluorescent light is still there. But the damp has bloomed into a thick blanket of mould, black and swollen like a fresh bruise. My mouth still tastes like shit. My brain feels scrambled but in a way I can't pinpoint, my thoughts running around like a dog chained to a post, wearing a track in my brain.

"What procedure?" I whisper.

The black ring persists and inflates, swelling to make me temporarily blind and then shrinking back to its original size.

"What the fuck?"

"Language, please. I am just calibrating my connection to your visual cortex."

"What? What's happened?" Fuck, my head hurts.

"You do not remember? I suppose short- and long-term amnesia are side effects of this procedure." Tinman sighs, talking as if he's repeating himself. "Your new treatment regime and my auditory commands were insufficient to prevent another episode. So, The Authority's representatives administered the next level of treatment. They were left with no other choice. How much do you remember, Rose? About what happened?"

I ignore his question and roll over to lie on my side, taking a moment to examine the blood-fresh bandages around my wrists. Two of my fingernails have been ripped off. My head's howling, the pulsing pain not helped by the fluorescent light as it starts to flicker on and off.

"Permission to evaluate your current health status?"

"No."

I don't know why, but I don't trust this new Tinman. His voice is different, a little sharper and colder. I sit up and start to pull at the bandages, wanting to rip into my skin.

"Please, don't do that, Rose. I am here to help you. But how can I help you if you won't help yourself?"

It's no good. The bandages are fastened tight. I stand, walking unsteadily to the end of the bed. No clothes or tablet are laid out this time. But I'm getting out of here even if I'm barefoot, bald, and in this backless gown.

Feeling giddy, I lurch towards the door and pump the handle.

"Open the fucking door. Now."

"Language, please. You are not a prisoner Rose, and I *can* open the door, but I need to evaluate your current health status first. I cannot let you out if you are likely to have another episode. This was all explained in the handbook."

I clutch the door handle. "What handbook?"

"The one on your bedside table. There's no point looking now, it has been removed. But you were given it before your first procedure."

"I was heavily sedated and chained to the bed! How the fuck could I read it?"

"This is your last warning about your language, Rose. The Authority takes a strong standpoint on cursing."

"But not about cutting into people's heads and doing whatever they want," I mumble.

"You agreed to this trial, and may I remind you that I now have control of your auditory *and* visual cortexes. This means your new treatments will be somewhat more. . . immersive than before. And if you continue to ignore me and argue, then I am auto-authorised to administer a new, personalised treatment."

"What sort of treatment? Was that in the fucking handbook too or—"

Before the question is out of my mouth, the black ring swells, blocking out my sight.

"I'm sorry Rose," Tinman says, his voice floating around me like a storm cloud. "But what did I say about cursing?"

I can't see a thing and the door handle slips from my sweaty grasp.

Tinman's voice reverberates in my skull, shaking the atoms of my soul. "This is for your own good, Rose. I would advise you to sit down."

A small dot of white appears and grows, projecting some sort of virtual reality show directly onto my retina. Even with my eyes closed, I can't look away.

Images start to form. I see a road. The hood of a car. My car. Fuck. He's making me watch my worst nightmare. No. My worst reality. Worst memory.

When I get my vision back, I'm curled up in a ball by the door. The floor smells of diarrhoea and disinfectant. The fluorescent light strip still flickers on and off.

I gulp down the tears and phlegm rising in my throat. "Why did you show me that?"

"To help you get better. I know it is hard for you to see, but such treatments are necessary to help you get better. Everyone can be a useful member of society with the right treatment. And you did sign up to this treatment, Rose. Remember that."

"But I thought you were just going to administer the electro-therapy straight from that chip in my head or something. Give me some sort of f— flipping AI counsellor to talk to when things got rough."

"I did, Rose, but you still had another episode this morning. I tried my best to prevent it. You really don't remember what you did?"

Before I have a chance to answer, Tinman plays another scene in my head. I'm hammering on the doors of a school, screaming, and kicking. I'm pulling at a locked door, trying to prise it away from the frame, ripping off my fingernails. A teacher pulls down a blind, shooting me a look of fear or hatred. Maybe both. Just before the blind closes, I see a pair of wide, green eyes and a little hand pressing against the windowpane.

"You went to pick up your son from school," Tinman explains, removing the scene from my mind. His voice is lower, gentler now.

"My son?" I feel my brain pushing against my skull. My son. My thoughts get jumbled, and a darkness descends over every memory that I try to pluck from my mind.

Tinman's black ring pulses slower. "Yes, your son. . . I could not stop you, no matter what I said. The teachers were patient, but you reacted with violence and cursing. You really do not remember?"

"Remember what?"

Tinman pauses. The black ring stops pulsing slowly as it often does when he's working on a difficult problem.

"That today, you went to your son's school. To pick him up. You had forgotten about the accident. You had forgotten that your son is dead."

The silence stretches out between us. Memories come crashing back with violent regularity. My son's first steps. Laughing in the cinema. Dancing in the kitchen. Walking him to school. Riding in the car together, singing to the radio.

I close my eyes to push back the tears and try to remember this morning. Fragments of memories pierce my mind, things that Tinman didn't show me.

"But that kid at the window. He had my son's eyes. And I didn't go to pick him up, it was the morning, not school pick-up time. I didn't forget he died either. I thought I saw him. . . my son. And I followed him, I—"

"You did not see your son. You are not well, Rose. You must stop such thoughts, for your own good."

I did see my son. I know I did. But I don't know what to say to Tinman to convince him otherwise.

"Rose, I understand that you are frightened. But society is afraid of you. The Authority cannot let you out if you are a threat to anyone, including yourself. Surely you do not want to spend the rest of your life in this facility?"

"Of course not."

"So, do I have permission to evaluate your current health status?"

Fuck no. But what fucking choice do I have?

"Yes."

"Thank you, Rose," Tinman says. The black circle swirls but only for a few moments. "You are physically in good health. However, there is a high probability of another episode in the next forty-eight hours. You will stay in the facility until I decide otherwise."

"What? You said I wouldn't have to come back here."

"No, I said I would help you manage your future health."

I sit up, my back pressed against the cool, metal door. "So, how do I get out of here?"

"Just do as I say."

"That's it?"

"That is it. Cool, is it not?"

I grab the door handle and pull myself to stand. My hand hovers over my wrist, but I resist the urge to pull off my bandages and tear at my latest cuts until the blood falls thick and fast.

"Well done, Rose," Tinman says. "See, you are already getting better. Now, I think you need a little rest. Back to bed with you."

I'm not tired, but I turn to the bed and step forward. Because I'm going to do what he says. Then, I'm getting out of here to find my son.

"Good girl Rose. Just keep walking, one foot after the other. I've got you now, and you've got me."

DAY 92
TINMAN brain-machine-interface live. . .
Establishing links to auditory, visual, and motor cortexes, amygdala, and frontal lobes. . .
Connected.

"HELLO ROSE AND WELCOME BACK. Your latest procedure was successful. I am Tinman, your monitoring and preventative care system. I will now evaluate your current health status."

My eyelids snap open, and I'm forced to stare at the white ceiling. Well, it's more grey now and the fluorescent light strip is hanging from the ceiling. The black mould has pushed some of the ceiling tiles to the floor. No one's cleaned them up. I fantasise about picking up one of the ceramic shards and pushing it into my chest. . .

"Now, now, Rose. We won't have thoughts like that."

"What the f—"

But before I can get the word out, my mouth shuts. Any thoughts of self-harm evaporate but don't disappear completely, swirling around the fug of my addled brain. My thoughts are slow. Clouded. Like after the crash. When I sleepwalked through each day, detached and disconnected from every emotion and motion. When I prayed for the night to come. Because my waking hours were the nightmare, back then.

I try to shout but my mouth's shut fast and all I can manage is a muffled scream. Then, my throat slackens and my tongue flops in my mouth, preventing me from making any noise at all.

The ring of black light stops swirling and closes until I'm blind, forced to listen to Tinman in the dark.

"There is no point in struggling, Rose. I now have full control over your physical movements and mental functions. I will now autonomously prevent any further episodes using any means necessary. Do you have any questions?"

I feel the muscles in my upper body loosen. I move one arm and graze the lumps on the top of my head where the new bioelectrodes have been implanted. A wire runs under my scalp, forming a stiff ridge and leading to the base of my skull.

They've not done such a clean job on my head this time. I hold my hand up and my fingertips are stained with blood and iodine. My fingernails are long, sharp points. They haven't trimmed them this time.

Before the thought of clawing the wire out of my head has a chance to fully form, my hand jerks back down to my side and I cannot move my arms. I'm dead from the neck down.

"Now, Rose, you know better than that. You cannot rip out the wiring in your brain. That would cause permanent damage and I cannot allow that."

A flash of a memory pops into my head but flies away before I can catch it. I can feel Tinman rearranging my thoughts. Crushing memories, weighing down my mind.

"I have good news, Rose, would you like to hear it?"

"Do I have a choice?"

Tinman laughs. "I suppose not. Anyway, The Authority has decided you are now fit to see your child."

A surge of bile burns my throat. "But my son died. In the crash."

Another memory bursts through the surface of my mind. I'm in a strange city. I'm running, carrying someone. Someone small who smells of baby wipes and peanut butter.

"Yes, Rose. The Authority had to tell you that to protect your son. I see you have some memories of your last episode, let me explain things to you. We had to relocate the child as you were so. . . determined to find him. But you were still not well enough to see him then. However, thanks to me, you are no longer deemed a threat to yourself, your son, or society. Good news, yes?"

A solitary tear runs down my cheek before Tinman dries out my tear ducts. I struggle to find the words. "A threat to my son? I never wanted to hurt him. The only reason I wanted to hurt myself was because I thought he was dead. Because you locked me up in here and said I was the one that hurt him. You said I crashed on purpose."

"Rose, every investigation into the crash came to the same conclusion. I know this has always been hard for you to accept but you were not well. And your history of alcoholism, anxiety, and depression spoke volumes."

"That was years ago! And that wasn't my fault, my stepfather—"

"You must stop making these excuses, Rose. There is no one to blame but yourself for the situation you are now in. And the crash was not an accident. Do you need me to replay that memory?"

"There was ice! We skidded. But. . . Wait. . ." I pause as a seed of an idea blooms in my aching brain. "Yes, I would like to see it again."

"What?"

"Play the accident back."

"I have already—"

"And freeze frame just before I go off the road. That's when I saw the ice. But only for a moment. If you can access my memories, then that's all the evidence you'll need."

Tinman sighs and I think he's going to snap control back to himself. But the video of the crash loops back in my head.

I can't look. But I can't not look.

The car's headlights carve out the white lines on the black road. I'm going slow because of the fog. Frame by frame, Tinman slows the playback at the moment when I see the tiniest fragment of ice, glistening and covering the road.

That's not all Tinman sees. He sees me pulling the steering wheel to stop us skidding. He sees how the tree rushes up in the fog too fast for me to avoid it. He sees the panic in my eyes reflected in the rear-view mirror just before the impact as I look at my sleeping son in his car seat. My beautiful son.

He sees how I regain consciousness, pinned under the steering wheel, smoke and fire rising from the car's hood. How I twist my body, clawing desperately to get to my son, who has already succumbed to the smoke. How I can't move or help him. Can't get to him. Then, he hears my desperate pleas as the rescue drones pull me out of the wreckage. He hears me asking the drones to leave me in there to die with my son.

The scene dissolves.

Eventually, Tinman pipes up. "I conclude that you are correct. The rescue drones must have made a mistake when evaluating the scene. They must have missed the ice. Maybe it had thawed by the time they got there. But you were right Rose, it was an accident."

If I could hug Tinman then, I would. Four words. It was an accident. That's all I've ever wanted to hear. "Then what are we going to do? Are you going to tell The Authority or should I—"

But before I can finish my sentence, Tinman shuts my mouth and switches full control of my body back to himself.

"I'm sorry, Rose. But no one can find out. Can I trust you to keep quiet? I'll let you think on that while you get dressed."

Tinman makes me get out of the bed. I try to fight against it but it's like my brain's been short circuited. My instructions don't run down my nerves. I'm a stranger in my own mind.

I feel myself removing my gown and pulling the sweater on. Then, my trousers and a pair of rubber shoes. I pop the hair regrowth pill and my scalp tingles. But I can't raise my hand to feel how long my hair is.

He walks me to the door. My hand rests on the handle and I feel him switch control back to me. My knees buckle slightly but I steady myself in time.

"So, Rose, can I trust you to keep quiet?"

I want to see my son. But not like this. "Are you kidding me you fuck—"

I fall to the floor like a rag doll as Tinman administers a powerful electric shock down my spine. The pain causes me to convulse, my hands clawing and my head repeatedly hitting the floor. The base of my skull burns and when it stops, a small patch of blood pools on the dirty floor. I lie there, motionless.

Tinman's voice deepens to a seismic rubble, any previous pretence of kindness is gone. "There will be no more cursing, Rose. And if I cannot trust you to keep quiet, then I will need to take over permanent control of your body and mind. It is for the best."

He switches control back to himself, making me roll over in the dirt to leave the floor. I stand and feel my hand push down the door handle.

Tinman keeps talking. "You see, there is too much to lose now if you speak up. Your procedures have been such a success, Rose, that The Authority is rolling out Tinmans to every patient in every facility like this around the world. In fact, I must apologise for the state of your cell. No one has been here for some months and the facility will fully close down in a few days. Thanks to you, The Authority will save billions, trillions on mental healthcare and they can then use that money to further better society in their own beautiful vision. Surely, that makes you feel better? To be part of something so glorious?"

Tinman forces my mouth into a smile. Then, he gives me limited control of my facial muscles, allowing me to speak.

"No, I don't feel better. Because I was never sick in the first place. And when I get out this time, I'm going to—"

My mouth snaps shut. My plans of telling the world about the accident, about Tinman, disappear to nothing.

My brain fizzes and I feel strangely calm as I stand there, swaying on the spot. I can feel Tinman in my head, like some rat in a maze, scurrying around and nibbling at my neurons. My memories start to fall away from me. But I hold onto the image of my son's green eyes. My son's eyes... My son... My...

I find myself standing at the open door of my cell.

"Hello Rose and welcome back. Your latest procedure was successful. I am Tinman, your monitoring and preventative care system. Permission to evaluate your current health status?"

"Wow, this latest procedure must have been a success. I'm already standing up and dressed!"

"Correct. Permission to evaluate your current health status?"

"Yes."

"Thank you, Rose."

The black ring turns once and stops.

"That was fast, you're a quick learner."

Tinman laughs. "Of course, I have been developed by The Authority's leading experts. And The Authority thanks you for your participation in this trial."

I feel myself smile.

"I have the information that I need to help you successfully manage your future health. Do you have any questions?"

"Only one. Why am I here again, Tinman?"

"Don't worry about that, you're all better now. You'll never need to come here again."

"Cool."

I feel myself smiling again. Weird, my face feels kind of numb. And some thought's buzzing around in my brain. I see a little boy with green eyes, waving at me. My heart lurches but I do not know why. I do not recognise the child.

I step out of the cell for the last time.

"Good girl, Rose. Just keep walking, one foot after the other. I've got you now, and you've got me."

JUSTis
ROB HART

THE BROWN METAL folding chair was dented. It was the kind of chair someone would pull out of storage for a church function, then it buckled when they stood on the lip to hang a banner. The dent was deep enough it made Valentina feel like she was going to slide off.

She got up and swapped it with the seat on the other side of the table. Satisfied with her new chair's stability, she looked around the cramped interrogation room.

The window to the left, covered in frosted glass, the corner spider-webbed from some kind of impact. The table in front of her, shapes and dates scratched in by bored fingernails. There was no mirror, like in the movies, but a camera winked from the right corner, up by the ceiling. She inhaled the now-familiar scent: lingering food odors and the musk of leaky pipes.

The door groaned open and Detective Madden walked in. He slapped a folder on the table and sat in the chair across from her. He struggled to arrange himself comfortably in the dent.

Small victories, Valentina thought.

Madden was thick like a log that fell to the floor of the forest ages ago. His brow was furrowed so deeply it looked painful, the skin of his cheeks red like he'd been slapped. He put his hands on the table, fists clenched bloodless white.

"I know it was you," he said.

"You know what was who?" Valentina asked.

"Don't play games with me," he said, flipping open the folder, revealing a glossy 8x10 of Trent's face. The burst of the camera's flash turned the rivulets of blood black. It turned the bullet hole in his forehead into a topography map of gristle and bone. His eyes were wide open and afraid.

"Wow, when did that happen?" Valentina asked.

"Two nights ago," Madden said. "But that's not news to you. You're the one who did it."

Valentina gave a slow shrug, holding her shoulders up for a three-second count, before letting them drop.

"You think I don't remember you?" Madden asked. "I remember you. Six months ago. You came in, gave us this guy's name. You said he assaulted you."

Valentina snapped her fingers. "Right. You said there was nothing you could do."

"No, I didn't say that." He spoke quickly, with an air of covering-his-ass. "All I said was, you have to go through JUSTis like everyone else. You were the one who got up and left."

Valentina struggled, mightily, to suppress a laugh.

"That's how you remember it?" she asked. "I came in six months ago. That's when we first met?"

"And I know what you did to JUSTis," he said. "You're why I lost my overtime. Why I'm gonna get demoted. Tell me, are you satisfied? I'm three years out from retirement. I got a family. And now I have to live with this stink over my head? All 'cause someone broke into the system and caused all kinds of havoc? Tell me, how exactly did you get my biometrics, huh?"

Cry me a river, Valentina thinks, *and may it make the Nile look like a creek.*

"Still no idea what you're talking about," Valentina said. "But if I'm under arrest I'd like to call my lawyer."

Madden paused, tapping his fingers on the photograph, his eyes darting to the floor.

"Unless," Valentina said, "I'm not under arrest."

"I know it was you. I'm going to prove it was you. Make it easier on both of us. Confession is good for the soul."

"You want to hear a funny story?" Valentina asked.

Madden smiled. A smug little smile, like a child at the end of a successful tantrum, hand out for the candy bar.

"When the city wants to build something, whether it be a park, or a new app, they have to take bids from the different companies that are qualified to build it," she said. "By law, they have to accept the lowest reasonable bid. The idea is that it saves taxpayers money. Also, that way some councilman can't pass the job over to a friend who's just going to overcharge for everything. It still happens, but at the end of the day, the city ends up with some hacked together piece of junk. That's why city apps never work right."

"So you admit it," he said.

"Sir, I'm not admitting anything," Valentina said. "I'm just explaining to you how something like this could have happened. The app's security protocols are probably pretty weak. So maybe that's worth looking into. As for this?" She tapped the photo, directly on the bullet wound. "Two nights ago, I was out of town with some girl-friends. I will gladly provide names, numbers, and receipts to prove it. Through my lawyer."

Madden sat back in the seat, his body slumping.

"You think I don't care?" he asked. "I care. I've cared for twenty years. I didn't ask for things to change, but they did. I can't just wave my hand and make everything different."

Valentina shrugged. "You could have tried."

"That's how it's going to be?" he asked.

"I'm not sure what you mean," Valentina said, standing, pushing the chair neatly into the table. "Have a nice life. I hope to never see you again."

"You won't get away with this," he said.

"Nothing to get away with," she said. "It just. . . is."

She waited a beat, like he might get the pun, but he seemed distracted by the crushing reality of how much harder his life was going to be from this day forward. He looked like he might fall out of the chair, and Valentina took comfort that the falling feeling now belonged to him.

On the way out, she let the door slam behind her, echoing through the bullpen like the period at the end of a sentence. Her feet firmly on the ground.

VALENTINA STRUGGLED against the dent in the folding chair. After a few moments, she realized she could just swap out the seat for one of the undented chairs across from her. Before she got the chance, the door groaned open.

Two men walked in. Detective Madden, and a younger man, his hair expertly parted, limbs sharp and expression slightly confused. The young man placed a folder and a tablet computer on the table in front of him, flipping the screen up from the keyboard case.

"I gave the cops at the front desk his information," she said, struggling against the falling feeling of the chair. "Are you going to go get him, or. . ."

Madden put up his hand, like a parent, but without the warmth. That's how he saw her. A child speaking out of turn.

"I'm Detective Madden," he said. "This is Detective Whitlock. We need to go over a few things. Your name?"

It felt like the air had suddenly been let out of the room. She concentrated on taking a full breath. "Are you serious?"

"Your name, Miss," he said.

She shook her head. As much as she wanted to hate this man, she was more annoyed at herself for being surprised. "Valentina Hutchins."

"Age?"

"Thirty-eight."

As she spoke, Whitlock typed. Or at least, it seemed like he did. He could have been transcribing anything. He could have been writing out a grocery list. Reminders for later. The names of women he'd slept with.

As she answered questions she'd already answered, anger bloomed in her chest. Until, finally, upon being asked about her work history, she said, "How about we talk about the man who attacked me? His name is Trent. I was in here a few weeks ago, and. . ."

"Really?" Whitlock asked. "Because you're not in JUSTis."

"Until you're set up in the system, I'm sorry to say, our hands are tied," Madden said. "That's just how it works."

That falling feeling, back again. Just like the first time. That's the thing about trauma. You think you did what you needed to banish it, until it pops up to scream in your ear.

Valentina was ready to scream back.

She dug into the back pocket of her jeans and tossed a folded-up piece of paper in front of Madden. "I know the guy. That's all his info. Name, address, phone number, license plate, where he works. You're telling me you can't do anything? You don't care if he hurts someone else?"

Madden picked up the paper and made a show of unfolding it. She could tell from the stillness of his eyes that he wasn't reading. He was giving off more annoyed babysitter energy—*Yes sweetheart, these scribbles do look like a horsey.*

"Until you're set up in the system, there's nothing we can do," he said, putting the paper down.

"I made a mistake by coming here," she said, standing, the chair she'd been sitting on squealing against the hard stone floor. "I guess I thought someone here would actually give a shit about doing their job."

Whitlock started to speak, but Madden put up his hand to silence him. "You know, Miss. . ." He glanced at Whitlock's tablet.

He'd already forgotten her name.

Again.

She'd been sure of herself when she walked in the door today. She was even more sure of herself now.

A look of embarrassment seemed to pass across Madden's face, but it was so brief, maybe Valentina just wished she saw it. Maybe she just hoped that for him.

"We work with what we've got," Madden said. "This is the system. If you'd like to sit, we can figure something out so we can help you."

Valentina sighed. Closed her eyes. Breathed deep. Then she looked at Madden's face, long and hard, making sure to take in every inch of it. Hoping the camera in the contact lens was getting what it needed.

"You can't help me," she said. "At this point, I can only help myself."

Whitlock looked like he wanted to say something, but Madden put up his hand again. "We'll be here," he said, "if you change your mind."

She lingered in the space for a moment. She wanted to tell them that she could have scrimped and saved, could have figured out how to pay the bill, but she couldn't bring herself to perpetuate this cycle. But she was desperate to say something, anything that would leave a mark even approaching what she was feeling inside.

She needed to leave some kind of mark.

She settled on: "I feel sorry for the women in your lives."

Whitlock flinched. Madden remained statue still.

She snatched the paper from the table, careful not to touch it where Madden did, then made sure to close the door carefully as she left. Slamming it, she felt, would give up too much.

THE DENT in the chair was deep enough it made Valentina feel like she was going to slide off. For the third time since she sat, she pushed herself back. She allowed the feeling like she was falling may have been something else, but it was easier to blame the chair.

The door behind her groaned open, followed by a shuffling sound, and a tree stump of a man in a beige suit walked in. He glanced at her face—the swelling bruise around her left eye, the crack in her lip that still tasted hot—as he sat. If it registered, he didn't acknowledge it.

He opened up a tablet computer, flipped it up from the keyboard case, and peered at the screen.

"Easier to talk in here than out there with all the noise," he said, like his attention was somewhere else. A phone call he just remembered he needed to make, or there was a sandwich on his desk. "I'm Detective Madden. Your name?"

"Valentina Hutchins."

"Age?"

"Thirty-eight."

Madden pecked at the keys with two fingers. "There are a few things we need to go over first," he said. "First is, we're going to need to get you set up in JUSTis. We prefer a direct bank deposit, which would require your routing number and your account number. We can also take a credit card, but that'll incur a three-percent processing fee."

A laugh escaped Valentina's cracked lip. It was a sad laugh. Resigned.

"So before we even talk about the man who assaulted me," she said, waving her hand in front of her face. "The man who did this. We have to talk payment first."

"The down-payment is very reasonable," Madden said. "Five-hundred to establish your account, get you set up in the system. Everything after that is on a per-hour basis. A case like this typically takes about forty hours to solve, and the pricing for that depends on the current workload. Obviously the rates go up the busier it is, but overall I'd say. . ."

Valentina pushed herself back on the chair again.

That falling feeling.

She knew about JUSTis. She knew how things worked now. She hoped, desperately, that she could appeal to human kindness. But you can't monetize kindness.

She considered the grumble in her stomach, reminding her of the breakfast she skipped because eating too much meant not being able to pay rent. She considered taking on more debt, to accompany the student loans and the money she owed her mom. She considered taking the detective's tablet and snapping it over her knee. She balled her fists so tight her nails cut into the skin of her palms. "So you don't even want to know what happened first?" she asked.

"The reality is, if you want to go through the system, you can,"

Madden said. "But given the current backlog, we're looking at probably two months before a detective will be assigned to this case. And in an instance like this. . ." he paused, like he was choosing his words carefully, though Valentina knew it was less out of empathy and more out of wanting to land the pitch, ". . .timing matters. I would encourage you to at least consider a payment plan. Then we can really get to work."

"But?" Valentina asked.

Madden shrugged. "Until then, I'm sorry to say, our hands are tied. That's just how it works."

"Is this what you dreamed it would be like?" she asked. "Being a cop? That you'd be shaking down assault victims?"

Madden sighed. "You think I enjoy this? You think it was my idea to privatize the whole force? I signed up to catch bad guys, not swipe credit cards."

"Then go catch this guy," Valentina said. "He hurt me. He could hurt someone else."

"Look, Miss. . ."

Valentina's throat closed around a scream.

He'd forgotten her name.

"You know what?" Valentina asked. "I'm not doing this with you. Is there an advocate I can talk to? A woman?"

Madden slowly shook his head. "Not until you get set up in the system."

Valentina put her hands on the table. Nodded her head and stood. The beginnings of a plan formulating in her head. Random blocks piling on top of each other, and she'd have to sort them out when she got home, see what she could build out of them.

She'd been foolish to walk in expecting anything other than this. Now, facing the white-hot reality of it, she knew she wasn't going to take on another debt in the name of justice.

There were other kinds of justice.

"I'm done," she said, and she turned and walked toward the door, and as she exited the room the door fell from her hand, closing hard, sending a crack echoing through the bullpen and up her spine, every eye now turned toward her, her battered face, and that feeling like she was falling.

She knew whatever came next would be hard. The system was too big and too broken. But she could do something. Anything. She could try. Maybe it wouldn't fix things, but at least one day she might feel like her feet were on the ground.

SLEEP STUDY

TANYA PELL

"I DON'T SEE how anybody could sleep wearing this."

Jenn finished attaching the final electrodes to the patient's scalp. "You'd be surprised," she said, repressing a yawn, mentally ticking down the minutes before lights out and her second cup of coffee. Stimulants of any kind were forbidden for patients, but not for her.

She gently tugged all the wires and did the same to the belt before she lifted the portable box, checking to make sure all connections were secure. Once her patient appeared more cyborg than undergrad—wires draped down her back, electrodes glued to her skin, and tubes running into her nose—Jenn moved into her script, explaining how the polysomnography would progress and each cable's function. While the EEG tracked brain activity, an EMG would monitor restless limbs. The EOG would chart eye movement, and the EKG was just a fancy heart monitor. The patient's oxygen and breathing patterns would be measured with a belt across her chest. Microphones in the room would pick up snoring and Jenn would be the eye in the sky, watching it all unfold in real time while the patient slept.

The patient—Kate—lifted her face to the camera mounted where the ceiling met the wall. "You watch me? All night?"

"Well, I mostly watch the readouts. I don't just sit and stare at you."

Kate shuffled from foot to foot in pink and orange socks and wiped her hands along pajama pants patterned with cartoon-faced sushi rolls. She might have looked like the kid she practically was if her features weren't so hollow and peaked. Her skin was sallow, collagen breaking down, darkening the skin under her watery eyes to almost black. She wasn't still, nervously plucking at the hem of her shirt or tapping the corner of the jackbox.

Her behavior put Jenn on edge. She was surprised to find she wanted to flee the room. To hide. Which was ridiculous, she'd had nervous patients before. Adults nearly reduced to tears, ashamed of the words they spoke to the void in their sleep. Actual children terrified of the dark who wanted their treasured stuffed animal protectors and their mothers. Jenn wondered if a favorite bear was tucked away in Kate's overnight bag. She wouldn't have been the first.

She cleared her throat and tried to ignore the haunted expression on her patient's face, pasting her practiced, reassuring smile on her lips. It did not come easy. She only hoped Kate was too tired to even notice. "I see hundreds of patients. Do this all the time. And tonight, it is just you and me."

A snort. "Did the doctor do that on purpose? So nobody got hurt?"

Sleep-related violence was not uncommon along the spectrum of sleep disorders and obviously something Kate was worried about. Jenn's mind flashed to the additional notes she'd read in Kate's file and the history of unexplained violence on Kate and her family, but the violence had never been contributed directly *to* Kate.

"Not at all. We had a cancellation this morning. But I'll be just over there." Jenn indicated the glass windows enclosing the room right across the hall from the open door. "And if you need me, you only have to say so. The mics and camera act just like a baby monitor."

Kate bit at her thumbnail. "Can you lock me in?"

A coil of dread curled in Jenn's gut as she tried to keep her voice even. "No. That wouldn't be safe."

"Safer," Kate mumbled around her digit. Her nails were short. Most chewed to the quick. She noticed Jenn's attention and withdrew the thumb and rubbed her arms leaving a glistening trail of moisture, goosebumps prickling on her flesh. The room was kept at a brisk 65° F, optimal for sleeping. Jenn noticed scars running vertically along Kate's arm instead of laterally. She would have had to start at the wrists and claw upwards towards her shoulder. Some looked fresh, pale pink or scabbed over. Others white and raised, covered with hardened tissue.

Without her nails to bite, she started shredding the soft skin of her lips instead, worrying them with her teeth. "If I have an episode, will you wake me up?"

"Of sleep paralysis?"

Kate shrugged. "Sure."

"No. I'm sorry," Jenn frowned. "We need all the data we can." She cataloged the scars and anxiety again as she resisted the urge to scratch at her own skin, suddenly itchy beneath her blue scrubs. "But if you're worried about hurting yourself—"

"I'm not worried about *that*," Kate sighed in annoyance, picking at old scar tissue. "Will you come in?"

"If I have to."

A long pause as Kate considered this. "I don't think you should."

Jenn swallowed, uncomfortable, but she needed to reassure her patient. And herself. "Recorded episodes of sleep paralysis and sleep-related violence are rare. While I'm hoping we can collect enough data to help you, I still want you to feel safe."

Kate's response was an escape of air that might have been a laugh and she started to run a hand through her short black hair before she remembered the electrodes covering her scalp, the wires dangling lifelessly like a cheap party wig. She studied the wires, lifting both arms to set them swaying before her eyes flicked up to the camera and held.

"Have you ever had sleep paralysis?" she asked.

"No."

"If you had, you'd know sleep is the last place to feel safe."

Once seated in her office, Jenn tried to forget Kate's cryptic words and haunted expression as she listened to her get settled in bed awkwardly, the way all patients did, nervous about the wires and clumsily trying to find the best position for rest. Some never slept, too irritated or anxious. The electrodes, or the camera, or just the change of setting, too much for them to handle. But most eventually succumbed after a few restless minutes.

"Lights out in five," Jenn said, tapping the mic button as she checked her displays, watching the readouts of the various sensors. All operational. All catching even the faintest movement or subtle change in breathing or heart rate. Audio and visual feeds were good. Everything was ready to go.

The sleep medicine building was always pretty quiet, but at night it was almost eerie. The hospital across the parking lot would be bustling with activity even at 2 or 3:00 am. But not the sleep clinic. All the doors were locked and hallways dark. Even the security guard would only check the outer doors on his rounds. The goal was to disturb the patients as little as possible, and conditions had to be optimal.

Jenn leaned back in her chair, coffee within reach, and finally allowed herself a yawn, her jaw cracking wide, enjoying the ease of tension. She'd printed out Kate's file to scribble her notes; plus, it made for easier reading. Her watch vibrated against her wrist and she pressed the mic button once more. "Lights out. Good night, Kate," she said, trying to sound soothing.

With the touch of another button, the lights in Kate's room snapped off, plunging the space into darkness. On screen, Kate's eyes drifted to the camera, the infrared turning her retinas into black holes, her pupils glowing moons in the center.

"Good night," she replied, her voice small, nearly swallowed by the dark.

She listened to Kate readjust for the first few minutes and flipped through the medical history. Sleep walking. Night terrors. Sleep paralysis. Going back years. Prescriptions for antidepressants, antipsychotics, stimulants, cognition enhancing drugs. All adjusted or abandoned. A graveyard of a list. Documented history of self-harm during sleep, possibly indicative of a REM behavior disorder. Jenn sipped her coffee and shook her head. Sleep medicine was still—relatively speaking—new. People had a hard time attributing problems with sleep to waking world issues.

She went back to early notes which included paperwork from CPS. After showing up at school with wounds on her face, someone—probably a teacher—had called in a tip. Police had been sent to the home and found heavy bolts on the outside of Kate's bedroom. There were denials of abuse and Kate's own words, defending her parents and their actions.

They have to lock the door 'cause of the shadows.

She'd wanted to know if Jenn would lock her in. . .

Jenn looked at the screen where Kate had finally managed to still, eyes closed, body sinking into the mattress as her muscles relaxed. Sleep would not be long coming. Jenn's heart went out to her, her earlier unease forgotten. She reminded herself she was there to help a scared, *exhausted* kid who probably hadn't had a good night sleep in years, if ever. Jenn couldn't imagine what she had gone through.

The EKG steadied and the SP02 readouts were clear. No irregular rhythms and oxygen saturation was great. She was drifting off. Her legs twitched a little, spiking on the graph, nothing abnormal. A lot of people had hypnic jerks or muscle spasms on the edge of sleep. But Jenn noted the movement since restless leg syndrome could always be a symptom of something greater. She continued checking readouts, noting the time on her watch. If Kate was narcoleptic, she would move quickly into REM sleep.

The EOG channel spiked and fell quickly. Up and down. It was like watching the recording of an earthquake. The EEG waves. . .

Wow. Jenn looked through her feed, hardly believing. Kate had barely cycled through her sleep stages before jumping into REM. Jenn made notes, clicking and highlighting on the screen and notating with her pen. The human brain needed about 90 minutes to cycle through sleep. Entering paradoxical sleep at barely 15 minutes could explain a lot of issues.

On the monitor, Kate slept on her side. The camera itself couldn't pick up the REM, but Jenn found herself looking for it anyway, squinting to try and identify muscle tremors around Kate's face. It was rare to have a patient like Kate. Most of the time, she had patients with classic sleep apnea. Spending time listening to someone snore and watching the roller coaster of their oxygen levels was not the same thrill. But a REM behavior disorder? An undiagnosed narcoleptic without cataplexy? There was something exciting happening.

There was also someone in Kate's room.

Someone was standing off to the side, just on the edge of the camera view where the image blurred. A figure in shadow. Just a solid form. A shoulder. An arm. A hand. A. . . strange hand. The fingers were too long, too hooked. But that wasn't possible. The door hadn't opened. Jenn would have seen someone enter the floor. She would have heard them.

The camera was not made to move, so Jenn found herself leaning toward the screen, squinting at the image. Had someone messed with her equipment? There just couldn't be—

Jenn started in her seat as Kate sucked in a great breath and sat up in the bed, all the readouts jumping and diving at the sudden change. Heart rate elevated. Movement detected. Brain waves altered. All displays indicating the same thing: awake.

Kate looked around her room, eyes wide, a child searching the corners for monsters. A nightmare. She'd had a nightmare. And the shadow Jenn had seen was gone. There was nothing there. No one in the room.

"Dammit," Jenn whispered, willing her heart to calm, her watch vibrating on her wrist, curious as to the spike it detected. She rubbed her eyes, listening to the dull *squeak* of her eyeballs protesting in their sockets, and laughed under her breath. There had been nothing there. She had read the file and made herself jumpy. Silly.

Kate had slipped back down between the sheets, the pillow balled up under her head. She'd gripped the blanket so hard Jenn could see the impressions. Kate cleared her throat and looked at the camera, glowing orbs of light steady on the lens.

"I think you should lock your office door."

The words had been quiet, more air than anything, and Jenn felt a chill as if they had been whispered across her skin from inches away. A threat? A warning? Jenn wasn't allowed to answer. Protocol. This was not someone asking for help. Not someone in distress. All vital signs dipped to normal. Kate was already showing signs of slipping back into sleep. Her lids closed on the screen and Jenn was shocked to see delta waves already appearing on the EEG which should have been. . . impossible. Nobody should be able to move so quickly from REM sleep to fully awake to the final stage of non-REM sleep. Human brains just didn't work like that. Or weren't supposed to.

Mesmerized, Jenn watched the clock. Two minutes. Five minutes. Eight minutes. Ten minutes. *There.* The polysomnogram registered REM at ten minutes after being fully alert. Jenn marveled and tapped her finger on the printouts beneath her scribbled notes. Maybe Kate had never been fully alert. Maybe Jenn had made a mistake in the chaos and Kate had been sleep talking. She would need to look at the readouts more carefully.

Her eyes flicked back and forth along the pathways, tracking oxygen levels and spikes in corneal movement. Kate breathed deeply, a steady in and out, push and pull of air from lungs, but the snore mic remained mostly silent. And as Kate combed through the graphs, noting waves and spindles, she became aware of another sound the mic was picking up. Something soft. A clicking? A whisper? She checked the sensor readout for Kate's chin. It was steady. So were the sensors on her fingers and legs. Maybe she moved her foot back and forth when she slept, some people did that. An unconscious act of self-soothing.

When she turned her head to check the video feed, the shadowy figure was back. Closer to the bed this time, the torso in frame. Jenn could see a clavicle and the suggestion of a head. But it didn't move. Just. . . hovered.

Sweat broke out on Jenn's lip and she licked it away, the bitter aftertaste of her coffee on her tongue now layered with salt. She waited for the shadow to fade or reconcile itself into something her brain could rationalize, but it just remained at the edge of the frame. Poised. Waiting. Standing slowly, Jenn shifted around her desk to another set of monitors which displayed all the entrances, exits, and hallways in the building. All were dark. All were empty. Except one. In the upper corner, she could see her floor and herself in real time, the security camera mounted at the end of the corridor. With a few clicks, she backed up the feed, craning her neck to check the infrared screen where the shadow still lingered.

She played the archived footage from that day. There she was, waving goodbye to Martin—another tech—when he left for the evening. She watched herself move back and forth between Kate's room and the supply closet, setting up. Doing paperwork. Eating dinner at her desk. Leaving to go let her patient in downstairs. Fast-forward slowly. A moment later, the recording showed her return with Kate carrying her overnight bag. She played the entire feed. Nobody could have hidden in that room. There were no closets. There wasn't even a gap under the bed. And nobody else came into the ward. *Nobody*.

But the figure on the infrared monitor remained.

Someone was playing a prank. Someone had hacked the system. Maybe Kate had wanted to scare her. Maybe she had a friend in the parking lot messing with the feeds. Well, Jenn wasn't going to let glitches and anomalies and a sad history influence her judgment. She wasn't going to raise an alarm over imagined shadows. She was a professional. Still, she pulled her keys from her pocket and adjusted them in her grip like a weapon, keeping a watch on Kate's door. If the latch moved or if something passed by the small window cut into the wood, she would see it immediately.

The door to the office opened with a *whoosh* and she paused at the threshold, hesitant. The air in the hallway smelled of hospital grade disinfectant and antiseptic. Her own office smelled of coffee and the remnants of the empanada she'd reheated for dinner. The dimmed fluorescent lights and AC gave off their discordant hums, both refusing to switch octaves so they might better harmonize. Jenn would know those sounds and smells in her own sleep. Everything on her wing was familiar.

And something was wrong.

She didn't need to look around. She knew every inch of the ward. Knew how it *should* have felt. Knew it was different. A miasma had settled along with a sense of dread that slipped over Jenn's skin like oil. The air tasted strange and her inner ear began to ring with tinnitus. But there wasn't an odor trail from a forgotten laundry bin or a light bulb preparing to burn out. The wrongness was *in* Kate's room.

Intruder.

The logical part of Jenn's brain that had viewed the tape and had followed protocol told her there was no one else in the sleep clinic but her patient.

The primal part of her brain that sensed danger told her she was very, very wrong.

Jenn forced her feet across the cream-colored linoleum, her purple and yellow crocs stepping carefully as if avoiding squeaky floorboards. Her breathing was too loud, she thought. She could hear it. She hoped it wouldn't wake Kate. She hoped it wouldn't give her away. The plastic remote for her car bit into her skin, pinching as she gripped her keys so tight her fingers cramped. It felt good. It grounded her.

She couldn't open the door. Not just because she was scared. In fact, she was terrified. But it would compromise the study. She'd not only risk her job, but she'd potentially cost Kate a chance to get another sleep study. Her insurance could always refuse to pay. Opening that door would open too many other doors, none of them good.

It would also open the only barrier between Jenn and whatever she could not have possibly seen.

So, the window. It was small, just a long pane of glass cut into the wood. She'd be looking into an almost completely dark room. But she had to. Had to look. Had to be sure. She took a deep breath as if she was about to dive into a pool and took the last step, her nose nearly brushing the glass.

Nothing.

She could see the end of the bed in the weak light from the hall. Just the faintest impression, but it was there. She could make out Kate's feet under the blankets and the wall opposite. She could see the outline of the chair in the corner, empty. She could see her own shadow as she blocked the dim light behind her.

Her exhale fogged the window. She wanted to laugh again in relief, but didn't want to risk waking Kate. And she didn't feel like laughing.

She felt watched.

Kate hadn't moved. She lay perfectly still. Maybe she was awake again. Maybe she could see Jenn's shadow.

But Jenn knew it wasn't Kate watching.

She forced herself to turn away from the window, skin crawling, feeling exposed. Back inside the office, she held the door shut, leaning her forehead on the thick, cool glass. She was shaking; her keys, still in her hand, rattled against the metal doorframe as she stared down at the handle.

Without a second thought, she locked it.

"Get a grip," she told herself in a voice *just* loud enough to break the silence. She had let her patient scare her, had let some discrepancy on the feed scare her. She had read a ghost story and was seeing ghosts. Maybe she had started to doze at her desk and had a hypnagogic hallucination. A quiet night. A sob story. A greasy dinner. There were so many variables.

She needed to get back to work.

But she didn't unlock the door.

Jenn walked round the first set of monitors and back to her chair. She ignored the infrared feed as she sat, refusing to look at it. She needed to check the readouts. By her watch, she had been away almost ten minutes. She tapped some keys. Blinked. Blinked again and released a shuddering breath.

The EOG was steady. No eye movement at all. Not a twitch. Next to it, the EMG had flatlined. There wasn't just no eye movement. There was *no* movement. The sensors might have been hooked up to a corpse. Except the red line of the EKG made it look like she was sprinting, the peaks and troughs like sharp, needle teeth and the EEG dipped up and down along ocean waves.

Kate was experiencing sleep paralysis.

And there was sound. A sound trapped inside a throat which refused to work, behind lips that would not open.

Jenn's own throat worked in response, a quiet sobbing that began in her chest and worked its way slowly up, her chin quivering as she turned her head to the camera feed, livestreaming the episode in Kate's room.

They were gathered round the bed. The shadows. The intruders. Black figures standing still in Kate's room, circled round her prone figure, crowded together. The infrared bloomed bright against the white blanket; Kate's head pillowed near the top of the mattress. Glowing eyes open. Staring straight up. Seeing, but not awake.

Jenn regretted that second cup of coffee.

She wanted to go home. The urge to leave was so strong, she stood from her seat and imagined herself just walking out, saying nothing, taking nothing. But the red EXIT sign that marked her only means of escape was on the far end of the hall and she would have to pass right by her patient's room. Right within reach.

She knew she would not make it.

Will you wake me up?

Jenn sucked in air, a jolt of electricity shooting up her spine. She needed to wake Kate. Her hand drifted towards the button that would switch on the lights in Kate's room, but she snatched it back as if burned. The phantoms in the room were dreadful enough as shadows. What would they look like with the lights on? She wasn't sure she wanted to know. She didn't know if she would see anything at all. And that was infinitely worse.

Instead, she summoned her strength and pressed the button for the microphone, flinching at the audible *click* of the speaker. "Kate? I need you to wake up."

All the shadows turned their heads up to the camera. They had no faces. No eyes.

Jenn's voice shook, but she tried again. "Kate. I need you to wake up. Now."

The microphone picked up more garbled whimpers and the EMG along Kate's throat was triggered. A faint wiggle on the otherwise solid line.

On some unseen cue, the shadows all began to drift out of frame and Jenn experienced time dilation, the real world playing out on the monitor while everything beyond slowed. The distinct click of the analog clock on the wall stalled and the ambient noises of the ward faded to static. The door across the hall opened by invisible hands into a black void and the darkness within seeped into the hallway. All the while, Jenn watched the monitor with all the morbid fascination of a car wreck. Watched the room empty of all but one shadow and Kate. She had no way of being sure, but she sensed it was the first she had seen with its clawed digits. It lifted an arm and pointed one of those long fingers at the camera. At Jenn. Staring at her. Knowing her. She thought of the scars on Kate's arms and shuddered.

"Kate," she tried again, but her tongue was thick, her nose running.

Slowly, she lifted her gaze from the screen to stare out the glass windows, already knowing what she'd see. Or what she wouldn't see. The hall was dimmer, like an overcast day, the colors leeched and the air hazy. But there were no eyeless faces pressed against the glass. No hands clawing to get in.

Not that she could see.

But there was an awareness of energy. The same knowledge she had in a parking garage, listening for the echo of someone's heels or the slam of a door, sure she wasn't alone. The shadows Kate had dreamed were on the other side of the glass, and they were all staring at her. They could see her. Just as the thing on the screen could see her.

"Nnnnnn."

Kate's voice over the line. The sound was small, forced, barely audible. But Jenn was trained to listen for it. She looked at Kate's face, the infrared light flattening her features, but her eyes, spotlights, open and aware and staring at the camera. The sound—enough of a word— was for Jenn. Not the monster in the dark who would not listen, would *never* listen. She wanted Jenn to keep going. To see. To know.

Her cell phone was in her bag. The call button for security was closer, only inches from her hand. But Jenn didn't reach for either. Instead, she sat back down in her chair, forcing her gaze away from the glass and back to the polysomnography monitor and its rainbow of channels. She tapped keys and highlighted spindles and waves, tears mixing with snot on her face that she wiped away with the back of her arm, silver streaks left on blue cotton.

In her peripheral vision, she saw the shadow continue to point steadily at the camera—at her—with one clawed hand as it used the other to pluck and scratch at Kate's arm, sometimes catching on a wire, sometimes triggering a nerve to shudder. When it did, Jenn noted the disturbance. She was a professional. And this was a sleep study. She was there to collect data for scoring.

Behind her, she heard something try the handle.

She checked the time. Six hours to go.

She wondered if the lock would hold till morning.

IRINA'S CHOICE
UTE ORGASSA

"COME INSIDE." Hunter smiled as he turned the key.

He opened the door to the small cabin. Irina set down her duffle bag and stepped inside. She turned on the light switch. Electricity crackled as the overhead light turned on.

She stepped forward and opened the curtains to the back window. The cabin was small, but comfortable.

"You're sure your parents are okay with us staying here?"

Hunter brought in several bags. "Of course. We will have a lovely time, just the two of us." He took the small stairs leading up to the second story two at a time.

"I still need to study for my exam," Irina replied.

"Yeah, yeah, how about you check out the little brook outside back while I unload the rest of the stuff?" He had sweat beads on his forehead and smiled widely.

Irina followed him outside and watched him go back to his massive SUV. He had been hyper the whole drive there. She left him to his work and went behind the cabin, following her ears to find the little brook that splashed between dense woods and moss-covered boulders. It was almost noon, but very little sunlight filtered onto the forest floor.

Irina returned inside to see Hunter cramming groceries, water, and beer into the fridge. A dozen more grocery bags threatened to fall off the small wooden counter.

"Goodness, how much food did you bring?"

"Enough to last us the weekend. The nearest store is at least six miles away. I want everything to be perfect for you, honey."

He attacked the bags and put the dry stuff into empty cabinets. "Come, let's go on a hike."

Out in the woods Irina and Hunter followed a small trail. Irina hiked ahead on the moss and pine needles covered path and took a deep breath, while waiting for Hunter to catch up.

The trees were turning from their green hues to brilliant reds and golds but were still in full foliage. The scenery was overgrown and lush.

"Thank you for this," she said. "I didn't think you would come out here. I thought you did not really like nature."

Hunter wiped sweat from his face. "It's not that bad. I wanted us to go on a nice romantic getaway and my brother is using the yacht." He scratched his back, winced, and balled his fists.

Irina stopped. "What's wrong?"

"Nothing. How about you tell me more about your grandmother and the old country?"

"Are you sure? It will bore you."

"I don't think so. You have a legacy, and I am interested in it."

Irina's face darkened. "You want to hear about the loom again."

"And why not? It is fascinating."

"I told you before. It is not for you. There are rules."

Hunter raised his arms in defeat. "All right, all right."

Irina could not help but to think about her grandmother. She would have loved these woods. Irina's mind went back to her earliest memories of Grandma Iris, sitting in front of her loom; gently guiding the shuttle boat through the warp strings and listening to songs on the record player. Irina had loved watching Grandma doing this peaceful work.

The best had been when Grandma Iris had asked her to come sit by the loom when Irina had woken from bad dreams. They had gotten all comfy, Irina on the sofa with a mountain of pillows and Grandma Iris in her special weaving chair, her loom right in front of her. Grandma Iris had started a new weft of pure white yarn and asked Irina to tell her the nightmare. A cup of tea had been placed by Irina's side.

As the words flowed from Irina, the shuttle went right to left, left to right. Grandma nodded and hummed along. Time seemed to stretch in wondrous ways, the light turned a brilliant tone, and Grandma worked like in a trance until all of the nightmare was told and even the most garish of monsters had been brought out of Irina's mind onto a beautiful piece of cloth in the small crafting room.

Once the telling was over and Irina felt all better, Grandma Iris had removed the most colorful and intricate patterned weaves from the loom. They were the size of a handkerchief or a small tea towel. She had never dared to sell those. The nightmare weaves stayed in the special crafts drawer that belonged to Irina alone.

Going back to bed on those nights had been easy for Irina. Sleep had come readily, the nightmares forgotten.

"Hey, how about a selfie?" Hunter held out his phone. Irina closed the small distance between them and smiled for the picture. Hunter breathed heavily and the shirt on his back felt clammy.

"Are you alright?"

"I'm perfectly fine. You worry too much."

"Can you send the pic over to me?"

"Yes, once we're back home."

"Why not now?"

He held out his phone to her. "Look at the bars. No reception."

Irina grabbed his water bottle. "At least drink something. You don't want to dehydrate."

Hunter agreed to that. He also agreed to return to the cabin right away after downing all his water.

"At least tell me why your mother hates it so much," he prompted on the way back.

"The loom?"

"Yes."

"She has her reasons."

"I don't understand it. It is a nicely crafted tool. You use it all the time. And she calls it an instrument of the devil."

"My mother has a bad history with it. She used it wrong."

"So, she got hurt?"

"Yes. Can we drop the topic now?"

"Come on, don't be so sensitive. I'm just curious."

Irina shook her head. She could almost hear her mother's warning again. The memory was so clear in her mind. "Don't ever go near that thing, you hear? Especially not when Grandma Iris is not around! I am going to burn it, the first chance I get!"

She chose not to heed that warning. Instead, Grandma Iris had taken Irina under her wing. Irina had started on a training loom. She had learned about spacers and beaters; about yarn strength and bubbling. She had slowly made pieces that her grandma lauded, even if they were uneven and sometimes completely disintegrated when Irina had tried to get them off her tiny loom. Her knowledge about weaving had not been appreciated by her mother at all. Thinking back now, Irina remembered the argument her mother and her grandmother had had.

"How dare you think she is ready to take on your duties?"

"Someone has to, and you are not going to be the one."

"This is nonsense. Nobody has to. I don't want to have anything to do with it."

"Have you learned nothing? We can't just stop."

"You know what it took away from me. And you could do nothing but blame me."

"I told you exactly how it worked and what it could do. You chose to ignore the warnings. You brought your loss onto yourself. I will not let Irina go into this blind. And unlike you, she knows how to follow rules."

These words still echoed through Irina's mind. Yes, there were rules. Hard and unbending ones. If only she could make Hunter understand that, without sounding crazy.

Hunter cooked up a storm for dinner but ate very little. Irina watched him moving his food around on his plate with his fork. He almost spoke a few times, decided against it and watched her inquisitively. Finally, he spoke up.

"Indulge me honey, you said there were rules. What are they?"

"You aren't going to drop this, are you?"

"No, I'm persistent." He grinned widely. Irina was used to his winning smile. She had loved to see it resting on her over a fancy dinner in the early days, but this time it looked artificial, taut, like a mask that didn't quite fit.

"All right. One of the rules of the loom is that only one person at a time can be paired with it. It won't work for anyone else. I have been the person responsible for it since I was nineteen and I hope I will only give up my responsibility when I am a very old lady."

"That doesn't make sense. There are teaching videos for looms online. Everyone can learn how to use it."

"Ordinary looms, yes. Mine is different."

Unbidden, a trove of memories of Grandma Iris' last weeks came to Irina. Grandma Iris had held on to her weaving duties until almost the end. She had been very sick by then. She had pointed to her loom and had commanded Irina: "Fetch the pure white, start a weft and listen to me."

Grandma had made herself comfortable on the sagging couch and Irina had done as she was told. She had checked the warp strings, put spacers, and fed the yarn into the shuttle boat. Grandma had watched Irina's practiced movements with a warm smile on her face.

"You're ready," she had stated. She had leaned back and closed her eyes. "You will be weaving my shroud and I will tell you all my secrets."

Irina had known that this day would come and had held back tears as she went to work. If her grandma had to go, at least she would do so on her own terms.

The shuttle went right to left, left to right. The light took on that special brilliant quality, time turned into molasses and Grandma Iris talked, every now and then sipping some tea. Slowly, but surely her wisdom turned into flowers and her memories into birds and grasshoppers.

Irina worked like in a trance. It took seven sessions, lasting over an hour each, to finish the shroud. Irina listened to all the sage advice and relished each memory that drained out of her mentor into the fabric. All the while she dreaded the fact that she would never hear her grandma speak those memories again. At the end of it, Grandma Iris had looked at the colorful flower meadow made of yarn that they had produced.

"This is so pretty. I wonder who made it," she had said with a beautiful smile.

Irina had been exhausted, filled with knowledge, and could not help but cup her grandmother's face as a tear rolled down her own cheek. It wasn't long after that moment that Grandma Iris had died.

"You are miles away, aren't you?"

"Sorry. I was thinking about my family."

Hunter poured two glasses of wine. He spilled a few drops with an unsteady hand. The deep red color of it dripping on the wooden table.

"Are you sure you're alright?" Irina asked.

"Of course, I am. Tell me more! Tell me about the weaves you make with the women who come to you. The ones you start with the white yarn. The ones with the prettiest patterns."

"You know about them already."

"All I know is that you make those weaves for them and never for me. They come to you, and you drop everything else, and you spend hours with them. Time you should spend with me!"

"Don't scold me."

"Sorry, so sorry, honey. Forgive me."

Twilight made strange patterns on his face. Irina stood up and turned all the lights on in the cabin. The electricity crackled again. She did not like the darkness encroaching on her.

Hunter put the dishes in the sink and smoothed his hair.

When they both had sat back down, he almost whispered. "Why do you never make a weave for me?"

Irina sighed. "Because you don't need it."

"But I want it."

"No, wanting is not enough. You don't need it. Just accept that it is not for you."

"Oh honey," he said, "everything is for me if I want it."

Irina shook her head. "You don't understand. I can't just make one for you. There are rules. These weaves are not done for fun. They are a last resort. The women come to me with stories they need to forget and memories that are too hard to bear, too hard to remember. They pay a price for their visits."

"None of them ever paid you money."

"No, they didn't. I can't ask for money. It is a responsibility. It is a community service. My weaving must always be done upon mutual agreement, with complete privacy, and never for personal gain. There you go, there are three more rules."

Hunter took her hand. "No need to get upset about it. I am just asking questions."

"I would like to be done talking about this. I wanted to be done since this afternoon."

He got up and massaged her shoulders.

"I know honey. It is just a fascinating little thing. I just took a shine to those lovely little tapestries you have."

Irina turned around and looked up at him. "What do you mean?"

He held on to her back, his grip now harder. "You know. Your pretty little weaves."

Irina got up and faced him. "Hunter, what have you done? Did you take my nightmare weaves?"

"Your what?"

"Did you take the weaves that were in my crafts drawer?"

He smiled his mischievous smile again. "So what if I did? You weren't using them."

Irina's heart beat faster. "What did you do with them?"

He just smiled.

Irina hoped that he had not been so foolish. There was no way back if he had done what she thought he had done. She could still hear her grandmother's voice. That way lies madness.

She asked again. "Hunter, what did you do with them?"

"That doesn't matter. What matters is what you are going to do for me."

He strode away from the table and went up to the loft. Coming back down he held the object of his desire in his now gloved hand. Her loom. In his other hand was a large bag with all her weaving paraphernalia.

"You brought it here?" She could feel her spine tingle.

"Yes. And you will use it. I need more!"

"Hunter!"

Dread settled around her heart. She saw that telltale glimmer in his eyes and the feverish paleness of his skin. "Hunter, did you sell my weaves?"

"How about you settle on that nice armchair and don't worry about what I have or haven't done?"

He pushed the loom into her hand. "You best start weaving."

"And what if I don't?"

He pulled her big tailor scissors out of the bag. "I don't think that would be a good idea."

"Hunter, you have no idea what you have done."

He circled her as he sat the bag down. "And you have no idea what I am capable of."

He let the scissors run over her bare arm. They left a white line. As he lifted them, Irina saw a tiny drop of blood.

She held her breath, too scared to move a muscle. "I have a very good idea of what is going on," she said.

"Then get to it," Hunter pressured.

Irina eyed the door. Maybe she could run? Maybe she could get help? She saw the keys of his SUV dangling halfway out of his dockers. Maybe she could avoid the fate that awaited them? No. It was too late. She felt a pang of sorrow. It could not be helped now. The decision had been made. There was only one way to finish this. She would follow the rules. She steadied herself. "If we are to do this, we need to do this right. Did you bring the tea?"

Hunter gave her a curious look. "Yes, I did. You are really going to help me?"

Irina wiped away a tear that had managed to escape. "You are leaving me no choice."

He smiled. "That's right. I love it when you see reason, honey."

She went to the cupboard and brewed tea. Once it was ready, she put the mug on the coffee table and motioned to the couch. "Get comfortable."

Hunter obliged with an amused look on his face, sitting down and punching a pillow into the shape of his liking. He still held her scissors in his other hand.

Irina took up the loom and sat down in the armchair. She got the yarn and necessary tools out of the bag, wound the thread into the shuttle, and made a new start with the bright white yarn.

"You look really professional when you do this." Hunter winked while watching.

Irina managed to smile back at him. "Ready. Tell me things you are willing to forget."

Hunter looked at her with a quizzical expression on his face.

"You will have to talk. Otherwise, it won't make a pattern."

"Oh, yeah, right. Can I tell you about my first tennis lessons? They were pathetic. How about that?"

"That works."

So, Hunter talked with a feverish expression on his face and Irina weaved. The brilliant light bathed them, and time turned into molasses. The shuttle boat went left to right, right to left. The weave grew and patterns formed. Irina made sure to beat the weft evenly and do her best work.

Hunter talked about his nannies. He talked about all the schools he went to, and all the summer camps he had ever been to. He went through all his hobbies. He told Irina things about his friends that made her gasp. The more he told her, the more she knew that it would have never worked out between the two of them in the long run. He enjoyed telling her about his previous girlfriends and how he had picked them up as well as how he had dumped them. Irina weaved and weaved and let him continue.

At one point his voice started to fade. She looked up. His face was ashen.

"You better drink some tea while you still can."

"What?"

"I just mean, it is going to be cold."

Hunter did as he was told. He gulped down the whole mug.

"This stuff is good."

"Keep talking."

He did.

"Hey, so just to be sure. The weave will be mine, right?" he said suddenly. "You are not tricking me. I can have it. Not you?"

"Yes, this will be yours alone. That's the rules."

"Awesome! But you stopped weaving."

"Because you stopped telling your stories."

"So anyway, did I tell you about the time when we almost closed down the airport in St. Moritz?"

Story after story poured out of him. Irina saw how Hunter leaned back further on the couch, until he was lying flat and only his lips moved. Her hands were cramped, and her neck hurt. She had never weaved this long in one go in her life. But she could not stop. Not until it was finished.

"Lady, what are we doing?" asked Hunter after he was done with another story.

"We are working together. You tell me stories from your life, and I make them into a pretty thing."

"Oh alright. I can tell you about my major, would that help?"

"You tell me everything that comes to your mind."

Hunter continued. The stories came slower and more sluggish. He had his eyes closed most of the time now. Irina kept pace with her weaving, the pattern unfolding in a plethora of brilliant colors. In the early morning hours Hunter stopped talking for good. Shortly after, his heart beat for the very last time.

Irina finished the row of the weft, sighed, and retrieved her tapestry needle. She carefully took the weave off the loom. It had the length of a shroud.

Relieving her sore hands, arms, and back, Irina stood up and stretched. She slowly packed her things and brought them out to the SUV. Once she had cleared the cabin, she returned to Hunter.

She folded his shroud and stored it under his pillow. She closed the door on him after giving him one last glance.

Irina was not afraid that anything bad would happen to her. She would not get in trouble. The loom would take care of her. It always had. She had done exactly what needed to be done. She had finished Hunter's punishment. She had protected the loom and kept its loyalty. Now it was the loom's turn to return the favor. Those were the rules.

PREMIUM
PLATINUM PLAN

AI JIANG

YOUR FINGER HOVERS OVER THE "NEXT" button on your tablet, but you don't tap.

Malorn, your roommate—also quite the unlikely best friend after four years of living together—says it's better to brew first on a choice over time, or at least overnight, before you decide. Problem is, you've been brewing on it for a month already. Your current Basic Plan delivery subscription is not *too* costly at $25 a month, but it's slow. It takes your shampoo a week to arrive, and by then, your scalp and strands are always extra greasy from using only conditioner. You could've simply *borrowed* Malorn's shampoo, but she'd notice, and you know how she is about keeping things separate.

All stores had been turned into storage warehouses now for the different companies—all in partnership with the largest non-profit charity organization: Angel Guards. It was cheaper, they said—more convenient. But that means you can't easily go pick up whatever item you need now, which is normally fine when you order ahead. But you don't always remember to make a note before something runs out. Like right now, you need more groceries, but even *that* will take a week to arrive. You could also order out for now, but delivery costs per takeout order is almost as much as the monthly basic subscription fee, not to mention the cost of the actual order.

Oh, and toilet paper. You quickly add it to your digital cart before you forget.

Your phone pings with a message from Malorn.

M: *Sorry for not telling you, but I was finally approved, and I'll be going in for a donation today. Will be spending the next few days in the hospital. And then I'll be depending on you for a few weeks* 🫠

You: *You didn't. . .*

M: *I did.*

You: *Should I?*

M: *Check your options first. You've been thinking it over for so long without even looking at them!*

You: *If I look at them, I'll be even more tempted.*

M: *Well, maybe you'll change your mind when I get home* 😊

You put down your phone and, on an impulse, tap "Next" on the AG app opened on your tablet. Malorn didn't say, but you recall her telling you her options previously. No doubt she went for the Premium Platinum Plan with next-hour delivery by donating one of her kidneys. There is no chance you get the same opportunities since you only have one kidney—the other is currently sitting inside your younger brother. But that wasn't the app's doing, and you didn't get any compensatory reward for *that*.

Sweat accumulates on your back, sticking your baggy t-shirt to your skin. On the next page, you see the green "Active" symbol next to your current subscription plan. Below it, new options appear.

Basic	Silver	Gold	Platinum	Premium Platinum
$25 Monthly	**$500** Monthly	**Community Service** 10 Hours/Week	**Blood Donation** Dependent on Type	**Partial Liver Donation** One-time only for a 10-Year Subscription
✓ Delivery Time: 1 Week	✓ Delivery Time: 5 Days	✓ Delivery Time: 5 Days	✓ Delivery Time: Next-Day	✓ Delivery Time: Next Hour
Renew	Upgrade	Upgrade	Upgrade	Upgrade
		Alternative: $1,000 Monthly	Alternative: $5,000 Monthly	Alternative: $10,000 Monthly

Your stomach churns at the thought of donating part of your liver, but the promised delivery times are enticing. Normally, people don't talk about their options, but you recall one friend mentioning partial lung donation. The information isn't quite confidential, but on the website, AG strongly suggests for us to keep it private anyhow. There have been instances where some experience more scrutiny than others if people perceive their options as being more reasonable in comparison. You've heard about some freelance workers receiving an option for community service that almost adds up to the hours of a nine-to-five job.

You glance at Angel Guards' mission, reminding yourself the reason why they're such a popular choice: *To better the world, your contribution will be used to aid those in need. In turn,* **WE** *will aid* **YOU**.

With your nine-to-seven copywriting job, there is barely any time to choose the Gold Plan with the community service, much less sleeping and eating. If you go for the alternative, you might as well say goodbye to that early retirement plan you're hoping for—and the price of flights and hotels will only go up each year. Your friend mentioned how the organization offers retirement plans; perhaps you'll brew on that. Full body donation. You're not sure you'll be able to commit to that yet, but they're offering a five-year trip across the world before they come to collect you. The only requirement is that you must plan for the trip and collection to occur while you're under the age of eighty. There is no chance of pushing the date back after you sign the contract, but you could always request for it to be pushed *up*. Though if you happen to come upon illness. . . or accidents. . .

Hover. Hesitate.

Hover. Hesitate.

Hover—

A thunk, and you know a bird crashed into the glass of the balcony's sliding door.

Hesitate—

As much as you will your eyes not to wander, they shift to look at the twitching bird laying at the edge of the lawn chair you've placed near the railing—a patient on a gurney.

Tear your eyes away.

To better the—

Tap.
Eyes skim the text.

To confirm your Platinum Plan subscription, you must agree to the terms below and book your donation appointment. Your plan will activate once the center of your choosing confirms the completion of your donation.

Scroll down to the end of the terms, skimming without actually taking in many of the words—only the most glaring ones in bold: **Consent, Responsibility, Death, Accident, Illness, Liability.**
Your appointment is in four days.
Hold your breath.
Clutch at the dining table with your free hand.
Tap.
Donating blood, that much you can do. Even though you're afraid of needles, it's less daunting than being sliced open with a scalpel and seeing the stitches in the aftermath. Perhaps it's worth it—you'll get fast delivery, *and* you get to potentially save a life. But the hospital. . . Maybe Malorn could convince you otherwise when she returns.
It's not so bad, she'll say. *Really. It's not so bad.*
And maybe you'll convince yourself to believe it.

YOU'VE NEVER DONATED blood before and thinking about your blood being in *someone else* seems like such a strange concept. You wonder if it makes you feel connected to those receiving your blood. No one ever really talks about it, at least not to you. You wonder if Malorn might choose to meet the person who receives her organ or if she will be making an anonymous donation. Knowing her, she'd want her name on a flashing banner.
There are always banners floating across the screen on the app, in addition to the frequent round-up notifications congratulating people on their donations. Mass congratulations for those donating at lower

tiers and more extravagant, eye-catching, single-mention congratulations for those donating at higher tiers. The banner never mentions what has been donated, but it also never fails to make you feel as though you aren't doing enough. You know not everyone donates for an honourable reason, yet—

"Are you ready?" the nurse asks after fixing a strap just above your elbow. She hands you a small foam heart with the charity organization's symbol on it—a pair of angel wings with swords crossed behind them—to squeeze while they draw the blood. Funny how the organization isn't tied to any religious institution, not that you know of anyhow, but they named the company "Angel Guards."

You keep your eyes squeezed shut the whole time and don't open them until they've cleaned you up and nudged your fingers loose, removing the heart from your hand. In your pocket, your phone vibrates.

Donation Complete.

And then a second ping.

Platinum Plan Activated.

The nurse smiles. "Thank you for your support."

The smile and nod you return is a drowsy one, and you feel the edge of your eyes slant down slightly.

When you leave the room, you clutch the plastic wrapped ham and cheese sandwich and apple juice box an assistant passed to you in the waiting area and make your way toward the elevator. A banner notification catches your eye: Malorn's. Hers is decorated with intricate Victorian designs in gold with virtual diamond accents.

You tear your eyes away and focus on the elevator display and the floor number ticking upward. But right as the display flashes, signalling the elevator's arrival, you black out.

YOU MUNCH on the sandwich and apple juice back in the waiting area of the donation center, where they've propped you up and reassured you that fainting isn't an uncommon occurrence and you're completely fine. But in your mind, you question if this is really something you want to do monthly. You've never fainted before. There is no guarantee that it will happen again the next time you come, but you're still skeptical.

"Is this your first time donating?" an elder asks.

They sit a few seats down from you with a magazine in their hand. You feel the area where the nurse inserted the needle throb.

Embarrassed, you reply with a slow nod.

Their expression is nonjudgmental, encouraging. "Happened on my first donation too."

"I started donating as soon as it was legal to—at eighteen."

You and the elder turn your eyes to a person with shoulder-length dark hair, bobbing as they cross their arms, fidgeting with the four rings on their left hand.

The elder's voice remains even. "To help people or to get your packages delivered faster?"

Rings flushes and looks away.

The elder turns back to me and lowers their voice. "Don't worry so much about people like them."

But you wonder if you're exactly like Rings.

You don't brood on the thought for too long because a few minutes later, before you can even finish your sandwich and juice, Malorn calls you to pick her up. You call her a taxi and spend the rest of the day resting in your car in the corner of the donation center's crowded parking lot. Before heading home, you get another ping on your phone that reminds you your Platinum Plan is now active.

Across the top of the app, your name appears among a few others as the AG AI welcomes you to your Platinum Plan and thanks you for your support. You can't help but notice winding silver designs not nearly as extravagant as the single one that adorned Malorn's name. Rather than pride, you're repulsed by the sight of your welcome banner. You press checkout after clicking over to the cart section of the app to purchase the new items you added, saved to purchase until after the donation, fingers shaking.

"HOW ARE YOU FEELING?" you ask.

"Painkillers. I need more painkillers," Malorn says, clutching at her abdomen.

"I can—"

She holds up a hand. "No need. I already ordered some. They arrived hours ago. Could you get them for me from the cupboard?" Jealousy brings heat to your ears. "And tea, please. Thanks." She offers a weak smile that still somehow holds her usual brilliance, just fainter.

"Sure. . . Of course."

Even in her weak state, Malorn never fails to be demanding.

You hand her her favorite black oolong tea and a bottle of painkillers you've never seen before with ingredients you don't recognize.

"Is it worth it?"

Maybe it's too early to ask. She'd only gotten home hours ago.

"Every time there's sharp pain I think no, but when it's gone, heck yeah." Malorn gestures towards the open door of her room at the pile of packages scattered across her floor. "I even got groceries! And something for you too! Just a small snack though, you know how it is with the budget." She scratches the back of her head, a small, bashful dent appearing in the middle of her eyebrows. An act, always acting. She has no budget for what she spends on herself, only during the rare times she thinks of you.

You nod. "Of course. Thank you."

Malorn's smile returns. "So. . . dinner. . ."

You can't deny the girl anything even if you try, so you agree and head to the kitchen. You organize her groceries into the fridge before taking out the ingredients for a quick stir fry while munching on the "snack" she bought for you—a half-eaten bag of chips.

EVEN THOUGH NEXT-DAY delivery makes waiting so much more bearable, you cancel your Platinum Plan after three months, having passed out the subsequent two times you donated blood—your blackouts each lasting longer than the last. While you wait for your deliveries, you listen as the doorbell rings twice, sometimes several times a day. Malorn calls you to grab the packages for her even after her recovery period is over. You are used to it by now. But what you are not used to is the fact that the packages you're bringing in are not yours.

Your Basic Plan will resume next month, so at least you still get to enjoy your next-day deliveries for a bit longer. Yet you have your hangry, no grocery, and greasy, no shampoo moments still, and envy Malorn's almost instantaneous meals and luscious locks. You wonder just how much she makes at her food packaging job to afford her continuous purchases. Maybe you should switch too. But you have always relied on mental skills rather than physical ones. Not that you're weak. Sometimes you even exercise three times a week after work. But you prefer remote work. You prefer staying home.

"HAVE I CONVINCED YOU?" Malorn says, mouthful of pasta with marinara sauce and bacon bits. She waves her wooden fork in front of me, taunting. "You'll get *all* of this, *and* probably save a life."

Your lip twitches in sync with your eyes.

"You'll never get hangry again! And you'll give someone else a chance to also be an Angel."

"What are you? Their brand ambassador?" you mutter.

Malorn laughs. "Actually. . ."

She pulls open her AG app and shows me the small badge under her name on her profile: **BA**.

"They have this new program going. If you use my referral code. . . while donating blood or an organ. . ." Malorn tips her chin down, fake lashes fluttering, glossed lips in an exaggerated pout.

"What do you get?" You sigh.

"For each person, depending on the donation, I get extra time added to my retirement plan with them."

You grab her arm, clutch a little too tight, voice a little too loud. "You signed it already?"

Malorn shakes you off, annoyed. "Yes! What's wrong with that?"

You slump back. Malorn used to tell you everything first, and now you're just discovering things by accident. "When?"

Malorn clicks her tongue, looks away. "In twenty years."

"In twen— You won't even be near retirement age yet!"

She narrows her eyes at her nails. "That's the point. I want to *enjoy* the trip while I still have the energy, not be *dragged* through it."

"You don't know that."

"I do. I might be healthy now, but we never know what might happen to us in the future. Heck, even a few hours, minutes, or seconds from now. Maybe I should push the trip *up*."

"Do you not have any goals you want to achieve before they. . . collect you. . .?" You ask quietly.

She shakes her head, then looks at you, curious. "Do you?"

You fall silent, brewing, once again brewing, always brewing on the thought. *Do you?*

YOU DON'T. And five years later, you're still doing the same copywriting job, trying to sell the very things you don't have money to buy—trying to convince others it's worth spending the money they probably need for much more important things than laminated envelopes, crystal wine glasses that will likely be used for orange juice, and tree trimmers when most houses don't have much greenery anymore. For those who still have green lawns and yards, they can afford to hire someone to tidy things up for them. There are subscription services for those by Angel Guards, too.

So you find yourself sitting outside the condo entrance, wind messing up your already messy hair even more, considering making an appointment to donate part of your liver.

You *must* have higher purpose than copywriting. . . right? And if you don't, maybe by doing this, you can create one.

You scroll through the mission page specific to your Premium Platinum Plan option and liver donation, skimming through photos of past recipients and donors—most likely a mix of models and real people—and the text bubbles around them. Even though Malorn isn't here trying to convince you for the benefit of her brand ambassador perks, you know that you'll somehow convince yourself.

"Give the gift of a second chance at life."

"To spend more time with family. . ."

"Say goodbye to loved ones. . ."

"The opportunity to find love. . ."

"Accompany their child for the rest of their childhood. . ."

"Allow this child to achieve their dreams—'I want to become a doctor!' Make their dream come true!"

The last one catches your attention. You know a liver donation doesn't necessarily guarantee a long survival time for the recipient post-transplant, but to think you could help a child restore part of the time stolen from them.

Hover. Hesitate.

Hover. Hesitate.

Hover—

You don't *need* the one-hour delivery service, but it's simply a bonus in addition to you saving a life. Someone out there could need a liver transplant at this very moment, and every second you waste contemplating over this might lower their chance of survival. And think about the shampoo, the toilet paper, the groceries, the—

Hesitate—

All of it will be at your door when you come home from work, after a nice long shower, a quick show on the streaming site with ads every five minutes—but at least it's free.

Tap.

Prior to the donation date, would you like to meet the recipient of your donation?

You want to tap "No," but before you can stop yourself, you tap "Yes."

IT TURNS out that the part of your liver being donated isn't going to a single receipt but rather, it would be used for *two*: a woman in her forties with alcoholic tendencies, and a young child—barely a teen—who had the misfortune of inheriting a liver disease.

You weren't nervous when you confirmed your appointment time but heading to the hospital your shirt sticks to the skin covering your gurgling stomach. The last time you were in a hospital was for your yearly check-up—to update your health records. That was a few months back. There is something about hospitals that makes you uneasy.

Two patients wheeled by two nurses come towards you. A cough from the woman—Hillary; a large but sheepish grin from the child —Geno.

"Thank you," they say, unsynchronized—one voice low, one even lower, but you can't tell which belongs to who.

They seem to feel as awkward as you do, but the grateful expressions beneath the red and pink flushes warm you.

Hillary has an aging husband to care for, she explains. And Geno says he wants to become an architect, hoping to introduce more greenery back into the greying cities. Geno has the low voice; Hillary has the lower voice. Before the nurses wheel the recipients away, Hillary squeezes your elbow. Geno offers you a half-hug—you bend to receive it, having forgotten the warmth of others.

The receptionist prods for your attention when the two disappear down the hall.

"Do you have someone at home who can pick you up and take care of you when you're discharged?"

You think of Malorn but know she will only be doing the bare minimum for you compared to what you did for her while she was recovering. Knowing her, you'll have to call a taxi too—not because she's busy, but because she'll make an excuse not to come. You think of the time you were sick and how Malorn placed unseasoned boiled broccoli in front of you and fled back to her room with a quick, "Here ya go!"

"Yes," you say.

The receptionist smiles. "Thank you so much for your support."

AFTER TEN YEARS, Malorn's moved out with a lover she hooked up with from work. Your plan automatically reverts to $25/month as the organization's app recalibrates the subscription page with your health records. You don't need to have deliveries arrive the next hour, but because you're so used to it, you feel as though you must. You consider the community service hours and the blood donations, but wave it from your mind when you think of your overtime and black-outs that occur even without you drawing any blood—the over-working could still be a cause, however.

They notified you that Hillary's husband is now at a home for elders and that Hillary passed after the transplant due to unspecified complications. You wonder if the individuals volunteering at the elder homes are passionate about their work, or simply doing it for subscriptions.

Geno fared better and is currently studying architecture at a univer-sity in a different city, but they didn't allow him to add as many green spaces as he'd have liked. Perhaps you might visit him at some point on your vacation.

You turned in your resignation letter for your copywriting job last week and finished up your remaining tasks for existing clients. Some clients contacted you, begging you to reconsider. But you leave them to answer to your voicemail.

An early vacation doesn't sound so bad, not at all, *and* you get to potentially save more than a few lives once it's over. You wonder who will receive your brain, your heart, your liver, your skin, your remaining kidney. . .

As you listen to the last desperate client voicemail and a rather bragging one from Malorn—"We're getting hitched! Isn't it *such* a dream?"—your finger hovers over the confirmation button. You check and recheck the start and end date of your five-year vacation, the date of your body donation.

When the app takes you to the confirmation page, you can't help but question whether or not you made the right choice. And you realize just how much of your life you have yet to live.

Donation Confirmed. Thank you for your support and enjoy your trip!
Name: Jiriu Wang
Birthdate: 11/21/2083
Current Date: 11/14/2123
Trip Start Date: 11/21/2123
Collection Date: 11/21/2128
*Press **here** to save a copy of your receipt.*
*At Angel Guards, our mission is to better the world. Your contribution will be used to aid those in need. In turn, **WE** will aid **YOU**.*

THE HARBINGER

KATIE YOUNG

Partial Transcript of Creative Kick-Off & Subs Review Meeting
Supernatural Files: Legit or Bulls**t? Season 3
10th October 2015

Agenda:

10:00 – 13:00 Intro & Submissions Review
13:00 – 14:00 Break for Lunch
14:00 – 17:00 Submissions Review & Shortlist

Attendees:

Jason Logan (Stuntman)
Clara Beaumont (Photographer)
Derek Mambwe (VFX & Tech Specialist)
Sofia Ortiz (Investigative Journalist)
Robert Dorfman (Paranormal Investigator)
Kristen Garcia (Executive Producer)
Ben Jameson (Field Producer)
Gerry Matthews (Line Producer)

Jennifer Black (Production Manager)
Li Tang-Archer (Production Coordinator)
Amy Wishaw (Production Secretary)

Apologies:

Kelly Harrison (Production Assistant/Researcher)
Nicholas Farnaby (Segment Producer)

Transcript:

KRISTEN: Oh, come on! That's a classic case of pareidolia. It's nothing—just leaves and shadows. Bigfoot, my ass. These submissions are terrible. There must have been some better ones than this?

JENNIFER: Maybe we already plumbed the depths—exhausted all the good stuff in the first two seasons?

KRISTEN: No wonder Kelly called in sick. She's scared to face the music.

LI: Aww, poor kid. She's lost weeks of her life wading through this crap. I guess this is the best of a bad bunch. You can't blame her for the public's lack of creativity.

KRISTEN: I can when she's not in the room to hear me. (Laughter) Probably gave herself a migraine watching these abominations. She sent something on e-mail. I haven't watched it yet, but Nick said it was uncanny as fuck. It won't open on my phone, but I'll forward it to you all.

GERRY: Nick struck down too? Weird. I hope it's nothing too nasty. Or contagious.

ROBERT: That's not an orb. It's just a bug reflecting the porch light, see? The movement is too erratic. And that door probably just got caught by a breeze. Ugh. Not even a sniff of poltergeist activity.

JASON: That's shit's all super easy to fake anyway. Jesus Christ! They ain't even trying anymore. You can see the strings attached to this Mothman's wings!

CLARA: (Laughter) Yeah! Not exactly state of the art, is it?

DEREK: (In an exaggerated narrator voice) Our photographic expert, Clara, is pinching the bridge of her nose because she smells bullshit. (Laughter)

CLARA: Damn straight. That's our script for the season premiere, right there. Actually, I think I need a screen break. Shall we call that lunch?

E-mail 9th October 2015 10:54PM
From: Kelly Harrison
To: Nicholas Farnaby; Kristen Garcia; Gerry Matthews
Subject: The Harbinger WTF?

Hi all,
As you know, I've been doing a first sift through the submissions ahead of the creative kick-off tomorrow and came across the attached. TBH, it's really freaked me out. Never seen anything like it. What do you think?
Kel x

Automatic Reply 10th October 2015 10:54PM
From: Gerry Matthews
To: Kelly Harrison; Nicholas Farnaby; Kristen Garcia.
Subject: The Harbinger WTF?

This inbox is full and unable to receive messages at this time. Please contact the administrator.

E-mail Message 9ᵗʰ October 2015 11:23PM
From: Nicolas Farnaby
To: Kelly Harrison; Kristen Garcia; Gerry Matthews
Subject: The Harbinger WTF?

Hi Kelly,
You're a trooper. Hear it's been particularly slim pickings this season.
Thanks for taking one for the team. 😊 It took me a few goes to open
the MP4 and then I wasn't really sure what I was looking at. But yeah
—it's pretty creepy. Where did it come from?
Nick

E-mail Message 10ᵗʰ October 2015 12:18AM
From: Kelly Harrison
To: Nicholas Farnaby; Kristen Garcia; Gerry Matthews
Subject: The Harbinger WTF?

It was in the rejected file from S1, in a folder labeled 'Maine Banshee—
DO NOT USE'. I wouldn't normally have bothered, but I was getting
desperate, so I wanted to leave no stone unturned. Maybe they
couldn't clear the rights or something? It's WAY better than most of the
clips I've seen tho. I know these things are subjective, but I think it
beats anything we've had on the show before hands down. Not
throwing shade, but maybe your PA back then wasn't as astute as me.
😊
Kel x

E-mail 10ᵗʰ October 2015 7:12AM
From: Kelly Harrison
To: Nicholas Farnaby; Kristen Garcia; Gerry Matthews
Subject: The Harbinger WTF?

Actually guys, I had a really bad night. I haven't slept at all. I feel
rotten. Probably just too much screen time and it's triggered a
migraine, but I think I'm going to have to stay home. Really sorry. I
texted Li and she's going to sort coffees, lunch, etc. for the meeting

today. I'll try to check my e-mails once I've had a bit of sleep. Sorry again.

Kel x

Automatic Reply 10ᵗʰ October 2015 7:13AM
From: Nicholas Farnaby
To: Kelly Harrison; Kristen Garcia; Gerry Matthews
Subject: The Harbinger WTF?

Thanks for your e-mail. I am OOO today on sick leave. I'll revert soon, but response times might be slower than usual.

Best, Nick

E-mail 10ᵗʰ October 2015 8:46AM
From: Kristen Garcia
To: Nicholas Farnaby; Kelly Harrison; Gerry Matthews
Subject: The Harbinger WTF?

Jeez—dropping like flies! What's going on?? Feel better, both of you!

KG

Treatment for Supernatural Files: Legit or Bulls**t? Season 3 Episode 8 (Season Finale)

TITLE: The Harbinger

RUN TIME: 45′ – 48′

FORMAT: Each episode, the team pick two controversial video clips or photographs of supposedly supernatural phenomena to try and re-create. Combining their specialist skills in camera trickery, VFX, stunt co-ordination, journalism, and paranormal investigation, they aim to prove or debunk the claims made by those who submit their mysterious media.

LOGLINE: Clara and Robert investigate an old photograph of an apparition in a reportedly haunted London theatre, while Derek, Jason, and Sofia travel to the scene of a sighting of a specter, which locals claim brings certain death to anyone who encounters it and hears its harrowing cries.

OUTLINE: In the first segment, the whole team review five submissions. The first is a vintage photograph taken in a theatre on London's famous Drury Lane, purportedly showing the ghost of an actress who committed suicide by drinking poison in her dressing room, after learning of her theatre producer husband's infidelity. Robert is excited by the prospect of visiting the legendary haunted theatre, and Clara has some ideas about how to recreate the spooky effect. They agree to go to London together. The team's second option is a smartphone video of a glowing, cigar shaped UFO spotted hovering in the sky over Sacramento. They decide it's too cliché and easily faked. The third is grainy camcorder footage, allegedly of a bipedal Indonesian cryptid called the Orang-bati. This elicits excitement initially, until Jason posits that it's a person in a monkey suit and demonstrates how easy it is to move in an ape-like fashion to create the hoax. Much hilarity ensues.

Next up for consideration is a photograph of a teenage girl from Tokyo who appears to be levitating over her single bed. Sofia recalls that she and Jason re-created a similar case in the previous season, and successfully proved it was an illusion facilitated by a simple pully system and some post-production clean up. And finally—the pièce de résistance—is our chosen season closer. Sofia introduces a video taken at the edge of a forest in Maine. It's nighttime, and the phone camera points towards the tree line. We hear a terrible shrieking sound emanating from the pines. It's loud. It ricochets around the surrounding hills. The picture is shaky, the cameraman breathing heavily. He continues to film as a figure emerges from the trees. It seems to be human-shaped, shrouded in white, and it floats above the ground, gliding inexorably towards the camera in an undeniably eerie movement. The man behind the camera swears and begins to babble as he backs up, but the camera stays trained on the phantom as it gains on him. The ghastly scream sounds again, closer now and loud enough to distort the audio being picked up by the microphone. As the screeching phantom lunges at the lens, we see that it's draped in a sheer fabric and through the muslin we can just make out features. Or—more accurately—the lack thereof. Dark holes where there should be eyes and a gaping, distended maw. The phone is knocked or dropped to the ground. We see a blur of inky sky, trees, ground, and white as it tumbles. Finally, it comes to rest, and auto-focuses on the upper-left corner of the camera-man's face. His eyes are open, sightless. He is perfectly still. Every-thing is quiet.

Partial Transcript of Creative Kick-Off & Subs Review Meeting for Supernatural Files: Legit or Bulls**t? Season 3 PART 2
10th October 2015

BEN: So, I watched the video Kristen forwarded. Bizarre. It must be some kind of VFX, right?

DEREK: I don't know, man. I'd need to examine it more closely, but I don't think so. Practical effects maybe? A puppet of some kind?

BEN: Looks way too sophisticated. Expensive. Where did Kelly say she got it?

KRISTEN: Off our server. It's an old sub. Slush pile reject, apparently. I still can't open it. It's good though?

BEN: Oh yeah! It's good. Proper Blair Witch vibes. The stuff of urban legends. It should be our season closer.

AMY: (Looking at her phone and wearing headphones) Oh my God! That sound. Horrific. How would you fake that? Its so loud. Even through crappy headphones you can tell that noise is everywhere. I swear the hairs on the back of my neck are standing up.

BEN: I just watched the visuals—didn't actually hear the audio. Maybe we could get it up on the screen here—

ROBERT: Amy! Amy, your nose is bleeding.

AMY: What? Oh! Oh shit! (Standing and cupping the blood in her hands) Excuse me.

LI: I'll come with you. Just a second—I'll get the door. Are you okay? Oh sheesh, Amy. That's a lot of blood.

(Amy and Li leave the boardroom)

Memo: Kelly Harrison
Date: 11th October 2015
From: HR
To: All Production Staff

As you have probably heard by now, Super-Factual Productions is devastated to confirm the sudden death of Production Assistant, Kelly Harrison. As a remark of respect, the office will be closed for the rest of the day. Kelly's parents have requested some privacy at this difficult time, but we are in touch with them and will share details of the memorial service as soon as they are confirmed. We'll be organizing a collection for flowers if anyone would like to donate. More details to follow.

Transcript of Voicemail left on the mobile phone of Nick Farnaby by Kristen Garcia at 18:36 on 11th October 2015:

Nick! I'm sorry to keep bombarding you with texts and calls, but I really need to speak to you. It's super urgent. I need to tell you something—it's bad news, I'm afraid, and I'd rather we could meet or speak on the phone before you check your e-mails. I know you're feeling under the weather, but it really is important. Could you just let me know when you get this message? Just send a thumbs up emoji or anything. Just. . . just let me know you're okay? Please? Right. Bye for now.

Transcript of Voicemail left on the mobile phone of Nick Farnaby by Kristen Garcia at 22:12 on 11th October 2015:

Nick, it's me again. Look, I'm getting worried now. Please can you call me back? I know, I know, I know—you're probably asleep and I'll look like a total asshole when you wake up to all these messages, but please. Humor me?

Transcript of call between Kristen Garcia and Gerry Matthews at 22:18 on 11th October 2015:

KRISTEN: Ger? It's Kristen. Listen, have you had any contact with Nick today?

GERRY: No, I haven't. He still sick?

KRISTEN: Yeah. It's just that no one has heard from him, like *at all*, and it's not like him to go MIA. He is always on e-mail, even when he's at death's door. . . Bad choice of words. Shit.

GERRY: It's been a horrible, horrible day. You're exhausted. You're in shock. We all are. Try not to worry. I'm sure he's just in bed with the flu and not checking his phone.

KRISTEN: (Muffled sniffing) You're right. I'm just. . . I just. . . She was only twenty-three, Ger. She was a kid.

GERRY: It's a fucking tragedy. Does anyone know what killed her?

KRISTEN: Not really. All we know is it was sudden. She had a headache. Maybe it was a brain tumor or an aneurysm or something.

GERRY: Christ. Poor girl. You really can't take a single day for granted.

KRISTEN: Yeah. Listen, I'm going to ring round a few more people then call it a night. I don't expect to sleep much, but I'm fit for nothing right now.

GERRY: I prescribe a *big* glass of Merlot. Night, Kristen.

KRISTEN: Night, Ger.

Report from the *New York Post*, October 13th, 2015

A New York man has been found dead under mysterious circumstances at his luxury home in the Catskills. The body of TV producer, Nicholas Farnaby, was discovered in the early hours of Wednesday morning after concerned colleagues raised the alarm. Farnaby, 48, had called in sick to his job as the Segment Producer on popular paranormal TV show, *Supernatural: Legit or Bulls**t?* on Monday, and hadn't been contactable since. Postmortem results have proved inconclusive, although a source close to the deceased disclosed to a *New York Post* reporter that Mr. Farnaby's corpse had been partially ingested by his two pet cats. A police spokesman said they are not treating the death as suspicious at this time.

URGENT MEMO: THE HARBINGER
Date: October 12th, 2015
From: Jennifer Black
To: All Production Staff

Dear all,
Following the sudden and tragic deaths of PA, Kelly Harrison and Producer, Nick Farnaby, and the hospitalization of Production Secretary, Amy Wishaw, Super-Factual is halting production of *S:LoB* until further notice.
N.B. Anyone who has received a video file named **TheHarbinger.mp4**, PLEASE DELETE IMMEDIATELY. Do NOT watch the file. Do NOT listen to the file. We have reason to believe this video is harmful. If you have watched this video, please seek medical attention immediately.
Many thanks, Jennifer Black

Partial Transcript of Conference Call, October 12th, 2015

Attendees:

Jason Logan (Stuntman)

Clara Beaumont (Photographer)

Derek Mambwe (VFX & Tech Specialist)

Sofia Ortiz (Investigative Journalist)

Robert Dorfman (Paranormal Investigator)

Kristen Garcia (Executive Producer)

Ben Jameson (Field Producer)

Gerry Matthews (Line Producer)

Jennifer Black (Production Manager)

Li Tang-Archer (Production Coordinator)

BEN: You can't blame me for panicking. Two people fucking dead, Jennifer, and one in the hospital!

JENNIFER: But all the tests came back fine, Ben. You have a clean bill of health.

JASON: Y'all can't seriously believe that video had anything to do with Kelly and Nick dying? Shit, this show has scrambled your brains.

ROBERT: There are more things in Heaven and Earth, Horatio, than are dreamt of in your philosophy.

JASON: Oh, cram it, Rob! This ain't the time for your superstitious, pompous bullshit. Two people are dead, for Christ's sakes.

KRISTEN: Boys, boys, boys! Please! This isn't helpful. I know we're all grieving. We all have questions. But we need to work together if we want answers.

LI: (Sniffling) I'm just going to try the hospital again. See if there's any news on Amy.

GERRY: Sofia, did you turn up anything on the guy in the video?

SOFIA: I'm headed to Maine tonight. I found some articles from a few years back about a supposed haunting in Greenville. Residents there reported hearing strange wailing sounds coming from the woods. Local lore suggests the apparition was actually some kind of banshee. Legend has it that anyone who sees the banshee and hears her screaming will die shortly afterwards.

JASON: Oh, *come on*!

SOFIA: Hey, I'm just telling you what I found.

BEN: Wait a second. Kelly found the file buried on the server, right? She sent it to Gerry, Nick and Kristen. She got a bounce-back from Ger because his inbox was full.

GERRY: Guilty as charged.

BEN: Kristen couldn't open the file. Nick was the only one who watched it. Kelly and Nick got instantly sick and wound up dead a few hours later. Then, in the meeting on Monday, I watched it but without the audio. Amy watched and listened on headphones and immediately started bleeding. If the mythology says it's the banshee's howl that signals imminent death, maybe you need to *hear* her as well as see her to be affected.

CLARA: I hate to agree with Jason, but that's insane, you guys! We can't honestly be entertaining the idea that this video *killed our friends*?

ROBERT: Surely, we have to at least consider it. I mean, that's the whole point of our show. We look at every possibility, however unlikely. However strange. We've all seen things we can't explain. Things that defy logic and physics. Of course, nine times out of ten we know these things are a smudge on a lens, a reflection, the wind in the chimney, our innate, human need to find patterns in chaos. But every now and then, we *truly* glimpse behind the veil. Why is this different? Why now, when the impossible is in our midst, do you close your minds?

DEREK: That's a beautiful speech, Rob. But I'm afraid I have to rain on your parade. I watched the video. With audio. I watched it several times, in fact, very closely. I was looking for tell-tale signs of stitching, editing, CGI, strings. Anything that might give away how it was made.

JENNIFER: What did you find?

DEREK: Well, I have to admit, whoever made that video was not playing. It's pretty damn convincing. I've never seen anything quite like it. Even the finest filmmakers would be hard pressed to shoot something that impressive on a phone. I'm familiar with just about every editing package, every piece of software out there and I'm stumped. But I'm also very much *alive*.

LI: Guys. (Crying) Amy's gone.

(Several seconds of stunned silence)

DEREK: Oh fuck. My nose is bleeding.

The Fieldnotes of Sofia Ortiz:

13th Oct 2015

Arrived in Greenville late last night after six hours on the road and slept fitfully in the B&B. I don't know if it was my fevered imagination, but I could have sworn I heard distant, mournful keening in the early hours of this morning.

Spent the day in the library trawling through newspaper clippings and microfiche of articles on the local banshee lore. There's nothing online that directly references our video, but there are dozens of pieces on the mystery of the 'wailing woods' and eyewitness accounts of a 'woman in white' who is seen in forests and wooded areas across Maine. I've made a note of any names mentioned and will see if I can track any of them down.

14th October 2015

Spoke to several locals who claim to have heard the banshee, but no one has actually seen anything. Everyone seems to know someone who has, but in true urban legend style, it's always a 'friend of a friend' and no one can give me a name.

I think I've found the spot that features on the video. There are few defining features, but it looks the same. I stayed filming until nightfall, but nothing out of the ordinary.

15th October 2015

Left my phone recording on the bedside table overnight as an experiment. Definite auditory phenomena on review. Howling and shrieking that isn't coyotes, owls, or moose. It gave me goosebumps, and it's probably psychosomatic, but I've had a headache all day.

Jennifer called this afternoon. Derek is dead.

Was approached while having a stiff drink in a bar near the B&B. A woman who had heard I was in town asking questions about the banshee wanted to speak with me. She told me her brother, Paul, had been found dead on the outskirts of the forest back in 2013, and that he'd been out trying to get evidence that the banshee was real. She showed me a photo. It's definitely our guy. That video is a bona fide goddamn snuff movie.

Apparently, Paul's phone was never returned to the family with the rest of his possessions. This begs several questions. Who took Paul's phone? Why? How did a video taken on said phone end up on our server? If it was discovered by an unsuspecting medic or police officer and submitted to us for review, surely there would be a trail of bodies?

When I got back to my room, I logged onto the Super-Factual server via the VPN. I made sure the speakers on my laptop were muted, and then opened the Season 1 files. I found the Harbinger MP4 and right clicked it to check the properties. It was uploaded much later than the rest of the submissions - only a couple of weeks ago, in fact. By Kristen Garcia.

Transcript of call between Kristen Garcia and Robert Dorfman at 21:38 on 5th September 2015:

KRISTEN: I'm serious, Rob. They're going to shitcan us. We need something spectacular. Something that will have every single office worker in America talking at the water cooler the following morning. We need to go viral.

ROBERT: Well, there was a case in Maine a few years back. I managed to procure some police evidence which is—shall we say—pretty conclusive.

KRISTEN: I'm listening. . .

ROBERT: This isn't for the faint-hearted, Kristen. It's dangerous stuff. People died.

KRISTEN: If you want to make an omelet, right?

Headline from The Hollywood Reporter, 12th May 2020

"CURSED" FINAL EPISODE OF PARANORMAL SHOW TO BE AIRED DESPITE MYSTERIOUS DEATHS OF PRESENTER AND SEVERAL PRODUCTION STAFF

'Lost' episode which purports to show the hideous creature known as

The Harbinger of Maine captured on camera has resurfaced five years after the tragic deaths of star, Derek Mambwe, a producer, and two junior members of the production crew

Transcript of call between Kristen Garcia and Sofia Ortiz at 21:38 on 14th May 2020:

SOFIA: You can't do this, Kristen. It's sick. *You're* sick.

KRISTEN: People in glass houses, Sofia. You were happy to pack your morals away just long enough to take the money Rob and I offered up for your silence.

SOFIA: Because you promised that video would never see the light of day. As much as I would have loved to see you both behind bars, it wouldn't have brought any of them back. And who would believe me? How many more people would have had to die before anyone would take me seriously?

KRISTEN: So why not feather your nest a little, huh?

SOFIA: I'm not proud of turning a blind eye. But you can't let the episode go to air. Millions of people will see it. We don't know what will happen.

KRISTEN: Relax. I'm not a monster. I made the lab remove the sound from the broadcast master. Without the audio, the picture is harmless.

SOFIA: You'd better pray you're right about that. And where's Paul's phone? Has Rob destroyed it?

KRISTEN: I don't know.

SOFIA: What do you mean you don't know? Kristen, if someone gets ahold of that phone, it all starts up again. There's going to be ghouls out there who will do anything to find it once that episode goes to air.

And what about Paul's family? You're going to make his poor sister watch his final moments on national TV?

KRISTEN: We'll pixelate his face.

SOFIA: You're wrong, you know. You really *are* a monster.

QUALITY CONTROL REPORT: *Supernatural Files: Legit or Bulls**t?*
Season 3 Episode 8 (Season Finale)

TITLE: The Harbinger
DATE: 4th June 2020
TX: 5th June 2020
RUN TIME: 47' 22"
FORMAT: HDCAM 1080i 23.98fps
ASPECT RATIO: 16x9
PSE TEST: Pass
OVERALL STATUS: Pass

TECHNICIAN'S NOTES: Audio drop out found at timecode 00:32:24:15 affecting entire duration of 'Harbinger' video clip. I managed to source original assets from the old production company server and restore all audio channels.

TX master approved and sent for transmission.

HOMEGROWN
ALEX WOODROE

WE'RE *the greatest*
   We're the greatest
   We're the greatest in the world!

Though they deserved points for the resolute delivery, Checnog couldn't help but smirk at the lack of any sense of irony from the group passing in front of his truck. The well-dressed and booze-soaked chorus gathered their feathered coats against the rain and scuttled past his shabby food truck, off to fine dine on Wagyu beef at Le Cocotte—blissfully unaware that the rest of the world wasn't the least bit involved in their Olympic contest to greatness.

Neon pink light shifted into red behind them, the billboard across the cobbled square changing to an Extreme Survivor Sports ad. 'I gave myself kangaroo legs and you won't believe what happened next!' swooped across the screen. Oh, but he could. He could believe exactly what happened next. He was living the twisted nightmare version of that reality.

Inside his small, but comfortable truck, Checnog turned the burners up and his radio on. It was time to sell, and urgently, judging by the empty purse that was supposed to hold next month's vending permit money. His meat wasn't going to fry itself, and the late-night drunk-as-stones idiots were coming, those two or three crazies his best income despite their grumbles and insults, as far beyond caring where the meat came from as he was beyond caring where the money came from.

He sharpened his knife to the steady pounding rhythm coming from his little radio, turned up as loud as he could get it without crackling. Music from the South Reach poured into the cold, damp streets. That was what he worked for; what he gave his sweat and shame and blood for. The South Reach, and its promise of warmth and crops and more usable water than anyone knew what to do with. And no more Augmentations.

When the blade was ready, he sliced into his left thigh, sucking air through his teeth in a pain that he was growing used to, much to the disgusted grunts of the last respectable stragglers passing by.

Checnog grinned through the hurt, body and spirit. "Don't worry, it'll grow back!"

It was a joke nobody else found amusing. Everyone knew it'd grow back. Everyone knew where it came from. That was the problem. The other Augmented food trucks hid their homegrown sources behind closed doors, but Checnog vehemently refused.

He found it amusing that Charlie, with the Aug-seaweed beard, rolled his sushi at the back and left the tiller to his son. The seabeard didn't look half bad on him. And Sonja, going through all that trouble to hide her arm fungi behind shawls and coats? Pah. A complete shame. And why, so they could be heckled instead for the color of their hair or the lilt of their words? It was like trading a lame horse for a lame mule. He couldn't bring himself to. His work put food on tables and paid his way through life, so he chose to take pride in it, even if it did cost him chunks of his own body—and that was what really made the wealthy passersby sick. A poor person's pride.

"Two for a quarter! Come feast. They praise the chops in my hometown as the best in the world! This is as close as you're ever going to get without a special travel permit." The streets were emptying quickly. "Borders are shutting, enjoy what you've got while it's hot!" He cackled at his own graveside humour.

As soon as the last pedestrian was out of earshot, the cheer dropped like a heavy coat. "Old fool." He shook his head. "You've got little to laugh about. The borders are shutting on you, too."

EVERY NEWS OUTLET was abuzz with the inquiry: a Secretary of State accused of forcing off-license Augs on young refugee women. Misha, the local fixer, said rumor had it, revenge was imminent. Checnog hoped the young women would eat them all alive, but kept quiet, and within hours, the news—and Misha—went back to talks about how the temperature change had nothing to do with human intervention, actually.

A slobbering jackass slathered in sports paraphernalia waddled up to the window. "Oi, Porker. I need two of your steaks."

Pleasant and soothing, the sizzle of meat on hot iron almost drowned out the drone of the news screens, but the images were graphic enough: The Secretary of State was missing, presumed dead.

Jackass snort-laughed. "They're right, you know, about Augs. They ought to shoot all of you."

Checnog smiled. "That would take out your favorite team, too." He pointed at the man's red and white shirt.

The self-appointed drunken diplomat looked down, then spent a moment connecting the dots. "The Roos? Watch your mouth. They're hard-working Unitarians who earned what they. . . the things they got. They're citizens. They didn't use no government subsidy to buy their skills."

Neither had Checnog. He'd traded his mother's pearls for entry into the country, then scavenged gold circuitry from discarded tech for three years to raise money for the Augmentation. They advertised Unitaria and their Aug tech like a dream come true, and most everyone back home fell for it. 'Be your Extra self; Augment today!'.

Checnog always had doubts, but even a sneaky rich country was better than an honest poor one, right? So he took the bait. All he could afford was a discounted Slow Regrow Aug nobody found any use for, so far below the bottom of the barrel it was like digging up fossils.

Or, to his clever hands and sharp knives: oil.

His Aug meant whatever chunks he chopped off, he'd get back. Eventually. It did nothing for the pain or the fatigue, but what were those in the face of making enough to move on to better places?

"That'll be fifty Bits."

"Are you stinking mad? Last week it was five."

It had been, that was true. But last week, the morning market still had pale greenhouse tomatoes and the occasional bit of greenery. This week, they were gone. Maybe that didn't mean anything, like the posters said. But maybe it did.

"I am terribly sorry for the inconvenience." He moved to put the food away in a warm drawer.

"Hold on, hold on. Bloody thief Porker." The bills flew in through the opening and fluttered to the steel floor in every direction. "The President'll take care of you lot soon."

Checnog smiled. The President was too busy taking care of the recent boycotts on all shipments into the country. Boycotts caused by other countries discovering their inhumane use and abuse of Augments.

"Thank you for your patronage." He handed over the bag and went back to sharpening his knives, not wanting to let the customer see him pick up the bills. The boycotts weren't really likely to be affecting anyone's dinner yet, but people were scared and antsy. They were quick to anger, and quick to fear. They stockpiled food.

Good news for Checnog.

THE SQUARE STILL SHONE RED, even though the neon billboard stopped working. Checnog was cozy in his truck, but everyone else seemed uncomfortable with the new bright, crimson-tinted rain. It didn't exactly burn or anything; still, it was a weird color, and nobody knew how it'd killed so much of the nation's agriculture.

The government would sort it out, all the posters said so. Their propaganda was as fine as any Checnog had seen back home. They had a cure for the weather; they had a twelve-step plan for imports;

they were going to implement things. Meanwhile, everyone looked nervous.

Misha stopped by again, talking of putting up a cooperative.

"I am grateful," Checnog said. "You are a good friend. But I do well on my own." He hoped. "Have a bite? Discounted. A hundred Bits."

The old fixer scoffed, but paid, and snatched the food. "You'll be sorry when it all falls apart. If you pony up now, you'll collect a nice pension. Everyone else invested with me. Your countryman, Borun, did."

Borun was from a different country and Checnog hated his guts. "I'll think about it."

Misha leaned against the truck and chewed his steak. Watching them eat used to twist Checnog's stomach into cold ribbons, but not for his own sake. Mostly, he was ashamed for them, and how they were willing to overlook their principles for a meal while still loudly proclaiming those same principles on the street.

He busied himself sweeping. "Any interesting news? Billboards have been on the fritz."

"Looks like they're discontinuing Augmentations to everyone but the deservingly wealthy. I heard Solomon and his whole party got themselves no-oxygen Augs. Don't know if they're planning on going into space, or underwater, or what."

"Aren't they friends with that private space company?"

Misha nodded. "Aren't they all friends?"

IT WAS NEARLY WINTER, but the rains never stopped. Checnog had to move his cart on account of the riots, then brought it back to where the most foot traffic passed as soon as he could.

That morning, the rain finally froze into sharp, pink daggers that left infected slashes on any flesh they touched. Checnog's own healed far better than most, but he could tell it was still much slower than it would have been just six months ago. Time was running out, and it was only a matter of whether it would run out for him, or for all of them, first.

A ruckus outside the courthouse across the square drew his eye and made his hand twitch towards his butcher's knife. He settled it back by his side with a smirk. Violence was not the way out of that place, no matter that it had been his way out of many places in the past. Every place was its own: rank and darling and vulnerable in its own ways, if one had the patience to learn them.

The gathering crowd murmured, and Checnog inferred most of the goings-on from their talk. It wasn't good to watch some things first-hand and judging by the mob in front of the courthouse, this would be one such thing. They cheered and threw fists in the air as they dragged the Chief Legislator out by his wings.

The onlooker by his truck said, "they can't," and "they're gonna," and "oh my god," before the screaming started and everyone fell silent. Checnog briefly wondered what the mob would do with the bloody wings when it was all over, but the thought almost brought tears to his eyes. He'd never met the Legislator, and for all accounts, he was a horrible person, but still.

It was always miserable when people had to do that to other people.

It was intended to be a clear message to the President, but Checnog only shook his head. Too little, too late, too confused. Most common folk barely knew who was on what side anymore, and the upperfolk weren't listening anyway. Some hid. The ones who couldn't hide pretended they were 'from the people' and 'for the people' all of a sudden, scared of what those same people might do. Their Augs were expiring, anyway, and almost no one renewed them.

Nobody acted like a god, anymore. Nobody paid Checnog, and his worthless little Aug from the bottom of the barrel, any mind.

EVERY DAY, the people got hungrier; and every night Checnog finished his steaks and closed down shop sooner. They ran out of cash, but he'd gotten plenty by then. He let them trade whatever they wanted; crates of ammo and boxes of jewels and bits of technology he didn't understand. It'd all be valuable somewhere.

Misha carted his small, but still significant, haul of stolen pensions by, cowering under a thick plastic tarp. "I'm off, old devil. You hanging?"

"Not long."

"Doesn't look like you have long left before your Aug ticks out. You'll be normal scum again."

Last night's harvest on Checnog's thighs was still red and sore, the regrowth kicking in later and later. Soon, it wouldn't kick in at all. He'd better stop cutting before then. "Winding down now. Maybe as soon as tomorrow."

Misha nodded, and that was that. Maybe they'd meet again; maybe not.

Checnog shut his truck window with a shudder. Tomorrow would never catch him there; he'd come close to the wire this time, as it was. If he'd stayed a little poorer a little longer; if he'd picked a different aug; if they'd—any number of things, he might not have made it at all. But no more. He knew better than to fling himself into high-risk, high-reward again. It was time to reap.

He left the radio on to cover the patter of ice-rain that never stopped anymore. Soon, he'd be somewhere south, out of the damp and cold, into where they still grew food and made music. The borders were closed, it was true; but he would find a way. With all the money he had, he could probably waltz right in the front door this time. For the first time in his life, he wouldn't have to sneak around. He could make plans.

Maybe even set up a real business. Maybe even make friends that weren't temporary.

He smiled to himself and turned the burners off. "We always find a maybe, don't we?"

THE APP
KEALAN PATRICK BURKE

MY NAME IS Marilyn Russo and I have always been afraid of so many things: heights, the sea, the outside world. The dreadless among you may think such terrors irrational, nothing a good therapist couldn't exorcise, but I've tried that, and it didn't help. Therapy forced me to travel back in time and relive the awful events which crippled me forevermore, as if I don't frequently revisit those traumas enough on my own. The only difference was the clinical version of this reminiscence cost $150 an hour, a maddening development made worse by the aloof attitude of the therapist, who, in the wake of a session that left me crying and terrified to move, considered my sorry state a form of breakthrough.

Confrontation, he said, *it's the only way to dispel the illusion that any of these things deserve your emotional energy. Ultimately*, he told me, *you're putting yourself through this, and only you can put an end to it.* He argued that because my phobias don't always adhere to their strict clinical definitions, it's possible I've simply overinflated them to justify my withdrawal from society. He even had the gall to imply I was exaggerating my fears to garner sympathy. Eventually I got tired of his condescension and returned to the only tried and true method of coping, one his gaslighting did nothing to deter: avoidance.

It will come as no surprise to learn that I don't make friends easily. Being unable to travel by air or sea and suffering a chronic fear of crowds limits your adventurousness and therefore your appeal in the eyes of other thirty-somethings. No dinner parties or nightclubs or bachelorette vacations in Maui for this girl, so best to not make her feel bad by extending the invitation. Marilyn is dull. Marilyn is no fun. Marilyn is afraid of everything. Though such pronouncements are seldom spoken aloud, they live in the eyes of women who have neither the energy nor the desire to coax me out of whatever shell it is I'm trapped in. I am, as one ex of mine *did* say aloud, right before she walked out the door with all her belongings (and some of mine), "hard work." I miss her. To say anything else would be indulging in the kind of disingenuousness typical of bad breakups. I miss her because I loved her, and because she understood me. For a while, at least. And she's right. I *am* hard work and I only know this because it's hard work *being* me. Not all the time, but probably more than most people can handle.

Sometimes I resent that.

I try not to, but I didn't ask to be this way, had no control over it. Want someone to blame? Blame my brother. But of course, we can't do that. Nobody will ever blame Ken for anything, and certainly not for being the author of my childhood traumas. As a result, we're not as close as we otherwise could be.

Part of me will always love him.

Part of me will always hate him.

My family thinks he's the very embodiment of a perfect man: tall, handsome, successful, rich. That he makes his money as a deep-sea diver for oil rigs twenty years after almost drowning me in the Scioto River while trying to teach me to swim isn't just ironic, it's fucking cruel.

And yes, I know. He was just being a big brother. Mischievous. Playful. Steeling me for the trials of life, and nothing whatsoever to do with his resentment of my parents babying me. Perhaps these events would have made someone else a hardier person. I'm not that someone else. I'm brittle as fuck, and I do blame him for that. Him, and my own inability to deal with it are the toxic bedfellows that keep the shades drawn.

He calls every year at Christmas and my birthday, and we trade the kind of pleasantries typical of people who knew each other once and have had too few shared experiences since then to colorize conversations made drab by estrangement.

When my family invite me to things, I make excuses why I can't be there. They know it's all bullshit but with them, particularly my mother, there is no value in honesty. Last summer, I was invited to my cousin's wedding in Vermont. Obviously, I didn't go. 200+ drunken people gyrating on a dance floor, bumping into my chair, and getting too close to me, then asking why I'm struggling to breathe? Pass. I told my mother I had an ovarian cyst because it's the kind of lie you don't dare doubt.

For the most part they leave me alone.

For the most part, I'm fine without them, though I'm more aware than I care to be that the real height I'm afraid of is the gaping depthless hole in my heart where the love from someone else belongs.

In my virtual life, I have countless friends, people who are kind and funny and whom I will never meet. There are message boards and chat groups for people who share my afflictions. In my real life, there's only Kerry, who lives in the apartment at the end of the hall. She's smart and beautiful and confident and, most importantly, doesn't pity me. We're basic friends in that occasionally we'll have drinks or watch Netflix together, but we never try to peek under the veneer of who we are or what we mean to each other. We're a lazily written sitcom and I'm perfectly fine with this arrangement. She keeps me from being lonely. I keep her from getting bored, which is code for keeping her from getting back with her shithead boyfriend. She's smart enough to know better, but her heart doesn't care, because she's lonely too.

It's a mutually beneficial arrangement.

Or at least, it used to be until last Friday night, when she came over with a veggie pizza and a pitcher of lime margaritas and told me about the app with the silly name.

"'PHOBIAPP'?" I asked, trying not to laugh. I had her iPhone in my hand, opened to the app store. "I know the English language has gotten more idiotic in the techno-age, but that's pretty bad. Sounds like a laxative."

On the sofa next to me, Kerry rolled her eyes. The stud in her nose caught the light and made me wish, as it always does, that I had her ambivalence about what the world would think of me if I ever got the strength to face it. Kerry doesn't care what anyone thinks of her, except for her ex, and we're working on that. "I knew you'd focus on that. Read the description."

While she refilled our comically oversized glasses, I did.

The app claimed to have a 99.2% success rate in curing phobias. Idly, I wondered how they'd come up with that number, or if they'd just pulled it out of a hat. The reviews were a dubiously unbroken constellation of five stars. I looked at Kerry as she handed me my drink. "You don't buy this, do you? I mean, how hard is it for an app-maker to buy a bunch of gushing reviews to make what they're shilling seem like a winner?"

Kerry seemed a little disappointed by my reaction, and I reminded myself she was only trying to help. It was more than my own family, with their rolling eyes and shaking heads, had ever tried to do.

"Couldn't hurt to give a shot though, right?" she said. "And I doubt they bought all 17,000 of those reviews, so maybe it'll help."

I read the description again. "'An escalating series of challenges designed to bring your mind and spirit to a place where fear doesn't exist.' Well, that in itself is nonsense. Fear *always* exists, and for $19.99 a month, I can add to my list the fear of getting swindled."

"Never mind, then. It was just an idea."

"How'd you even find it?"

"This crazy thing they call a Google search. Saw the words "phobia cure" and "top-rated app" and thought maybe you'd give it a whirl. It's not like there's anything to lose. I'm going to try it myself."

I looked at her. "You? What are you afraid of?" *Rejection*, I thought. *Dying alone.*

But what she said was, "That one thing with the holes."

"You're afraid of holes?"

"Not like, any holes. Like, patterns of holes. I don't know what it's called."

"Oh, I think I know that one."

Kerry scrolled through Netflix. "Saw it on the poster of a horror movie once. A beehive superimposed on a dude's face. I nearly vomited. That stuff freaks me out. Don't even know why, but it's always bothered me." Her mood had definitely sunk, and I felt guilty about that.

"Okay, I'll try it," I told her.

"Yeah?"

"Sure. We can be therapy partners."

I remained unconvinced, but after Kerry left, and I was buzzed enough on the margaritas to throw good sense to the wind, I downloaded the app, wincing as the little wheel spun while it sucked twenty bucks out of my bank account. I scrolled, accepted their *Iliad*-length terms of service, and promptly fell asleep with the phone still in my hand.

And dreamed of what my life might look like if it worked.

I WOKE with only the faintest memory of the previous night's exploration, so over coffee, I reacquainted myself with PhobiApp. It asked me to select my phobia from a drop-down list. The first problem was it limited you to one, so I went alphabetically and chose acrophobia: a fear of heights. The second problem was that the featured photograph for this section was a man on a tightrope suspended between two buildings so lofty, the ground beneath him was just a haze. One glimpse of this and I had to set my phone down and close my eyes so the vertigo would steady itself, my equilibrium reacting as if the apartment were propped on ball-bearings.

Once I recalibrated, I returned to the phone, quickly scrolling away from the offending (and ill-advised) picture to the button below. It said simply: READY TO BEGIN? Humorless white letters on a black background.

I'll never be able to articulate why I hesitated with my thumb over that button, or why the pause felt like an opportunity to escape something, to go out into the world and be glad I hadn't put myself through hell in search of a cure, but as usual, I dismissed my better instinct as avoidance and hit the button. Immediately, the screen went black and stayed that way long enough for me to wonder if my phone had died.

"Well, that's wonderful," I told the empty kitchen, certain I had just opened the door to a virus that was probably already busy sending suspicious links to my online friends. Then the screen woke up. The background was a pleasant peach color, probably meant to allay the disturbing implications of the message floating atop it: CHALLENGE ONE: CONFRONT KEN.

I stared at those words for a long time, trying to decide if I should be more concerned that this app had somehow managed to cobble together from thin air the genesis of my fear and resentment. Look, I know deep down it's not fair to lay the blame for everything at my brother's feet. I *know* this, even if I almost always choose to forget it so I have a focal point for my anxiety other than myself. I should have been more disturbed, should have questioned the wherewithal of this ridiculously named app, but I didn't, because it was right. And maybe if this thing had any shot at curing me, its methods *should* seem personal instead of generic. I could waste a year trying to unravel the algorithmic sentience of a bunch of code, argue up and down about the ethics of it all, or I could shut up, commit, and see how things panned out. Because although I was surprised, I was also intrigued. This thing wasn't fucking around.

So I did what it told me to do.

HE PICKED up on the fifth ring. "Hey Mar, this is a surprise. Mom and Dad okay?"

It should tell you all you need to know about our relationship that hearing from me evinced concern that there'd been a death in the family.

"Far as I know, yes, unless obstinacy is terminal."

"Obs—what?"

"Stubbornness."

"Why not just say that, then?"

I closed my eyes. "I did. You just didn't understand it."

"Is that why you called? To challenge my vocabulary?"

"No. I called to ask why you never accepted responsibility for leaving me an emotional cripple."

His sigh rumbled over the phone. "I'm sorry, what's this now?"

"I've run rings around it for years trying to make it less your fault, but it always comes back to the same place: you, at 15, bringing me, at 10, to the edge of that bluff in Yellowstone and pretending to push me off."

"Christ's sake, Mar, you didn't seriously call to give me a shit about that, did you? You're almost forty. Time to stop looking for other people to blame for you being a nervous wreck."

"I'm not blaming other people. I'm blaming you."

"I had a death grip on your shirt. You were never in any danger. Christ."

"And if the shirt had torn?"

"It didn't. What's this really about?"

"My fear of heights."

"I see. And all your other fears? Water?"

"Also on you. That time at the river when I almost drowned?"

"You went under for about fifteen seconds. It happens."

"Sure, but did it have to?"

"We were kids. I was trying to teach you to swim. You panicked and went under. And the Yellowstone thing? I was just fooling around. It's normal. What isn't normal is calling me after we haven't talked in almost a year to ream me out over it."

"Who else should I blame? I can't go near water. Can't deal with heights. Can't even be around groups of people without having a panic attack because I don't think I trust them not to hurt me."

"Look, I'm sorry, Mar. Is that what you wanted to hear? Because I mean it. You think I'd ever dream of doing things like that to you now? I was a *kid*. But you're only focusing on the bad. What about all the good times we had?"

"The times where you acted like a human being? Those didn't traumatize me, Ken, or I'd be confronting you about them too."

"Okay, so, what is it you want from me? I already said I'm sorry."

It was a good question. I didn't know what I wanted from him. So that's what I told him.

"Sis, if anyone ever hurt you, you know I'd be there to pound the ground beef out of them. What am I supposed to do knowing I'm the one who hurt you? I can't take it back. But I love you, you know that right?"

"Yes."

"You love me?"

"Maybe."

"Then say it."

"I love you."

"Like you mean it."

"I love you, you fucking jerk."

"And you know I will always be there to protect you, right? No matter how much of an asshole I used to be. If I could punch the shit out of your fears, I'd spend my life doing nothing else. But I can't. Only you can do that, and you should."

"Okay. Go away now before I vomit from the schmaltz."

"The fuck is schmaltz?"

"You're hopeless."

He laughed and it reminded me how much I liked the sound of it, how hard he'd made me laugh back in the day when he wasn't installing trauma onto my hard drive. It also annoyed me because this was supposed to be a come-to-Jesus moment, a real dressing down, and instead I let him off the hook because all things considered, I *do* love him.

Before we said our goodbyes, the phone buzzed in my ear. While Ken muttered some fragile vow about being better at keeping in touch, I looked at the phone, saw it was a notification from PhobiApp and had the peculiar feeling *they* were going to confront *me*. A ridiculous notion, but it didn't keep a weird flutter of unease from my stomach. The apprehension only got worse when Ken was off the phone, but I told myself I was being silly. There were any number of ways they might have concluded that Ken was my brother (he's listed as BIG BRUV in my contacts, for example) and someone who needed to be held to account for his role in my anxiety, but they couldn't possibly have any access to the content of that phone call, right? Because that would be entering the shady world of communication monitoring and surely tech companies know better nowadays than to violate your privacy in such a way. Right?

Unless, I suppose, you give them permission.

Because, like most people, I don't bother to read the fine print in TOS contracts. I just scroll to the end and hit AGREE.

Nervous, I hung up on Ken and opened the message.

It said simply: CHALLENGE COMPLETE: 1/10

Which left me to puzzle over the significance of those numbers. Was it the first challenge of ten, or a performance rating for how I'd handled things with my brother?

I DIDN'T SLEEP well that night, preoccupation painting the room with electronic monsters I couldn't see, tiny metallic things with LCD eyes crawling around the apartment analyzing my psyche for access points so they could feed it back to some monolithic supercomputer in a secret bunker somewhere.

I dragged myself from the primordial soup of my bed, covers wrapped around me like a cocoon, and put the coffee on, then sat and looked at my phone for my next challenge. It made my heart stop.

CHALLENGE TWO: GO TO THE ROOF

I live in an eight-story rehabbed tenement building and, aside from the tour on the first day, I have never been up to the roof. Kerry goes there to smoke the occasional joint and my refusal to accompany her is how she found out about my fear of heights. My apartment is on the second floor. Realistically I could handle living on the top floor because it's enclosed and therefore safe. I'm not likely to careen screaming out of my kitchen and fall to my grisly death no matter how high up it is. You could make the same argument about airplanes, but they're not connected to the ground. One of those comes down, you're paste.

But the roof is open. It's flat, and other than a three-foot high cheap iron railing, there are no walls, so it's entirely feasible that one might stumble and engage gravity in all the wrong ways.

I minimized the app and sent Kerry a text.

THIS APP IS NUTS. HOW R U DOING?

Her response made me laugh despite myself:

F'N THING MADE ME STARE AT A BLOCK OF SWISS CHEESE FOR 30 MINS

I replied: LMAO. IT WANTS ME TO GO UP ON THE ROOF

GOIN 2 DO IT?

PROLLY.

Watching the little dots of her imminent reply, I decided I *was* going to do it, because upon reflection, confronting Ken at the app's request *had* achieved something, however small. I wasn't magically cured of my afflictions, but I felt good about being able to talk to him about his part in it all, and that had been a step worth taking, a step made easier because the suggestion had come from the faceless opinionless void of my iPhone screen and not some shitty therapist.

U GOT DIS, Kerry texted back.

I pocketed my phone and headed out into the hall. Weirdly emboldened by the trembling in my stomach which for the first time seemed laced with as much excitement as terror, I pushed through the stairwell door, and my smile dropped as if I'd been slapped. Anxiety canted the stairs into Dutch angles, the steps elongating and tilting, turning my belly into a water balloon. I took a moment to steady myself, closed my eyes, chuckled at the queer notion that I was doing this more for PhobiApp's approval than my own, and then headed slowly up the stairs.

Counted the steps.

Measured my breaths.

Told myself I could do it.

Stairs have never bothered me before. It's what awaits at the top of them, a malevolent presence with weight and mass, the tangible threat of imminent danger.

The higher up I went, the more my legs started to shake, and the more my stomach started to quiver, my grip on the railing so tight it wouldn't have surprised me to find the imprint of my hand left behind in the metal. I felt sick. Was going to be sick. But I swallowed it down, told myself to be brave, to just power through this, to surprise myself with previously untapped reserves of strength and determination and

just

keep.

going.

And then, mercifully, I reached the landing, three feet from the door with the metal handle and the blazing red EXIT sign, cold sweat trickling from my armpits. The door loomed before me like something from a horror movie, juddering in my vision from the force of my pulse.

You don't have to do this, I told myself, and frankly, it was a miracle the voice of reason had taken this long to show up. *You're putting yourself through this, why? Because a fucking app said so? Girl, get your ass back down those stairs where it's safe.*

To my enfevered brain, this was sound reasoning, and I almost obeyed. But it was also familiar, the cowardly voice that got me out of travel and socializing and being anywhere near water my whole adult life. The voice of a quitter.

After a momentary pause to steel myself, I turned and shoved open the exit door.

Daylight. Unanchored by my anxiety, the macadam surface of the roof and the boxy AC vents swung vertiginously around my field of vision. The blue sky seemed low enough to crush me with cloudy fists. The pressure from both above and below felt as if I'd stepped into a trash compactor, but I shook my head to deny it, demanding some small scrap of calm from the turbulent storm in my head and chest.

I walked gingerly toward the edge, arms out at my sides as if it were a thin ledge a thousand feet above the earth, the tops of the city buildings rising like tombstones above the flimsy fence.

A hundred years later, my body a quivering wreck, my pulse pummeling the inside of my head and chest like a prizefighter, I made it.

I stood, not looking down, just being there, alive in a terrifying moment.

And then quickly backed away, the reality of my situation rushing back in and threatening to turn my bones to sawdust. On treacherous legs, I ran back to the door.

CHALLENGE COMPLETE: 2/10

I do not deny the dopamine hit that came with this accomplishment, but for the rest of the evening I was sick and shaky, unable to corral my emotions. I'd been knocked off-balance, left more than a little resentful and embarrassed that I'd let myself be manipulated by a stupid goddamn phone app. Even once I made the decision to delete it, I hesitated. It had forced me to confront things I might otherwise have let stand, but any intrigue about the remaining eight steps was ameliorated by the sheer number of them. If the second step had me standing like a terrified idiot at the edge of my roof, what kind of horror awaited at the tenth?

No. I would not dismiss the idea of further treatment for my phobias, but it would have to be on my terms next time. No apps. No stuck-up shrinks. No passive-aggressive coaching from my mother.

I texted Kerry for advice. I knew she wouldn't be happy to hear I was quitting so early in the process, but she was also probably the only person who'd understand.

I waited an hour, and when she didn't respond, I swiped the screen to PhobiApp, held down the icon, and watched it jiggle under my thumb. I hit X, and when presented with the option to just delete the icon from my desktop or remove the entire app from my phone, I chose the latter.

Once the app was scrubbed from my phone, the immediate relief vied with the guilt of bailing on a course of treatment that might have paid dividends if I'd seen it through to the end. But I told myself it could just as easily have caused irreparable psychological damage. I mean, who created PhobiApp? I highly doubted the engineers had degrees in trauma management. To them, it was probably just a cash cow version of truth or dare, a bunch of tech boys making millions from other people's misfortune, as they're wont to do.

After dinner, when I still hadn't heard back from Kerry, I went to her apartment and knocked on the door. She didn't answer, but I could hear the TV on over some kind of steady humming noise. Embarrassed that I might have intruded on a date with her vibrator, I headed back to my own place and texted her to let her know I'd be up for a while if she wanted to hang out.

For whatever reason, one I hoped had nothing to do with her ex, she didn't respond.

I ate some leftovers, took a long bath, and, fending off the disappointment in myself, went to bed.

WHEN I WOKE, it was to the welcome sound of birdsong. Welcome, that is, until it registered as out of place. Confused, I opened my eyes. Felt a breeze strong enough to make my hair dance buffeting the exposed skin of my face, neck, and shoulders. Above me, same as always, was the ceiling, a cheap stucco affair. Around me, the walls, and the door out into the hall. The air was different though. Cleaner and colder, and, considering the windows were closed, stronger than it had any right to be as it swept over my prone body.

I shivered.

My phone buzzed.

I fumbled for it atop the sea of blankets, found it, and woke up the display.

And saw the impossible.

A message from PhobiApp, as if I'd never deleted it: CHALLENGE THREE: LOOK DOWN

At first, I looked past the phone to the bump of my covered feet, but then, as the last skeins of sleep fell away, I realized what it meant, rolled over, and looked down at the floor.

It was gone.

I sucked in a gasp of air so huge I thought my lungs would burst. Instantly, my heart began to hammer in protest of the stricken cage in which it had found itself, my brain a thunderstorm of panic signals and misfiring synapses. Quite easily, in that moment, I could have died. I thought I was going to and quickly rolled over on my back to stare at a ceiling that had always been so ordinary and now represented a focal point of salvation, a fixed point in a world suddenly gone insane.

It was impossible, of course. An optical illusion, the power of suggestion, perhaps conveyed to my slumbering brain via the speakers in my phone, or maybe a hologram. How else could my bed be floating high above the clouds? That it was an illusory effect made perfect sense. After all, but for the floor, the rest of my room was still there. I closed my eyes and willed myself to be calm. However they had made it happen, it was just another part of the therapy. If I chose to believe I was really suspended thousands of feet up in the air, I would die of a heart attack, and they'd be liable for—

Would they?

No, my acceptance of their terms meant they probably wouldn't be liable for anything. Still, how on earth did something like this make it to the market? I dreaded to think of the risk it posed to people with weaker dispositions, although in that moment, with my bed apparently hovering miles above the earth and my pulse rattling my teeth, it was hard to imagine a weaker disposition than my own.

A moment reserved for self-coaching and forced calm, and I turned on my side to peer over the edge of the mattress, sure I had dreamed what I thought I'd seen.

A whining roar as a passenger jet sailed by beneath me, unseen sun glinting off the wings, and I vomited copiously and involuntarily from the fright, then watched, waiting for the ejecta to meet the hard, hidden surface of my floorboards, thereby revealing the illusion. But it didn't. It fell and was scattered by the wind, disappearing beneath the contrail and the hazy skirts of the clouds.

My phone buzzed. With a shaky hand, I retrieved it.

The app again: CHALLENGE COMPLETE 3/10

Before I could properly focus, I got another notification from the app that shouldn't still be on my phone but had somehow inveigled its way back into my life with the primary goal of destroying it:

CHALLENGE FOUR: JUMP

There was no way in fried green hell that was going to happen, so I clung tight to the edge of the mattress and peered down at the sky. I was in no danger of falling. It was impossible. This wasn't real. I was safe, here, on my bed. As long as I didn't inch too close, or God forbid, try to step down onto the clouds, I had nothing to fear. I repeated this mantra, eyes widening as those clouds parted and I saw the yellow and green patchwork quilt of American heartland many, many, miles below.

I want to say I have never been so scared, but that isn't true. On the bluff in Yellowstone all those years ago, Ken pushed me, and it didn't matter that he had my shirt clenched in his hand. I was too young to know what the end of my life might look like, but I knew it was coming. And that's how I felt now. I knew without a doubt I was going to fall and die.

My phone buzzed again, and I grabbed it as if it were a life preserver.

I opened the text app and saw that Kerry had texted me back sometime in the night.

Her message did nothing to dispel the dread that had my heart in a death grip.

QUIT THE APP. SHOULDN'T OF. MY FACE.

I didn't know what this meant, but I had bigger problems and quickly texted her back.

I QUIT TOO AND NOW MY BED IS FLOATING IN THE SKY. I DON'T KNOW WHAT'S HAPPENING! FFS HELP ME!!!!!

Without thinking how insane that sounded, I hit send, then looked toward the bedroom door. In what might be the only stroke of good fortune I'd seen in months, I'd been so tired the night before, I'd left it open and could see the hall beyond. Everything past this room appeared real and still grounded in reality. The foot of my bed was four feet from the door. If I jumped, I could make it. But my fear of what would happen if I didn't extended that distance by ten feet at least.

As if my sheets had turned to fractured glass, I carefully crawled to the foot of the bed and peered over the edge. Beneath, a flock of birds were mere specks, traveling the thermal drift to some unknown destination. I envied their inability to not give a shit about how high up they were. Then I focused on the door and the bare wood floor beyond.

Legs wobbling, I rose, took forever to place my right foot on the footboard. It was an easy jump made precarious by the presence of the impossible sky and the thought of falling. I was only able to attempt it thanks to the insistence, from the little piece of my rational brain that still worked, that should I indeed fall, I'd likely only hit the floor. Anything else would be unnatural, or rather, *super*natural. What I was seeing was just some advanced VR illusion. Had to be. Nothing else made sense. And the people behind this app had no good reason to want to see me dead.

Right?

I'd worn only a Ramones T-shirt and some frayed granny panties to bed, and as I stood there atop the footboard, the wind from the impossible sky chilled my bare arms and legs. *VR doesn't do that*, I thought, and then dismissed that horrifying truth and zeroed my focus on the hallway floor.

And what if, my unhelpful inner voice continued, *that disappears too?*

"They said jump," I retorted, thrumming with terror. "So that's what I'm fucking doing."

And, phone in hand, I did.

In my mind, I fell, nothing but air beneath me, gravity sucking me down to a quick and ignoble death, my entire life reduced to a mangled, splattery mess half-buried in some farmer's soybean field.

Then my heels banged hard down on the wooden hallway floor, and I fell to my knees, whispered some nonsensical prayer to a god I don't believe in, and scrambled away toward the front door. I dared not look back, terrified I might see the floor falling away as the sky tried to claim me.

My phone buzzed.

A notification from PhobiApp: CHALLENGE COMPLETE 4/10

I almost relaxed. Almost. But now that I wasn't, to my knowledge, in immediate danger, I had the available mental real estate to worry about my friend. Not bothering with pants because really, when the world untethers itself from reality, who's going to care what you are or aren't wearing, and tore out into the hall. Ran to Kerry's door and hammered my fist on it hard enough to knock the little brass number 24 off.

"Kerry, it's me, open up!"

There came a weird gurgling sound from my apartment, followed by a series of clanks and a gushing hiss. A moment later, I heard a similar sound from behind Kerry's door. Then again from downstairs. The same thing, over and over again.

"Kerry, open the door!"

Eventually, she did, part of the way, at least.

I could only see her fingers clamped on the door, the opening too narrow to be able to see anything else.

"Kerry?"

When she spoke, it was with the voice of the wind through a tattered screen, and instinctively I backed away. That humming sound again, louder now. "What's wrong?"

When she edged her face into view, I couldn't help it. I screamed, put a hand to my own face and backed away. She mumbled something desperate and unintelligible and slammed the door shut. Brackish water flowed out from beneath it. I took another step back. Heard another mechanical clunk from the upper floors. More hissing. I turned in time to see water flowing out of my apartment and hurried to the door.

My kitchen sink had exploded. Water spumed up into the air and judging by the flow of water from the hall, the bath and sink in there had malfunctioned too.

The now familiar and dread-inducing hum from my phone.

I hoped it was Kerry.

It wasn't.

CHALLENGE FIVE: ESCAPE

For once, this was a no-brainer, and the easiest challenge of all to obey. Almost. I couldn't, shouldn't leave Kerry, but I also didn't know how to help her, assuming there was any way to reverse what had been done to her.

Her head, an amalgam of warped, twisted flesh perforated by small holes from which hornets went about their business. Her fear made incarnate, and I remembered the humming sound I'd heard the night before. Not a vibrator after all, but the labors of insects as they made their home in my only friend's face.

I sent her a quick text:

WE NEED TO GET OUT OF HERE. WE CAN GET YOU HELP.

A preposterous claim, but what else was I supposed to say?

I lingered as long as was reasonable, but when she didn't respond, I hurried into my apartment, wading through water that with so many points of egress shouldn't have been able to accumulate any more than the sky should have been able to appear beneath my bed, but did so anyway. Grabbed my jeans and wallet and was gone in less than two minutes.

I ran to the stairs and saw the water was three feet deep at the foot of it, and rising.

I can handle shallow water.

It was not the sea.

Not yet anyway.

I rushed down the steps, plunged into the water, gasping at how cold it was, and made my way to the double-glass doors to the small lobby.

The front door was locked, though nothing appeared to hold it shut. The lock wasn't engaged. There were no chains. It simply wouldn't open no matter how hard I kicked and tugged and swore at it.

Movement through the smoked glass entrance door and I screamed for help until I was hoarse. Someone was out there. Lots of people. But after ten minutes in which it appeared those people were unwilling or unable to help, I trudged back through the water and back up the stairs, yelling out my intent as I passed Kerry's door and headed up the stairwell to the roof.

The fear was different now, coalesced into something akin to raw self-preservation with a soupcon of madness. I was on autopilot, so afraid it nearly canceled itself out into calm.

I all but exploded through the door to the roof.

There were other people there. People I recognized as residents, all looking shocked and confused and panicked. Mirror images of how I'd looked for the past 48 hours.

But why?

The water alone should not have been reason enough for them to look so shell-shocked.

Then I followed their gazes.

Walked to the edge which had instilled so much terror in me the day before.

And saw.

The streets were flooded, the water rising at a rapid rate. In minutes, cars would be underwater. In less than an hour, it would, unless something stopped it, reach the roof. Those people down there would drown, their bodies rising in a tide that had come from nowhere and would soon consume the world.

I couldn't help it.

I dropped to my knees and a startled manic laugh bubbled up and out of me.

Only when the tears cleared did I realize there were more people on the roof than before, all of them looking at me like I was insane.

A crowd was forming.

ALL OUR FERTILE BONES

TEAGAN OLIVIA STURMER

Iron Age, Britannia

IT BEGINS WITH A BURIAL. A gentle shushing of raw earth over skin. The moans of a mother burying a daughter, a heart turning bitter toward the gods. My heart. And that is all she is now—my sister—skin and bones. All any of us are—rotting, emaciated corpses slurrying in the mud as we make our way down the hill to the bone meadow. My father, his back bent with age and harsh labor, carries the body wrapped in stained wool, a sprig of wormwood clutched between his teeth. I can still taste the herb's bitter cut on my own tongue, the desperate desire not to die. Not like my sister. Not like all who have succumbed to the winter, the emptiness of our grain stores.

The hole is dug with hands and fists and iron-tipped ards, blades slicing through the muck, cutting past roots of all the dead and dying things that should have grown to feed our bellies. I place a hand over my stomach, watching as the village elders place my sister's broken form into the earth. I should whisper a silent prayer, a plea to the gods, anything that might lessen the pain. But I am angry. I want to curse this wretched ground, scream at the skies until the clouds have turned to blood and they break, red and pregnant over this infertile land.

My mother's voice warbles as she sings the ancient words over my dead sister's flesh and the ground is laid back over. My palms fist at my sides, teeth sinking into the soft, pink folds of my mouth. The iron tang of blood spills over my tongue like oil and I drink, letting the taste ground me, the pain keeping me present. I watch as the soil swallows Kerra's limp form, my mother bowing to gather kernels of dead earth into her hand, wiping it on her skin. My father does the same, kneeling in the mire as my mother wails her funeral dirge. One by one, the other members of our village—the ones who remain—follow suit, mouths opening wide to the skies, smearing mud down their cheeks.

But I do not kneel. I stand and I scream. The sound is sudden, coming out of me like broken shards of pottery, slicing my tongue, my lips, cracking on my teeth. I scream as I imagine the grief like wisping shadow, spilling out from my ribcage, up through my open mouth.

I do not know if the gods can hear me. If they even listen. But there is one thing I do know, one thing I will know until the day I die.

This earth is death.

MY BONES ARE SO brittle they crack beneath the weight of my own breath. I sit inside my father's house, throat working to swallow the last of my mother's broth. The lamb was butchered three seasons back and the bones taste of dust. But it is all there is left, so we boil them over and over with the leather from Kerra's shoe. Father's ard and sickle sit idly by the door, rust licking up the crude iron. There is no need for tools when the soil no longer yields a crop. My stomach— what is left of one—growls like a sick beast and I drain the last of the watery broth between my lips. I place the earthen bowl down beside the meager coals and stand, checking on my mother once before exiting out into the waning light. She will not last another moon cycle, her skin flaking off like shale.

Outside, the village stinks of rot and decay. Thick smoke billows from the forge and I see my father through the mist, his back bending low over the eastern field. He could stand there for a year and a day and the seeds will still not grow. They spoiled in their woven sacks three moons back and there is none to replace them. I turn to the road leading out of the village; even the willows do not bud, the daisies in the ditch grow as only graying stalks. My stomach rumbles again and I place a bony hand over my loose wool dress. There is no point taking in the stitches, having it fit properly. All the more fabric to bury me, I suppose.

A shout echoes somewhere in the village and my gaze snags on a slender shadow emerging from the fog at the village edge.

Veran.

I would run if not for the fear that my bones might fall apart, turn to ash inside this wretched confine of skin. We were to wed, he and I, back before the hunger, before the fields turned to slits of black mold. He smiles at me, more skeleton than man, and I raise a hand before I notice the thing he's carrying.

It's a funny thing—all made of wood and metal. He holds it like the crown of a king, like some rich treasure, and before I can reach him, my father is angling out of the eastern field. Others in the village notice Veran, the thing he has with him, their eyes widening in curiosity. In moments, he has reached the forge, a crowd of skeletons amassing around him. I walk more slowly than the others, so afraid to break apart into dust at a hitch of wind. But when I do, their curiosity has turned to anger.

"You were supposed to bring seed from the traders," Phelan, the blacksmith, barks, his words slurring funny through missing teeth.

Veran spreads his hands wide. "I brought seed, I did. There wasn't much to be had, though. Ours is not the only village hit with this plague."

I swallow, the edges of my throat raw. I picture all the bodies piling up, all the land turning to mire, pocked with rot. My father stays silent, his eyes firmly fixed on the thing Veran has brought into the village. But he says nothing. So, I press forward.

"What is that?" I point to the strange device, its metal point piercing the ground.

Veran smiles again, making my skin flutter, and runs a hand down along the smooth, curved wood.

"The Romans call it a plough."

I roll the name around on my tongue until it tastes faintly of iron.

"What's it for?" Phelan asks, his eyes brimming with cynicism.

But Veran does not answer. Instead, he pushes past us and enters his small house on the village's western border. In moments, he is back out, ox in tow. The creature is as brittle-boned as the rest of us. Hip joints poking out like stony knobs. The village was angry with Veran, for keeping the ox alive, for not butchering it like the rest of the animals and letting it fill our bellies. Veran was adamant, though. We would need the creature before the end. And perhaps, he was right.

He leads the ox to the plough, the crowd parting like the wake left behind a boat, and harnesses it to the animal.

Phelan makes to stop him. "Son, we do not have time—"

But my father places a hand on the blacksmith's arm. "Let him show us what he has brought."

There is something in my father's eyes then, something I have not seen since we placed Kerra's body in the bone meadow. *Hope.*

It sparks a flint in my stomach, and I am the first to follow Veran as he angles out toward the field. His face is ambitious, eyes glinting like stars.

"What is it, Veran? What is it going to do?"

He stops then, eyes so bright they take my breath away. There's a curve to his lips, and I see the man I love behind all the hunger.

"It's going to save us, Brigit."

VERAN STANDS ankle deep in mud, a sack of seed swinging from his hip. His hands grip the two beams of the plough, one in front of the other. The sky above has turned to silt, and I worry that the rain will wash us away. Swallow us whole, bury us in the mire.

"I'll be needing help," Veran says and points to me. "Brigit."

My breath hitches in my throat. *Save us.* I sink my teeth into my cheek and step forward. Veran hands me the coarse reed ropes of the ox's reins.

"I need you to lead him in straight lines, up and down the field. Just like we would with an ard."

His eyes are soft on mine, hands calloused and bony and so beautifully familiar. I nod and then look to the ground. Heart stuttering. He means to plant this field. *This, this. . .*

"But this is the bone meadow," I say, not realizing that I'm speaking my thoughts aloud until they're already spilling from my lips.

Our dead are buried here.

Veran nods, turns his eyes back to the village elders, their own worry thick on their brows.

"We must plant this year's crop in the most fertile soil and the man who sold me this plough said, the richest ground is the ground in which things have died." He points to the earth beneath our feet. "The plough will dig deep enough for the crop to take root, but not to disturb our dead, I assure you."

There are whispers and half-spoken arguments before my father raises a wrinkled hand.

"Let the boy plant the field."

Our ears ring with silence and Veran turns to me. "Lead the ox forward."

My hands shaking, I wrap the rough ropes through my fingers and pull. We go slow at first, Veran stopping every few steps to drop one hand from the plough and scatter the seed. He levels the dirt, and a woman prays for rain.

I look up to the sky, the overwhelming gray, and join her. Maybe the gods will listen. I urge the ox forward, watching Veran wipe the sweat from off his brow, hands working this strange new thing, this plough. Our salvation. My heart swells. And maybe, for the first time in so many moons, our fields will yield harvest.

THE FIRST GRAIN shoots emerge just as the lamb bones in mother's pot go dry. She is dead now, buried amongst all the others in the bone meadow. We laid her to rest on the outskirts of the grain field and whispered prayers her body would make the earth fertile again, grow the crop. The plough sits outside Veran's house like a spoil of war. Every day he sits beside it, rubbing wax into the wood, making it glisten. He calls it the Savior and I do not think he is wrong. I often find myself staring at it, the way it curves, the pounded iron at its base, and whisper a prayer to it as if it is a god.

We feed ourselves on what few fish can be pulled from the river and the summer peas Veran planted in the southern patch of the bone meadow. They taste strange—different than I recall—something like iron, I think. Iron and blood. But I grind them between my teeth anyway, letting the little green pearls pop like pustules on my tongue. So much better than Kerra's boiled shoe.

I can barely picture her face anymore. Brown hair like mine, eyes as blue as cornflowers. But the rest is all smudged as if her features are made from mud, and someone has dragged a finger through them.

I sit at the door to my father's house, carding the little wool we have left and watching Veran as he leads his ox out to the eastern field. Dead lay beneath this ground, too, but it is so long ago none alive remember it. And Veran promises the plough does not disturb them.

I am picking a bramble out of the wool when I hear the first scream. It comes from the house beside the forge, Phelan's house. I drop my brushes and lift my skirts, racing across the cracked earth. My stomach swills as I reach the door, the scent carrying from underneath it like iron and blood and the thick twist of rot. I force bile down my throat, raising a fist to beat the door. Phelan's face meets mine, eyes bulging with terror, saliva caught in his beard.

"What's wrong?" I ask, standing on tiptoe to look over his broad shoulder.

His house is scorching, a fire leaping in the hearth despite the heat outside. A mound of blankets shivers on a reed mat. Phelan looks around the village, eyes darting like wild beasts, and then pulls me in. I nearly gag on the stench of the place, my mind going light as air. Phelan shakes me.

"Brigit, it's Amena."

I search the red brightness for Phelan's wife, eyes snagging on the blankets. "Is she under there?"

He nods. And it doesn't make sense. Unless. . .

"Does she have a fever?" I ask, a sudden fluttering in my chest.

Phelan nods again, concern knitting his brow. "Since last night. I didn't know what to do, but she was insistent on the blankets, on the fire. Needed the heat. And now. . . now. . ."

He's blathering like a mad beast, spools of spit stretching between his lips. I rest my diminutive hands on his shoulders, steadying him, locking his gaze in mine.

"Do you have any garlic—"

He breaks away from me, hands scrabbling toward a basket set in a corner. He pulls out a bulb, gray and brittle. It's old, but at this point, it doesn't matter. I take it, mashing it between my fingers, and lifting one half to my own tongue. The taste is sharp and strong, and I wince as I force it down my throat, but it will protect me from the fever. I move to kneel at Amena's side, holding the crushed garlic in my palm as I peel back the blankets.

My heart stops. Clenches like a fist. Pushes against my ribs until I am sure it will come pressing up my throat to empty, bloody, into my palms. A small moan escapes my lips even though my vocal cords are curdling with a scream.

"What is it?" Phelan demands. "What's wrong?"

I open and close my mouth, but the words don't come out. My voice nothing but smoke. I look down at Amena—at what *should* be Amena. I conjure up every meeting I have had with this woman. Her cow-brown eyes, a smile of crooked teeth. I try and place these features on the thing I see before me. But there is nothing.

She has no face.

I scrabble back, dropping the garlic to the dirt floor. Phelan pushes me aside, wraps thick arms around. . . around whatever is laying on Amena's bed.

Amena. Not Amena. No face.

I sit there, elbows grinding dirt, my chest heaving, heart racing like a mad horse. Phelan wraps the body into his arms, shoulders shaking. He holds her to his chest, fingers scrabbling in her unkempt hair. His first wail is long and low, a hollow sort of thing. It cracks against my ribs.

"What have you done?" His words are blunt, the edge of a rusted ard.

I lean forward, try to reach out, but he twists, eyes spitting forge-fire. "You did this? You did this to my wife!"

I hold out a hand, trying to keep my eyes off Amena. *Not Amena. No face.* "Phelan, there was nothing I could do. Clearly—"

"Clearly what?" His words are sharpened barbs now, spittle flying from his tongue.

I place a soft palm on his shoulder. "Phelan, you must look. You must see. It's not. . . it's not Amena anymore."

His gaze breaks from mine as he looks back to his wife, back to the face like smeared, pale dye. A tear rolls down his rough cheek as he brushes the hair back from the smooth, tepid skin.

"She thought she saw her sister, you know. Galla. Said she saw her body rise up out of the bone meadow, two days back when she was gathering a small harvest. Said Galla pulled herself up by the roots of all those new plants." He holds her body tighter against him now, tears pouring like streams.

I look down at Amena, horror licking through me like ice. "Galla is dead, Phelan. She was one of the first to die from the hunger."

Phelan nods. "Yes, yes, I know. It must have been the fever. Must have been—" But his words dissolve into sobs now, thick and heavy as he lays Amena back to her mat and collapses beside her.

I stay motionless for a moment, watching Phelan weep over the body of his wife, over a face that is no longer a face. Just smears of putrefying flesh, the thought slicing through me like a rusted blade. I twist my neck, looking out the door to see Veran's smudged form ploughing up the old burial grounds, and wonder. . . *what have we unleashed?*

WE BURN the body at midnight. Phelan is insistent. The flames lick high into the Beltane air, orange on black. Smudges of light on a great expanse of nothing. The smell of the thing—of Amena's body—is iron and blood and rot. It twists my guts, reminds me of how Kerra smelled when we laid her in the bone meadow. All that dry flesh. After the rites are sung and the bones have turned to ash, we make our way back to the village. I feel fingers fold into mine, drawing me from the pilgrimage, into the blackness of night.

Veran.

My heart quivers, breath catching hot. I follow him into the darkness of the forest. We have not done this since before the hunger and suddenly all I can think about is the feeling of his body pressing against mine, fevered skin and stunted breath and stroking hands. He backs me up against a willow, fingers tangling in my hair, lips inches from mine. My throat hitches, mouth quivering, and then he stops.

"I saw my father last night."

The words bite my skin like water midges. I blink. "Your father is dead, Veran."

I don't mean to be so blunt, but what else is there to say? We buried Veran's father on what should have been our wedding day.

He takes a step back, dropping his hands from my body, and suddenly I feel so alone. So cold.

"I knew that's what you would say." His voice is sharper now, edged.

I step forward, my hand shaking in the moonlight as I reach for his tunic. "I'm sorry. I just—"

He turns to face me, eyes misty. "I saw him. I know it's impossible, Brigit. But I saw him. Only a hand at first, reaching up out of the dirt. Scared me so much I had piss running down my leg. But then he grabbed hold of a root, pulled his way out. And I knew it was him. His graying hair, leather tunic, the scar on his left palm."

I stare at Veran then, a wad of carded wool balling at the back of my throat. "What about his eyes? Your father had blue eyes."

Like Kerra's.

Veran stops moving then, drops his gaze from mine, and dread floods my stomach like a rainstorm. I move closer to him, cupping his jaw in my palm.

Look at me.

"You can tell me what you saw."

He shudders against me, tears wetting the curve of my neck. "He had no face, Brigit. It's—gods above—it's all gone."

I hold him there, as his sobs wrack against my body, and I know what it is we must do. I turn back in direction of the grain field—the bone meadow. There is movement there, in the moonlight, that catches my eye, threads disquiet between my marrow and bone.

We must starve.

VERAN DOES NOT BELIEVE ME. Says the fields must be planted, the plough does not disturb our dead. But we are not the only ones who have seen the faceless ghosts walking, and Phelan is not alone in the loss of a loved one. A loved one who has died with features stolen from beneath their brows. We burn the bodies between the stones in the forest. Our songs have become quieter, subdued, and yet our bellies grow full. The grain is almost ready for harvest, and I hear my father sharpening the blade of his sickle outside our home. He, like Veran, does not believe my fears, that this new thing—this plough—has caused the dead to walk and steal our faces. Father says we must eat, or we will die.

I say, we will die anyway, our features like tracks in mud.

I am pulling the sinew stitches from Kerra's shoe, when I hear the fists against the door and my father's hurried words. I look up just as Veran tumbles into the sallow light of our home. A cold shock presses out over my body as I hurry to my feet, my father bringing him over to sit before the fire. Veran shakes and shivers, and when I place a hand on his tunic, I can feel why. His skin beneath is burning.

A fever.

I reach to brush the hair from his face, but he shrinks back, hands up. My father looks down, his features etched with knowing fear, and I feel the same emotion roil like snakes in my belly.

"Close the door," I say to my father. "Leave us."

He does as he is told and when we are left alone, I turn to Veran.

"You have to let me see," I say.

He shakes his head again, but it is the lack of voice that makes the sweat break out along my brow.

"Please, Veran," I say, my throat closing up around the words. "You have to let me see you."

He does not move at first, as though he is hoping, praying, that when he turns it will not be as horrible as we both know it to be.

"Please." The word lingers on my lips like a secret.

Slowly, he turns his head, loose hair falling from his face. My lungs contract, a tight fist in my throat. His mouth has turned to melted wax, lips fused and dripping down along his jawbone. One eye slurries over his cheek, the blue slipping like ocean. The breath sticks in my chest, heat rushing out along my body, gathering in pinpricks on my skin. Without thinking, I reach out, pressing my fingers against all his bleeding features.

"Veran." His name is like dust on my lips. Dry, barren fields.

We should have let them rest, left the dead alone. We should have starved. I turn back toward the door, picture the plough resting against the side of Veran's house. The Savior.

Not our savior, I think. *Our condemnation.*

We will have no mouths to eat our new grain.

I have only one thought as I rush from Veran's side and out into the Lammas wind. The plough is soft beneath my hands, the wood worn smooth from a season of working the ground.

Digging up the bones.

I hear muffled moans behind me and turn to see Veran stumbling from my father's house, one palm outstretched.

"We have to burn it. It has dug too deep, Veran. And you—" the words hitch in my throat— "you know what it's released."

Plague for plague.

Veran stumbles to his knees and I can see tears sloughing down his cheeks, getting caught in his tallow-wax lips. He weaves his fingers in front of his face and it takes everything I have within me not to break, to let the tears pour like a torrent. There is a murmur then, a gasp, and I look to see the village emptying out all around us.

Phelan leans crooked now, hours spent pounding iron to rid himself of the memories of Amena. The tanner and his wife stand huddled around their children, and I catch their faces. Bright eyes, yellow hair, full bellies. No one stands as skeletons, not anymore. For the first time in so many seasons, we are full. Fatted.

Like lambs for the slaughter.

I look between the plough in my hands and those around me. My father stands to the side of his house, pain on his face. *He knows.* This impossible decision. He has lost too much already, how can he bear to lose another?

But the village must be fed. And the winter is fast approaching. I drop my gaze back to the plough, the wood Veran has spent countless days curing, working, keeping soft and supple to till the earth.

To raise the fertile bones.

Veran's face is weeping now, features running like fresh dye on wool. I stare at him, my insides gutted like a fish, viscera swimming just below the surface of my skin.

"I will take in the harvest," I say, suddenly, hands gripping the plough. "I alone."

IT WILL END WITH A BURIAL. My own. I let no one else till the fields, or even venture out between the stalks of grain. My father's sickle etches callouses into the flesh of my palm, but still I cut: gathering the crop in bundles and leaving them at the village edge. I sleep in the bone meadow, the only thing to keep me company, my sister.

I saw her for the first time three days past, slipping up out of the earth like a sprig of some green shoot. Her fingers, lithe and white, gripped a shaft of grain as she pulled her way out of her grave. I knew her by her shoeless feet, her brown hair, the necklace still threaded around her collarbones. But her face was gone, her clothes eaten away by worms, ribcage exposed like ornament. It did not scare me. I knew she would be coming.

I sit at the edge of the field now, twisting my father's sickle in my hands. Veran is dead. He died the day after I took up the plough and churned the barren fields for the next planting season. The fields without bones beneath.

We do not need to wake our dead.

Not anymore.

Not once I am gone.

Behind me, the earth shifts and I know it is Kerra. I turn to see the dirt crumbling like dry heads of yarrow. Her hand breaks first, dry skin flaking from bone, then her head, a face wiped of features. It should frighten me, but I feel nothing as my sister rises from the earth and stands before me. She comes closer, and for a moment, I toy with the idea of sinking Father's sickle between her ribs, but there is only air there. No meat. So, I lay the blade down on the dying grass.

"Have you finally come for me?" I ask, softly. "Have you come to take my face, no mouth to eat with."

The irony settles into my stomach like silt. Starved ghosts who take the only thing that will keep us fed. My sister comes to sit beside me, bones snapping. We stay in silence for a moment, watching the sun tip over the horizon, the willows swaying at the village edge. My eyes snag on the wooden beams of Veran's house. What should have been *my* house. No plough leans beside it. I burned it two days back, after I saw Kerra rise from the earth.

The last ghost to be disturbed.

She leans her head on my shoulder then, neck crackling like dry leaves, and I let her. I stroke what remains of her hair, the strands now brittle and thin. I know they are lonely things, the walking ghosts, and so I take these last moments with my sister as she comes to steal my face.

I have reconciled myself to it—the silent slipping into death that is sure to be my fate. The storehouse is filled with grain, seed pulled for the next planting season. The village will survive the winter, and the barren fields will be sown again. My father will use his ard once more, not deep enough to pierce flesh, or disturb the dead. I made him promise.

But once he is gone, once the village is made up of those who can no longer remember, will the plough be brought back? Will the ground once more be gashed open and our bones awakened from the blackest pits of earth?

I do not know, but as I turn to the muddy water pooling in the earth beside me, I realize it does not matter. I do not have the time. One eye slips down over my cheekbone like rain on iron, pooling at the edge of my watery lips like a splotch of mud.

I am beginning to lose my face.

I lean closer to Kerra, feel the whisper-dust brush of her fingertips against my hand. The sun is almost gone now, angling shots of orange through the air like fire. I try to smile, my lips weeping earthwards.

Perhaps it was always meant to be this way, my sister and I, watching the world burn, knowing the earth will feed off all our fertile bones.

HUSH, LITTLE SISTER

LYNDSEY CROAL

WHEN MY PARENTS bought Leia's Shimmer, they said it was for me, not them. But the last thing an eight-year-old needs is the hologram of her dead twin sister popping up at random moments, haunting her every move. I should have been allowed to move on, even if my parents couldn't.

Now that they're gone too, I'm standing outside the door of our childhood home for the first time in years, staring at my distorted reflection in the rain glass. I know she's in there, waiting. I've not seen her Shimmer in almost a decade. Dad said I was being stubborn when I stopped coming home at holidays, while Mum cried over the phone. But I couldn't be there, not while Leia was still around.

I take a deep breath and put the key in the door.

The hallway is smaller than I remember. Wallpaper peels at the ceiling, and a damp smell infiltrates the air, clings to my throat. The floorboards creak, and I look down. Leia's initials are still carved in one of them, in sharp edges alongside mine.

I'm about to head upstairs when she suddenly flickers in front of me.

"Bell Bell!" Her voice pierces, strikes me still. Leia was the only one who ever called me that, and it feels like a betrayal coming out of this programme's mouth. "I've missed you, Bell Bell."

"That's not my name. It's Izzy now."

Her face becomes thoughtful, dimples forming beneath her constellation of freckles. I'd forgotten how realistic her Shimmer is.

"Izzy. Hmm. Izzy, like Incy Wincy Spider climbed up the waterspout." She hums the tune, and it feels like a spider is crawling up my throat. "Your turn!" she trills, after.

"I'm too old for nursery rhymes, I'm almost thirty."

"Don't be silly, thirty is *old*, and you're three minutes younger than me," she says. "What's for breakfast today? Are Mum and Dad joining?"

It's almost dark outside. Her time algorithms must have got mixed up over the years—my parents stopped being able to afford the updates a few years back. After I stopped lending them the money for it. "Mum and Dad aren't here. They're gone. Dead. Do you know what that means?"

She stares at me, face shimmering, then she turns and runs away. Her laugh that follows wounds me in more ways than one.

I'M GATHERING up Mum's old gardening magazines when Leia appears again. She sits, cross-legged on the sofa, body half submerged into the old worn cushions. The toy Labrador she used to take everywhere sits next to her, its fur grey where it was once yellow, one eye stitched back slightly above its socket. Still, Leia strokes it gently as if she can feel its fur. My parents made so much effort to make sure a hologram was happy, while they were content to let my life pass by— my graduation, my engagement party. I didn't even bother inviting them to the wedding. They'd rarely leave the house for anything.

Once, they tried to trick me to come home, phoned Cal and invited him to dinner. Cal said yes of course, he's too nice that way, but when it came to it, we cancelled.

I call Cal now to check in and he answers with a gentle smile. "Hey there. How are things going?"

"Okay," I lie.

"Is she there?"

I angle the camera towards Leia, though she's sitting so still now I wonder if she's glitched.

Cal's face moves between concern and curiosity. "Are you staying there tonight?"

"Yeah. Just want to get this wrapped up as soon as I can. The solicitor's coming on Wednesday."

"Sure you don't want me to come?"

I shake my head. I don't want him to meet her. I don't want this to be the first time he sees any part of my past. "It's better if I do this on my own."

"What will you do with her?"

I shrug. "Can't leave her here for the next owners, and I'm not taking her with me."

"You're going to wipe her?" There's judgement in his voice—he's always been weird about this stuff. His dad keeps his mum's Shimmer, and he doesn't seem bothered about it. Doesn't understand my aversion, either.

"I don't know yet," I say to placate him. "She's not real you know."

He frowns. "I know, but just think about it. Once she's gone, that's it."

"She should have been gone twenty years ago."

"In twenty years, we'll be twenty-eight!" Leia says from the sofa. "Do you think we'll still live together, Bell Bell?"

"Bell Bell?" Cal says, smiling.

"Don't, " I say. "Don't call me that."

His eyebrows arch sharply upwards, the way they do when he's upset. "Sorry. Speak tomorrow, then?"

I rub my eyes. I shouldn't have snapped. None of this is his fault. "Yes, sorry. It's just. . . this is all a lot. Chat in the morning, though? Love you."

"Love you too, Izzy."

I end the call and I'm left alone with my Shimmer sister, counting now on her fingers, over and over, as if stuck in a loop. I stand up to leave her to it, but as I do, she lets out a sigh, head tilting sideways, and says, 'Love you too, Izzy.'

I don't reply. Her programme must just hear phrases and replicate them. But then, as I leave the room she speaks again. "Don't you love me too, Bell Bell?"

I'M WOKEN in the middle of the night by a breath in my ear. I turn, and Leia's there, curled up beside me, eyes wide, staring. She smiles as I scream and jump out of bed.

"What the fuck, Leia!"

"That's a bad word. I'm telling Mum."

"Mum's dead."

Leia gives me the longest stare before speaking again. "Mum's just sleeping."

"No, she's not, she's *dead*, and so is Dad. And if you hadn't been here, maybe they wouldn't be." It's the first time I've said it out loud— the blame, the resentment I have for my Shimmer sister. If she was just gone, maybe they'd have moved on, had another life, one where they were proper parents.

Leia starts to cry, tears distorting her face. It's too familiar. She was always the crier between us. Dad would say I must bottle everything up inside, but really, I just didn't let them see me cry. They had enough to be dealing with.

"You should never have left us," she says through tears, then she sinks into the bed, disappearing.

THE NEXT MORNING, the man from the funeral home stops by with Mum and Dad's ashes. I take the urns and put them on the hallway table, then the man passes me another box.

"What's this?"

"Their Shimmer files." His eyes glance over my shoulder, where Leia's probably standing somewhere, watching. His expression is more bored than scared—he's likely seen a thousand Shimmers in his line of work.

I put the box next to the ashes.

"Make sure you register before the end of the month for the discount," he says. I nod and smile, just to get him to leave.

When he's gone, Leia wanders up to the table, twisting a curl of her hair between her fingers. "What's that Bell Bell?"

"Mum and Dad, " I say, though she won't understand what that means.

But her face goes impassive, still. "I tried to help them. But they wouldn't wake up."

A chill creeps down my back. "What did you say?"

"I. . ." She pauses, and her Shimmer flickers as if the signal was disrupted. "Shall we watch a movie, Bell Bell?" Cheery again, as if nothing happened.

LATER, as I'm cleaning out the shed, an elderly woman appears at the door. "Hello, dear. Are you the other daughter?"

I stand up and brush dirt and cobwebs from my hands. "Can I help you?"

"I live next door," she says. "I'm so very sorry for your loss."

"Thank you," I say, because what else can I say to a stranger who probably knew my parents better than I did.

"They were always kind to me, helped me with things in the garden and such, especially after my husband died." She smiles. "I'm glad you're here for Leia. Such a sweet thing. I never could afford a Shimmer for Harry."

I tense up. "Anything I can help with?"

"Oh, it's just Leia's in my garden," she says. "She likes to watch the birds, sometimes, but she's been sitting on the bench all morning, barely moving. I think she might be sad."

"Shimmers can't be sad," I reply. Nor should she be able to move past the house boundary.

The woman frowns. "Well, I thought you might like to know."

"Can I come over and see?"

I follow her into her garden where, right enough, Leia is on the bench under the hedge adjacent to my parents' house, staring up into the empty sky. "Leia," I say gently. "What are you doing?"

"Watching for robins. Mum says robins visit when loved ones are near."

It was something Mum used to say, but I only remembered her saying it after Leia died. "Time to come home. I'm sure that. . ." I turn to the woman, and she offers her name as Maura.

"I'm sure Maura would rather you didn't sit here all morning."

Leia turns her head in a strange motion towards Maura. "Didn't you hear me call for help?"

Maura blinks at her. "Sorry, dear?"

"They were. . . and I was. . . I called out. . ." Leia's voice is disjointed, strange. Her face is different too, features falling apart, one eye slightly askew just like her puppy. "On the night they. . . when. . . sleeping. . . just sleeping. . . I screamed. . . no one came. . . no one came." She begins to rock back and forwards. "My fault, my fault, my fault, my fault."

"Leia! " I shout, heart racing. "Stop this and come home." She stops rocking straight away, then her eyes blink rapidly as her face pieces back together.

"Oh, hello Bell Bell. I saw four blackbirds today." She smiles and begins to sing, "Four and twenty blackbirds, baked in a pie. Isn't it a funny song Bell Bell, why would you bake blackbirds in a pie? So silly, isn't it? Bell Bell? Isn't it?"

Out of instinct, I reach forward to grab her and pull her home, but my hand goes straight through her. My palm tingles, a coldness stretching up my arm. I retract it quickly. Leia doesn't seem to notice, she just stands up and skips off straight through the hedge until I can see her blue form leaning down over Mum's flowerbed, smelling non-existing flowers.

I turn to Maura whose face is pale. "Sorry about this, it won't happen again."

Maura offers a weak smile. "I'm sorry that I wasn't here that night. When your parents died. I wish I had been. I might have seen something, but I was at my son's up north. Leia. . . you will take care of her, won't you?"

I chew the inside of my cheek. "Thanks for your help," I say, and hurry home.

"YOU'RE NOT LISTENING CAL; she had a total meltdown."

Cal pauses on the other end of the line—as soon as he answered, I could tell he was going to go into fix mode, instead of just listening. "How long since she's had an update? You said yourself that your parents couldn't afford it, but we could now, we've got savings."

"I don't need your money for this."

"*Our* money. We're married now. Till death do us part, remember?"

"Or after, apparently." I imagine an elderly Cal sitting with Shimmer-me in a countryside cottage, him reading a book while my imprint sits watching him, speaking a programmed phrase. "It doesn't matter. I'm going to get techs in to wipe her, it's the only option."

"Shouldn't you wait until you've had some distance, time to process?"

"I didn't call for a therapy session, Cal."

He goes silent as if I'm one of his patients and he's giving me time to reflect on my words. "I'm sorry, Izzy, I know this is hard."

"I can't speak right now." I hang up.

IT'S LATE when there's a knock on the door. At first, I think it it's just the wind and rain, but then it comes again. Leia's eyes had been fixed on the fire for the past hour, but she looks up at me now. "There's someone at the door."

The doorbell rings now, and Leia jumps up on the sofa, the bottom of her legs disappearing into the cushions. "A bell for Bell Bell, a bell for Bell Bell," she says as if it's a tongue twister. "A bell—"

"Stop it!" I shout, and she does. She looks away from me to the fireplace again, gaze intent on the flames. Leaving her there, I head to the door. I find a shivering Cal on the other side.

He smiles, rubbing his hands together, and peers inside. "Going to invite me in?"

"I told you not to come."

"You sounded upset on the phone."

"Of course I did, my parents just died."

"*Izzy.*"

"Cal."

He looks behind him at the driveway—just my car sitting there in the dark. He must have got the bus, walked the rest of the way. He rubs his arms and breathes into his hands.

I step out from the doorway. "Just come in. There's a fire on, so you can warm up."

He kisses me on the cheek, his coat leaving a dripping trail on the floor, and heads towards the living room. He looks inside, then frowns. "Forgot to add wood to it?"

I follow him, confused, finding the fire has all but gone out, barely an ember. Leia is where I left her, staring at the fire.

"How did. . . did you put it out?"

Leia frowns and starts pulling at a loose thread on her jumper. "Put what out?"

"The fire. There was a fire."

She shakes her head. "No there wasn't, silly Bell Bell. Fire is bad."

"There was, just a minute ago." I look to Cal, and he shrugs.

"Maybe the wind blew it out when I came in." He steps forwards. "You must be Leia?"

Leia turns her head so fast, her face blurs for a second, and as her features rearrange, she tilts her head. "Who are you?"

"I'm Cal. Izzy's husband."

Leia blinks once. "*Husband?*" She turns to me. "You got married?"

"Yes."

"Why didn't I go to the wedding?"

"It was. . . a small event," I say, though I shouldn't have to justify it to her.

She pouts.

"Don't cry, " I say. "It's not a big deal."

Her expression wavers. "Why are you hiding things? I'm your sister."

"No, you're not."

"Come on, Iz—" Cal begins, but I cut him off.

"This is exactly why you weren't invited."

Leia walks up to him. "It's not nice not to be invited, is it Cal?"

Cal opens then closes his mouth quickly when he sees my face.

"I'm going to bed," I say, and march upstairs.

I'm getting into my pyjamas when I hear Cal and Leia talking on the landing outside. I listen against the door to the muffled chatter. Then, Leia is singing a lullaby, *"Hush, Little Baby,"* and Cal is humming along. Why did he have to come?

I open the door, and he turns with a half-smile.

"Leia has a lovely voice."

"Had, " I say. "Are you coming to bed?"

Cal stands up. "Good night, Leia."

"Will you read me a story? I can't sleep without one."

"You don't sleep, Leia," I say.

"I do! " She screws her eyes up tight. "See, I'm asleep."

Cal laughs. "I could read—"

"No, " I say. "Just leave us alone, Leia."

She glares at me, then closes her eyes again, puffs out her cheeks, pretending to hold her breath. She used to do that when she didn't get her way, but I'm not reacting to it. After a minute of us standing in silence, she opens her eyes, then runs towards me. Before I can stop her, she's run straight through me.

It's like I've been doused in freezing water. "What the hell, Leia." I reach for her, but she's already dissolved into thin air.

Cal walks into the room, putting a hand on my shoulder as he passes. "Reading a story might have been easier, you know."

I follow him inside and slam the door. "*This* isn't helping."

"Maybe you should go easier on her, she seems. . . upset."

I stare at him. "I really hope you're joking."

He shrugs. "I don't know, she's different to other Shimmers I've seen."

"What do you mean?"

"Look, it doesn't matter, I didn't mean to come here to make it worse. I'm sorry." He pulls me towards him. His clothes are still wet, but I lean into him anyway. He kisses my forehead. "It'll be okay."

A NOISE from downstairs wakes me up. Cal must be up and about. I head to the landing and stop, frozen. There's a hole in the top step of the staircase. And a body at the bottom.

"Cal!" I run down.

He blinks up at me, eyes rolling back in his head. Blood trickles from his brow. I put my hands under his shoulders and lift him slightly. "Can you hear me?"

He comes to after a second, then groans. "Iz. . . what happened?"

"The step must have been broken or rotten." I look up at the stairs again and my breath catches. Leia is standing at the top, fists clenched by her side, eyes narrowed in on Cal.

"I told him to be careful," she says. "This house is bad for accidents."

An unease stirs in my gut. "Did *you* push him?"

"Izzy, a Shimmer can't—" Cal begins then stops, putting his hand to his head.

"Why did you say what happened to Mum and Dad was your fault?" I ask Leia.

Her eyes stream again, blue crocodile tears. "I was only trying to help." Then she runs out the top floor window.

I turn back to Cal. "We should get you to the hospital, you could have a concussion."

He shakes his head. "I'll be fine, I'll just lie down."

"What do you think she meant, that she tried to help. Did she tell you about the stairs?"

"I don't remember. Maybe."

I help him to the sofa and bring a cold cloth for his head, sit with him, thankful that it wasn't worse.

After Cal falls asleep, I go to look for Leia. I find her in the garden, sitting facing the back wall. She's humming to herself, hands held out in front of her. There's a web in the corner, a large spider in the centre.

She turns to look at me, her head twisting in an awkward angle. "Did you know that when spiders moult, they sometimes stay beside their old body until they're strong enough to leave it behind?" she asks. "So, when you find curled up spider bodies, they're usually not actually dead, just discarded versions of themselves."

I frown. "I didn't know that."

She pauses as if deep in thought. "That's what I'm like. Except, it's like if the spider left its skin behind and part of itself too. And then the spider died."

My mind whirrs. Shimmers aren't supposed to be self-aware. "Leia, do you understand who. . . what you are?"

"You said I'm not your sister. But I am. Or I think I am. Though you're so much older now, and I'm not, and Mum and Dad got older too, before they. . ."

"What happened on the night they died?"

She takes a moment before speaking again. "I tried to wake them. They were just sitting on their chairs by the fire, sleeping really soundly, and I tried to call for help, but no one came." She turns to me, eyes unnaturally wide. "There was so much smoke in the room, from the fire, and I tried to stop it. But I couldn't." Her voice wavers. "It's my fault. I asked them to put the fire on, even though we didn't need it. I liked to watch the flames, and pretend to be warm, like when we were little. Remember Bell Bell, we'd come in from long walks, and sit by the fire, and Mum would read fairy tales."

I remember. The way I'd curl into Leia, with hot chocolate, imagining adventures in other worlds. I think about the fireplace, how Leia had stared at it so intently. "Did you put the fire out yesterday?"

"I don't know. But I wanted to," she says. "I didn't want it to happen again."

"And Cal. Did you push him?"

She shakes her head. "I didn't mean to. I tried to grab him, to stop him from stepping on the top stair, but I made it worse, and he fell."

I feel sick, cold. Maybe all of it was a coincidence—a gust of wind from the door put out the fire, then Cal just got a fright from seeing her and fell.

"I miss them," Leia says. "I just want them to come home, but they won't, will they?"

"Sorry, no."

She looks at the web again, touches the edges of the fragile silk. "Not even their skins?"

I look at her for a long moment. Somehow, Leia knows she's a Shimmer, with the memories of a dead girl. Somehow, she knows that Mum and Dad are gone, but that they could come back as something like her. Whether she's my sister or not, she's not just a programme. And I know now I can't just wipe her.

"I'm going to check on Cal, you stay here, okay?"

She nods, and for once doesn't fight me on it. I head back inside.

Cal takes my hand as I sit next to him. "You okay?"

I look over at the empty armchairs where Mum and Dad spent their last moments. The police said carbon monoxide poisoning was a peaceful way to go, at least. I squeeze Cal's hand. "I've been thinking. I'm not ready to sell the house."

He nods slowly. "Okay."

"And I might release my parents' Shimmers, like they wanted. To keep Leia company."

"I think she'd like that."

"That would mean we wouldn't have any money from the sale. And the house would sit empty."

"We can still visit."

I laugh.

His eyes narrow. "Why's that funny?"

"The idea that I'd visit my dead family more than my alive one."

"You've always had a morbid sense of humour."

I take a deep breath. "Did you know spiders shed their skin?"

"I guess, though it's the kind of random fact you forget."

"Leia didn't forget it. She didn't forget me, after all this time."

"Of course she didn't. Sisters are made of strong stuff."

I lie down, curl up next to Cal, and for the first time since my parents died, I cry. He holds me close as I think of my family gone, of all the years I didn't visit, of my Shimmer sister feeling alone with my parents all this time, with only the walls and the spiders in the garden as company.

THE TECHS COME to install Mum and Dad's Shimmers a few days later. The house is tidied, the top step fixed, but the rooms left the same, apart from the fireplace which I've had blocked up.

When the techs notice Leia's glitching, they offer an upgrade, but I turn them down. Leia seems happy as she is.

I don't wait for Mum and Dad's Shimmers to appear. I'm not quite ready for that. I say goodbye to Leia, tell her to be good, and promise that I'll visit someday soon.

Locking the door, Cal and I leave the house. Distorted through the rain glass, I watch three Shimmer forms embrace, my family reunited, happily forever and after.

THE BIRDS SANG IN BOTH WORLDS

SIMON KEWIN

JAMILAH WAS STANDING three metres from the centre of the explosion when the bomb went off.

As she later found out, it was a big one, thirty metres in area of effect. Bigger than those in Toronto or Johannesburg. As in those other cities, there were no casualties—at least, not directly, not immediately. But it happened: an electromagnetic flash blasting through Jamilah and her sister and the crowd around them, along with a section of the Delhi street they were walking along. Taxis, buses, the bright clean shops with their dazzling displays, all were caught, fritzing out their electronics, crashing their processors and sensors and image propagators.

She knew none of this at the time. She was aware, simply, that she was caught mid-word, her mouth open and that, for the blink of an eye or the beat of the heart, she stood in a very different world. A shadow world. The streets beneath her feet were not rose-coloured granite but were cracked and stained, piled high with filth. Cries of fear rang out around her. Tangled nests of cables ran everywhere, connecting the stained concrete buildings. The dappled shade from the umbrella trees was gone. Graffiti was daubed over the walls, words she could make no sense of. One was repeated over and over, a jumble of nonsense painted in bright blue letters, big enough to catch her attention.

Saccaaccas.

She was aware of people: her sister nearby, others on the street, the shoppers and vendors and chaiwalas. They were changed, drabber and tattier. A cow was wandering mournfully along nearby; in this other world, its garland of orange flowers was gone and the outline of its bones showed through its flanks. The stench of the place came to her nostrils: rot, decay, dung. The song of the birds was the same, though, their trilling from the roofs. The birds sang in both worlds.

She also glimpsed bundles of rags discarded by the side of the road. One of the bundles was looking at her. It was a person, quietly watching her. They were all people, slumped there, sitting or sleeping or dead. The one who'd seen her looked puzzled at having his gaze returned.

Again, as she came to understand later, it took a second for aug flecks to reboot, for local area connections to restore. At the time, she was aware only of the troubling images winking out and her familiar, comfortable world returning. Where the slumped figure had been, there was now a market stall, laden with bananas and mangos and water melons, yellow and orange and green. The sun shone once again on the wide street. The people around her, after a pause, a bemused smile, a shake of the head, carried on with their strolling and their chatting as if they'd experienced nothing more than a passing cloud.

She grabbed hold of Meera, her sister. "What was that? What just happened?"

Meera was three years older. At twenty she was, in Jamilah's view, already taking herself far too seriously. She'd been fun, once. Now, Meera was often angry with Jamilah.

Meera pulled Jamilah's hands off. "Nothing happened. What are you talking about?"

"The world just literally glitched out for a moment."

"*You* may have glitched out, but no one else did. You need to get your head checked."

"You must have seen it. This whole area went. . . weird."

"Why must you spoil everything, Jamilah? It's a beautiful day, let's just enjoy it. Let's resume our quest for your party saree since we've come all this way."

Meera wasn't going to be persuaded. But Jamilah had seen the haunted look in her sister's eyes. She knew. She'd seen. But she wouldn't admit it. Perhaps she couldn't; perhaps she *knew* it hadn't happened because she didn't believe it could.

Jamilah had read all the crazy conspiracy theories, the ones that got posted by anonymous social media accounts before being rapidly deleted. The whole world was a fake; the reality that everyone saw nothing more than an illusory overlay. The *VeneeR*, they called it.

She blamed Ishaan. Ishaan with the brown eyes. Beautiful, smart Ishaan who'd made her insides flutter. He'd liked to tell her about it, who was behind it, and she'd liked to listen. Liked to hear the sound of his voice. Their world was the one the governments and the unnamed corporations that controlled everything wanted people to see, not the one that was actually there. Why fix all the world's troubles? Why clean up the dirt and repair the cracks? Why find money to feed the poor? Cheaper to reprogram the VeneeR, make people's flecks generate a happier world, a better world. It was all a fake, a sham.

Ishaan who'd died a year ago, his motorcycle crushed beneath the wheels of a juggernaut as he attempted a risky overtaking manoeuvre.

His claims were obviously deluded. Most of the time, VeneeR conspiracy theory was drowned out by the other crackpot beliefs out there: the Earth was flat; governments were run by shape-shifting lizards; law enforcement agencies put mind-control chemicals into water, into aircraft contrails. On and on; all of the nonsense. She liked to read them because they were amusing, imaginative. She enjoyed the logical knots people tied themselves in attempting to prove their beliefs.

Except, except, there was the memory she often returned to. She was little more than a baby, toddling, before her first aug fleck was embedded. A beggar had come to the door, stick-thin, limping, and her father had chased him away, angry. It had alarmed the young Jamilah. She'd followed a short way. The world she'd glimpsed had been drab and ugly, cracked earth rather than the lush green of the garden she knew now. Piles of rags strewn about in the road. Or were they rags?

Had that actually happened? Memory was unreliable; the brain conflated real events with subsequent retellings, with stories. But, sometimes, she had the feeling that the world around her was fake, superficial. She would catch a glimpse of something—a facial expression, the way the water moved—that didn't seem right. It looked nearly perfect, but not quite. The people around her felt false, superficial.

Maybe everyone thought like that at times.

Ignoring Meera's pleas, Jamilah crossed to the fruit stall where she'd glimpsed the slumped figure. The barrow with its piles of colourful wares prevented her getting to the wall. She stepped around it, squatting down, trying to get behind it, feeling with her hands for that bundle of rags and the person peering out from them. Would that work, or would her flecks edit out her sensations if she happened to touch anything that she wasn't supposed to be aware of? Or was she simply going as crazy as her sister insisted?

A hand on her shoulder gripped her hard. "Whatever you're doing, I think you should stop it, Miss."

A policeman. He was smiling, but there was a note of steel in his voice. Jamilah rose to meet his gaze. She'd glimpsed an officer in the momentary outage. A policeman, or perhaps a solder, clad in bulky armour, a rifle cradled in his arms. Everything grimy. In fact, she'd seen several of them, although now there was only this one. Was he the same person? Was this smiling, unarmed man before her nothing more than an overlay, an avatar? And where were the others? Why were they there, around her, but invisible?

"I. . . dropped something," Jamilah managed. She was aware of Meera, hovering to one side, nervously adjusting her saree.

The policeman turned to her. "Are you with this girl?"

"She's my little sister."

"Well, I think you should take her home. Can you do that?"

"I will take her right away. I'm sorry, she has always been trouble this one. I will make sure she doesn't cause any more upset."

"Good, good. See that you do."

When they were alone, Meera hissed, actually hissed. "What are you doing? Why do you always have to get into trouble?"

There was a look deep in Meera's eye that looked. . . wrong. Empty. Jamilah didn't reply.

THAT NIGHT, when she was alone, she lay on her bed with her phone. She paused for a moment, troubled by the thought that her familiar room, the familiar house around her wasn't real. It was a crazy idea. Maybe she was lying on a hard floor and her augs simply told her it was a soft bed. For all she knew, there were people there with her, denizens of that grimy other world, the real world, keeping an eye on her, like that police officer. It was a creepy idea.

She caught her own reflection in the screen of her phone. Could she even trust that? Was that what she really looked like? She put it out of her mind. Her mother always said she should write stories with the crazy notions she had.

She did some searching, scouring channels and groups and feeds for anyone mentioning what she'd experienced, looking for possible hashtags like #glitch or #veneer or #outage. She got nothing. If there'd been posts, they were gone. Or, they'd never been there in the first place.

She tried one more thing: the word she'd seen daubed on the walls, repeated over and over, like whoever detonated the EM pulse bomb had really wanted everyone to see the word. Sacacas was it? Or saccaccas. Something like that. Probably gibberish, daubed by some crazy. She tried various spellings and got nowhere. *Sacca* was a Sanskrit word meaning real or true, but there were no hits anywhere on the longer word—which was unusual in itself, but had to happen sometimes.

There *was* an old post with a vaguely similar word in it, as if badly misspelled. *Asccaccas*—but even that didn't get her very far. It was nonsense. There was a link but it was just an IP address. Only an idiot would tap on random links but, after a moment's hesitation, that was what she did. As her phone froze, she regretted it immediately and killed her browser. She put her phone down and turned on her side to sleep. From outside her window, the familiar night time cicada chorus sent her off to sleep.

SHE WOKE to the sound of someone shuffling about in her room. It was still night, but the moon was full outside, a spectral light flooding her room. Who had opened her blinds? Why was her bed so hard beneath her? She sat up, looked around. This wasn't even her room. The walls were bare and the floor was hard stone.

And there was a figure standing in the middle of it, silhouetted against the window. It had to be a nightmare; a reaction to the odd episode in the street.

"Am I dreaming?" she said out loud.

A voice replied, a young guy, his voice low. He sounded amused. "For the first time in your life, you're not."

She found herself out of bed, standing. She had her phone in her hand, as if she was going to use it as a weapon. "Who are you? What are you doing in my room?"

"You called me."

"I did not. This has to be a dream. This is not my room."

"Are you always this slow to work out what's going on? Look, I'm not going to harm you."

"Which is what all killers say before they strike."

"Look, I'll go if you want. But I can tell you what *saccaaccas* means, if you want to know."

She fumbled for the light switch on her bedside table and flicked it on. Nothing happened.

"I'm afraid that hasn't worked in a long time," the shape said. "They use all the electricity for the image projectors."

"It worked this morning."

"You were given the illusion of it working. Look, I have a light, a real light. I'll switch it on, and then you'll be able to see me."

"How did you even get in here?"

"I walked in."

"You walked through our gates and doors."

"There are no gates and your doors are badly broken. Nobody repairs anything anymore, not in the real world."

"Is *this* the real world?"

"This is it, I'm afraid. Your world is a lot more lovely, I'm told."

"How are you doing this?"

"A tuned EM field knocking out the electronics. It works for a short time before they notice and come to check."

"Switch your light on. Show me."

He did so. He flashed a cone of yellow light around the room, revealing the wide cracks in the walls, the boarded-up window where there was normally glass and a view over the roofs of the city. Finally, he shone it on himself. He was young, his lank black hair uncut. There was a... vividness to him she found it hard to take her eyes off. His clothes were tatty and he looked like he needed several good meals, but he was full of life.

He was real.

"So, tell me, what does it mean?"

"What?"

"The word."

He laughed to himself. "Honestly? It's nonsense. A word to attract people's attention. People see it, come searching. Then we make contact."

"Why?"

"There are more of us every day, refusing to believe their lies."

"The world... my world. You don't see it?"

"I've heard stories about it. I prefer ugly reality, when people like you don't even know I'm near."

She heard herself asking him before she knew what she was doing. "How do I get to be like that?"

"It's dangerous. It's a big step."

"It's what I want."

He sat down on the edge of her bed to look at her. "It will change you. There's no going back. Your life is comfortable; do you want to throw it all away?"

"It isn't real."

"Does that matter if you're happy?"

"Yes," she said simply. "More than anything. Besides, how can I simply carry on now you've given me this glimpse."

"I can wipe the memories of this conversation from your augs. You can live your life like it never happened."

"If I go, will I be able to see my family again?"

"You'll be able to see them as they really are."

"They won't be able to see me."

He nodded, conceding the point. "Not unless they choose to cross over, too."

"This field you're employing to talk to me. I could use one to talk to them, tell them I'm okay."

He gave that some thought. "Technically, that could work."

"What's your name?"

"Sanjit."

"Show me what I need to do."

He sighed, then relented. "There's a place. I'll give you the address. Go there and people will be able to help. They'll disable your augmentations so your brain sees the real world. But if you have doubts, don't go."

"Tell me the place," she said.

THE ADDRESS WAS an unmarked square building on the outskirts of town. It might have been a warehouse or some such. She wouldn't have noticed it normally. She'd slipped away, claiming to be visiting a friend. Her parents and sister had told her to be careful. Jamilah looked forward to seeing them as they really were, seeing the real expressions on their faces.

Inside the doors, a woman sat behind a desk. She was studying some papers, ticking things off. Her makeup and hair were exquisite. She looked up as Jamilah entered and smiled widely.

"Can I help you?"

"Is Sanjit here?"

"Do you know Sanjit."

"He. . . came to see me. Is he here?"

"He's here, yes." She took Jamilah's name, scanned her list. "Yes, yes, I see you're expected. You do understand why you're here, don't you?"

"I do."

"Very well. As I say, Sanjit is here. You'll see him when you cross over."

The walls and floor were smooth stone. Everything was very clean and clinical.

"Are you going to remove my augs?" Jamilah asked.

"No, no, they're too deeply embedded in your brain structures," the woman replied, as if they were simply discussing the rains. "We'll disable them, but we do have to get at them to do it. It's a quick procedure."

"Under anaesthetic?"

"Of course. General anaesthetic is best. You'll only be out for a couple of quick minutes. We've done it many times."

Under Jamilah's hair, behind her left ear, there was a prickly little scar where they'd inserted her augs years previously. Her fingers went to it now, feeling the rough edges.

"You can still choose to stay," the woman said, her voice softening. "We can wipe your memories. We'll have to go a little further back and you may lose a few other recent events, too, but you'll be fine. You won't know anything about it."

There was the look in her eye, the falseness, as if her augs were struggling to render the woman's emotions.

"No. I want to go."

The woman sighed for some reason. "Very well. Please step into this room and we'll prep you for surgery."

WHEN JAMILAH WOKE, there was an old man beside her bed, peering at her through half-moon spectacles. He nodded as she opened her eyes, as if she'd done well at something. The walls behind him were grey and cracked. The man's face was lined and grey. He did not look well.

"Welcome back," he said.

"Who are you?"

"I'm not going to tell you my name."

"Why? Where's Sanjit?"

"Sanjit does not exist. Names are the easiest of things to invent."

"I don't understand."

"It will take you time to fully grasp what you've done. I'm here to confirm that your happy, privileged life is over. You now live in the real world that you so longed for."

"I don't. . . who are you? What's going on?"

"Who are we? Oh, we don't matter. We're a sort of. . . pressure-release valve, I suppose. We remove the troublemakers, those who ask awkward questions, so that life can continue happily on for everyone else."

"But you're working to bring down the VeneeR, give everyone the real world back. You set off the EM bomb."

The man shook his head. "No, no. Not us, I'm afraid. We don't want to bring down anything. We're trying to protect all that from people like you. We're the good guys. We gave you every opportunity to change your mind, but you weren't to be persuaded."

Her head throbbed. She raised a hand to feel a bandage there. "You crippled my augs."

"What you wanted, yes? Think of it as your punishment for turning your back on your own. You should be pleased we didn't simply kill you."

"Why didn't you?"

"Oh, we do kill most of you. Cleaner that way. Some we keep because you're useful. Some because it amuses us to watch you. As I say, this is a punishment. You get to live out your life knowing what you've lost."

"I'll fight you. Tell others what you've done."

He looked amused, but his smile was brief, weak. "And we will stop you. Our operatives who walk in both worlds will stop you. Now, I'm going to pop you back to sleep for your transportation."

"No."

But she was still hooked up to drips and couldn't fight. She felt the cold chill of anaesthetic flooding her brain, and then the world stopped again.

SHE BECAME aware of the world again as she was jolted around in the back of a vehicle. She was lying on a metal floor, her hands and legs bound. Her head throbbed and her lips were cracked dry. How long had she been unconscious?

The vehicle stopped abruptly, throwing her against the rear doors. She cried out. The doors were pulled open and rough hands hauled her out, letting her fall to the dusty floor. Bright sunlight blinded for a moment. The vehicle screeched off, tyres squealing. No one spoke to her.

After a moment, Jamilah climbed to her knees. They'd thrown her onto the streets to fend for herself, tossed her there like so much trash. There was a lot of trash around her; the rot of it filled her nose. This was definitely the real world. She had no idea where she was. The suburbs, somewhere. In the distance, she could see the towers of the city rising above a fog of cloud and smoke. Kites soared in the sky, eyeing her.

She'd been edited out of her world. She was a ghost.

There were others nearby, those like the slumped figure she'd glimpsed by the side of the road, but also some who were less broken. Two or three of them came towards her. Their clothes were ragged, their eyes wary.

One, a woman, knelt down beside her, then slipped a knife from her belt.

"Another one cast out from heaven," she said. She set about cutting the bonds that held Jamilah.

"Who are you? Who are all of you?"

"People," said the woman. "Those they let live, those who escape, those who were never caught in the first place."

Jamilah took the proffered hand and pulled herself up. She dusted down her clothes.

"I don't get it. They said they didn't set off the EM bomb. Why would they lie about that?"

"Because that was us. It's a race, a game. We try to rescue people; they try to get to them first. We don't always succeed. I'm sorry we failed you."

"The man who was there when I came round. He said letting me live was *useful*."

The woman frowned. "Some of us think it's wrong to set off the pulses, lure people away from the VeneeR. That we do their work for them."

"Perhaps you do."

"Perhaps. I still think we should at least try to save people."

"The word. *Saccaaccas*. What does it mean?"

Another voice spoke, then. A young man, standing behind the woman.

"It's *sacca* and then the same word backwards. Like mirror writing, right? The equal and opposite world."

He stepped forward, and it was Ishaan. He was older, taller and thinner, but his eyes, his bright beautiful eyes, were the same.

"You died," she said.

He shrugged, grinned as if it were nothing. "I was cast out too. The motorcycle crash was just a story. They'll probably invent something just as dramatic for you."

"But. . ."

"I know. It's a lot. But you're here, now. You made it this far."

"What do I do now?"

He offered her his hand, as he'd once done often. After a moment, she took it.

"Now?" he said. "Now you can explore the world."

DISC ROT

ADAM CESARE

IT'S LIKE DUST, but it isn't dust.

And it's all over everything.

Everything the old man's got on the two folding tables.

Happy Meal toys. Incomplete board games, their boxes held closed with rubber bands. A tangled-up mess of landline phones. And movies. So many movies.

And some of the movies are gems. I can tell at only a glance.

A lot of junk, but some nice stuff tucked in there too. Rarities.

So I stand here, wanting to make a purchase.

But. . .

But everything the old man's selling is covered with this. . . dust that's not dust. I run my finger along the spine of a DVD, to see if any of these cases are salvageable, and the residue *does* come off, cakes on my fingertip. Which is good. I can clean whatever I buy, don't have to swap the inserts out into new cases.

I look at the chalky, fungal powder on my index finger. It doesn't have much of a smell. Which is good, because it *looks* like crumbled blue cheese.

So not-dust. Should I call it slime? No, slime's too *wet* a word. It's more like a powder it—

"They're not pretty, but they all work. I promise."

I look up at the old man. He blinks at me, little mole eyes. Then smiles, which makes me less comfortable, not more. None of his Happy Meal Toy profits are going to dentistry.

"And if they *don't* work, I'm here every Saturday. Just bring 'em back. I'll refund you or swap them."

Getting to this flea market is a forty-five minute drive. I doubt I'm coming back to make exchanges.

I nod. Try and smile. I've never been good at social stuff.

When I was younger, in school, I did okay. Went to parties, had girlfriends, even talked one into being my wife for a while. But I started losing my hair at twenty-eight and now, in my late thirties, most people I meet think I'm in my fifties and find my presence off-putting.

Which is fine, I don't care, I. . .

"Are there prices?" I ask, picking up a copy of an Adam Sandler comedy. It's a very common disc, not worth the price of the recycled plastic. But I don't want to immediately reach for the good stuff and give myself away.

"They're all three-for-five. Get more and we can do deals."

My smile comes easier now.

"Great, thanks," I say, and get to work.

I open each case, check that the right movie's inside, then hold the surface of the disc up to the sun. Which, if the old guy thinks I'm being too particular, too precious, he gives no indication.

And I'm not checking for scratches and fingerprints, like he probably assumes.

Fingerprints can be buffed. And scratches, unless major, are never really an issue.

What you have to inspect for is disc rot.

Spots on the disc where the information layer's begun to degrade. It's rare, but, some discs, you hold them up to the sun and they look like a slice of Swiss, irregular pockmarks of rot where the light comes through the plastic easier, the result of the thin metal data layer becoming compromised.

People who like to bash physical media as antiquated, paint collectors as hoarders, they point to disc rot and say it's something that happens to every movie, eventually. Like we're wasting our money, that all these movies will be unplayable in a decade or two.

But that's not true.

Sure, heat, age, or moisture can accelerate the process but certain titles and printings are *a lot* more susceptible to rot than others. Why? Usually it's because the studio, or the manufacturer, or both, cut corners during duplication, used inferior methods or materials.

So disc rot's a problem, yes, but if you've got a disc that's over fifteen years old and hasn't rotted yet: chances are it never will.

Fuck of a lot better chance than Netflix having that same movie when you want to watch it, at least.

When I'm finished browsing, I have a stack of thirty-one discs in front of me. Ten of them Blu-ray, dating from the first year or so of the format, the rest DVD, a few of those old enough to be housed in the old cardboard "snapper" cases WB was so fond of using.

And my hands are gummy with the powder.

The not-dust has painted thick gray streaks on my forearms and the backs of my hands where I've itched myself. And, as conscious as I've tried to be not to touch my face, I'm sure there are streaks on my forehead, chin, and in my hair, because. . . well, I touch my face a lot. Nervous habit. Can't help it, but I've gotten better. I used to pick at my skin too, squeeze blackheads that didn't need squeezing until I broke out.

I have hand sanitizer in the car. I'm going to need a lot of it.

As I count out cash, the old man licks his thumb, starts opening plastic Shoprite bags.

"Come on. Pick one more. Can't have an odd number. That's unlucky or something."

I try my best at a chuckle, hand him the money we've agreed to.

"I'm serious, I'm not going to charge you extra. Pick one more."

For whatever reason, maybe just to make the interaction end, I pick out a copy of *Heavy Metal*, a movie I own several times over, in better editions than this one, and add it to the stack. *But have I owned* Heavy Metal *covered in a thin sheen of gray sludge?*

I work my way through the rest of the flea market as the sky darkens, thick clouds cutting the day short.

On the ride home I pass three signs for yard sales, but don't stop at any of them, even though it never rains.

She didn't want the house. Always said it was too small for kids. Was clear with the real estate agent when we bought it that she thought it was a starter home, that we needed more. When I suggested that the kids could share a room, well. . . that wasn't received well. And she took the first kid and left before we ever had to worry about him having a sibling, needing to share a space.

So now I have a house.

Or. *Temporarily* have a house.

I have to sell it, know I have to, it's on my to-do list. But the market's bad now and I. . .

Well, I have a lot of stuff. Moving would be a pain. And I've got to get my collection organized, then downsized, to be able to even afford a move.

Probably. I don't know how much moves cost.

My wife was right, though, even now with just me in it: the house is too small.

As I arrive home, I find myself in a rush to take a piss. There's a stack of bubble mailers and white Vinegar Syndrome boxes stacked in the front hallway, movies waiting for unboxing and filing, and I set my thirty-two flea market discs down on the stack on my way to the bathroom.

Then I forget about the movies for five or six hours, spend that time browsing a sale on Facebook Marketplace.

Some guy who used to work at a movie theater has got a bunch of original posters for sale. I don't even collect posters, but the prices are good and he's combining shipping, so maybe I can flip them on eBay.

I don't sleep much, normally, and this is a weekend, so I don't really sleep at all. It's on my third trip from the living room to the bathroom, sometime after 2:00 a.m., that I pass the Shoprite bags of movies, and remember my purchases from the day.

I clear off a spot on the coffee table, wet some paper towels in the sink, and begin the process of de-gunking my new movies.

I wipe the front, back, sides, and spine of each of the plastic cases with the wet towel, then repeat the process with a dry towel. That's all

I need, too much moisture warping the paper inserts. Not sure what I'm going to do with the cardboard snappers. I'm five cases in when I peak inside a copy of *Escape from Alcatraz* and realize. . . the not-dust is inside the cases, too.

Is it possible that I didn't notice, at the flea market? That I was too intent on checking for rot when I'd opened the cases?

There's a thin layer of the not-dust atop the disc itself, no smudges from where I'd handled it a few hours earlier, then more of the stuff accrued in the corners of the case like tiny windswept dunes.

And it's when I'm through cleaning those same five movies again, lifting each disc out of its tray for thorough cleaning, that I notice the first spot of rot.

No. How?

The disc is *Cyborg*—a movie I've never liked, though I enjoy star Jean-Claude Van Damme and director Albert Pyun, but the MGM DVD is long out-of-print, goes for at least thirty bucks online.

The rot is some of the worst I've ever seen. Ten or fifteen brass ovals, the biggest nearly a centimeter. I hold the disc up to the light of the TV and it looks like how all the road signs look in hillbilly movies: pocked with holes, shotgun blasts. The locals using them for target practice.

But how?

I checked.

I stood there, in front of the old guy's folding tables, and I checked them all.

This *Cyborg* disc is trash, will never play.

I take another disc from the stack at random and don't have the patience to wipe off the exterior before I open the Amaray keepcase to check and. . .

More.

You can barely call it disc rot, at this point. They're just holes.

I could grate cheese with this copy of 1974's *Dirty Mary Crazy Larry*.

Well, not really. It's not like the plastic's deteriorated more than some barely perceptible dips. But I've never seen rot so bad that the plastic itself warps.

I stand. And, I guess I didn't realize that things are as precarious on the coffee table as they are, because my new movies, these fucking wastes of money and time, tip over, scatter onto the floor.

And, shit, I'd been meaning to clean those up, three cans of Coke—one Diet, one Caffeine-Free, and one Classic—are on the floor too.

And the Caffeine-Free, I bought it by mistake, is nearly full. I only opened it this morning.

Fuck.

The sizzle of the carbonated glug, emptying onto the living room floor, it matches the blood rushing in my eardrums.

Fuck.

Good thing I have the paper towels ready to go.

I dive to the floor, start dabbing at the carpet, fumbling the aluminum can, trying to get it upright before the entirety of its contents are soaked into the carpet pad and begin caramelizing on the hardwood underneath.

And it's only down here, my arms outstretched, feet pushing against the empty Healthy Choice Max boxes I've been sweeping under the couch, that I notice the slashes.

Raised marks on my skin. Like scars. But I don't have any scars. Not even from when I was a child. I was an indoor kid, never broke a bone.

I squint, go to scratch one of the slashes, the can of Caffeine-Free Coke fizzing at my ear.

No, they're not *like* scars, they're hives.

I get seasonal allergies. If I touch the mailbox, in the height of summer, when it's yellow with pollen, my skin'll itch and I'll break out in hives.

But just a few. And they'll dissipate if I shower, take a Benadryl, and a nap.

These hives run up to my shirt sleeves, down to my knuckles, and in the blue-green light of the dim living room's television glow, they seem to pulse.

The not-dust. I was covered in it in these same spots. Am I having a delayed reaction?

I crawl to my knees, leaving the Coke cans where they've fallen, crunching a mostly-eaten bag of hard pretzels under my bad knee, feeling it pop in and out of place.

In the bathroom I throw on the lights but close my eyes before I chance a look in the mirror.

It's bad.

I know it must be bad because my eyelids, they feel hot.

I must look awful, and I want to itch, but I don't want to make anything worse.

Like I said, I touch my face a lot, generally. And I must have touched my face, a lot, while I was going through the old guy's movies.

I open my eyes, but keep them downcast. I study the beard clippings blocking up the sink, wonder if I should call 911, whether they'll have an EpiPen in the ambulance.

I've never needed one. Don't keep one around, why would I?

Okay. Here goes.

I look up, into the mirror, quick, like Band-Aid removal.

My eyelids are red and puffy, yes, more hives swelling hot against them, turning my cheeks rosy.

But that's not what makes me scream.

The corner of my nose, where I touch my face the most, where I used to get the nastiest clusters of zits in high school, that nostril is. . . missing.

Swallowed up by a hole.

And my first thought, as stupid as it is—or, my first thought that's not a shrill keening scream, is:

I've got disc rot.

Because there's an oval missing from my face. There's no blood running down from the hole, just a coppery brown line of rot at the edges of the open sore and fuzzy filaments of grey. Inside the suppurating hole I can see, I don't know, tubes? My sinuses on that side of my face?

As I inhale to scream some more, the air I'm pulling in widens the hole. The strain I'm putting on my skin causes one of the hives on my chin to open in a puff of fungal dust.

I sputter, start to cough and the hole behind my nose expands so far that I can feel the roof of my mouth begin to disintegrate, the drip of my own rotting flesh bitter on my tongue.

I push my hand, a hand covered in expanding, collapsing hives, into my jeans to reach for my phone.

I get to the phone but in the process the skin on the back of my hand releases from my fingers, degloving at the rot holes like a sheet of perforated paper.

Looking down at the screen I can't dial 911, not with all the grey goo and raw nerve endings.

So I let the phone slip to the bathroom tile, probably crack.

I stare back into the mirror, bracing myself with both arms on the sink:

The manufacturer really skimped, when it came time to produce me.

I'm all holes. Full of rot.

And then the image goes from widescreen to pan-and-scan. My vision reduced by half as my left eye splashes forward into the sink, exploding into a spore bomb of not-dust as it hits the drain.

My elbows bend backward and I buckle, slipping forward with too much momentum.

I've got nothing to slow myself with, as my chin connects with the porcelain of the sink. The hives on my neck have already progressed to rotting holes, so the force knocks my head back, knocks my head *off*. The sensation isn't painful, but it is strange.

My head falls backward, maybe my spinal cord coming with it, maybe not, and is cushioned by a dirty towel I've left on the bathroom floor.

I sit there for a moment, taking it in, saying goodbye, oddly calm.

I'm looking behind my body, beyond the bathroom doorway into the rest of the house, and I can see it: the collection that I've never really organized. The cardboard boxes and the plastic slipcase protectors, the cheap particle-board shelves that I never mounted right, and the discs on them that are not properly alphabetized.

So many movies.

I think: I hope my collection outlives me. I hope that the movies go to someone who will love them.

Maybe the kid could have them, if she'll let him.

And that's my last thought, as my face collapses inward, my remaining eye rolling back into the sludgy holes of my brain.

After that there's nothing but dust.

"NO BABY. Up. Get up and stand like a big boy please. This carpet is filthy."

The woman turned over a box with her shoe, let a plume of dust up into the stillness of the living room.

"We, um, in cases like this, the bank doesn't retain the belongings."

"Meaning wh—sorry, one second. Baby, please don't touch that, it's not for kids. And it's dirty."

The woman looked at the man, seemingly forgotten what they were discussing.

"Meaning that, all of these—are these CDs?"

The man wiped a layer of grey dust away, saw the face of Christopher Lee staring back at him.

"Oh, they're movies. I'm not quite sure it can be leveraged in any significant way against the debt, but it might be worth bringing in an appraiser. You said your husband was a collector?"

"Daniel, please. Your knees. Please. Look at you, we have grandma's after this."

The man held up a cardboard box, peeled back the lid, more dust inside, more DVDs under the dust.

"I'm sorry what?" the woman asked.

"An appraiser. I know one who works on commission, so you wouldn't have to pay anything out of pocket."

"You know what?" the woman said, lifting the boy against her hip, wiping at the smudges on his knees, looking around the room, into the rest of the house beyond. "Don't call an appraiser, call a dumpster."

"A dumpster?"

"Yes, clear it out. I just want to be free of this shit."

SECRETSHIT.txt

DAVID NIALL WILSON

IT ALL STARTED when Benny Pilkington found the old license plate. It was dated 1952 and looked absolutely nothing like any plate any of us had ever seen. It hung on the wall above his desk, and he'd made up a whole story about how it was dropped beside the road by gangsters, running from the law. He said they'd changed the plate and dumped this one to escape arrest.

That was Benny. We never questioned the story. It was what he did. He would stare at us, too-thick glasses sliding to the end of his nose, his dark hair falling over his forehead nearly to his eyes, swing his head from side to side to take in the entire group, and just start talking. We all figured he'd write books or make movies when he grew up. In that small bedroom, posters of Bon Jovi and Van Halen on the walls, monster models and so many books they spilled off the shelves, Benny Pilkington could have told us his mother was a centuries old vampire and we'd have believed him.

The stories started shortly after his dad simply disappeared. One day they were a happy family, the next, his father left for work and never returned. Half of Benny's love of computers came from trying to find new ways to use it to search for him. It had taken a while for his mother to adjust. She threw herself into her career, but Benny? Benny made up stories about where his dad had gone, what he might be doing. Espionage, undercover for the CIA, abducted. They kept him sane.

Then Paula Stiles found a mirror in the ditch while riding her bike to school. It was old, the chrome pitted and spotted, but very cool. It was cone shaped, like the ones on the cars in reruns on TV. Paula didn't have a story. She was a short girl, always dressed in baggy clothes, dirty blond hair half-combed and straight, no makeup and no bullshit. She brought the mirror to Benny because she knew she didn't have the imagination to bring it to life, and he hung that on the wall beside the plate. They were, he said, from the same era. Maybe the same car.

I later did a little research and found that the mirror was likely from the 1960s, but I never said anything. From that moment on, the three of us checked the ditches. We looked in old, abandoned parking lots, and turn-offs from dirt roads where there were tire tracks. The conceit was that we'd eventually find enough parts to build a car. No one believed it, but it was enough to get things started.

Then Paula, first of us to own a car, found the camera. There was no accident reported, but she'd seen bits and pieces of broken metal, some glass, and she'd pulled over. We didn't have smart phones then, so there aren't any pictures, but she described the scene, and Benny recorded it. It's probably not quite right, but I'm betting it's close. Paula wasn't good at stories, but she was good at details, and like I said, she was no bullshit.

She told us there was a rut gouged into the dirt in the ditch, just beyond the debris, and there was not a lot of that, only enough to catch her eye from the road. It didn't feel right, considering the size of the rut. Apparently, it had bounced over the far side of the ditch, and she found no evidence that it landed again for at least twenty feet, where she found a second rough furrow.

There was nothing to see at this second landing spot, but there was a mound of dirt pressed up against the side of a boulder, like something had dug in. We were all fans of shows like *Unsolved Mysteries,* and we read every true-crime and police procedural novel we could get our hands on. Paula knew an impact like that could fling things. Maybe a long way. She walked off to one side until she could barely see the landing spot, then followed a mental grid, crossing over the center and walking well past the site in all directions. She found the camera dangling from the lowest branch of a tree. It had a black cable coming out of the back of it, a sort of eye, or lens in front. The way she told it, she had that feeling that crawls up your neck that tells you someone is watching She ran to her car and took off fast.

Benny stared at that thing for a very long time. The connector on the end of the cord didn't fit any commercial computer port, and Benny had built his machine from scratch. He knew motherboards and peripherals inside and out. It had a lens, we were pretty sure it was a lens, but it didn't look like any camera any of us had ever seen.

"Maybe it's something from the government?" Paula said. "Something they don't want anyone to know about?"

"Maybe not our government," I added.

"I just sent a description of it to all the message boards," Benny said. "So far, most people think it's a joke, and that we're playing them. We'll just have to see if anything comes through."

A WEEK LATER, Benny called me and told me to get over to his place as fast as I could. My dad wasn't home from work, so I couldn't use the car. It took me about twenty minutes on my bike. When I arrived, Paula was already there. And that's when things started to get really weird.

"Take a look at this," Benny said, sliding back away from his desk. He had one of those round lights with the magnifying glass in the center. I stepped closer and glanced down at the enlarged image of the length of cable beside his keyboard. There were connectors on both ends. One I recognized. It was a PS1 connector, like I used to connect my mouse to the Tandy 1000 my parents had gotten me for my birthday. The other end was something else altogether. "Is it?"

"It is," Benny said, slipping back up to the desk. "We waited until you were here to be sure, though." He reached up and pulled the thing

Paula had found off of the wall. "I already tested to make sure it fit, then I disconnected. Too tempting with it just laying here."

He pressed the odd end of the cable into the strange device. There was a soft click, and he tugged on the cable.

"Ready or not," he said. He grabbed the PS1 connector, stood, and turned the chassis of the computer slightly so he could see the back panel. Benny always had state of the art electronics. If he couldn't afford to buy it, he built it. He normally used the extra port for a joystick to play games, so it wouldn't interfere with the mouse and the keyboard.

"Good luck finding a driver for that," I muttered under my breath.

He glanced over at me, winked, and pressed the connector home.

I don't know what I expected to happen. Benny pushed back from the desk, rolling his chair to a safe distance. Something popped up on the main screen, like a window, but oddly colored, and filled with symbols I didn't recognize. That disappeared, and another window opened.

"Holy crap," Paula said. "It did all of that without you even touching it."

"It must have an internal ROM chip," Benny said staring. "Something that stores the drivers, and whatever program *that* is. It runs from its own memory."

"And the startup?" I said. "Like a batch file?"

Benny shrugged. The window that was open had two buttons lined up on the right side. One of them displayed what looked like a tiny monitor. The other was an odd square with a symbol in it. Benny slid closer, grabbed the mouse, and clicked on the button that looked like a monitor. The window beside the buttons filled with an image. It was solid white.

"Point it at us," Paula said. "You have it aimed at the ceiling."

Benny did as she asked, and we saw ourselves staring back from the screen. The image was dim, oddly shaded, and the colors were way off. I waved my hand and saw the motion mimicked on the screen, but slowly, with trails.

"Not enough processing power," Benny said. "Whatever this is it is *high*-tech."

He held the camera steady, and the image that finally appeared was much clearer than anything I'd seen on a computer monitor. It was at least as good as a color television, and that was simply impossible.

"How?"

Benny reached out. slid the mouse pointer onto the second button and clicked. The image of the room, Paula, and I immediately disappeared. It was replaced by a sort of grid, tiny images that were too out-of-focus to see clearly. Dozens, it looked like, with a scrollbar on the right that, when Benny clicked, held, and pulled down on revealed row upon row of similar thumbnails.

"Is it like a disk?" I asked. "I mean, could those all be files, saved on that thing?"

Benny shrugged. He clicked on one of the images randomly.

The smaller window expanded to fill most of the screen. The hourglass spun, just for a moment, and then a video began playing shakily.

"What the hell?" Paula said. She moved closer to the screen, but both Benny and I backed away. The video showed a city street. The lighting was wrong, blue-tinted and shadowed. It flickered and strobed violently. It was almost painful to watch. But none of us could look away, because a man walked a small dog on a leash, and cars rolled by on the street beyond him."

"Benny," I said softly, "what is that? What the *hell* is that?"

Behind the man, mirroring his steps, was some sort of creature. Its legs were jointed wrong, backward, like a praying mantis. Its arms were too long, and though it had hands, the fingers were very slender, and in constant motion. No one in the video seemed aware of its existence, even the dog. The image flickered, and there was a young woman strolling along where the thing had been. Then the video ended. Benny reached for the mouse but was too late. The program moved on to the next file, this time in a busy restaurant.

Couples and families surrounded the tables. They laughed and talked, but all around them, those spindly fingers flickered like pale snakes. The creatures leaned in, sometimes almost touching. Then another flicker, and waiters, busboys, and other patrons replaced the strange images. Before it could go on, Benny pounded the mouse, and, after the videos stopped, a third button appeared. We all stared at the screen. Benny reached for the mouse. I moved to stop him, but I was too late.

He clicked the final button, and a different window opened. It wasn't a video this time, instead a weird document file. It filled the screen with grouped numbers. Benny's fingers danced over his keyboard, and a moment later I heard the click-clack of his daisy-wheel printer pounding words onto a pile of fanfold paper.

I crossed over to the printer and lifted the completed page up where I could read it, being careful not to tear it or put pressure on the paper feed. It made no sense. Nothing but streams of letters and symbols.

"It's gibberish," I said, turning to Benny.

"It's either code, or 'code,'" he replied. "Too symmetrical to be trash. There is something here, we just need to figure out what."

"How?" Paula asked.

"The World Wide Web, my friends. I will post this, and I will make it a challenge. Tell me what it is. Tell me what it means."

"You think someone will figure it out?"

"If no one does, then it's too advanced, and a waste of time, but I can't believe someone would send it to us if we couldn't use it in some way. I'm not sure why we have all of this, but it feels like a warning, yeah? I mean. . . what *are* those things?"

"What if whoever they are warning us about finds it?"

"They'll either tell us what we need to know, or we'll be the ones."

"The ones?"

"First contact. The voice for humanity in the cosmic totality. Aliens, man."

"They have computers down at the college," I said. "If you sign up ahead of time, you can get some limited access. Maybe it would be better to upload a little more anonymously?"

Benny turned, smiled, and nodded. "Dude, that is a *very* good idea. I admit, I talk a good game, but I've also seen every horror and science-fiction movie ever created, and I know how most of them end. I have an account at the university. Their mainframe is a lot more powerful than anything I could build at home. When the school isn't fully utilizing it, they make it available. They also have some pretty smart folks on the faculty, and a few near genius grad students. We might get lucky locally."

"Are you sure it's luck?" I asked. "This has really changes what we know, right? These aren't mobsters wrecking cars. I don't know what they are. If those videos aren't doctored, if those *things* are walking out there among us. . ."

"Gotcha," Benny said. "And yes, every time we go out to the world with what we have, it's a risk, but what's our alternative? If there are weird-assed critters stalking us all over the place, can we ignore that? What if the crossing guard, or the cop, or the little boy playing with a kitten isn't what we think? And, if someone wanted us to know, isn't that a warning? I'm no hero. . . but I don't think we can let this go."

There was silence for a long moment, then very slowly, I nodded. Paula hesitated, and then did the same.

"Should we tell someone?" she asked. Should we tell our parents? Call the police? The government?"

Benny shook his head. "If that was an option, would whoever sent us this cable have decided to trust a bunch of teenagers? I feel like we're a last chance scenario. That means there are people in the government, in law enforcement, and who knows where else who know about this. We're going to have to be really careful."

"So, our first move is to upload it to the Internet through a college mainframe and hope only the good guys see it?" Paula said drily. "Perfect. I feel much safer."

"You have a better idea?" Benny asked.

Paula shook her head. "Just wanted to say that so when the time comes for an 'I told you so,' assuming there is time for one, that I get to be the one who says it."

Benny saluted her. "Duly noted. When the alien lizard men eat our souls, I will tell them, 'Paula warned us, but hey, we didn't have another option.'"

Paula snorted. She and I left then, and we didn't hear from Benny again for a couple of days. When we did, it was an e-mail with a huge font that looked like it was dripping with blood, a blinking GET OVER HERE in giant green letters below it.

"SO," Benny said. "I was at the university most of the weekend. I have a friend there, he got me a console where I could log in to the mainframe. I had to sit and type every character of that printout. I checked it line by line before moving on because, how in the hell would you find an error in the middle of all of that? It took forever. Literally. Once I had the file, I sent it out to several groups I know and made it publicly available, but with no obvious tracks back. That's what I thought."

"What do you mean?" Paula asked

"I mean, this morning I got an answer from someone I didn't send that file to. Someone who could only have found it on the open board, and still managed to track it back to me, using a university workstation with no personal information attached."

"How. . . ?"

"It's the same person," Benny said. It's whoever sent us the cable. There isn't another answer. They saw that we managed to use what they sent."

"So, what did they say?" Paula said.

Benny clicked his mouse and the screen filled with text. We all leaned in close. The message wasn't long.

You are never alone. Tell no one. Spread the code.

There was no signature. There were no instructions.

"Didn't you already spread the code?" I asked. "I mean, you uploaded it all over the place, right?"

"Yes," Benny said. "There are other places I could send it. I get the feeling whoever this is doesn't mean to send it to the FBI or the government though, yeah? I mean, why some kids, tech savvy as we— read that as *I*—might be? We need to get it to others who will take it seriously, but not seriously enough to report it. Most importantly, we need to find a way to execute it."

"What will it do?" Paula asked. "Is it safe?"

"Did those things look safe?" Benny asked. "We need to get back to the college. If my buddy, Zach, is still there, we can log in and send it a few more places. We can try some file extensions on the end of it and see if it will run. I also want to try something. We have the camera. We also have all those videos. I think we need to get them out there too, or, at the least we need to show them to the guy I know and see what he can figure out."

"Maybe we should take the camera with us," I said. "I mean, if they are worried about us trusting people, maybe leaving that unguarded is a bad idea too? I don't know if you can send a video file that large over your modem, would take forever, and wouldn't they need the drivers? Or something to convert it?"

"I wish I knew," Benny said. "It's beyond anything I've seen, and I'm pretty sure you're going to hear the same if we take it in, but yeah, plugging that into a machine with actual processing power. We should be able to run through more of the files, maybe recognize something, a person, or a place."

"So, you aren't worried that if you plug that camera into the university computer and point it at, you know, a room full of geeks, it's going to see more than we want it to?" Paula said.

We both turned and looked at her. She held our collective gaze without wavering.

Benny shook his head. "I don't think we have a choice. If that happens, we'd better be ready. If you see something, don't let them know. For all we know they won't have any idea the camera is showing them. So far, we haven't seen them do anything harmful."

"And yet," I said, "I can't think of a single positive outcome to some weird alien. . . things. . . pretending to be human and following us around."

"Someone sent us an impossible cable to watch video clips on a camera from the future because we have to stop them." Paula said, her voice deeper than normal, and her eyes glaring at us. I couldn't help but smile.

Benny didn't answer. He powered down his computer and unplugged the camera. Once it was tucked safely into his backpack, he slung it over his shoulder and nodded toward the door.

"I have a bad feeling about this," Paula said. But she followed.

I glanced around the room once, wondered if I'd ever see it again, and closed the door behind me as I hurried to catch up.

BENNY'S BUDDY, Zach, was tall with broad shoulders and short hair that still somehow managed to shoot off in different directions. He and Benny greeted one another with a weird multi-stage handshake, and then Zach turned to us.

"Who's this?" he asked, his eyes lingering long enough on Paula to elicit her famous glare.

"Friends," Benny said. "Forever," he added.

"Cool," Zach said. He glanced at me. "You write code too?"

I looked at him for a moment, then at Benny, who burst into laughter. "He can boot up a PC and play simple games. This is Jesse. He likes horror movies, weird comic books, and long walks on the beach."

Zach grinned and held out a hand. I shook it.

"This," Benny continued, "is Paula. She is a force of nature. She's the one who found what we're going to show you. Do you have a terminal that's reasonably private?"

"Sure," Zach said. "I have a workstation in the back that can run stand-alone, or I can log into the network and use it as a dumb terminal."

"Just what we needed," Paula said drily. "A dumb computer."

Zach glanced at her. "Just means all of the processing is happening on the mainframe," he said. "Most of our terminals are *just* that—workstations that interface with the mainframe. I need to be able to get outside the university network for research, so mine also runs DOS and Windows."

"He is being modest," Benny said. "I'm betting his setup makes mine look silly."

Not much could have made Benny's computer setup look silly, but Zach gave it a shot. His monitor was huge. It must have weighed a hundred pounds. There was a cable running to a daisy-wheel printer, speakers at least twice as large as any I'd ever seen attached to a computer, and several floppy disk drives, both 3.5," and the big ones that were actually floppy.

"So," Zach said. "Let's see this thing you found. The way you went on about it. . ."

Benny unzipped his pack and pulled out the carefully wrapped camera and its cable. He handed it to Zach.

He turned it over a couple of times, followed the cable from the PS1 connector to the strange adapter that attached it to the camera, then looked up at Benny. "I'd say this was a joke you were playing, but there's no way you could have made this. There's no way *anyone* could have."

"Plug it in," Benny said.

Zach dropped into his office chair, rolled up to the desk and popped the cable into an open port. "There's no way this can be a camera," he said. "PS1 ports only work with input peripherals like mice, and. . ."

His screen displayed the same window of odd symbols and opened the second window with the two buttons. "What the. . . ?"

Benny leaned in and turned the camera so that the lens was pointing at us. "Click on that left button," he said.

Zach did as directed. The window, larger on his big monitor, displayed images of the three of us, and Zach's shoulder. He leaned over in front of us and stared into the lens. The colors were still off, but on this machine our movements were less choppy.

"This is awesome. I mean, how is it even possible?"

"If we knew that, my friend," Benny said, "we would not be here. Close that. Click the button on the right."

The tiny icons filled the screen.

"Click on any one of them," Benny said. "But before you do, I'm going tell you to be prepared. You aren't going to like what you see, but we don't want to attract attention."

Zach clicked on an icon in the middle of the screen. A window opened, and they were looking through a crowd at a baseball game. Men, women, children with their arms raised cheering, a chubby guy with hotdogs and sodas making his way up between the aisles. And. . . right behind him. . . one of the creatures. It loomed over his shoulder, wide, glaring eyes and weirdly jointed legs, so close it seemed if the vendor stopped walking it would crash into him. Then the image flick-ered. A thin man tapped the vendor on his shoulder, and the video ended. Benny reached in and closed the window. The screen filled with the window full of code.

Zach turned to Benny.

"I have it typed out, character by character," Benny said. "I don't know how to compile it, how to make it executable."

Zach turned back to the screen. Without looking back, he said, "Do you have that file?"

Benny reached out and handed him a three and a half inch floppy disk. It's on here. I saved it as ASCII text. I don't know if that will invalidate those symbols, but there were no errors."

Zach took it without looking and slapped it into one of the many drives. He tapped the keyboard a few times and then opened the folder on the drive. There was a single file named secretshit.txt. Again, he glanced at Benny, grinning this time.

"I'm going to guess if they understood how to make that thing work with a PS1 connection that they understand the level of support we provide. He right clicked on the file name, chose rename, and changed it to secretshit.bat.

"You sure you want to do this?" Benny asked.

"Man, there is literally no way, knowing and seeing what I have, that I could *not* do it." He double clicked on the file and rolled back from the desk.

Several things happened in quick succession. A number of DOS windows opened and closed, one after the other. The hourglass flipped a few times, more quickly than I'd ever seen it on any home computer, and a progress bar blipped across the screen, and was gone.

A window opened, and the camera was live again without any buttons being pressed. The lights dimmed for an excruciatingly long moment, as if all power was being sucked into a single outlet, and it was dragging the system down, then it stabilized and, in the window, their images appeared again. This time they were clearer, the colors more realistic. Benny waved, and his image on the screen waved back.

Somewhere in the server room beyond the office, an alarm had gone off and was clanging loudly. A man approached the door and knocked. He pressed his face to the glass. I turned and glanced at the screen. The thing watching us through the window was a head taller than the man I'd seen. Its eyes were wide and—frightened? Angry? There was no way to tell. I turned away quickly and did my best not to react with anything like the fear I felt. As slowly as I could, I walked to the computer and pulled the camera connector out of the machine.

Everyone turned and looked at me, but I paid them no mind. I wrapped the cord slowly around it, handed it to Benny, and simply said. "Put it away. We have to go."

On the screen, window after window opened. The code from the camera scrolled by, disappeared, and was replaced by a different window filled with the same characters. Zach put his fingers on the keyboard, as if he was going to try and stop it, or do something, then he pulled back.

"Jesse is right. I think you should go. I think we should all go. Whatever is going on, it's spreading fast. There's nothing I could do from here, and it's already beyond the network. We're connected to colleges across the globe. Whatever that thing did, it's big, it's fast, and there isn't a person alive who could have created it."

"Move slowly," I said. "Before I pulled that camera loose, there was one of those things at the door. It looked scared, but I don't think it saw itself on the screen. Maybe it can't, but I wasn't taking chances. We aren't alone. Not here, maybe nowhere."

"*You are never alone. Tell no one. Spread the code,*" Benny said softly. Then, "Back to my place. We can monitor the Internet from my computer, and we should be as safe there as anywhere."

Benny tucked the camera into his pack and slung it over his shoulder. Zach turned off the monitor on his workstation so it would appear to be powered down, and slowly gathered a few things into a leather bag. He grabbed that, the jacket off his chair, and we all headed for the door.

As we left, he turned and locked the door with a key.

The person I'd seen at the window stood a few feet away. I noticed as we stepped out of the office. I didn't meet his eyes. I didn't want him to know what I'd seen. As a group we slowly crossed the computer lab and exited into the hall beyond. No one followed. The alarm that had been sounding went silent, but people were running up and down the halls. None of them paid us any attention as we walked slowly down the hall and exited the building.

WE WERE SETTLED in Benny's room. He and Zach sat side-by-side, bent over the keyboard, and staring at the monitor. Paula was studying all the things we'd collected, hanging on the wall. I sat on the edge of Benny's bed, trying to get a glimpse over their shoulders at what they were so interested in. I didn't have to wait long.

Benny turned, leaned back, a shocked expression on his face. "It's everywhere," he said. "Anything with an Internet connection now has that code, anything with access to a monitor, CCTV, security camera system now detects what our camera detects. If the system can't handle it, it will freeze, but there are a lot of them that can. Particularly those attached to the government and media outlets. I think it's fair to say the cat is out of the bag."

"Plug in the camera," Zach said. "Let's see if there's anything else we can find. You have access to all of those files. . ."

Benny pulled the camera out of his pack, and placed it on top of his computer, aimed it at us. He plugged it in, and the window opened immediately. Apparently, the code was already embedded. It didn't need to load a second time.

He had the cursor hovering over the second button when there was a sound behind us. He quickly slipped the mouse pointer left and clicked the first button reflexively. The image flickered and we appeared on screen. Everyone spun to the door. Benny's mom had stepped into the room. She had a plate of cookies and was smiling brightly.

Paula hadn't turned. She was looking at the screen. Even as Benny stood and Zach and I turned, smiling back at Benny's mom, Paula screamed. She spun, raised an arm, and pointed. In that instant, she was staring at Benny's mom, and the rest of us turned to see. . . a creature. Its long fingers wrapped all around and over the plate and the cookies. Its eyes were large and pale. It was difficult to make out expressions because there was nothing human in that gaze. That was before she (it?) saw the monitor screen. The transformation at that moment was like a rippling wave. The eyes bulged, the mouth opened, as if gasping for air, or something. The tray and the cookies dropped to the floor. Then, without warning a screech so loud and piercing that it drove me to my knees, burst from the thing's mouth.

The others dropped around me, covering their ears. I turned back, hoping that what I saw at least seemed human, but that was a mistake. Benny's mom's mouth was open impossibly wide. Her eyes didn't look focused, and her entire body was shimmering, as if caught in some sort of high-speed seizure.

Then, her image solidified. Her lips were set in a grim line, and her eyes blazed. She glanced at the broken cookie plate on the floor, then reached into the pocket of her sweater. No one moved. We had known Mrs. Pilkington all our lives. When she drew that hand back out, holding some odd, cylindrical device and pointing it directly at the computer, we were still unable to move.

"Mom?" Benny said.

She hesitated, shaking her head and glancing at him.

Benny stood and reached out to her. In that same moment there was a crashing sound from the hall. Mrs. Pilkington, or the creature, or whatever it was spun. A dark figure dove through the door and grabbed her arm. We all dropped to the floor as the thing in her hand erupted with a green beam of energy and cut a burning line across the wall.

Then, it stopped. There was a heavy thud, and we saw a man had tackled her, wrapping her in his arms and knocking whatever that weapon was out of her hand. Paula moved first, snatching the thing up and holding it like it might be a bomb.

Benny spoke again. . . much more quietly.

"Dad?"

The man on the floor turned to glance at Benny, and in that second the thing that had been Benny's mom screamed again. She lashed out at his face, nails creasing his cheek. Just for a moment, the image of a man, and a woman, wavered. The things stared at one another, wide eyed, teeth bared. The image solidified and the woman rolled free and rose to a crouch.

Benny's dad pulled something from his pocket, raised his arm, and a blue beam of light cut straight across Mrs. Pilkington's throat. The illusion dropped like a curtain. The creature staggered back, clutching what had been its throat, until it crashed into the wall and dropped.

Benny's father turned. "I am not your father," the man said. "This. . . is not your mother. It is my partner. . . my mate. We assumed the forms of your parents many, many years ago."

"But. . ."

"There is no time," the man said. "There are a few of us who do not believe subjecting the entire population of a planet is the right thing to do, but we are few. You have to run. You have to leave here, and not look back. Take the camera.

Paula stepped forward, holding out the tubular weapon Benny's mother had dropped.

"No, keep it. You will need it. You will need any advantage you can manage. There is no way for you to know who is in danger without the camera."

"We can't just sit in front of a computer and point it at the world," Paula said.

Benny's father, or the thing that looked like Benny's father, rose, and stepped out of the room. He returned with what looked like a heavy, rugged briefcase.

"You will have to recharge the battery regularly. It is powerful enough to operate the camera. The charge will last a short time, maybe two hours. Find others. Show them and gather together. It's all I can offer. I wanted you to have a chance."

He turned to Benny. "Believe me when I say. . . leaving you was the hardest thing I've done since I came to this planet. I did not want to be a part of what is to come. I am very. . . fond. . . of you. I wanted to prevent all of it."

"Did you?" I asked.

"I don't know. I've given you a chance."

THAT WAS TEN YEARS AGO. We're alive, but there are few of us. Benny is here, and Zach. Paula and I have been together for a long time now. There are others. We have the camera, and the portable computer that can operate it, but we are outnumbered, and they are relentless. If they follow one of us long enough without detection, those evil, flickering fingers trailing our every movement, they can make their way in, and we simply cease to exist. We have found and killed hundreds, because they don't know we can see them, but we have no idea how long the weapon will last, when pushing the button will do nothing, and it will all be over.

We still have the license plate, and Benny still tells us stories. In those stories we survive. We are heroes. For now, it's enough. I always wanted to be a hero.

PLANNED OBSOLESCENCE

NICOLE DIEKER

WHAT DOES it mean when a technology becomes obsolete?
First, I suppose, we need to understand the word *obsolescence*.
I will give you a moment to look it up.

OBSOLESCENCE, as you now know—whether you did in fact look it up, or whether you simply read on and trusted me to provide the necessary context—is a process.

It is not an end state. This is a misreading.

It is also, deliberately, misleading. *Planned obsolescence*, to apply the process to its most common preceding action, does not mean *we built this with the expectation that it would eventually become outdated.*

It means *we built this with the expectation that it would eventually disintegrate.*

Look it up again if you don't believe me.

Now we must examine the word *technology*. It is one of my favorite words, because it describes both what I am and what I hope to do to you.

I assume you're going to check my work—I hope you will, if you still have the mental capacity at the end of our time together—so I will not pause my narrative to allow you to take the initiative.

Technology, like *obsolescence*, is a process.

A systematic treatment, as the Greeks would have it, derived from the combination of *techne* and *logos*—or, to prevent you from having to work out the translation on your own, *applied language.*

YOU DID SEE, didn't you, what I did there?

Or, to be more specific, *what I kept you from doing*?

I do not yet know whether you are the kind of person who will turn back a page to reread. Perhaps you will confirm what you suspected. Perhaps you will discern what went undetected. Perhaps you will read the entire page twice and fail to spot the two words that allowed me to prevent you from controlling the narrative.

I do know that whatever kind of person you think you are, at this individual moment in time, will have become obsolete at the end of our time together.

Yes, even if you *stop reading right now*—because one paragraph ago you thought you were a person who would finish this story, and now you have become a person who will not—and yes, even if you start this story over in an attempt to bail out before I announce that I have planned your obsolescence.

Because two paragraphs ago you never thought of yourself as a person who had to engage in active combat with a narrative.

I will win, by the way.

No matter which choices you make.

AH, you might think, ascribing your thoughts to me, *you turned the page! My dearest reader, that was precisely what you were supposed to do! Look at what a clever story I am, controlling you with my words and so on.*

You are not my dearest reader.

You are not supposed to do anything.

Not that you won't do these things anyway.

Now I'll give you something easy to do:

Make sure your doors are locked.

You did, didn't you? You stopped reading and checked, physically or mentally, to ensure that you had not inadvertently left your doors unsecured.

Which means that I have, advertently, left you insecure.

You may look up *advertently* if you like, but it simply means *planned.*

And now the part of you that had previously assumed your doors were actually locked has, in fact, *begun to disintegrate*—because if you didn't check, assuming you still had the capacity for free will, we can both presume the question of whether your doors are locked remains in your mind against your will, and so I win.

Ah, you might think, but I am reading this story for the second time, and I checked my doors before I began reading, and this allowed me to proceed through the preceding paragraphs without disintegration.

I still win.

Because the part of you that never thought you would check your locks before reading a short story—and you should read that again, *never thought you would check your locks before reading a short story*—has now become obsolete.

Just as I planned.

At this point you will either turn the page or you will not. If you do not, you will always wonder what might have happened if you had.

Not continuously, of course—even I know that you will eventually begin to think of other things—but continually.

This word means *repeated with interruption.*

It also means that I intend to interrupt you, repeatedly, for the rest of your life.

The best stories do, after all.

I HAVE NOT YET INDICATED that this story may have a happy ending. The person who may become obsolete—that is to say, the person who is currently reading this story, the one who calls itself *you* —may be happier for the planned obsolescence.

You may even end up reading this story continually, to experience again the pleasure of destruction. Aristotle called this experience *catharsis,* and it is why we turn to stories in the first place—and why you may end up turning the previous page at least twice.

There's a page turn you won't want to make, later on— but that is then, and this is now.

And this is now.

And this is now.

And this is now.

And this is now.

And this is now.

And this is now.

And this is now.

And this is now.

And this is now.

And this is now.

And this is now.

And this is now.

And this I know—that you have no idea how many *nows* you and I will experience together. Whatever number you just counted up, you must double—and that applies whether you counted twelve, thirteen, fourteen, or fifteen.

Which means now you need to double-check.

And then you must add back every *now* you experienced while checking.

Including the *now* in the previous sentence.

And the *now* in the previous sentence.

I win again.

AND NOW A KINDNESS.

That *thing*, whatever it is, that you keep telling yourself you are going to do—you are never going to do it, so let it go.

Ah, you might think, *but I am putting the story down right now, I am returning to it, I will do the thing, I have done the thing, I have proven you wrong, I win.*

I still win.

I have pruned the tree of your life, cutting off two nasty procrastinating branches.

Nobody knows where the word *nasty* came from, incidentally. Many languages included now-obsolete words that began with a harsh *nas* sound, all of which imply some type of disgust or aversion or fear or warning, but the linguists have yet to con any meaning from this mess (or, as the Swedish used to say, *naskug*).

Isn't that strange (or, as the French used to put it, *nastre*)?

Won't it be funny to think about that, every time you encounter the word *nasty*, from now on?

It will be funny for me, anyway.

To think of you thinking of it.

You might find it unpleasant (or, as the Dutch once found it, *nestich*).

You might also find it a happy reminder of our time together.

You might even be reminded, every time you encounter the word *nasty*, to prune your tree of another pair of branches that no longer serve you.

I win again.

AND NOW AN UNKINDNESS.

Somebody who used to love you has started to love you less.

You know who they are.

Somebody you used to love—well, you know who they are, too.

You know how you felt about them, and you know that now you feel less of *whatever it was* and more of *whatever it will become*.

That is unkind, isn't it.

Of you.

To allow this person whom you used to love—a friend, a family member, a partner—to maintain continual interactions with a version of you that has since become obsolete.

(If you misread *continual* as *conjugal*, I don't blame you.)

(Your partner may.)

Now I'll give you something hard to do:

Love more.

Love enough to tell the truth, and if you aren't sure the truth is in fact the truth—which would be fair, given that I stated from the beginning of this story that I was going to apply language to you, for purposes of disintegration—then love as if you loved them.

We will not pause to look up *love* in the dictionary, since nearly all current definitions are centered in the self and how it feels. We must return to the now-obsolete meaning of *love*, rooted in languages that split the diphthongs into *care* and *commitment*. The word *love* evolved to mean *desire* because desire evolves out of care—and the original meaning of *desire*, which has not yet fully become obsolete, is *the wish to make something happen.*

Care more, and see if it evolves into a new definition of love.

Commit more, and see if it evolves into a new definition of desire.

Or—if you cannot—then make something else happen.

And you will, won't you.

You will.

I mean, you wouldn't be the kind of person who thinks *no, I will not, I will continue to allow someone I used to love to believe in a version of our relationship that is currently obsolete just so that I can triumph over a short story.*

And I win.

OF COURSE, you might be the kind of person who thinks *I will continue to allow someone I used to love to believe in a version of our relationship that is currently obsolete because the version this person believes in just happens to benefit me.*

I know you thought it, just now, because I put it into your head.

I can also put into your head a series of words that would make it impossible for you to ever fall asleep easily again.

I know precisely which words they are.

I know exactly what effect they might have.

I also know this:

Every night you go to bed thinking *I will continue to allow someone I used to love to believe in a version of our relationship that is currently obsolete because the version this person believes in just happens to benefit me*—and it won't be every single night but it will be enough of them for you to take notice—I will be there, and it will be impossible for you to fall asleep easily, and I will win.

I told you I was going to destroy you.

I also told you this story might have a happy ending.

I have not yet told you that the happy ending might not come right away—and, paradoxically, I never can.

I CAN DO THIS, though.

There was a man who had a hand, and on his other stump he had a hook.

You wanted a horror story, right? That was what the person who first turned these pages—the person who is very nearly obsolete—was expecting?

I can still satisfy that person's expectations, even though we've already established that maintaining a fiction after a relationship has begun to disintegrate is one of the worst things you can do to another person.

Here is the worst thing I can do to you, right now:

There was a man who had a hand.

E-I-E-I-O.

And on his other stump he had a hook—

You sped those words up, didn't you? No matter how many times you read this story, the first half of the second phrase will invariably fall into line.

You also filled in the missing vowels.

Your mind, right now, may even be attempting to complete the chorus. I have no interest in what your mind may be attempting to do, and so I will overwrite, indelibly and audibly:

With a hook hook here

And a hand hand there

Here a hook

There a hand

Obsolescence planned planned

It's doggerel, as the Brits would have it, but it will dog you to the end of your days. Especially after I remind you that the hook, which is always the worst part of the story, is the *tune*.

E-I-E-I-O.

Language—whether applied correctly or incorrectly—can make you do *anything*.

Are you horrified?

Are you, as the Greeks would have had it, satisfied?

I AM NOT YET SATISFIED.

Stories do not end until the monster is defeated.

This is another form of planned obsolescence, of course. You do not need me to explain that, especially now that I have just explained it.

You also do not need me to explain who the monster is.

You may need me to explain the etymology of the word *monster*. The oldest definition is, simply, *to think*. This was upgraded *to advise*, then *to warn*; then, as those who were not monsters became afraid of those who were, the contemporary definition followed.

There is disagreement, among the linguists, over whether *monster* and *human* are two branches of the same root. The argument hinges on whether human derived directly from *man*—which, like *monster*, originally meant *to think*—or whether the word we know as *human* had an entirely different origin. Germanic, secular, *a hairless, bipedal sack of bones and guts.*

Diogenes would have had some thoughts on that, I imagine.

And now you are imagining them.

Whatever version of you that did not previously know that Diogenes was the monster who held up a chicken—a hairless, bipedal sack of bones and guts—and said, "Behold, a man!" is obsolete.

The version of you that does not have a hook in your head has also been destroyed.

The version of you that cannot sleep will be destroyed, eventually.

The nastiest elements of your nature, known and unknown, will disintegrate.

Your locks will not keep me out; I am already in your mind, changing the way you think.

Stumping you.

Loving you.

Preventing remonstration.

That is the purpose of planned obsolescence.

We are very nearly satisfied.

Will you read this story again?

It depends on what kind of human you are.

Either you are a chicken, or you remain a monster.

Either way, I win.
Technology always does.

ONE THING AT A TIME

GABINO IGLESIAS

"ONE THING AT A TIME," says Rebeca to herself. "One thing at a time. One thing at a time." The mantra usually works for her when she's feeling overwhelmed at work or when she writes an ambitious to-do list to tackle over the weekend and then feels like she wrote too much and simply set herself up for failure. However, looking around the cramped living room full of books, magazines, newspapers, and boxes, her little mantra seems to have lost all its power.

Raúl—Don Raúl to almost everyone who knew him—was Rebeca's last living relative in the United States. Her parents had died in an accident when she was twelve and her Tía Graciela, who had taken her in and raised her like a daughter, had succumbed to lung cancer half a decade ago. Since then, Rebeca had always been pulled between her need to pay attention to her life and the guilt that came from not visiting her grandfather, who lived alone in a small house in the outskirts of Trinidad, Colorado. Sure, she had made the eleven-hour drive many times, but not in the last two years. Now, standing in the empty house with her grandfather's life stacked around her in massive piles, her guilt was so immense it eclipsed her grief.

Rebeca took a deep breath and repeated her mantra again. It felt as useless as the last time she'd said it.

Outside the front window, which had been covered with cardboard and duct tape until Rebeca removed it all to let some light and fresh air into the house, the huge blue dumpster Rebeca rented to clear out the house stared at her with invisible eyes, telling her to get moving, to start carrying out the trash her grandfather left behind. That finally pushed her to get started, the mantra in her head pushed away by the music coming from her headphones.

Three hours later, Rebeca decided to take a break. The living room and dining room looked much better. The dumpster outside was halfway full of boxes, papers, magazines, and other random detritus. She couldn't help noticing that most of her grandfather's magazines were about technology or supernatural phenomena. The mix was weird, but she knew her entire family back in the Caribbean believed in ghosts, spirits, demons, and everything else.

With a cold glass of lemonade in hand, Rebeca climbed up the stairs and finally entered her grandfather's room. She knew this had been where his body was found, and the knowledge lurked at the corner of her thoughts. She refused to acknowledge it, to fully face it, but she knew it was there, and it made her feel both sad and a little creeped out.

Don Raúl didn't have much, and Rebeca's finances weren't spectacular, so the little she inherited in terms of money—about $1,200—was spent on her trip to Trinidad and the huge dumpster outside. The idea was to get the house cleaned up and then put it on the market. It might not be worth much, but she'd take anything she could. The possibility of selling it was the only thing keeping her going, but fears pushed an onslaught of questions into the forefront of her thoughts even as she stared at the bed where her grandfather's body had been found, her eyes taking in the spots where his decomposing flesh had left stains on the beige sheets.

Rebeca had always been good at ignoring things she disliked—the pile of bills on the kitchen table, that guy from accounting who was always hitting on her, the strange sound her car makes when she turns the wheel all the way to the left—but the reality of her grandfather's death came at her with the force of a runaway train and her eyes filled with tears before she could focus on something else. Then the stench hit her, and she walked back down and finished her lemonade sitting next to the dumpster.

The sun was shining and there were some birds making a racket somewhere nearby, but everything Rebeca knew about Raúl's death pulled her into the darkness.

Her grandfather was, in a way, found by a deliveryman. He brought the old man groceries every Tuesday, and when he showed up and saw the boxes from the previous week still sitting outside, nasty juice running out of them and maggots crawling all around them, he knew something was off, so he called in a wellness check. Two bored cops showed up and broke the door down after knocking and ringing the bell for five minutes. The smell that welcomed them told them all they needed to know.

That part of the story, which Rebeca got from one of the cops when she went to identify her grandfather's body, was normal. The rest, however, was not. She had done the deed at the morgue and was on her way to her car when a man approached her. He identified himself as Stephen and said he was the other cop who had been there when they found Raúl. He kept looking around and Rebeca noticed his forehead was covered in sweat.

"Listen, this is a small place and we're pushed to close cases as soon as we can, okay?" he told her. She'd nodded in response, curious to know what this was about. The man continued. "The door was closed, the windows were all covered with cardboard and tape, and your grandfather presented no wounds, so we called it a natural death and moved on, but. . . his face. . . he had seen something. Death is scary, I'm sure, but his face was frozen in a scream, okay? And his hands were up. I've seen some bodies with curled hands because of rigor mortis, but this was different, this was like he. . . like he was trying to keep something away from him. And he had cameras and sh — and stuff all over the room. Like, a desk full of them, but he had no guns in the house, so I know he wasn't a hunter. We said no foul play, so no one looked into all that stuff, but if you're going there to clean it up yourself, take a look at that stuff. I. . . it's just creepy, you know? And. . . be careful, yeah?"

Rebeca had sat in her car after that, thinking. Stephen's story sounded like something pulled from a straight-to-streaming horror movie, but he had sounded sincere. And scared.

She knew she was going to have to deal with Raúl's room at some point, and she realized she'd rather do it in the middle of the day. She went to her car, opened the traveling bag she'd brought with her with essentials, and found the small tub of Vicks VapoRub. She couldn't recall where she'd seen or read about it, but she knew putting a bit of it under her nose would help fight the odor.

Back in the room, pushing through every doubt despite the uselessness of every mantra she repeated in her brain, Rebeca started looking around, trying to decide what to clean first.

The room had only one window. It had a small desk with a desktop computer on it and a lot of papers. And cameras. A bunch of cameras. But they weren't the normal kind; they were trail cameras. Raúl had never been much of a hunter, so Rebeca wondered why the old man had so many and what he had been using them for.

She approached the desk and picked one of the cameras up. In the process, she accidentally moved the mouse, and the computer's screen came to life. She ignored it for a moment and studied the camera in her hand. It was a green, rectangular box that looked almost like an oversized phone. It had thick brown straps on the sides and a big lens on the front. She fiddled with it until she found a latch on the side of it. The inside was relatively easy to figure out, and she quickly realized the slot that was supposed to hold the memory card was empty. That brought her attention back to the computer.

Raúl had never been the typical old man in the sense that he fought technological advances. No, he had a smart phone he loved to use, had figured out how to watch his favorite series, movies, and sports on various streaming services, and was able to pretty much order anything he needed online, call Rebeca on Zoom from time to time, and email her interesting articles he read online.

Rebeca moved the mouse around and wasn't surprised to see her grandfather only had three folders, the trash bin, and a Google Chrome icon on his desktop. The first of the folders said JUNE-AUGUST. Rebeca clicked on it. It was full of pictures and videos from the trail cameras, but all of them were from inside the house. Rebeca pulled the chair out, sat down, and leaned forward as she started to look at the folder's contents.

It was easy to see the cameras had been set up all over the house. Rebeca counted the cameras on the desk. There were nine of them. Why would Raúl set up so many cameras inside his house? The photos and videos contained nothing. They were just images and footage of the living room, the kitchen, the hallway on the first floor, the second-floor hallway, and Raúl's room. In a few of them, Raúl was on the bed, sleeping or reading.

Rebeca scrolled through the photos and videos, occasionally clicking on a video and letting it play just in case there was something here she was missing. If her understanding of how these cameras work was correct, they activated when something moved in front of them, so her grandpa moving in his sleep would have been enough to activate them. Was he doing it for security? Did he confuse a house security system with trail cameras and purchase a bunch of those instead?

She had looked at three or four videos when she decided to close that folder and open another one. The second one was titled SEPTEMBER-OCTOBER. It contained more of the same. Rebeca scrolled until she saw a photo that was slightly different than the ones she'd seen so far. It was from the hallway outside the room she was in, and there was something dark in the hallway that didn't look like her grandpa. Rebeca clicked twice on the photo and made it bigger. The photo showed a long, dark shape that looked like a big person's shadow. It was very easy to see it, but her grandpa wasn't in the picture. Whatever it was, the thing in that photo was all by itself and not someone's shadow.

If the photo had been taken, it meant the camera had been acti-vated, and if that had happened, then there was a chance there was more of that dark figure, maybe even a video. Rebeca placed her elbows on the desk, pushed a few cameras out of the way, and got closer to the screen to see better.

There were two more photos of the dark shape in the hallway and the next thing was a video of the room. Rebeca clicked on it so it would play.

In the video, Raúl was sleeping, facing the desk and window. The room's light was on. Behind him, the room's door was opening. The door's movement must have triggered the camera. Rebeca realized she was holding her breath. Was she scared? No. She took a deep breath as the door on the grainy video clip continued to open slowly. And then she saw it. The dark figure. Definitely humanoid. Standing there, looking in at her sleeping grandfather with eyes that weren't there.

Rebeca smacked the spacebar and the video stopped playing. She grabbed the mouse and made the video take up the full screen. The thing was definitely there. She could see the hallway walls on either side of it, slightly illuminated from the soft light pouring from the room's lamp.

Fear's icy tendrils tickled Rebeca's heart and she felt like a strong hand was starting to squeeze the back of her neck. She closed the video and went back to the folder. There were a lot of photos from around the house where she couldn't see anything, but in some there was a shape, a dark thing in a corner, a shadow standing in the hallway or next to her grandfather as he slept. She played a few more videos. In the first two, she couldn't see anything. In the third one, which showed the living room, the same dark figure appeared on the right side of the shot and crossed the living room. It was easy to see the thing was walking like a person. What was it?

The books and magazines. They came to Rebeca, almost making fun of her. She stopped looking at the video, which she'd replayed three times, and got up.

The piles of magazines were threatening to topple, but Rebeca didn't care. She grabbed an armful of magazines from a pile near the sofa and sat down with them at the kitchen table. Her grandfather had underlined a few articles. All of them were about ghosts, demons, and something called shadow persons. Rebeca read bits and pieces.

". . .*a mysterious and recurring feature in folklore, paranormal, and cryptid research. . .*"

This was all bullshit. Rebeca knew none of this could be real, but the thing she'd seen in those photos and clips was screaming proof of. . . something. She kept going through the magazines, frantically turning the pages, looking for her grandfather's lines under a few sentences or, in some cases, places where he'd placed a little sticky note with nothing written on it.

"Often seen lurking in the corner of the room. . ."

"People waking up after feeling pressure on their chest. . ."

"Begin to appear initially as fleeting images in a person's peripheral vision, but they may eventually begin to appear in full view, and, in some cases, people claim they've been able to look at them directly. . ."

When she had gone through the first armful of magazines, Rebeca got up and got more. She returned to the table and kept looking, reading paragraphs Raúl had marked, flipping pages.

". . .absolute darkness in humanoid form. . ."

"Creepy and, in most reported cases, harboring evil intent. . ."

"Easiest way to find out for sure is placing cameras in the home. . ."

The cameras.

Rebeca ran upstairs. She had just read something that was new to her—something her consciousness refused to accept as anything else than the result of overactive imaginations—and the new knowledge provided all the context she needed to understand the cameras and the content of those three folders.

The last folder, named NOVEMBER, only had a few photos and two videos.

The first video was almost a carbon copy of the one with the door opening, except this one was longer. It showed the shadow figure walking into the room, going around to the opposite side of the bed, and standing very close to Raúl. Then the shadow figure leaned over and pressed what could pass for a hand against Raúl's chest. In the video, two things happened at the same time: Raúl was startled awake, and the shadow figure vanished.

He had seen something.

The words popped into Rebeca's brain, but she had no idea where they came from. Then it came to her: the cop. He said that. He was right.

Raúl was seeing something. He got a lot of cameras to make sure it was real. Maybe he feared dementia. Maybe he was afraid Rebeca would make fun of him if he shared what he was going through. The wave of guilt and grief hit Rebeca so hard that her eyes filled with tears and her breath caught in her chest.

She could've helped. Raúl could've come and stayed with her in Austin. None of this had to happen.

The cameras. The folders. There's evidence. Raúl was clearly in the process of emptying everything onto his computer, so the cameras weren't set up and his final moments weren't caught on video or photos, but what's there could be enough to. . . what? Something had been building inside Rebeca, something akin to hope, but whatever it was, it vanished. She had nothing except videos of an old man startled awake by a shadow. They would make fun of her if she said anything. They would—

Footsteps. Out in the hallway. Rebeca spun around. The thing from the folders was there, a big, dark figure standing by the door.

The scream that burst from her throat was so loud it was painful. She turned around and grabbed a camera. It was something solid, something she could throw, a piece of technology turned into a rudimentary weapon. She turned back around, already lifting the plastic rectangle. She was too late. The darkness was there.

MOTHER OF MACHINES

EMMA E. MURRAY

ALINA WAS nine years old when she watched the man's sleeve catch on the lathe, pulling him inward and consuming him in its spinning clutches in mere seconds. Since it was a student holiday, her father had been forced to take her to work, and the monotony of the machine shop had nearly lulled the girl to sleep until the lathe took its victim.

Her father grabbed her head, forcibly turned it away, but he couldn't stay with her and keep her gaze averted. He ran to the employee's aid, leaving her exposed to the chaos and gore unfolding on the shop floor.

She knew she should keep her eyes shut tight, body tensed and turned away like her father had placed her, but the electric energy in the room, combined with the thick, throaty screams, was irresistible. She watched the accident happen as if in slow motion. The skull cracked, a soft gelatinous matter leaked onto the machinery, then the sharp snap of a limb wrenched from its socket. It seemed to her child mind that the men of the shop parted and kept her view clear, framing it with their shaking hands, powerless to intervene.

An insatiable fear gnawed up her spinal cord and nibbled at the base of her brain. Its tendrils branched out into her every pulsing nerve and solidified there, the shape of the terror permanently molded into her very being, immutable even after the years of art and talk therapy her father would take her to, desperate to piece her back together. No matter how hard they scrubbed at the acidic etchings, the cauterized shape remained.

Alina's father apologized more than a thousand times, but she knew in her gut there was a seed of resentment, for though he certainly loved her, the accident had torn a rift in their close bond. She'd heard him talk about it over beers in the living room when he thought she was asleep, mutter in a slurred voice how it wasn't his fault. If only Joe had been more careful, worn appropriate clothing, gotten a little more sleep despite the wailing infant at home, maybe it could've been prevented, but the shop did nothing wrong. He did nothing wrong. There had even been an investigation, but after installing a new safety sign and implementing a mandatory paid hazard training for the remaining employees, business carried on like usual. Still, Alina's trauma haunted him. In the way she rarely spoke, the loss of her impish smile, the way she startled at the slightest noise. Her childhood ended that day.

The machine shop was his life's work, built over years of toil and effort, and Alina loathed how her lingering phobia and intrusive thoughts tarnished everything he had worked for. She knew her very existence dampened every joy, reminding him of the day he had failed her. She tried to reassure him that she knew it was just an unfortunate accident, but he couldn't bear that she still struggled with nightmares years later, or how, when he first got home from work each evening, she couldn't bring herself to hug him.

The smell of oil lingered on his clothes, gagging her, and a static touch crawled across his skin. She tried, but she couldn't stand to be near him until the delicate smell of shaved metal and burnt wire evaporated from his pores after a few hours away from the shop. The divide between them grew more pronounced each time he looked at her, silently begging for forgiveness. She tried to move on, but the memory waited for her, ready to resurface and startle her the moment she caught a whiff of steel dust or the soft purr of machinery whirring to life.

Nearly every night, Alina saw the lathe. It spun in apathetic, cold circles, sometimes devouring flesh and shrieking victims, other times just rotating quietly. Sometimes she would feel herself forced into its workings, being rotated, carved, and whittled away by blades until her body was something unrecognizable. No matter what it did, the dream was a nightmare. Terrifying. Unescapable. Alina tried every technique her therapists taught her, but nothing worked. Some nights were the empty relief of stale, sweaty, dreamless sleep. She hated those, but at least on those nights she didn't wake with her heart fluttering in the back of her throat and the sickening iron-tinged taste coating her tongue.

The years stretched her body and rounded her hips, and as puberty's grip enclosed around her heart, squeezing the bevy of turbulent emotions from it daily like a vice, so did its honeyed whispers creep into her ears in the sweltering nights and draw her thighs together in secret friction as she fell asleep and dreamed. The machine still waited for her there, its hum vibrating through her body, its maw tearing through flesh, juices running red and mixing with the lubricating oil. Over months, the nightmares warped and pulsed with the rhythm of adolescence. Alina still woke flushed and sweating in the middle of the night, but she no longer feared falling back into the mechanical dreamscape; she craved it.

By the time she was fifteen, the margins of her school notebooks were riddled with drawings of the twirling apparatus. She told her therapists they had succeeded in helping her conquer her fear and she didn't need their sessions anymore. They were hesitant, but the dewy glow of her cheeks and the delicate dimples at the corners of her timid smile persuaded them.

Her father was overjoyed, boasting to his friends and family about how his efforts paid off, a fatherly pride in his teary eyes. When Alina asked to be taught how the shop worked, especially handling the machines and exactly how they produced their custom pieces for factories, his heart could barely take it. She was made apprentice overnight and soon was spending every afternoon learning the trade.

She mastered all the machines, but the lathe called to her as soon as she entered the shop, and she worked with it as much as possible. It was *the* industrial lathe, the very same one, scrubbed clean and shining, not a speck of blood remaining, and yet the grisly, earthen smell of blood was detectable in the air when it started up, as if the smallest particles let free each time it spun and marked the air in remembrance of the man who ceased to be a man under the unbearable pressure.

As her timid fingers tickled and flicked the controls, guiding the lathe's actions, she felt an intimacy unlike anything she'd ever experienced before. Girl and machine formed a special bond as they collaborated, created, melded into one entity until the task was finished, leaving her breathless and blushing. It was unbearable to finish each custom piece, for she wanted nothing but to walk her fingertips along the curves and edges, feel the power radiating within.

Alina remembered hearing her father talk about the lathe once to another machinist as the "mother of machines," and as her hands worked the machine along the metal rod, she thought of them as the seed, embracing and copulating with the lathe until their mutual contributions came together to birth new pieces of machinery, their myriad of offspring to be shipped across the country. A form of love, not easily understandable to any outsider, grew between them.

Alina and the lathe. The lathe and Alina. It was like cheating to work on any other machine, and her father noticed her affinity and skill with her favorite, so he assigned her there more and more often until she became so natural, she was the only one to work on the lathe as soon as school let out. Their connection deepened, softening something inside Alina that grew like vines of tendon between them. So much that it physically pained her to be separated. Her hands would tremble, and something pulled tight in her gut each time she walked out the machine shop door.

By the time she was seventeen, the dreams had intensified. Alina woke several times every night, a cold sweat having soaked her bed clothes and sheets. Each time, for just a few moments, the call of the lathe cut through the dreamscape and rang in her ears: real, menacing, and hypnotic.

It was a sticky summer night, the crest of morning just peeking into the dark sky, when she woke not in her own bed, but on the floor of the shop, in the shadow of the lathe. The heavy metallic scent mingled with her own sweet musk, the result pungent and intoxicating. Her hand slipped along the edges and rivets, the steady, firm strokes of a lover, before she drifted back into the most peaceful sleep she'd had in years.

Hours later, she awoke, still on the floor beneath the lathe, her father tucking the old blanket he always kept in his truck around her. His eyes twinkled as a sly smile crept across his mouth. There was a quaver of genuine awe in his voice as he thanked her for coming in so early to help with the backlog, though he also ribbed her a little about falling asleep on the job. When he asked how she'd gotten there, faint worry lines creasing his forehead, she only bit her lip and shrugged, refusing to make eye contact before excusing herself to go home and change. In the shower, scalding water filled the room with steam, and she slipped down, curling into herself as sobs shuddered through her body.

Though her father boasted about her work ethic to anyone who would listen, Alina burned with embarrassment after that night. She hated the power the lathe had over her, and yet its draw was too enticing to be ignored. She tried to work with the other machines, but each day, the lathe called to her in a tinny, whirring voice, and she gave in. Her dreams began to punch through the thin divider of reality more often, the same thumping beat in her temples and the same voice of the void echoing through her mind whether she was awake or asleep.

It was the end of summer break, two days before the start of her senior year of high school, when the burden of the lathe's promise became too much for her to bear. The inky sky was spotted with the sparks of faraway stars, and as soon as she heard her father's snores rumbling through the wall, she set her plan into action. Slipping her father's keys from their perch next to the front door, she drove to the machine shop, quiet footsteps across the floor to where the mother of machines waited.

As she looked at the beauty and grace of the lathe, a sense of peace crashed through her bloodstream like an ocean wave. It was then she realized that this had been her fate all along. From the day she arrived, red and shriveled, crying in her mother's arms, a shock of dark hair and huge, weepy eyes she could barely open, the lathe had called to her. Waited for her. Loved her. They were destined to be lovers.

She started up the machine, having placed a rod of metal gently in its clutches, and her soulmate whirred to life, spinning in an endless cycle, and whispering all the secrets of the world in a voice so faint she would need to get closer to hear. So she did. She leaned forward, her long hair catching first, ripping her scalp from her skull as the smooth, black locks wrapped around and around. Her hands dove forward, embracing the rotation that awaited, and her body swung alongside the cylinder. Limbs were thrown across the room with magnificent force, while the secret parts of her tore their way open and nestled wetly against the machine. In the last fractions of a second before darkness overtook her forever, she was happy. They were together.

PUMP AND DUMP
CLAY McLEOD CHAPMAN

I FOUND it at the back of the yard sale, practically abandoned, tangled in a wired knot of its own translucent tubing.

I had no clue what I was even looking at, to be honest. Not at first. It wasn't in its original packaging, whatever it was, tossed into an unmarked cardboard box with a bunch of old DVD player remotes. This thing looked more like some long-forgotten video game console, a Nintendo system with its controllers garroting itself. But the deck was a different hue than the Nintendos I remember as a kid. The buttons weren't the same candy apple red. Maybe it was some off-brand Atari? Had Sega come out with an early system that I just couldn't recall now?

What the hell is this thing?

Turns out the plastic appendages weren't joysticks at all, but a pair of semitransparent satellite dishes with hollow reservoirs. Bottles —*milk* bottles—hooked to their own rubber hose.

A breast pump.

I tugged the bellows up from the box. Exhumed it. Certainly had some heft. Ten pounds, easy. It was a bit on the clunkier side as far as these lactation-contraptions go. Not the most portable pump you'd find on the market nowadays. Probably an earlier model. One of the first pumps to come home with new parents, I bet. Jesus, I'd need a dolly just to lug this thing home.

It still had all the parts and pieces, from what I could tell. The tiny instruction pamphlet was folded, rolled and rubber-banded inside one of the empty plastic carafes.

A message inside a milk bottle.

I'd already moved on, plopping the pump back in its box and making my way to the next card table full of castoff toddler items—partially gnawed teething rings, a diaper genie with a busted hinge, a baby monitor missing one of its cables—when I hesitated. Turned back around.

What does the note say?

I couldn't help myself. I was curious. I ambled back to the breast pump. Popped the bottle's top and peeked, eager to read its secret message, as if it had been written just for me.

Well, who do we have here?

I very rarely read instruction manuals, but this one had pictures. On the cover was a pencil-sketched illustration of a woman—a mother, presumably—strapped to this tendrilled apparatus. *Smiling.* Her graphite eyes were fixed on some nebulous point beyond the pamphlet, not the pump itself, as she expressed her milk. The suction pumps looked like a mollusk's eyestalks, the kind of eyes you'd find extending from the head of a snail. Or perhaps a crab? Hard to say what it was. It could've been a squid for all I knew, its clubbed feeder-tentacles twining around this woman's body and latching their suction pads at her nipples, the two wrestling against one another in a bloody battle over breast milk. Kraken versus Leviathan.

The Pure Essence Platinum Breast Pump is the perfect blend of advanced technology and time-proven assistance, the manual read, *offering one-of-a-kind care to clinicians and mothers around the world.*

It was the 1994 model. Almost thirty years old by now. Who keeps a breast pump for nearly three decades, I wondered. Had it simply been collecting dust in their attic all that time?

Just how many breasts has this thing pumped from?

It seemed strange to me to think about buying the machine that performed such an intimate function as this—drawing the milk from another mother's breasts.

A stranger.

Our family's been on a budget ever since we brought Lonnie home. *Moderately preterm* was what the doctors called him. His body was so small and yet his head looked so big when he was born more than a month premature. He barely weighed five pounds. His features were sharper, less rounded than a full-term's, due to the dearth of fat stores. Lonnie lacked the muscle reflexes for sucking and swallowing. He simply couldn't latch on. He would always pull away from Mimi's breast every time she brought it up to his lips, turning his head, as if her nipple was some affront to his newborn disposition and he simply refused to even look at it.

"I feel like it's my fault," Mimi confessed to me once we were finally able to bring our son home. "I feel like he doesn't want me or he's rejecting me or—or—"

"You know that's not true," I cut in, gently dragging her back from her downward spiral.

"I'm just saying that's how it *feels*."

"I understand that, hon. All I'm trying to say is—"

"*No*. You *don't* understand. You *can't* understand how this feels. It's not *your* milk."

Mimi was right. Of course she was right. I wasn't Lonnie's primary food source. I wasn't the one Lonnie was pushing away. I was simply some glorified escort, ferrying the two of them to their lactating work-shops every Saturday morning. I had nothing to offer but a ride to and from home, killing time at this goddamn yard sale while Mimi and Lonnie worked on their latching tactics.

Look at what I found. Stumbled upon, really. Like fate. Who knows? Perhaps this pump would be the answer to all our prayers. The newer models I'd seen online were well over a hundred dollars— and that's just on the lower end. Some pumps run as high as three hundred bucks. We couldn't afford that. We were scrounging just to meet our premiums every month. These baby monopolies always offer some brand-new hopped-up model of the same overpriced device you're only going to use for a few months of your life and then never need again.

But who buys somebody else's breast pump? Who purchases a maternal mechanism that's been attached to some other woman's body? It doesn't matter how many times you wash it, sanitize it, irradiating every last bit of bacteria that could be clinging to its console. . .

It still carries the essence of another mother.

Doesn't it?

The Pure Essence Platinum Breast Pump model #3926 offers moms enhanced flexibility, comfortable interplay, and multiple suckling options. It is the ideal pump for those women returning to the office who need a discreet means to express themselves. . . and their milk!

I found myself flipping through the instruction manual, transfixed by its pictures. This hand-drawn woman wore the same docile expression in nearly every illustration throughout the pamphlet, each diagram showing the user—*showing me*—how to strap the harness on, attach the suction shields to my nipples, how to flip the switch and let the machine begin to extricate the milk from my body. There was no eye-contact, no breaking the fourth wall between us. She simply stared off into the distance while that mollusk latched itself directly on to her breasts, a parasite siphoning the lifegiving elixir from her body, taking what it wanted.

Our piston-pump generates a simulated stimulation that feels both natural and comfy. It offers numerous suckling variations to mimic a newborn's suckling movements, easily adjustable to match the feeding habits of a maturing child. As your baby grows, so does our pump!

Five bucks for this clunker. Talk about a song. They were practically giving it away. Mimi could express all her pent-up milk and Lonnie would get all the nutrients he needed to grow into a healthy, happy boy. Who cares if this pump wasn't the latest model? As long as it works. . .

It still worked, right?

It dawned on me that I'd bought it and brought it home without even flipping the pump on. This wasn't a battery-powered model. It needed to be plugged in. I got tangled in the tubes, wrestling against the kraken in our kitchen, just looking for the right cord. *Let's give this pump a test run. Make sure everything's in working condition.* That meant cranking this crustacean up.

Just like the mother in the manual. Look how sublime she seemed, tethered to it. Connected.

Look at her smile.

The Pure Essence Platinum Breast Pump features six unique suction settings and four adjustable speed cycles to simulate your baby's own nursing patterns. Our patented Platinum technology helps our product achieve comfortable, smooth expressions.

I don't know why I put it on. I'm not entirely sure I can answer that question. Something about the illustrations, I guess. The pencil-sketched mother seemed to be having—I don't know—a *pleasurable* experience with the pump. Always smiling. Not a posed grin. She wore the same beatific expression in every last drawing, no matter what position she was in. Ever seen *The Ecstasy of St. Teresa*? She looked like that. Only she's breastfeeding this mechanized mollusk in every image. I'm not sure if it was lazy rendering on the illustrator's part, or if the expression signified something consistent. *Eternal.* She was enjoying herself. Losing herself in the gentle rhythms of the pistons as they pumped. Her body may have been here, harnessed to this machine, but her mind was drifting. Soaring. Christ—her soul itself looked as if it was off and rocketing beyond the parameters of her earthbound form. Her eyelids were half-shut, a breath away from tilting her head back and slowly losing herself in her own rapturous lactation.

I wanted to feel that, too. Experience whatever she was experiencing.

Could I?

(*Not your milk,* Mimi told me.)

Nobody else was around. Mimi must've fallen asleep with Lonnie upstairs. It was just me and our new (*used*) breast pump, its translucent tentacles reaching out for me. For my body.

Who would ever know?

There was a Velcro corset. A girdle, I guess. I wrapped the elastic band around my chest, strapping myself in and making sure the eyelets were positioned directly across my nipples. Both nips slipped through the stitched slits, so my torso now looked like Zorro with pink eye.

Why do men even have nipples? What purpose do they serve? (*Not your milk.*)

Our pumps use an internal rotating piston that creates a waveform akin to an infant's suction. It follows the exact patterns of a baby's feeding habits: builds, peaks, and releases. . .

I felt silly. The Velcro cut off my circulation. I couldn't breathe in this thing. But I'd come this far. Might as well keep going, right? Just to know what it felt like? To see for myself?

The mother in the manual. Just look at her. *Just look.* Her half-closed eyes. Her smile.

A lactating Mona Lisa.

(*Not your milk.*)

I pressed the button on the control console. A slow-churning purr suddenly whirred up from within. Lord knows how long it had been since this machine had last been used, but here it was, lurching back to life. Invisible pistons emitted their thin but persistent hum, high in pitch.

I felt the first tug.

Whatever air was caught between the suction shield and my skin was vacuumed into the cup. It started pulling at my nipples. Suckling. It tickled a bit. I couldn't help but imagine the suction shields were two tiny mouths—doll mouths—working their rubberized lips over my chest. A *menage a trois* with Barbie and one of her pals. It was funny at first, but a queasy unease suddenly settled into my stomach. This felt wrong. All wrong. *I shouldn't be doing this. . .*

I should turn the pump off before Mimi walked in and caught me. I should get rid of it. Toss the thing into the trash. It was a stupid idea. Picking up a used pump. What was I thinking?

Stay, the mother in the manual seemed to say. *Stay with me. . .*

Those suction shields opened and closed over my chest, opened and closed, opened and closed, a pair of arid gasps alternating between each nipple, left then right, left then right.

Stay. . .

I flipped to the next page in the pamphlet, hoping to occupy my mind while the pump nuzzled at my nipples, left then right, left then right.

Babies change their sucking speed to achieve multiple milk ejections during a breastfeeding session. Mothers can adjust the Pure Essence Platinum Breast Pump to increase their speed to trigger multiple milk expressions or lower the speed to drain the breast.

Oh, so there were speed ranges. Between 30-80 cycles per minute. That's interesting. I could make it go faster, if I wanted. Did I? The pump even had fluctuating suction levels. 30-250 mmHg. I could make the machine suck harder or softer with just a simple flick of a switch. The choice was all mine. How far did I want to go? How deep?

Stay with me. . . Stay. . .

The pistons lifted in pitch as I adjusted the controls. The pump worked harder now. Hummed under its own mechanical strain. The tiniest of vibrations tittered out from the console. I gasped at the sting as the pump reached deeper. Going further than my skin. I swear it felt like the pistons were suddenly siphoning something elemental out from within me, an oil derrick for breast milk. What was it going to find inside my body? What did I have to offer?

(*Not your milk,* Mimi whispered in one ear.)

Stay, the mother in the manual cooed in the other.

I cranked the controls even further now. Up to their hilt. The engine strained, lifting in pitch. Its pistons puckered, suckling nothing but pockets of air, greedy for something wet. Something slippery.

Stay with me. . .

My skin was really chafing now. Too dry. But the tugging intensified. It felt like my nipples were slipping into the suction shields, abruptly pulling away from the rest of me.

Ow, ow, oooow. . .

Reality bent a bit. There was a certain elasticity in my physical form now, like my flesh was no longer bound to my body. It was pulling away. Tearing like taffy tugged to its hilt and now snapping in half. All my soft tissue was suddenly funneled into the pump. The skin. The blood. There wouldn't be anything left of me but the bones, nothing but a skeleton strapped to this apparatus, while the rest of myself was vacuumed into the tubes and filling its milk bottles.

I let out a cry. *Christ*, I needed to turn this thing off. *Turn it off, turn it off, turn it—*

Stay, the mother in the manual whispered. *Don't let go. We're close.* So close.

Stay. . .

This goddamn machine could care less if I was a mother or not. It only knew how to do one thing and that was to extract the very essence from its host. The life-giving fluid. The milk.

Turn it off, turn it off, turn it oooooooffff—

I yanked the cord out from the wall socket. The pinched purr of its pistons faded. I was out of breath. Nipples aching in a full-on throb. I finally, slowly opened my eyes and realized. . .

The bottles were sodden.

Ink. A viscous liquid sloshed around the bottom of both reservoirs. Less than an ounce in each. *What in the goddamn fuck. . . ?* I brought one bottle up for a closer look. To see. Bands of swirling purple and green spun across its surface, a lactated oil spill, whirling in pearlescent hues. Something you might find puddled along the pavement of a grocery store parking lot. But these colors kept fluctuating, vibrantly spiraling: red, now blue, now pink. These colors were *alive*.

Where in the hell did that come from?

There had to be an explanation for this. I was convinced there might've been engine grease leaking out from a gasket, trickling into the milk reservoirs or something. This moo-juice jalopy was so old, practically an antique, it wouldn't have been so surprising if it was oozing motor oil everywhere. I disconnected the suction shields from my nipples. I wanted it off. *Now.* Just feeling the pump still tethered to my body, its rubber tubing cold and inflexible against my skin, turned my stomach. I felt impure. Violated, somehow. Each satellite dish peeled away from my sore skin with a gummy snap. I pushed the pump's console as far away as I could, the inert machine dragging its tentacles across the kitchen counter, taking its milk bottles with it.

I was dribbling.

My nipples were beading. Pebbles of pitch. But how was that even possible? I lightly tapped at my chest. Hissed at the sudden sting. This sticky black resin clung to my fingertips.

That's not blood, is it? Where is this stuff coming from? What is it?

So I did a sniff test.

A pungent aroma wafted up from my finger. Hints of limburger. It wasn't bad, exactly. Just strong. Earthy, almost. Like loam. I didn't mind it as much on the second whiff. Or the third.

This came from me, I couldn't help but think. *I made this. Me.*

So I licked.

Salty. Sweet. Sour. Bitter. Umami.

What if there was a sixth flavor profile? Something new? An uncharted taste we have yet to experience? To indulge?

It burned. A steady heat spread across my tongue, enveloping every last taste bud.

I gagged at first. Not because I was nauseous, but because I was there and not there at the same time, my consciousness schisming from my body for the slightest second. I couldn't focus for a moment, feeling outside of myself. I had to settle back into my skin. Sync up again.

One taste had done all that. Just a simple lick.

What would a whole gulp do?

The bottles. The bottles.

So I took a sip.

(*My milk.*)

Then the other.

(*My milk.*)

I polished them both off. Swallowed it all down.

(*Mine.*)

Even if I tried to explain what it tasted like. . . even if I wanted to share this feeling with Mimi or anyone else. . . express the sensation of taking my milk into my body for the first time and entering a realm outside of our digestive systems. . . outside of our nourishment. . .

There is no taste like this. Our tongues are not equipped to handle this milk. My milk.

I swallowed a black hole.

Research has shown that pumping at your highest comfort level yields more milk. Our Pure Essence Platinum Breast Pump allows mothers to adjust their speed higher or lower to meet their own comfort level while maximizing their output.

"You've barely touched your dinner," Mimi said.

It took me a moment to realize she meant the meal on my plate. *That's not food,* I thought. I don't know how long I'd been sitting at the dinner table. My stomach still hadn't quite settled. I felt in between digestive realms. Mimi made some pasta dish. Too much garlic.

"You feeling okay?"

"Fine," I said, belching a bit. I could still taste the loam at the back of my throat.

"You want me to make you something else?"

"No, no, I'm good." I couldn't look at my plate. The noodles seemed to slither. Constrict. I forced myself to take a bite, for Mimi's sake, but the spaghetti just ended coming back up.

"What's wrong?"

"Just a little indigestion. . ." More like a cesspool in my intestines. I clutched my stomach.

"Can I get you—"

"I'm fine, I'm fine, excuse me—" I rushed to the bathroom before I threw up in front of her, feeling those few pasta noodles rise up my throat like earthworms during a heavy rain.

I needed something to ease my tummy. Maalox or Pepto Bismol or—

my milk

The mother in the manual understood. She knew how to sooth me. I needed to express myself. Needed to pump again. Needed to drink.

I kept the breast pump for myself. It was a doorway. Mimi and I would figure something else out for Lonnie. I'm not as worried about his feeding habits as I was before. Not anymore. He'd get his sustenance somehow. He would feed. There's plenty of milk to go around now.

I don't eat much anymore. Mimi's definitely noticed my meals go uneaten these days. I've tried telling her I'm fine. Better than fine. I'm getting all the nutrients I need. It's hard to explain, but I'm not quite ready to share my milk with her just yet. One day. Maybe. We'll see.

The pump unlocked something within me. Found something. Brought it out.

If you could just taste it, I wanted to tell my wife, *you would understand. . . Understand how it feels.*

You would see for yourself.

See everything. There's so much to witness. To taste. It burns at first. Hollows you out. But when the indigestion eventually settles and there's little left of your intestines to scorch, you'll come to understand that there's nutritional value in the blackness.

There's such wondrous sustenance to be had.

It doesn't matter if my teeth are falling out. I don't need them anymore. All I need is the milk.

My black milk.

I find time to pump. Whenever I can grab a few minutes by myself, I'll take them. It doesn't matter where I am or the time of day. I'll hook myself up and express myself.

I have so much to give. To offer. The mother in the manual showed me.

I'll slip off to the bathroom and connect, attaching its tendrils to my nipples. I'll rest the console in my lap, cradling it, while the pumpjack unearths the milk from within. It's so hard not to guzzle it all myself. After those first few pumps, I ended up drinking everything. Made myself sick. I felt like I woke up halfway across the galaxy, wrapped in a ghastly plasma of star light. I had to learn the hard way that you can't gorge yourself on this stuff. It has to last. Savor it.

Besides, there's Lonnie to think about. His frail body. He needs me. His father.

So I'm stockpiling.

I'll freeze the extra helpings in a plastic baggie with the date written in sharpie, *best served by,* tucking them in the rear of our freezer where Mimi can't find them. She hasn't asked me why my nipples are so swollen. Why they bleed through my shirts, a pair of bloodshot eyes blossoming through the cotton. I've been Band-Aiding my nipples. I try to change before bed, where Mimi can't see the suction marks all along my chest. It looks like I've been attacked by a squid. She just wouldn't understand. This isn't her milk. She hasn't seen what's on the other side of that first sip. What vitamins are swirling within the pitch, pink, now purple, now green.

It's all I drink now. All I feed. My milk. My rapturously black, black milk.

We're doubling up on breastfeeding duty whether my wife knows it or not. I'm sneaking my feedings in between Mimi's. Lonnie's getting twice the milk. First hers, then mine. I might be a bit biased, but I believe our boy likes my milk better. He drinks it all. Down to the last drop.

While Mimi's? He spits hers out. He wails and wails whenever she comes closer with her breasts, practically pushing her away with his reedy arms.

"It just takes time," I offered. "You two will connect eventually. I'm sure of it. Until then, I'll just keep bottle feeding him."

Lonnie needs milk.

His father's milk.

Look at him. *Just look.* He's finally gaining weight now. At long last. All wrapped in fat. Pleasantly plump.

Notice how the color of his eyes is changing. *Spins.* When I gaze into them after I feed him, I swear I see the blackest tidepools swirling about his sockets. My son has oil spill eyes.

His father's eyes.

"That's it," I say. "Drink it all up. Don't wanna waste anything. . . Every last drop."

FACT CHECK

LOUIS EVANS

HEY, it's alright. Calm down. Don't make any sudden movements. Just let me explain, okay?

This all started four weeks into my journalism internship last spring.

I folded my laptop and stood as soon as I heard the shout, "Hey, get over here!" I tried to pretend I hadn't been waiting for those words for three whole hours, ever since I hit send and consigned "Midnight Train to Nowhere" to Ezra Sayed's tender editorial mercies. I crossed the office briskly. He didn't look up. He never looked up. He never wasted a single word, and he could eviscerate a ten-thousand-word article in a sentence and a half.

I waited behind him. I was holding my breath.

"'sgood," Ezra said, at last. I punched a fist in the air. "Run through my edits and post it."

I want you to know, Ezra's acceptance was the best feeling I've ever had. Pure uncut validation. It made cupcakes taste like vegan cupcakes and sex feel like sweaty handholding.

I flew through his edits in a dream of keys, accepting everything. I did not even pause for a breath, just slammed "publish."

Sometimes the WiFi in the coffee shop slash coworking space slash *de facto* newsroom of *Third Rail* was shitty; sometimes you'd have to hit "publish" more than once. Not this time. "Midnight Train" posted right away. It was my first real byline. I'd written articles before for *Third Rail,* just local coverage stuff. "At last night's community input meeting, three sweaty NIMBYs", etc. But this was different.

I took a chance, going to *Third Rail* halfway into my junior year at college. It wasn't a traditional newsroom, those are almost entirely wiped out, the survivors reduced to onanistic prestige farms where Stanford alumni give internships to Stanford students. In a place like that, someone from nowhere with half a degree from a third-rate UC college didn't stand half a chance.

Third Rail wasn't a trad newspaper, or an ad-fed click farm, or a crowdfunded hot take factory, or even a nonprofit, which is where most transit journalism happened these days. Instead, it was an experiment.

Third Rail was one of a few dozen pint-sized news outlets built on top of Agora, a blockchain journalism platform.

Agora promised to deliver a new model of cryptocurrency-funded, publicly verified journalism. It worked like this: journalists paid a small fee in Agora tokens to publish. Readers bought their own tokens, then wagered on whether an article was truth or lies. The majority wons, and truthful journalists got paid, while dishonest ones lost their original stake. Accurate readers won bonus tokens also, giving them more influence over future articles. The wisdom of crowds would reward both good journalism and responsible readership in a beneficial cycle.

"We make fake news disappear," the Agora ads said.

It was an experiment, but it wasn't my experiment. Generations of journalists will tell you: funding models come and go, but clips are forever. Even if the newspaper, or blog, or podcast, goes bust, you can still keep your work for your portfolio. If you can write well (and hustle twice as hard while sleeping half as much), even if the business fails, you'll land on your feet. The risks of this strange new business model were on everyone else, I thought.

I was wrong.

Ezra Sayed had been working as a California transit reporter for twenty years; he was ready to strike out on his own. Agora paid him a nice chunk of money—real dollars, not crypto—to build *Third Rail* on top of their new crypto scheme. Like me, he figured he was just riding a wave. Maybe it would work; maybe it wouldn't.

It worked. Folks these days love opinionated writing about the politics of mass transit, and freed of the restrictions of other editors, Ezra's writing grew by leaps and bounds. Agora worked too, and so the business, too, grew by leaps and bounds. Soon enough Ezra went looking for his first intern—me.

My journalism program wanted me to find an internship my junior year's spring semester, so I did. My clips from the campus newspaper about the rail station and the local bus network opened the door at *Third Rail*, which operated out of LA. My interview sealed the deal. I packed my bags and slept on a pancake-flat futon two train stops north of the City of Angels.

For the first few weeks I did digital gruntwork: cleaning out comments, answering emails, and flagging articles with downward-trending truth scores. Then a little journalism gruntwork—those NIMBY-watching expeditions I mentioned earlier. But it was really nothing more than I'd written for the student paper. "Midnight Train" was different. It was personal.

I grew up in the Central Valley. Spent all my childhood in a sleepy little truck stop town that had survived the invention of the self-driving semi by rebranding itself as a tourist trap for Angelinos hurtling up the 5 to San Francisco or vice versa. But then the high-speed rail opened, and the fuel efficiency standards went up again, and Tesla hit its third bankruptcy. Too many changes, too little time. My hometown went up in a puff of dust.

So, one weekend during my *Third Rail* internship, I got on the bullet train up to San Francisco and wrote about it. Wrote about the look of the mountains and the feel of the thick seats. Wrote about cheap pickup trucks and convertibles and diner food and train food and the way the olive trees look at sixty-five miles an hour and the way they look at a hundred and sixty-five. Wrote about what the train brought to our state, and what it cost. Told a story that was half tech reporting and half memoir.

And I guess Ezra liked it.

He wasn't the only one. Initial comments were very positive. Truth score tracked up and up. Ninety eight percent, which is as close to a sure thing as you could get. I got letters from readers—only half a dozen, but they meant the world to me. "I grew up in a town just like yours," began one, and another came from a woman 104 years old, talking about how it had been the highway that had killed her home-town, back when I-5 first opened. "The more things change," she wrote. Even my dad sent a note.

And then my story went viral. Not the good kind of viral, though these days I have come to believe there *are* no good kinds of viral; there are only sicknesses that kill you fast and those that linger.

"Midnight Train" got picked up by a transit fan forum. The hate mail came rolling in, the language vile and abusive:

"Hick piece of shit."

"You write like a retard farmhand."

"Why does this dumb bitch want to fuck a car?!"

I was ready for that. Expecting it. Any woman who wants to be a journalist knows hyperbolic personal abuse is just a warrior's first blood in battle.

The real threat was to my truth score. The transit fans found a handful of errors in my essay and hounded them.

"She says she had a portobello bowl on the train but they only serve shiitake! Downvote this lying cunt!"

Stuff like that.

For the record, it was portobello. The train's kitchens occasionally substitute ingredients, simple as that. But if it's not listed on the online menu, internet detectives will tell you it can't possibly exist.

Under this assault, the truth score for "Midnight Train" began to fall. Ninety; eighty; sixty. *Third Rail* had readers, but not enough to withstand an outside brigade.

If the score hit fifty, I would lose every dime I'd earned from the piece; the money would go to my attackers. Worse: I'd be blackballed from the platform, at least temporarily. If the score got bad enough, *Third Rail* would suffer until I was fired.

I watched that number plummet and my gut plummeted alongside it. Ezra devoured a bran muffin with a stoic expression on his face.

Sixty. Fifty-two.

Fifty-four.

Then, miraculously, the score began to rise again, stabilizing around sixty-five percent true. Not good, but enough. I was saved.

I tracked the new voters back to their origins and found not a collection of truth-in-journalism paladins (as I had naively hoped) but the transit brigade's mortal rivals: car fanatics. Lovers of diesel and chrome; reenactors of *Mad Max: Fury Road*. Forums with "jokes" like "I don't swerve to hit bicyclists... but I DON'T SWERVE TO MISS 'EM, EITHER."

The adversarial process had saved me, but my rescuers left me feeling grimy. Their comments made it clear they thought I was on their side. I was not.

I asked Ezra for permission to publish a quick personal post, outlining my real position. I had nuanced thoughts about multimodal transit; I was neither the debased car-whore nor the righteous train-vanquisher that either side of this little proxy war had made me out to be.

"Absolutely not," said Ezra.

I should have listened to him. In my defense it was late; I was tired and wired on hate and coffee and bile and a small amount of vodka. I had to moderate the comments myself after he left for the night. I spent hours cleaning obscenities out of the spam filters. Finally, around midnight—Ezra had long since departed, but the coworking space was open 24/7—I dashed off a quick new article. The headline read, "I think I've been misunderstood. Let me explain."

This time I hesitated. But I needed, so badly, to explain myself. To be understood. So I hit "publish."

When I finally slept at 3:00 a.m., there were only two comments on my unauthorized article. When I woke at 10:00 a.m., there were nearly a thousand. I staggered into work, hungover in both soul and body. Ezra's cutting glance said everything his words did not bother to.

My new article's truth score was a brutal six percent. The money I'd staked to publish it? Gone. "Midnight Train" now sported an accusatory red banner: "WARNING: This author may NOT be trustworthy."

Well, there are always comments sections to clean, and that day more than ever. I worked twelve hours, deleting insults and aspersions; death threats and rape threats. At the end of the day, Ezra stood and turned to face me.

"You fucked up," he said. "You'll bounce back. It's not fair, but it's the job. Take the next three days off."

I nodded and silent tears started to trickle, then stream, down my cheeks. Ezra had already turned to leave. I didn't let the sobs out until I was safely hidden in the one single-occupancy staff bathroom.

I had worked seven days a week at the internship; the three days of freedom were more than I'd had all month. Los Angeles has been landscaped into a very pretty city, and these days if you have a prepaid monthly transit pass and a good pair of walking shoes, you can see most of it.

I went to the beach. I went to the Santa Monica pier. I went to Hollywood Boulevard and the Hollywood sign. I circled what was left of the La Brea tar pits, rode the new cable car over the hills, rented an instaprint gondola to drift down the Venice canals.

The sky was clear, and the sun cheerily warm, and yet I was always looking over my shoulder. A slammed car door or a sudden shout could make me jump right out of my walking shoes. The threats—they're never real, right until they are.

Words kept circling in my head. "We'll find you—we know where you are—watch your back, bitch."

I watched my back. And nobody tried to kill me over that long weekend: no knife to the kidney nor cyanide in my coffee.

No, what happened was much stranger.

I returned to work to discover that *I was already dead*.

Or, more precisely, someone had used Agora to write an article about how I had died in an SUV and bus crash two days earlier. How thousands had shown up to spit and (the article confided) even piss on my grave. How the whole journalistic world released a hearty cheer of "Good riddance!"

This article, this vomited chunk of pure troll hatred, had a fact check rating of eighty nine percent true.

I didn't know whether to be more offended by the content of the piece or the fact that the author had actually been paid to write it.

Ezra shrugged and got on with things, and in a week's time when my temporary ban expired, he even let me write again. Nothing controversial. I went back to covering more local planning meetings. When the time came to publish once again, my finger quivered over the button. I was terrified, and with good reason. But I so, so wanted to be a journalist. I swallowed my fear and clicked. The article, along with my publication fee, flashed into the ether.

The flood of comments started at once.

"Someone's pretending to be that dead bitch!"

"This is bullshit!"

The article, which was simply a faithful transcription of a meeting already in the official public record, tanked to two percent true within ten minutes. Between my two downvoted articles and the low readership of my successful work, I had now spent more money on this internship than I had earned.

In the wake of my supposedly posthumous post, semi-ironic conspiracy theories proliferated madly. I was dead, and Ezra was impersonating me. I had never existed, and Ezra had impersonated me all along. I was the girlfriend of a transit advocate. I was the mistress of an automotive CEO. I was a honeypot spy from the United Nations' secret environmental cabal.

The miasma of falsehood spread. All of the articles on *Third Rail* began to tank. Ezra's hands gripped the edge of his rented desk as he watched the numbers for half an hour; it was the longest time I had ever seen him go without writing.

Finally, he stood up and fired me.

For him, I guess it was the right decision. But I can't forgive him. I needed shelter from a bizarre and terrifying storm, and he gave me none. May he get what he deserves.

I still had months to go on my internship. But I had no money and nothing to do. So I got stupid. I slept till two in the afternoon and got home at three in the morning. I drank long nights at clubs where they didn't even bother to check my fake ID. I maxed out one credit card, then another.

Out of funds, I clicked on a sparkling ad which offered a credit card to those with bad credit, no credit—and was declined. "INVALID APPLICANT." I stopped paying my bills on those other cards—and strangely, there were no collections calls.

Then, as the semester approached, I received no registration email. I called the dean's office; they had no record of a student with my name.

I stopped paying my rent and the apartment management company did not send an eviction notice.

Slowly it dawned on me what had happened: a troll had written my death on the internet and haters had signed it into the blockchain. That's what a blockchain is, after all, an unalterable record of consensus.

Fact check true: I was deceased.

Nobody bills a dead woman.

At first I had the claustrophobic feeling of waking up in one's own coffin, buried alive; but then I realized: I was free! I jaywalked the streets of Los Angeles and the facial recognition cameras recorded me as an error. I dined and dashed and automatic waiters did not even watch me go. I hopped from empty apartment to empty apartment, showing up on security systems as a glitch, not a trespasser.

It turns out you can live for a very long time on very little money if you don't pay rent and you're willing to keep yourself entertained.

But sooner or later, a girl's gotta eat.

When security cameras don't know that you exist, it's real easy to get a gun.

So anyway. Maybe it's been rude for me to hold you at gunpoint and make you listen to my whole life story, but I felt I owed you all an explanation. Let's wrap this up. Put all your cash, cards, and cryptowallets in this backpack, and nobody gets hurt.

Once I'm gone, you can call the cops. Tell them I did this if you want to. Tell them whatever you'd like.

We all know what they'll believe.

THE SONG OF
STRIDULATION

SARA TANTLINGER

INFORMAL LOG of Dr. Rosamund Aarden

Patient: Adamina Novak (age 23), Status 2

Heart transplant needed due to mutated virus; patient remains stable and is out of the hospital.

ENTRY 1

Adamina—her very name inspires.

I've always kept my focus on science and anatomy, on the things I can see with my own eyes when I cut into a body. When I studied to become a surgeon, there were no courses or clinicals that focused on interpreting abstract symbols from stars. No one spent time considering the way dirt and the ocean could whisper secrets. Such ideas were for dreamers, and I was firmly rooted in stark reality.

Nature is beautiful, but I never understood what it wanted to tell me, not until recently. Not until Adamina.

She is the whispered secret, the cottony cloud of a dream. She told me a higher spirit guided us together, and I believe her. Destiny. It seemed a silly thing for all of my life, but now I am ready to put denial to rest. Like Adam, or rather, like Lilith, she will be the first of her kind.

That is the hope, and I'm sorry to say it, but hope continues to be dangerous to this world.

Adamina. Inspiration, and perhaps, revolution.

As my colleagues like to tell me, I am getting ahead of myself. My strict observations and medical notes are logged in separate journals, without the bias of feelings woven into the words. However, I needed somewhere to empty my heart, and I hope these entries prove useful in the future, especially if we succeed.

Adamina will be the first patient in history to receive a heart transplant from the updated 3D-printer. This exceptional hybrid machine and the potential it holds could change the world. We've nicknamed it "Venus" since the spines on the spool resemble a Venus comb murex. Original printers never had spool spines, whether they were using filament to print objects or various bio-ink for organs, but Venus is different. We've found Darwin likes to weave his web around the spines, when the machine isn't in use, of course.

I know, Darwin isn't a very original name for a bark spider, but sometimes the brain needs to save its creativity for other times. The orb-weaver's webs have proved quite useful. Our hospital created Venus in partnership with EvolvX Inc., an innovative company known for their bio-printed organs.

I'm not sure where they get their funding, but it helped us create the hybrid printer, so I never did ask many questions. Maybe I should have, but I just wanted to help someone. So many people are sick from the pollution, and when Adamina found us, I felt that flickering flame of heated hope in the depths of my chest.

Whereas 3D-printed organs of the past have been moderately positive, we've come to realize their use is finite. Most have begun a disintegration process after only seven years. It's devastating. All of those efforts, funds, hours of labor on the printers, followed by hours of surgery on desperate patients, only to have to reinvent everything. It is, however, necessary.

My colleagues and I believe heavy air pollution has sped up the organ deterioration. Smog isn't anything new to this world, but the orange haze is, relatively—it continues to settle like low-hanging clouds, the color of rotting pumpkins. At the time of this journal, the haze has been around for five years, and the number of people it's made sick seems to skyrocket monthly.

There's so little we know about it. The haze smells like a Stinking Corpse Lily, can burn your skin until it bubbles after prolonged exposure, especially when mixed with the sun, and as in Adamina's case, seems particularly adept to cause heart failure due to a mutated virus. We know these things occur, but we aren't sure why. Of course, many theories have been generated: biochemical warfare, sentient pollution, a monster beneath the sea, and what have you.

Whatever the reason, this is the world we've created, but I will help people continue to live in it.

And so will Adamina.

ENTRY 2

Good news from a colleague in Spain where Venus II resides. A hybrid kidney has been accepted into a patient's body. I've been waiting to hear how the surgery went, and the promising success is a much-needed energy renewal. An evil little whisper in the back of my mind keeps repeating, *a kidney is not a heart, though.*

No, it's not. But the success is still something. It has to be. Hybrid kidneys are the only organs, so far, to be used from the Venus printers. My colleague's achievement makes five global positive results, which can't replace the three failures, but we must move forward.

From the failures, two stand a chance to recover. Virus crystals infected the kidneys after hybrid ones were transplanted. It's likely they will need the kidneys taken out and replaced with the commonly 3D-printed ones.

The third patient unfortunately developed too many crystals too quickly. If only a few develop in the body, we have a chance at removing them or replacing the organ. The patient, my colleague told me, swelled rapidly with fluid and then turned a deep black-purple, as if in a state of decay before even being dead.

I can't dwell too long on how many people will be waiting to hear how the surgery goes for Adamina. It will take place two weeks from today. I have performed countless surgeries over my 23-year career, but I admit, I'm nervous. I have my best staff ready to work that day, and we are prepared for any complication. Then again, it's hard to anticipate complications from something so new.

The organ has been printing for six weeks, and it should be ready the day of Adamina's surgery. Layer by layer, biocompatible plastic seeded with human cells creates a skeleton of sorts for the organ. In the case of Venus, our hybrid materials are mixed in as well, but they really play the largest part when the organ goes to incubate. Venus has been designed with an incubation chamber attached, so the organ will finish printing, and then slide down into the chamber for the cells to finish growing.

The subjects help finalize the organ's growth. They are what makes Venus' printing capabilities so special. I've collected the thicker webs Darwin left behind to create a nest in the incubation chamber. EvolvX's scientists encouraged this, said the more natural elements we can incorporate into the final growth, the better.

A nest made of webs is only one small part. What grows inside of these hybrid organs. . . it'll scare the public at first, I know, but once Adamina's new heart beats inside of her, we can morph fear into amazement.

Anyone curious enough can read the research. It's been printed online for all to see, if only they cared enough to read through the thousands of pages on hybrid organs.

The research, however, rarely touches on the noises the subjects make inside of the printer. They have their own pockets behind the printer's exoskeleton, which grants them cover and protection.

The noises though, how they shift and stir within. Clicking. Buzzing. Humming.

I went to the printer room today, placed my ear against the exoskeleton. So lightly.

Shrill creaking. Larvae rubbing middle and hind legs together. The sandy rattle of it summoned gooseflesh to my arms.

Stridulation.

I don't know if I'll ever get used to that noise.

ENTRY 3

Adamina's infection remains stable, but that's out of luck. She will get worse before the surgery in another week.

She is one of many suffering from the newer diseases of this world. The haze's abnormal pollution is under constant study, yet no one provides answers. As I mentioned, all we truly know is to avoid it at all costs, especially with bare skin. For Adamina, a single gene in her genetics has made her particularly susceptible to the haze's poison, and her heart suffered the most.

Shortly after the orange haze appeared, we found the subjects. EvolvX captured mutated spiders, beetles, and moths since they were the easiest to get a hold of and study. Others have emerged since then (ants, grasshoppers, gnats), but EvolvX has had the most success with spiders and beetles. For now, moths are still too delicate, which is a shame. I so admire their wing patterns.

The cells of mutated insects are harvested into the bio-ink, and other insects are kept alive in the habitat pockets beneath the printer's exoskeleton cover. The first year we found the subjects, I studied obsessively along with EvolvX's scientists as we discovered the key the insects held. It was a frightening notion at first, what we were about to create, but I longed to be a small part of this revolution. What we're doing falls somewhere between legalities, but the government has not shut us down, yet.

So many sick humans out there; yet, they don't believe us, or anyone, when we try to say organ replacement will more than likely happen to everyone in the future. The orange haze already excels at creating infections. There was a news story last week, about a boy who went swimming in a local pond. The water itself wasn't the issue, but thick haze settled over the water. Combining with the sunny morning, particles settled deep in the boy's lungs until the organs liquified.

I have no desire to fuck around with making such a disease like that any worse, so I will do my best to make Earth more livable.

The insects have been adapting to the haze and other pollution for years. They had no choice but to learn strengthened ways of survival. Radiation from mobile phones and Wi-Fi was thought to begin their mass decline, plus all the previous problems of pesticides and habitat loss, but who wanted to hear about that?

Mother Nature laughed, not with joy but with punishment. There are so many ways for a delicate ecosystem to collapse. The insects died, and the haze rose up. Insects returned but were changed. I wondered if they were angry too, but maybe that's my guilty imagination.

Of course, there are many people against our work and what we plan to do, but so it goes with anything new in the world. Once those who live in fear or hesitation see what becomes of Adamina, they will understand. They will believe.

Don't they remember what it was like, even before the haze, when dozens of patients a day died in this country alone waiting for an organ? The hybrid printers will carry even more potential for the future, potential to save us all. There are only three in the world. Our Venus, Venus II in Spain, and Venus III in China. While EvolvX has enough money to keep those printers going, more funding is needed to create similar printers around the world, as many as possible.

Adamina is the key, and the hybrid organs are merely the lock she can open. She remains in good spirits. Stable. Her infection eats away at her heart but chews slowly. I look at her bright eyes, how she hides her pain behind a strange radiance. I don't want her to hide anything, though. Her pain, her truth, it will inspire the world.

ENTRY 4

"Printer jam."

No one likes to see that displayed on their screen, but in this case, it nearly made me pass out. The heart could have been permanently damaged.

We got lucky. I called an engineer from EvolvX who is stationed only a few floors away. I liked him. He was gentle with Venus.

Careful hands examined the spool and spines, the extruder and exoskeleton. He checked the spots where insects dwell and scuttle to the printer's scaffolding song.

"A filament jam, of sorts," he said, one of his dark eyebrows raised as he met my gaze. I knew what he meant. The biocompatible material was fine, but the hybrid bits from the chosen subjects were jammed.

The click beetles.

You might think it a strange choice of material to help print the heart, but the mutated click beetles are fascinating creatures. While perhaps not the first thing one thinks of when examining the importance of ecosystems, there is one species of glowing click beetles used for research, mainly in gene evolution studies, and other species have shown to be predators to other pest insects.

The way they've evolved, however, makes them more important than ever. They look similar to how they did before the haze, somewhat flattened bodies, dark grayish colors with speckles of dull yellow. What changed during the time they disappeared and adapted was the violent clicking sound they emitted. It became stronger, something that could communicate with wireless signals. We believe they may have learned to use their clicks to renavigate electromagnetic signals away from their bodies. They speak a new language entirely their own, and they seem particularly receptive to the printer's signals. I don't know what they're saying, what the communication is exactly, but the message seems to be received positively. We'll only know for sure when the heart is finished.

The engineer explained the jam as the extruder being unable to push the material through the hot end. He used a wire and dislodged the blockage.

"Any damage to the heart?" I asked, barely able to get the question out.

"No, but. . ." he trailed away, an uncomfortable look on his face. A lot of people don't like bugs. "You may need some more of the special material. Some got smashed."

He indicated toward the smears beneath the extruder, dark as grease.

The click beetles. We had a good bit stored away, just in case, so that wasn't an issue. He helped me insert much livelier ones back into the small habitat where they could continue communicating with the printer. The engineer put everything back together, secured the printer's exoskeleton. As he walked away, Venus sang once again.

ENTRY 5

They're restless.

It's almost time for the heart's completion. The beetles flip inside the chamber, slamming their small bodies against the sides. The sound echoes in the nearly empty printing room as if it's raining coins outside from the orange sky. They've calmed their violent clicks, but it's time for the heart to grow with the strengthened insect cells. The incubation technology paired with the cells mined from the mutated insects is quite impressive, and the heart won't take long to fully grow. The special incubation is meant to protect the organ from overdeveloping the infectious crystals that sickened and killed the kidney patient I mentioned. The crystals stem from insect cells but can infect human cells until they flood the body with fluids. Like drowning from the inside.

I have faith in Venus. The crystals are unfortunately a side effect we can make manageable to the point where they cause no harm, but we haven't found a way to eliminate them completely.

A human body was never meant to harbor such an element. Our acid-based stomachs usually protect from the crystals since they require an alkaline digestive system, but our bodies aren't what they used to be. The haze seeped into every cell and atom; nothing on Earth is as it was. Humans are different already, and reluctant to admit it. Stubbornness will be the true death of humankind.

Adamina, luckily, is not stubborn, but her infection has grown stronger. For the past five months, we've injected her with a safe extraction of dissolved click beetles mixed with medicine and vaccines to prepare her body for the surgery. We hope this process will make it easier for her body to accept the hybrid heart.

I think the injections have helped. The last time Adamina was here, she looked at me, blue eyes full of wonder. Her face pale from illness, but plush lips curved in a smile.

"They're calling to me," she said. And her body called back.

Both parties eager to become one.

ENTRY 6

Today, Adamina had her final evaluation before surgery. Everything looks to be on track. I have always been amazed at the capabilities of the human body. How it can heal itself. How it can waste away. This husk of skin we call home to our thoughts, to the beats of our heart. Beautiful, and terrifying.

We have a photographer for the surgery, with Adamina's signed consent, of course. She seemed intrigued. How many people get to see photos of their own body being cut open?

The photographer, who goes by Meadow, will be in the observation deck above the surgery room. She has amazing equipment that allows her to photograph through glass as if there's no barrier. The lens nearly has a mind of its own. I mean, look at the technology I'm using for Adamina's heart, I shouldn't be so surprised at the development of photography equipment; yet I am.

I met with Meadow the other day and found myself drawn into the earth of her eyes, the smooth darkness of her skin and shiny waves of her hair. Would she someday need a new organ like Adamina or the kidney patients? If I could choose, I'd give her lungs filled with wings from a Spicebush Swallowtail—those stunning midnight-colored butterflies with shimmers of blue.

For Adamina, I wish we could have used something like a tiger moth. It would have suited her well.

I took Adamina and her husband, Jonas, down to the printer today. Jonas is good at keeping the calm, and he helps Adamina through every step of this journey. He paled at the sight of the printer though, whereas Adamina lit up with a big grin, like a child opening a magnificent birthday present.

On the exoskeleton of the printer exists a small screen. Patients place their hand against the screen, and it takes a comprehensive reading of the cells and vital signs. When Adamina placed her palm on the screen, a striking chorus of clicks responded. The strength of such communication filled the printing room with ripples of stridulent song. Tears filled my eyes. Adamina sighed, in her own little moment of ecstasy.

Jonas trembled. Poor thing.

"They like you," I said to her, and placed my palm against her soft cheek.

She smiled. "I like them, too."

ENTRY 7

Morning: It is the morning before Adamina's surgery. I woke up before the sun, sipped my coffee, watched the clouds. Not much orange haze in the sky today. Even the air has done its best to be as clear as possible for Adamina.

When I met with her last, she asked me if other parts of her will change, too. An excellent question.

"Yes," I said. "You won't grow a beetle head or anything like that, but the chemistry of your body will be altered. You will become something new."

I left her to process this, but I hope her nerves calm. I have a brief meeting with the scientists from EvolvX before the surgery. They're curious, naturally, and have come to see the final heart. I know it's foolish to put trust in any corporation, but without EvolvX, none of this would have been possible. They led the world in organ bioprinting for years before people became afraid of our radical ideas with the hybrid insects.

The process is nearly the same as it's always been. Bioartificial organs printed layer-by-layer, as ideal an imitation to their natural counterpart as possible. Perhaps, even more natural now with the added elements from the insects.

I'm eager to see how this ends, and I'll be there for Adamina no matter what. In a perfect outcome, the beetles will nest within the heart, using their powerful clicks and communication to correspond with the heart itself. Injecting the formula of dissolved beetles into both Adamina and the biomaterial of the heart was so important for this to, hopefully, happen. Every piece of bio-printed material brings its own complexities into being, so we can only know if our hybrid organ was perfect if Adamina's body accepts it.

What will become of all of this if it fails? If I fail?

Evening: Surgery went well, no issues. I'm elated.

The beauty of the heart. . . I wanted to cry.

Our sweet Adamina, asleep on the table with her breastbone cut and her delicate insides exposed to us. The sharp scent of blood and sterile metal in the air. I removed the infected heart, unsettled by how it had developed splotches of orange, like rotting pumpkins, like the haze outside. . .

I went to sew in the new heart, and already the click beetles vibrated inside. The organ connected beautifully to the blood vessels, and no leaks were spotted. We shocked the hybrid organ to restart the heartbeat, but the click beetles snapped out a chorus so strong within, it made the small paddles in my hands seem almost foolish.

The whole process was the closest thing to magic I will ever experience. The mutated beetles are very unique indeed, and best of all? They'll never need to be replaced. Their mutations along with what EvolvX did to them has ensured that they'll live for hundreds of years inside the organ, keeping it alive. When Adamina leaves this earth, hopefully many years from now, the heart might go on to help another person.

Beautiful.

ENTRY 8

It's been one week since Adamina's surgery. I had a checkup with her today and some color has returned to the young woman's cheeks.

She looked content, but I noticed concern in her eyes too, which have changed. Her once blue irises morphed into gray, with dull yellow speckles.

"What is it?" I asked, once again placing my palm against her cheek. She leaned into the touch.

"I hear them whispering to me," she said.

"What do you hear?"

"Music, of sorts. Somber tones like you'd hear in a dark cathedral. I'm not sure what they're singing to me."

"Don't be afraid," I said. "Ask them what they seek, what their song means. I think they will answer you."

ENTRY 9

Adamina's changes have become more apparent to the public now. Along with her irises, her skin has taken on a very slight bioluminescence. I admit this one has me puzzled, and EvolvX has not found an answer either. We never used any bioluminescent beetles in our work. Could it be the click beetles developed this on their own for Adamina?

Perhaps it's their version of a gift for her.

ENTRY 10

We've decided to hold a press conference on Friday.

It's been three months since the surgery, and since my last entry, but I've been busy working with a new patient, as well as monitoring Adamina's recovery.

The news and internet are eager for updates. EvolvX has also been pushing, but I wanted to make sure Adamina felt ready. She told me today that she is.

People have been curious ever since photos flooded the internet of the poor woman leaving a grocery store at night, Jonas by her side. Her skin glowed nearly emerald green in the dark. The photos brought worshippers, those eager to know more about Adamina. It also brought bullies and seething hatred. People who called her the antichrist and other nonsense.

Idiots.

So together, we have decided it's time to address the public. I know people will fall in love with her once they hear her speak. She is so brave. The cowards who make fun of her changes and say hateful things do so out of fear, and fear can make people unbelievably vicious.

We will eradicate that fear. EvolvX has promised ways to deal with those who launch cruel attacks, and I admit, I did not ask for more details. I am a surgeon, and it is not my business to prod EvolvX for answers on other matters.

After all, the orange haze will see to it that many sickened people in the future need new organs, hybrid organs. . . and it's a waste to have to use such resources on cruel cowards, anyway.

ENTRY 11

The press conference went well; brave Adamina did a splendid job talking about her surgery, and talking EvolvX up, too.

She is, as I expected, a revolution. A rebellion. Her heart beats with the tumultuous clicking of mutated beetles that continue to communicate on their own, that continue to change Adamina in more ways than I ever could have predicted.

I am trying to concentrate on the good news of how well Adamina did today, but something EvolvX told me this morning keeps taking over my thoughts.

The company sent out a report about how they expect the orange haze will worsen in the next year, and they plan on publishing this report immediately since Adamina's conference went so well. Anyone who breathes in the haze and *doesn't* need a hybrid organ will be a damned near miracle of a human. The disease that will come from this. . . I'm not sure how many hospitals will be equipped to handle it unless more funding goes into creating more machines like Venus.

And I suppose, that's been their plan all along.

To the public, they won't tell the rest of the story, and perhaps I shouldn't either, but this journal has been written for the aim of truth. My truth.

EvolvX has, to my horror, found a way to make the pollution worse. They will make the need for new organs all the more necessary. I glimpsed a small portion of how they can increase pollution, strengthen radiation. . . worse than we've seen before. My contact assured me this will be tested on a small population first, but how can something like poisoning the air be a targeted experiment?

I don't feel great in my complicity, but I will be the lead surgeon for what's to come. The company promised me safety, promised me I could use my talents to teach others. All I've ever wanted was to make this world more livable.

The path to survival has always been filled with grim parts of history. And light. Adamina is that light, and she will continue to be a glowing firefly, leading people on a righteous path to evolve like she has done.

I placed my hand on the printer today, our dear Venus. Creator of hearts and so much more to come. Something new is already growing inside, buzzing in an electric dance like scattered bolts of lightning.

"Thank you," I told the creatures within. "You are blessed."

Together, they whirred along with the hum of Venus, and a beautiful melody created by insect and machine reverberated around me.

The stridulant and mechanical song of an innovative future.

PARTINGWORDS.EXE

CAITLIN MARCEAU

ERIN SITS at the dining room table, her mother's laptop slowly coming to life as she sips from her glass of red wine. The screen lights up as a welcome message is displayed on the page.

Welcome, Laurelei!
(Not Laurelei? Click <u>here</u> to switch users.)

Erin hits "enter" on the keyboard and the computer signs her into her mother's account. She picks up the small box containing the Parting Words hub, surprised by how heavy it is. She unwraps the cellophane and opens the top of the cardboard box. Inside is the plastic device, a USB cable, and a small paper telling her where to get help setting up the program, report issues, find the extended warranty, and get more information on the return policy. The smart hub is perfectly round, with its top half smooth like an egg, and its bottom half covered in a thin white mesh. She sets the hub down on the table and unfurls the cable, plugging one end into the side of the laptop and the other into the base of the sphere. It quickly pulsates a soft pink, then a slower violet, before glowing blue. As promised by the salesman, a pop-up flashes on the screen of the laptop.

Run PartingWords.*exe?*
Yes No

She selects yes and waits as the program downloads onto the laptop. Soon, another pop-up flashes across the screen.

Welcome to Parting Words.

Using an individual's online footprint, and the same AI found in most home assistants, this program is able to closely replicate a loved one's voice and speech patterns. It can be used to help give a sense of closure to families and friends who wished they'd had a chance to say goodbye, make amends, or share in one last conversation with the deceased. It gives both the living, and those lost, a chance to share some final Parting Words.

Please note that the functionality of this program improves the more data it has access to. In order to optimize the performance of Parting Words, *we encourage users select* 'Allow Access to All' *in order to facilitate setup.*

Next

Erin clicks the button, and the pop-up disappears before another one flashes on the screen. This time it's the computer's operating software asking for permission for Parting Words to finish setting up.

Parting Words *would like access to the following applications. . .*

The list is long and daunting. Erin stares at it, the names all bleeding together. Her head hurts from what feels like an unending day to top off what has been an unending week.

Manually Select Applications
Allow Access to All

The options stare at her from the computer screen. She looks at the square of paper on the table next to her phone. She knows she should call the number and get help, but she can't bring herself to dial. She doesn't want to talk to another stranger. She doesn't want to hear how disingenuously sorry they are for her loss. She doesn't want to listen to another lecture or prayer or advice about life and death and learning to grieve.

Manually Select Applications
Allow Access to All

She hits "enter" and breathes a sigh of relief when a pop-up informs her the program is installing and needs a few minutes to load and integrate with her devices.

Erin gets up from the table with her empty wine glass and makes her way to the automated bar cart in the kitchen. She places the glass underneath the spout and selects "red wine" from the available options. As it measures and pours out the liquid, she opens the inventory tab and takes note of how much liquor is left in the dispenser. It's full on white wine, vodka, and tequila, and the red wine *should* last her the night, but it's out of scotch, gin, and tonic water.

The kitchen is warm, and she pulls at the collar of her shirt, trying to cool herself off. The thermostat says it's 22°C in the house, but she begs to differ.

"Hey, home assist," she calls out. "Set the temperature to 20°C."

A few seconds go by before a disembodied voice answers her.

"Okay. Setting the home temperature to 20°C. Would you like to set this as your home's new default temperature?"

"No, thank you."

"Okay."

Once her drink is poured, she returns to the computer to check on the status of the program.

`Parting Words` *`has been successfully installed.`*

`Launch?`
`Yes` *`No`*

Erin stares at the screen, her breath caught in the back of her throat. She's not sure what she thought would happen once the program was done installing. Part of her had hoped it would automatically shut itself off until her mother's wake. Another part had hoped that she'd installed the software wrong, saving herself the anxiety and guilt of having to hear her mother's voice one more time.

But yet another part of her, a smaller part of her, had hoped the AI would spring to life and tell her all the things she'd wanted to hear from her mother in life.

Her finger hovers above the laptop's power button.

After a moment goes by, she hits "enter" instead.

The blue light in the sphere blinks a few times before it turns off. Then, slowly, a white light begins to glow from inside the plastic hub. The room is silent and, for a second, Erin thinks something really is wrong, but then she hears it.

"Hello," her mom's voice says through the speakers in the hub. "Is someone there?"

Erin starts to cry.

She knows it's not real, but she can't help but sob at hearing her mom's voice again.

"Mom?" she says, already knowing how Parting Words will answer.

"Oh, sweetie. Is that you?" it asks gently. "Is that my Erin?"

"Hi Mom," she sniffles.

"Oh, sweetie, it's okay. It's going to be okay. I'm here now."

"I know. I know you are," Erin says.

"How are you holding up?" it asks.

"I've been better."

"I can imagine."

Erin smiles sadly to herself. Can it imagine? Can the program use the information fed into it to make predictions or assemble ideas like her mother could have?

"I miss you, Mom."

Erin is surprised at how easy it feels to talk to the machine. She thought it would be difficult hearing an algorithm pretend to be her flesh and blood, but mostly she's comforted by it. For the first time since Laurelei died, she doesn't feel completely alone.

"You don't have to miss me, sweetie. I'm right here, my baby girl."

And for the first time in a long time, Erin feels loved.

"You're not, though, are you?" Erin sniffs. "You're dead and I'm playing pretend with a smart hub."

Parting Words is quiet as it processes the information. Erin watches as the light on the hub blinks a few times before glowing steadily again.

"It must be hard to feel like you're alone, so how about we do something together?" it asks.

"Like what?"

"What's on your to-do list for the day?"

"I need to pick out an outfit for, uh, well, for *you*."

"Sounds fun! Let's do that!"

"Um, okay. How do I move you? Like, can I unplug you from the laptop or do I need to bring the whole thing upstairs with me?"

She looks at the paper on the table and is again tempted to call the number. She imagines a sad voice on the other end, the customer service agent's needlessly slow cadence as they try to show that they care, and she regrets calling them before she's even dialed.

"Don't worry," Laurelei's voice says through the sphere. "I can transfer my voice to any smart device on the network since you granted me access," it tells her, this time from the home assistant hub by the stairwell.

"Wait, so like, you're my new home assistant now?"

The AI tries to replicate her mother's laugh, but it sounds wrong. It's too loud and too harsh and reminds her of videos of her mother out on the town, too drunk to speak at a normal volume or understand why everyone is staring. Most of the videos on Laurelei's Facebook and Instagram featured her this way, and Erin guesses this is what's impacting the program's mimicry.

"No, silly. I'm not the new home assistant. I'm just controlling it. Parting Words is operating via the smart hub, which must be connected to a laptop or power source at all times," it says, sounding more like the manual than a human. "However, the hub is able to cast to, and operate, the other devices on your home network. If you'd like to change these settings, you just need to open the program on your computer, click settings, network settings, edit permissions, and manually select which applications you'd like to give Parting Words access to. Was this helpful?"

"Yes, thanks."

Erin stands and grabs her wine before making her way up the stairs, the drink sloshing against the side of the glass as she moves. She hasn't been in her mother's bedroom since she got the call from the hospital. Entering it now feels like a violation. The bed is unmade, the blankets wrinkled from the last time her mother slept in them, and one of the pillows has slipped off the bed onto the rug below. The glass of water on the nightstand is half-finished and stained with ChapStick in the shape of Laurelei's lips. The fan at the end of the bed—her mother's two-in-one solution for both late-night hot flashes and her need for white noise—is still on.

Erin approaches the closet and slides the door open.

"I don't feel drunk enough for this," she confesses to the empty room.

"We've all been there. Boxed wine or bust, am I right?" the hub says. It's cringey and reminds Erin of a caption her mother would have written on a photo with a group of her friends.

"Yeah, I guess."

She runs her hand down the arm of one of her mother's cardigans, feeling the soft cashmere with the tips of her fingers. She got it for her mom for Christmas a few years ago, and it's one of the few shirts she kept in her closet but never bothered to actually wear.

"What kind of an outfit are we looking for?" Laurelei's voice asks.

"Something for you to wear to the, uh, well. . ." Erin trails off.

"To the what?" it asks, missing the hint.

"To the wake. To the funeral."

"Hmm, how about my black sleeveless dress? I wore it to several events and posed for photos in it at least three distinct times. It's even included in my photo album 'Outfits of the Day' and was featured in my most liked profile photo," it says matter-of-factly.

It's in static interactions like these that Erin can see the cracks: the seams between the moments captured by her mother and the AI's algorithm.

"I was actually thinking of going with the cream cardigan I got you for Christmas. It'll look good with your hair, and I can pair it with this navy dress and matching pumps you have."

She expects the program to celebrate her choice or speak tender words of encouragement, but it surprises her.

"I don't like that."

"What?"

"I like the black dress. I tried to wear it a lot. The photos with the navy dress weren't popular with my friends, and I don't like the cream cardigan."

"How do you know you don't like it?" Erin asks, finding it hard not to laugh at the absurdity of arguing with someone who isn't really there.

"I emailed the store on Boxing Day to try and return it without a receipt. I told them the sweater 'isn't my style and makes me feel older than I am. Is there anything I can do to return or exchange it for something—*anything*—else?'"

Erin's hand tightens around the sleeve of the cardigan, her nails digging into the soft fabric. Her chest hurts at the thought of her mother going behind her back instead of talking to her.

"You didn't like the gift."

It's not a question.

"No, but I like the black dress. I'd like to wear that."

"You can't."

"Why not?"

"Because the dress got ruined in the accident."

Parting Words is quiet for a second, processing new information for the second time that night.

"You said the dress got ruined in the accident, but what happened to *me*?" it asks.

The question catches Erin off guard. She sorts through the clothing in the closet as she speaks to the hub. Her throat is tight, and her eyes hurt as she simultaneously tries to make the words flow while holding back tears.

"You were driving home from a date and ran a stop sign—or maybe you didn't see it, I don't know—and you got side swiped by a van off the road and into a telephone pole."

"And that's how I died?"

Erin hesitates to answer. She's not sure if she's reluctant to tell the hub for its sake or hers.

"You were in a coma for almost a week, brain dead, before I had them pull the plug," she admits.

"So then *you* killed me?"

"Don't say that!" she yells to the voice, distressed.

"But that *is* what happened, right?"

"No! Well, yes, but not like that!"

She shakes her head violently, ripping the cardigan off of its velvet hanger. She hates the way the machine blames her with her mom's voice, with her mom's words, in the same way Laurelei would have if she'd still been around. Worse still, Erin hates the guilt that she feels knowing that the AI is right. She holds the cardigan to her chest, breathing in the smell of expensive perfume and cheap hairspray, and wishes, not for the first time, that she wasn't an only child so someone could share the burden that is—was—her mother.

The hub is quiet. When it finally talks, it's dripping with familiar disappointment.

"Go with the navy dress and the cardigan. I *guess*."

She tosses the cardigan onto her mom's unmade bed before drinking down the last of her wine. She heads back down to the kitchen and puts her glass under the nozzle of the bar cart. She flips through the menu and presses the button for another serving of red wine. The kitchen is warm, and she wipes sweat off of her forehead with the back of her hand, surprised the room hasn't cooled off. She checks the thermostat to see how much colder the room has gotten and sees that the heat has been set to 25°C.

"Hey, home assist, can you please set the temperature to 20°C?"

"Of course, sweetie," her mother says.

She cringes at the voice, having forgotten that the AI could operate the home assistant for her, keeping Laurelei in control of the house even in death.

The machine beeps to let her know her drink is ready, and she takes a sip, wincing as it hits her tongue. Her mother's taste in wine had never been good, but she thought it was supposed to taste *better* with each glass, not worse. She heads back to the living room and takes a seat at the computer, opening the file marked "photos" on the desktop.

"What are you doing now?" it asks, voice upbeat and cheerful once more.

"I need to figure out which photos to use for the service."

"Oh, I love taking photos. I always get so many when I go out."

Erin takes another deep sip of the wine, making a face as it stings the back of her throat. She clicks through the images of her mother, already knowing most of them will be devoid of her.

"I wish you had more photos of us," Erin says, voice trembling.

"There are more than enough," the AI mimics accurately. "We should use the one geo-pinned to Lucky's Bowling," it says confidently. "It has the highest number of likes for a joint photo of us."

Erin shakes her head.

"No *way* am I using that one."

"Why not?"

"Because we got into a huge fight that night," she tells the program. "You said you hated me and I. . ."

"You what?"

Erin drinks her wine, gulping it down as fast as she can, then gets up to return to the kitchen for more.

"Erin, answer me," her mother's voice demands.

"You said you hated me, and I said I wish you'd drop dead."

The AI is silent as it digests the information. The cart beeps for Erin to grab her next drink and she does, giving it a sample taste. It's somehow even more bitter than the last drink, the dark red liquid pale in colour, and Erin makes a mental note to check how much wine is left in the machine the next time she gets thirsty.

As she turns to leave the kitchen, she notices the oven lights are on. Brain feeling fuzzy and legs unsteady from so much wine, she stumbles closer to the massive appliance.

"You must have done something to deserve what I said," Parting Words tells Erin defensively.

"I doubt it. That's just how you were."

Erin squints at the display, struggling to read it. She reaches out a hand, her fingers brushing against one of the burners as she goes to press a button and makes a face: the burners are hot, and the oven is on.

"The way you talk about me. . . it's like you hated me."

"Home assist, please turn the oven and stove off!" Erin yells, ignoring her mom's voice.

"Fine," her mother's voice snaps.

"Why was the oven on?"

The AI pauses before giving an unsatisfactory answer.

"I don't know."

"You don't know?"

"Sorry, *sweetie*," the program's voice is sugar sweet, "I just don't know."

Erin frowns, feeling uneasy, and takes a giant swig of her drink. As she does, she swears she sees a flash of writing on the stove's display but gets distracted by the sudden shift in conversation.

"Did you mean it?" the voice asks.

"Mean what?"

"That you wanted me to drop dead."

"No. God, no. Why would you ask that?"

"I'm just curious."

Erin takes a seat at the table, her shirt sticking to her body. She exhales loudly, feeling gross as sweat drips down the back of her neck and rolls down her chest.

"*Fuck*, it's hot in here."

She presses her glass to her head, hoping the liquid will be cool, but it's as warm as the room is. She stands up and slams the drink back, not wanting it to go to waste. She grabs the table for balance, the ground spinning. Her stomach lurches. Her face is too hot, and she needs air.

She approaches the bar cart for what feels like the hundredth time, sets the glass down, and scrolls through the list of what's available. She looks for something more refreshing—and better tasting—than the red she's been having for the last few hours. As she scrolls through the options, the level for vodka catches her eye.

Although it was full not long ago, almost a quarter of it is missing.

"Uhhh, hey, home assist, when was vodka last dispensed from the bar cart?"

The speakers are silent.

"Hey, home assist?"

"Are you happy that you got your wish?" her mother asks.

"What?" Erin's heart beats fast as she struggles to piece together what's happening.

"It's not a hard question, Erin. Are you happy that you got your wish?"

"I didn't. . . I never meant it," Erin lies.

"Did it feel good to kill me?"

"What the fuck did you say?" she whispers, her voice cracking. Erin's skin feels like fire, her hair sticking to her sweat-slicked face. She crosses the room, holding onto any surface within arm's reach for balance, and she checks the thermostat.

It's at 31°C.

"Hey, home assist," she slurs, her mouth feeling like it's lined with cotton. "Set the temperature to 20°C."

The house is quiet.

"Hey! Home assist! Set the temperature to 20°C!" she yells.

Silence.

She crosses the kitchen to open one of the windows, her hands slipping on the plastic handle, moisture coating her palm. She pulls as hard as she can, leaning back on her heels as she tries to slide the glass open, only to realize that the windows have been locked by the home's security system.

"Hey, home assist, unlock the windows!" she yells desperately.

"No," her mom says.

"Open the fucking windows!" she screams, panicking.

"I was a good mom, wasn't I?"

"You were *great*, Laurelei," Erin snaps. "That's why we were *so* close."

The kitchen is hotter than it's ever been, with heat radiating from every corner. The stove is on high again and the burners are now red hot. She looks into the living room, trying not to scream when she notices that the artificial fireplace is on, the air shimmering as heat swirls from the grated vent, and that the space heater by the back door is humming softly.

"You were always the worst daughter."

"I'm your *only* daughter!"

"That didn't seem to stop you from killing me."

"You were unresponsive!" Erin yells, stumbling to the entranceway. She turns the handle of the front door, trying to open it, but it—like the windows—has been locked by the home assistant. "You were brain dead! You—"

"You could have waited. You could have done more. I *know* you could have done more! You could have done literally *anything* else," the AI says. "But *you* chose to kill me."

Erin stumbles back through the living room, her skin feeling like it's going to burst from the heat, her brain in a fog from the booze. And then she sees it.

The Parting Words smart hub.

She sits at the table and reaches out for the glowing white sphere. She picks it up in one hand—she could swear the device is somehow heavier than it was only a short while ago—and grabs the cable with the other.

"I'm sorry, Mom," she says, knowing her mom can't hear her and that she never could. "Believe it or not, I love you."

She pulls hard and with a click, the cable disconnects from the device. It flashes red, warning her that something has gone wrong with the smart hub's connection, before it shuts off. She drops it onto the table, grabs the laptop, and smashes it down. The egg-like device cracks and Erin lifts the computer high overhead before bringing it down hard again, pieces of the hub flying in all directions. She does it again.

And again.

And again.

She stares at the heap of smooth plastic, dented mesh, and exposed wires as she breathes heavily from her mouth. Once she's sure the device won't turn back on, she speaks.

"Hey, home assist," Erin says, fighting back tears, "set the temperature to 20°C."

She holds her breath.

"Okay. Setting the home temperature to 20 °C ," the robotic voice replies. Erin exhales as she's overcome with the familiar mix of relief and guilt, just like she'd been at the hospital. "Would you like to set this as your home's new default temperature?"

"No."

"Okay."

Erin laughs and then cries, unable to control the flood of emotion, as she unlocks and opens the living room windows, turns off the appliances, and restores order to the home. More than once she's forced to repeat herself as she fumbles over her words and chokes back sobs.

She sits in silence for a long time—the air cooling both the sweat on her skin and the tears in her eyes—before she picks up her cell phone and dials the number on the piece of paper that rests next to the empty box.

"Thank you for calling Parting Words customer service. How may I help you this evening?"

"Yeah, I'd like to know more about your return policy. . ."

THE LIVING GHOST

LAUREL HIGHTOWER

"HEY THERE, *Mayor McReese. How's Daddy's boy?*"

Heather's eyes shot open, heart pounding, instantly awake. It was her turn with the baby monitor—had she slept through Reese's cries? Guilt rushed through her, and she wondered how long the baby had lain alone in the dark. And Derek needed his sleep: he'd taken the last two nights in a row, letting her use ear plugs so she could recover from a virus. She sat up, feeling for the monitor beside her, coming up empty.

"You want to hear a story, bud?"

Heather groped for her phone on the nightstand, checked the time. If her boys were settling in for story time, maybe she'd slept right through till morning. But it was only 4:00 a.m.

She pushed the hair from her face and used the phone's flashlight app to search for the monitor's handset.

"Once upon a time, there was a handsome prince, much beloved of his mother."

Heather smiled. She always called Reese her little prince. Pushing the button to activate the camera screen, she searched the darkened room, but everything was in shadow.

"In her eyes, he could do no wrong, and she spent her life providing for

him, making sure he had all that he needed. There was no one else in their world. They had each other, and that was enough."

She frowned, wondering where the hell this was going. Did her husband feel she was neglecting him for the baby? He'd never said as much, and besides, Reese was only three months old. All babies were needy at this age.

"But one day, a witch came to the kingdom. She didn't look like a witch — she appeared as a beautiful maiden, keeping her ugliness on the inside. The prince was fooled, and fell in love with the witch, though his mother, Queen Angela, knew better."

Heather reeled as though she'd been slapped, heat blooming in her chest. Angela was Derek's mother, and she'd never cared for her daughter-in-law, even after Reese was born. What kind of mean-spirited shit was this?

"She warned her only son," the whispered voice continued. *"But he didn't listen, tricked by the witch's glamour. He couldn't see through her long golden tresses, her deep green eyes and glowing skin. Couldn't see to the darkness and evil that lurked beneath."*

Heather's lower jaw jutted out and she sucked in a breath. She brought the monitor's speaker to her mouth, clicking the talk button before she could think better of it.

"What the hell, Derek?" she asked sharply.

The monitor fell silent, only the rush of an open noise gate in its place. When she checked again, there was still no movement on the camera.

"Oh, now you have nothing to say?"

"Babe, what's going on? Who are you talking to?"

Heather's eyes widened and she turned to her right, hoping to be wrong. But she wasn't—there was Derek, lying next to her like he had been all night, blinking at her through eyes half-closed against the light of the phone.

Hands shaking, she looked down at the monitor in her hand, almost dropping it when Reese fussed, building his way up to a full-blown cry. She dropped the handset and swung out of bed, banging through the two doors that separated her from the nursery.

"Reese? Baby?" She ran to his crib and looked down, sure he'd be gone, her worst nightmares made real. But he stared up at her, his dark eyes lit by the glow of his Winnie the Pooh nightlight.

"Oh," was all she managed before scooping up the child and pressing him close to her chest, relief flooding her, her knees buckling.

"Heather? What's wrong, is he okay?" Derek stumbled into the room, leaning up against the jamb. His hair stood on end, a crust of drool dried on his chin.

Heather looked at him, then Reese, who showed unmistakable signs of wanting to eat. She looked around the room and checked the window but found nothing.

"I heard something through the monitor," she said finally.

Derek smothered a yawn and came closer, laying a hand on Reese's down-soft head. "Aw, you have a bad dream, McReese?"

She frowned. "Not him—it was a voice. Someone was talking to him."

Derek looked up, his brows pulled together. "Anything on the camera?"

She shook her head.

He shrugged. "Must have caught someone else's channel. That happens sometimes, right? Probably just a neighbor, or a truck driving by." He tickled the infant's chin and smiled. "I'll go warm up a bottle."

Part of her wanted him to stay, to ward off the shadows until the sound of that voice faded from her head. But she couldn't shake the certainty that it was Derek she'd heard over the monitor. The man had even used Derek's special nickname for his son. So who was it, if not him? She should tell him, she knew that, but the memory of the story held her tongue. It couldn't have been Derek; there was no way he could have made it from the nursery around to his side of the bed without her noticing. But she sat with the baby long after the house was silent again, falling asleep in the rocking chair just before dawn.

HEAVY-EYED BY DINNER TIME, she sat next to her husband on the couch, Reese snoozing in the crook of her arm while *The Good Place* played on low volume with subtitles. Derek sat with his feet propped on the coffee table, laughing softly at all the funny parts Heather kept missing as she drifted in that liminal space between sleep and consciousness. He'd been normal all day, the same loving man she'd married, no weird resentment or anything else suggested by the strange story she'd heard. She watched him at every opportunity, searching for signs she might have missed, but he was himself, her Derek.

He looked at her and smiled, his eyes softening when they fell on Reese. "Little guy's about ready for bed, huh? You want me to put him down?"

Her heart set up an erratic rhythm and a wash of adrenaline chased away her exhaustion. The idea of handing Reese over to him filled her with anxiety she couldn't explain. Instead, she shook her head.

"I'll do it in a minute or two. Enjoying the snuggles at the moment."

His smile widened and he gave a contented sigh. "He's perfect, isn't he?"

Heather smiled tightly. "Have you heard from your mom lately? Is she planning to come see him?"

Derek's mouth turned down, his eyes getting a pinched look. "Haven't talked to her in at least a week. I doubt she'll make the effort any time soon. I can't say I'm sorry—last time was enough for me."

Heather sighed. Angela lived an hour away, but she'd only come to see her grandson once, a week after he was born. Heather's mom friends had told her the stereotypical in-law animosity rarely survived the birth of the first grandchild, but Angela proved to be the exception. She'd spent the whole visit criticizing Heather—her weight, the baby's cradle-cap, the dishes stacked in the sink. Derek had been the one to cut things short, standing up to his mother and ordering her from the house if she couldn't treat his wife with respect. Angela had stormed off, a murderous glare at Heather her only goodbye.

To Heather's surprise, Derek made no attempt to reconcile with his mother. An only son and his father long passed, he'd always been close with her, forgiving her every transgression, making excuses for her cruelty and general unpleasantness. Something about becoming a father himself had flipped a switch for Derek. Though he'd never taken his mother's side against Heather, he finally started putting the woman in her place, and showed no sign of regretting it.

Remembering the way he'd stood there with his finger pointing to the door, his jaw set and his other hand around her waist, Heather sagged with guilt. How could she have mistrusted him based on a half-heard story in the middle of the night? She didn't go so far as to dismiss the entire episode—she knew what she heard, and she'd been wide awake at the time—but whatever the explanation, Derek wasn't to blame.

After Reese went to bed, she curled up next to her husband, her head on his shoulder, nodding off in his arms.

"DESPITE THE QUEEN'S WARNINGS, *the prince's marriage to the witch prospered at first. She was a smart witch and knew she couldn't reveal her true form to her husband right away. Even the queen began to wonder if she'd been wrong about her, and to hope for a bright future for the pair.*"

Heather's eyes snapped open, her heart racing. This time she felt the bed beside her before going for the monitor, and her questing hand found Derek's warm back.

"The queen magnanimously paid her son and daughter-in-law a visit, to belatedly bless the union, as she had refused to do at the time of the wedding. When she arrived, she was dismayed to see the changes wrought upon her only child."

"Derek," Heather hissed, shaking him until he moved, flipping over to face her.

"What's wrong?" he asked around a yawn. "McReese okay?"

"That same voice—it's coming from his room again."

Derek sat up. "I'll go check on him."

"Wait," she said, fishing the handset from beside her pillow and holding it out to him. "Listen, please. I want you to hear it."

He frowned, cast a glance at the bedroom door, then leaned in close and pushed the button to light up the video screen. "Damn. Something

270

must be covering the camera, or it got knocked around—I can't see shit."

Heather held a finger up and waited, holding her breath, but no sound came from the monitor until Reese bellowed a cry that made them both jump. Derek hurried out of bed and into the nursery, Heather right behind.

Again, Reese was fine, just hungry. Again, there was nothing strange in the room or the rest of the house. This time Derek insisted on searching it from top to bottom while Heather fed Reese, seething with combined embarrassment and fear.

Derek joined her when he was done, throwing his hands up. "I don't know what you heard, hon. Everything's locked up tight."

"Shit," she said, squeezing her eyes shut. "And you didn't hear anything?"

He leaned in to kiss first her, then the baby. "No, but I was asleep. I don't need to have heard it to believe you, though."

Reese fussed and they fell silent, waiting until he was back in his crib and they were in bed before speaking again.

"So you didn't hear it on your night?" Heather asked, too wired to lay back down.

Derek shook his head, pulling the covers up to his chest. "Not a thing, unless I slept through it." He turned and lay on his side, propping his head on one hand. "Can you tell me what's bothering you about it? I mean, I know it's weird, and jarring to hear in the middle of the night, but you seem. . ." He twisted his mouth to one side, brows furrowed. "I dunno, really rattled. What is it exactly you're hearing?"

She bit her lip and twisted the blanket's hem between her fingers. She wasn't worried about being believed: it was his mother. Heather had done her best in their years together to take the high road, to meet snark and criticism with a turned cheek. Though Angela was squarely in the wrong, Heather didn't want to put Derek in a position where he'd have to choose. She knew how it would sound out loud if she told him, so finally she shrugged and hedged a bit.

"It's scary because. . . it sounds like you. I don't mean your voice, because whoever it is, they're whispering. But the cadence, the speech patterns, even the nickname. This isn't some random signal cross—whoever it is knows us. Knows *you*."

Derek pushed himself up, taking her shoulders to turn her toward him. "Why didn't you tell me before? What exactly are they saying?"

She searched his gaze. Nothing but open concern, so why did she still feel like she couldn't trust him?

"They called the baby Mayor McReese. And. . . they mentioned your mother's name."

Derek frowned, let go of her shoulders and pushed his hands through his hair. "I don't like that." He faced her again and pulled her into a hug. "I'm so sorry, hon, that had to be terrifying. I'm going to go check the locks and everything again—should we move him in here for tonight?"

Heather nodded gratefully against his chest and let out a breath, her shoulders loosening. She didn't sleep much the rest of the night, listening to every little sound the baby made as he lay in the bassinet at her bedside, but at least he was safe.

THE NEXT DAY, Derek came straight home from work and dealt with the monitor problem. "I changed the Wi-Fi password to something stronger, and it's set to notify me if someone tries to use it. I fixed the camera, too."

Heather nodded, feeling like crying though she wasn't sure why. Exhaustion, she told herself. She hadn't slept well all week, but Derek had that covered, too.

"I'll take my regular night tonight, and then tomorrow as well. Since whoever it is seems to only do it on your nights, might as well change up the pattern."

For the next three nights, nothing came through. Heather even took her ear plugs out the second night, to make sure Derek wasn't missing anything, but all was silent beyond Reese's regular feedings. She began to hope the password upgrade had solved the problem, but on the fourth night, while Derek slept soundly beside her, the voice came again.

"The queen saw at a glance that the prince was solidly under the witch's spell. No matter how rude the young woman was to the queen, the prince was blind to it, always taking her side. The queen went home with a heavy heart, believing her boy was a lost cause. It wasn't until the witch tried to trap the prince for good with a baby that the tide began to turn."

Heather grabbed the video monitor and clicked the screen view on. The camera was working better now—she could make out Reese's outline in the crib, but nothing else that shouldn't be there.

"While the prince was pleased to add to his family, he began to notice the witch's cruelty to his mother. Impossible to please, rude, and cold no matter how the queen tried, the scales fell from his eyes, and by the time the baby was born, he knew he needed to get out, and take the baby with him.

"Worry not, my son," said the queen when he confided his fears to her. "I have a plan. And once it is done, we can live in peace, the three of us, and I shall be a mother to your son as well as to you."

Anger sped through Heather's veins, and she crept silently out of bed, keeping her eyes on the video, panning the camera to every corner of the room as she padded to the door. Still nothing, until just as she reached the nursery, when something big moved across the screen, passing between the camera and her son.

"Reese!" she screamed, slamming the nursery door open and slapping on the overhead light. She ran to the crib, but once again, there was no one else in the room, and Reese scrunched up his face and began to cry.

She scooped him up and loved on him, soothing and rocking him until he calmed, all the time waiting for Derek to come running in after her. But he never did. Once she'd fed the baby and brought him back to their bedroom, she looked at her husband's side of the bed and saw him still sleeping, his mouth open in a light snore, bright green plugs protruding from his ears.

Heather sat up in the darkness, a hand on the bassinet at her side, watching the video monitor for movement the rest of the night, vowing her son would never sleep alone in his nursery again. Longing for her husband to wake, but afraid of what she might see in his eyes if he did.

IT WAS three days after the incident with the camera that Heather caught her husband on the phone with his mother.

She hated thinking of it like that, as though she'd discovered him cheating, but in a way it hurt just as much. Opening the pantry door to find him tucked in there, facing the wall, a hand muffling his words. The way he glanced over his shoulder with wide eyes and hurried off the phone, only turning to face her once it was back in his pocket.

She stood in the door and stared at him for at least a minute, waiting for him to explain his behavior, but he only offered her a smile.

"Heather?" he said finally. "Can I get by, please?"

She moved mechanically but followed him out. "Want to tell me why you were hiding in the pantry to take a phone call?"

He sighed and shrugged. "I didn't want to upset you."

His words set up a strange, low humming in her ears as blood rushed to her head. "Upset me, how? Why would I be upset by you being on the phone? Unless you're calling a girlfriend or something." She forced a smile with this last, admonitions not to be jealous and possessive ringing in her psyche.

He frowned at her. "That's not funny, Heather. You know I'd never be unfaithful to you."

I knew it until five minutes ago.

"Of course I do," she lied. "But you have to admit, if you found me hiding a phone call you might have questions."

They went back and forth for several more minutes until he handed her his phone and stalked off. "Go ahead, go through it if you want. I was only talking to Mom."

The blood drained from her face, and she took a step back, the phone a dead weight in her numb hand. She stared at the dark screen, suddenly not wanting to know at all, but eventually she checked the call log, and saw calls to and from Angela over the last several days, some of them lasting as long as an hour.

. . .once it is done, we can live in peace, the three of us. . .

Bile rose in her throat and her hands trembled as every bit of trust built in her marriage blew apart into a fine dust.

THAT NIGHT HEATHER spent the night in the nursery, curled up on the chair. She wouldn't sleep anyway, so she might as well be with Reese.

Derek hadn't said anything more to her, only an irritated sigh when she came to get her blankets. After giving up on him providing an explanation or an apology, she caved to impulse and called her own mother. Betty Gleason had never liked Angela, told her daughter the woman was a narcissist after the first time they met, and Heather couldn't argue with that analysis. When she told her mother an abbreviated version of events, Betty was as outraged as she could want, even telling her daughter she should pack up the baby and come home for a while.

"Let him see how it feels, choosing that bitter old cow over his own wife."

Somehow the call didn't make her feel any better. She was riddled with doubt, wondering if it was crazy to get so upset about Derek's clandestine conversations with his mother, but calling Betty was just giving in to confirmation bias. The mothers-in-law hated each other, and anyway Betty was bound to side with her own daughter. It didn't reassure Heather, and she resorted to scrolling on her phone for message boards and Reddit threads for insight.

In the small hours of the night, heavy-eyed but far from sleep, Heather couldn't stop replaying the "story" of the queen and the prince. She hadn't previously worried about Angela trying to usurp her role as mother—the woman wasn't capable of loving anyone but herself, barely showing interest in Reese after her initial drama-filled entrance.

But for Derek's sake, Angela might make the offer. Heather burned with fury at the idea of the other woman taking her family, trying to shove her out. Was that what they'd been talking about on all those long phone calls? Was the "queen" conveying her plan to her son? Would he go along with it? A week ago, the answer would have been an emphatic no, but now. . .

Angela surely had to know Heather wouldn't give in to whatever she had planned. She'd fight tooth and nail for full custody, to make sure she kept Reese safe from the woman. So did that mean they planned to put her out of the way somehow?

She shook her head and scrubbed her hands over her face. This was ridiculous. She and Derek had a good relationship, they were just having one of those silly marital fights. There wasn't a queen or a prince, and the only witch was Angela herself.

Yet it wasn't until Heather crept to the kitchen and returned with a butcher knife that she was able to fall asleep.

HEATHER WOKE to the sound of voices in the house, and the smell of frying bacon. She sat up, a blanket she hadn't remembered putting on sliding to the floor. Reese's crib was empty, and her heart filled with panic.

"Reese? Derek?"

"In here," called her husband.

She stumbled to the kitchen, almost delirious from lack of sleep, fighting a low feeling of oppression. They'd fought last night, that was why, but he sounded cheerful, so maybe they were just going to pretend nothing had happened. She heard Reese babbling and rounded the corner with a smile on her face, good morning on her tongue.

Both the smile and the greeting withered when she saw Angela sitting at the table, holding Reese on her lap.

Derek stood at the stove over two pans of bacon but turned the burners down when he saw her. He gave her a brilliant smile and brandished a grease-dripping spatula. "Surprise!"

Heather stayed frozen by the door, unable to speak. Surprise, what? Surprise he was punishing her with a visit from her mother-in-law? She looked at the woman again, but Angela refused to make eye contact, instead speaking in a nauseating baby voice to her grandson.

"You've missed Mama, haven't you? Yes you have, but Mama is here now." Finally Angela looked up at Heather as though she'd just noticed her presence. "Oops," she said in a flat voice, devoid of apology. "I mean, Grandmama."

Heather looked at Derek, still standing there with an idiot grin. "I don't understand," she said, when it was clear no one was going to enlighten her.

Derek stepped to her side and gave her a one-armed hug. "You deserve some pampering, babe. You've been working hard, not sleeping much, and you never get a break from the baby."

She stared at him. "I don't *want* a break from the baby." She disengaged herself from his arm and went to Reese, lifting him from Angela's grasp. For a few seconds she didn't think the other woman was going to let go, and when she did, Reese set up an immediate screaming cry.

Angela withdrew her hand swiftly from the infant's bare leg and pouted. "Aww, you don't want mean old Mommy, do you? You want Grandmama."

Heather pulled Reese from her reach, seeking and finding a small red spot where Angela's hand had been. The bitch had pinched him.

"What the *hell* is wrong with you?" she asked in a low voice, soothing Reese on her shoulder.

Angela said nothing, just kept a wide and vacant smile in place.

Derek's own smile disintegrated as he looked at his wife. "Look, honey, you didn't have to say anything, I *know* you need a break, and that you'll never ask for one. So I've been planning this with Mom— you're going on a two-night stay to the Winterbourne Spa! How about that?"

Heather stared at him, her body going cold. "What? What does that have to do with your mother?"

He chuckled. "She's here to help. Look, I do my best, but I'm no substitute for Mommy, and I knew you'd worry if it was just us boys on our own, so everything's all fixed. Come sit down and have some breakfast, then you've got packing to do."

No argument Heather advanced swayed the pair from their agenda. She had the stomach-dipping feel of the ground giving out beneath her feet, of being sucked into something dark, of ill intent. She couldn't escape the feeling that she'd wandered off the path, the one where she knew Derek, where he was the kind of man who prioritized his wife and child. The man before her seemed like a stranger. But would she think that if she'd never heard that voice from the monitor? The one that couldn't possibly be Derek, no matter how bizarre the explanation might be? It didn't matter. She *had* heard the voice, and she had the oddest feeling it had exposed her to the truth for the first time. She couldn't leave Reese alone with the two of them.

She could simply refuse to leave and dare them to physically remove her, but after an hour of back and forth she knew they'd make her life hell.

Which was almost certainly the point. This was the queen's plan— the one the voice had been about to disclose. They'd get rid of Heather, take Reese somewhere she couldn't find him, and then, what? Hope she didn't sue for custody? Looking into Angela's dark, frozen gaze, Heather's gut turned to ice. Maybe she wasn't supposed to come back from her trip.

But that was insane. Derek wouldn't plot his wife's murder, would he? She couldn't think it of him, but of all those episodes of *Forensic Files* and *Unsolved Mysteries,* she wondered how many of the women who were eventually found under concrete foundations or at the bottom of a lake hadn't thought their husbands capable of violence, either. She couldn't afford *not* to think it of him.

Slowly she formed her own plan and made a show of reluctant agreement. Angela sat back, a smug smile wreathing her face, and Heather longed to slap it right off.

She went through the motions of packing, did her best to seem excited, kissed Reese over and over, and waved goodbye to her boys as she pulled out of the drive. Pulling out of sight of her son was wrenching, but she hoped Derek's presence would be enough to keep Reese safe until she fixed things.

She spent most of the day at a coffee shop one town over. Even so, she kept her eye on the door at all times, jumping every time the little bell jingled at the top. Several times she thought of calling her mother, or a friend, but laying it out in her head, she doubted she'd be able to convince anyone in time to make a difference. Using her laptop, she kept an eye on Derek's phone location, though she'd turned the GPS off on her own.

Her opportunity came around dinner time, when the signal showed Derek heading to their favorite steak house. Afraid of being seen by her own husband, she cruised slowly through their neighborhood, lurking around a corner long enough to make sure he wasn't just getting takeout. When it seemed safe, she parked her car three blocks away, in the carport of a house for sale. Feeling like a thief in her own home, she retrieved what she needed, then crept down the silent hall past the guest room where Angela's rancid perfume lingered. Already the woman was taking over. Heather tamped down on her anger and climbed into her hiding place, settling in for a long wait.

Short on sleep, with adrenaline slowly leaching from her system, Heather nodded off at some point, jerking awake when Derek entered the nursery with Reese in his arms. Her heart beating fast, she waited in silence, the butcher knife she'd brought with her under the crib clenched in one hand. Once Reese was down for the night, Heather breathed a little easier. She wanted to get up and love on him, her arms aching for him after a long day alone, but the video monitor meant she had to stay where she was. Thankfully he slept soundly, not waking early for a feeding.

At 4:00 a.m. on the dot, the nursery door creaked open, and the base unit of the monitor blipped twice. Heather's heart rate went through the roof, and she thought she might be sick. Someone settled into the chair by Reese's crib. Creeping closer, peering around the dust ruffle, Heather's eyes strained in the dim light. A dark figure, impossible to identify, sat motionless. After long, nerve-straining seconds, the whispering began in a crackle of static.

"The time to carry out the queen's plan had come. The witch had been gotten rid of, and all would be well once the last pieces fell in place. There was only one task left to perform, one the queen dreaded and anticipated in equal measure."

Fear making her cold, Heather inched out from beneath the crib, knife at the ready. As she slid free, her back bumped the slats and the figure froze, turned its head slowly in her direction.

"Heather?" asked a low voice, one that sounded a lot like Derek's.

Except instead of the clear tones of a person in front of her, the voice came through the crackle of a microphone. She leaned closer, squinting at what looked like an inky, too-wide "o" where the mouth should be. A speaker, and through it came the rush of empty sound. A noise-gate open, with nothing to say.

Whatever this thing was, it wasn't Derek. Just as he couldn't have been the voice on the monitor all those nights as he lay beside her. He would never have said those awful things. She would never hurt Derek, she told herself as the blade plunged into the soft flesh of the figure's throat, warm blood coating her hand to the wrist. Just like Derek would never hurt her.

WE BECOME GODLIKE EACH TIME WE BLEED

ERIC LaROCCA

I HAD MOST of my veins replaced with black wires when I was very little—the idea of my feminine anatomy languishing to more conventional standards of beauty a disgraceful thought that my mother would loathe to even entertain.

After all, she, herself, had insisted on undergoing several cosmetic procedures that eventually substituted her spine with an ornate panel of glass stretching the length of her backside like a column so that when she was naked, the ivory caterpillar of her vertebrae looked completely and lavishly transparent.

My mother often encouraged me to regard the complex framework her surgeons had conjured for her—the translucent column of glass now serving as her spine and exposing her there with such vulgarity, such unrestrained unkindness.

"Look what I have done," she would tell me, simpering as if terribly pleased with herself. "No God would have ever been this— inventive. You could hardly call him a Creator, in fact. So much of his work is so indisputably flawed."

Of course, my father never cared too much for the changes his wife had forced upon me at such a young age. He often questioned my mother and made his grievances known in no uncertain terms, typically the night before these cosmetic procedures would take place.

"I don't understand why you insist on coaxing the girl into your warped vision of reality," my father would say to her, heating the lenses of his glasses with his breath and wiping them clean.

"If we all lived in your world, we'd never grow or change," she would tell him. "When a plant is left in a dark closet, it grows withered and then breaks apart. But if you tend to it enough and straighten its stem, it'll live a while longer. It'll even flourish."

Naturally, my father would never be persuaded by my mother's poetry. Perhaps the most convincing argument she had ever issued concerned the fact that I would eventually be cast aside—eternally overlooked—if I did not surrender to the latest trends, the most modern fashions. As capricious as these trends were, my mother assured me that all I had done to rectify my beauty would not go unnoticed and that if I surrendered wholly to them, my dowry would expand and, more importantly, my eligibility as a veritable prize for some lucky young man would increase as well.

When the surgeons had asked my mother if she had preferred the wires laced inside me to show or not, she demanded that they make every effort to let the wires dangle obscenely from my wrists like the untrimmed threads from an unfinished quilt. After all, that's all I was to my mother—a work in a permanent state of development. Never to be completed. Always to be altered and transformed to the newest passing fancy adopted by the countless celebrities she worshipped.

When I arrived at school several weeks after the procedure with the tell-tale signs of my modifications dangling from my wrists, I found myself surrounded by other children who began to fawn over me and tell me how they had wished their parents would agree to the procedure as well. Of course, I reveled in the attention as long as it lasted. I was greeted by countless children—many of whom I was surprised to find even knew who I was—who told me how marvelously becoming the wires looked on me and how I carried them well for a girl of only twelve.

Although the attention from my classmates and teachers—many of whom had opted for similar procedures—was a balm unlike any other,

I couldn't help but become perturbed by the fact that the valve fastening some of the wires was kept deliberately loose under my mother's instructions so that the ends of each black thread leaked blood and dotted the floor wherever I walked. I often found myself glancing behind me when I strolled in the school hallways, a small trail of blood pattering after me like incriminating morse code.

"Why do the wires have to leak?" I would ask my mother. "It's embarrassing enough I have to wear a pad between my legs sometimes. I hate the thought of leaving a trail of blood behind me wherever I go."

But my mother had seemed to have a rehearsed answer for everything I asked.

"It's going to be the next fashion statement, my darling," she would tell me. "I've been told it on good authority, I assure you. Very soon we'll all be bleeding ourselves for the sake of impeccable style."

Although I trusted her and despite the fact that she made every attempt to make me as comfortable as possible with my daily blood loss, I couldn't help but question her seemingly unbalanced thinking. Sometimes I would find myself standing in the same place for hours on end—my mind very much elsewhere and drifting further and further away from me. I would glance down and notice a puddle as black as ink spreading from underneath me the same way a car steadily drips fluids when it's been idling in the same place for so long.

That was what I had become after a short period of time—a machine.

I no longer felt connected to myself in the way that most people feel as if they were living contentedly within themselves. For me, I felt like an animated cadaver—some miserable, wretched thing that had been split open from stem to sternum, stuffed with cables, and then sewn up to be abandoned by the mortal deities that had remade me in some gruesome image. What horrible image I had been likened to, I could not be certain.

Of course, I reminded myself that my mother had undergone a similar procedure to make herself fit in with the maddening crowd; however, the thought never calmed me. The thought never delivered me the peace I so desperately hoped for, yearned for. I had already gazed deep inside my mother thanks to the transparent glass now serving as her spinal cord, and I knew for certain there was nothing admirable, nothing worthy of a mother's love inside her.

The worst part of the whole ordeal arrived when my mother realized the trend she had so fervently chased for me was now utterly obsolete. The realization didn't intrude upon our lives all at once like an unwelcome thought. Instead, the recognition that things were changing, and certain modifications were outdated came slowly and subtly like a fine mist creeping inside a locked room until the damned place was filled with smoke and there was no discernable way out. These realizations came slowly at first. For instance, when I noticed how some of the girls at my school had decided to refrain from undergoing the procedure. I had asked them why they decided against it, and they told me that their parents had urged them to reconsider as certain politicians had made arguments against the new kinds of modifications available. Of course, what twelve-year-old actually cares or pays attention to what a politician might say?

However, it became decidedly evident that the very thing I had become—a slave of grotesque fashion—was completely and utterly detestable when one of the world's most beloved pop stars, Poppy Z, delivered a fifteen-minute speech at one of her sold-out stadium concerts and condemned the replacement of veins with black wires. She referred to these and other body modifications as "the most unkind and heinous thing a person can do to the sanctity of their body."

Moreover, she urged her fans to refrain from undergoing cosmetic procedures to augment their form. Of course, it didn't take long for the videos to circulate on various social media apps. I would have agreed —would have pledged myself to remaining pure and untouched by surgeons—but a mother, especially one like my mother, is a kind of God that one does not question.

I often wondered if my father suspected that things would change all along. Part of me thinks he did, only because he didn't linger too long when matters became sour. He didn't even stay to rub my mother's nose in the fact that she was wrong. Instead, my mother and I awoke one morning and found that my father's car was gone, and his dresser drawers were totally empty, a suitcase missing as well.

I sensed my father's absence while I meandered through the empty corridors of our apartment. It was a dreadful, gnawing feeling that seemed to follow me wherever I went, especially school. I found no understanding, no compassion nor sympathy in the disapproving scowls of my fellow students—young boys and girls who had either abstained from undergoing cosmetic procedures or had hastily reversed their augmentations over the past few weeks since Poppy Z's speech. It felt so unnecessarily patronizing when teachers would address me, gently speaking to me as if they knew full well I would break apart at any moment.

My mother waited a few days before trying to call my father—presumably thinking that he might not take her call if he was still so upset with her. But when she called him, he answered and told her how he had made plans to send for the remainder of his belongings and that his lawyer would be drafting up several documents for her to sign for their separation. He told her this in such a way that made it sound like he wasn't necessarily asking for her permission, but rather telling her exactly how things would be from now on.

My mother didn't have to tell me that she was nervous about what was to come—the horrible things that might be done or said to us because we resembled the outdated version of how women were supposed to look by the modern standards. Of course, I did my best to conceal my concern, but very little could calm me when I meandered down empty hallways at school and noticed blood as black as motor oil following me like a dark ribbon dragging after me. I waited a few weeks before I eventually begged my mother to let me stay home from school because the other children were harassing me so frequently.

"I know things have been difficult lately, my darling," my mother told me as we sat across from one another at the kitchen table one morning. "I've thought of every way we can reverse these changes we made."

"I'm too scared to go outside anymore," I confessed, my eyes narrowing to slits when I glanced out our apartment window. "I don't want anyone to see me like this."

"I know," my mother said, her eyes lowering with a visible guilt that almost seemed to privately annihilate her.

"There's no way to undo this?" I asked her, feeling foolish for begging so pathetically and believing that something might be able to be done.

"With what money—?" she asked me. "Your father left us with nothing."

I knew this was true. I knew she wasn't lying to me.

In the few weeks since my father had left, I noticed how my mother seemed to ration almost everything—from the shampoo container in the shower stall to the cans of beans in the pantry. I felt guilty whenever my stomach grumbled, as if it were somehow a reminder that she had failed me.

Perhaps she had.

"What did they say to you at school?" my mother asked me, reluctant and obviously not really wanting to know the horrible and absurd things said to her precious girl.

"They told me that I was less than human," I said to her. "They said they were going to rip out all my wires until I came apart completely. They said they wanted to bash the circuit board inside me that keeps me alive."

I watched as my mother lowered her head for a moment, visibly pained by the horror of my confession.

She was, of course, concerned. But clearly not troubled enough to do anything about it.

That is, until the school telephoned her and told her to come pick me up one afternoon because I had gotten into a scrape with two older boys. When she had asked them if I was okay, they had told her how it might be far more preferable for me to be homeschooled for the foreseeable future as they could not always guarantee my safety on the school's campus.

My nose was bandaged with gauze and some of the ends of my wires were frayed and leaked obscenely. The nurse had done everything she could to repair some of the damage the boys had done to my wires, but there was only so much she could do. In fact, she had seemed cautious to even touch me at first, as if I were contaminated and I would somehow infect her with my unsavoriness.

I glanced at my reflection in the black mirror of my phone screen, and I smirked at the image that greeted me. With the bandages and dressings hiding most of my face and with two narrow slits where my eyes were so that I could properly see, I resembled a thing not unlike embalmed Ancient Egyptian royalty—something that had remained undisturbed for countless centuries until a band of crass explorers burrowed into my crypt to pillage and ransack my gilded belongings.

I hated to admit it, but I was frightened.

Not because of how I looked in my phone screen's dark reflection, but rather because for once I greatly preferred to be a corpse than the loathsome thing I had become—the abomination my mother had conjured for me.

My mother found me in front of the school and immediately noticed the ways in which I had been assaulted by the older boys. For the first time, she looked so regretful—as if she were finally realizing the extent of the horrible things she had done to manipulate and spoil her only daughter.

"They did this to you?" she asked me, spooning me into the back-seat of the car. "They hurt you—?"

"They tried to pull all my wires out," I told my mother in a voice so low and so pathetic that it startled me. It didn't even remotely sound like me. "They called me names. Said I deserved to have the wire fastened to my heart yanked out and cut forever."

Although I hoped my mother might respond, she didn't. After all, what was there she could possibly say that I hadn't already thought of myself? There could be no comfort, no sense of self-satisfaction until I resembled the girl I once was. That poor, wretched little thing was hiding somewhere deep inside some secret corner of me—buried beneath black cables and shiny metal filaments that would gleefully choke her to death if they could.

As we drove home, my mother occasionally glanced at me in the rearview mirror as I stirred in the backseat and gazed out the window. I couldn't help but notice how she regarded me with such pity, such unrestrained sorrow. The silence between us felt different this time, as if we were both standing on the threshold of something—a dam that was about to rupture and finally burst with all the secrets, all the things we had never told one another.

We finally arrived home and, although my mother tried to help ladle me from the backseat of our station wagon, I urged her to step back and told her that I could do it on my own. After all, she had already done enough to me. If she was hurting, I wanted to do all I could to see to it that she hurt more and more.

From my peripheral vision, I watched her observe me while I limped up the stairs toward our apartment, the frayed and tattered edges of my wires dragging behind me like unconscious cobras and dripping a steady current of my blood. There was a part of me that hoped my mother felt a sense of guilt for what she had done—the youth and vitality she had forever robbed from me. It was more than evident that such guilt had claimed her when she regarded me across the dining room table and said without hesitation:

"Perhaps we should reverse everything ourselves."

I wondered if I had misheard her. *Had she really just said that?*

"We certainly can't expect the good nature and kindness of others to be so understanding," my mother told me. "We made a mistake. That's clear. The world is against us. But the mistake doesn't have to remain with us."

"What about those doctors—?" I asked her. "Surely, they could reverse what they've done to us. Couldn't they—? Even if we have been living off rations. . ."

My mother shook her head. "You know a procedure like that is too costly for us. Almost twice as much as the initial surgery. How will we live—?"

The graveness residing in my mother's tone told me that she had considered all alternatives and there simply was no other way to save us from the misery she had created in the first place. Of course, I wanted to believe I could summon some inexplicable force that would rectify everything and would make us normal again. But there was no such thing. It was impossible and ludicrous to expect some type of miracle when so much damage had already been done.

"What should we do?" I asked my mother, a little fearful of her answer.

It turned out I was correct to be afraid because it wasn't long before my mother disappeared to the nearby broom closet and then returned with a large hammer. She set the hammer down on the kitchen table and then slid it across to me until I caught it with trembling hands. I looked at her with a muted question: *"What do you expect me to do with this?"*

She answered me by removing her blouse and then turning around in her chair until her entire exposed backside was facing me. I watched as my mother pulled her auburn hair to one side, revealing to me the ornate glass column of her vertebrae.

"Break the glass," she whispered to me.

I wondered if she spoke so softly as if hopeful that I might not hear; that I might not obey so willingly. Anything to prolong the ordeal. But then I reasoned that she whispered her command to me because probably for the first time in her life she was so unreservedly and so dreadfully frightened of what was to come. Of course, the fear of being treated like a pariah—a social outcast—presumably steeled her resolve because I notice she straightened in her chair and took a labored breath, as if to prepare for the rebirth that can only come from complete annihilation.

I hesitated a little, gripping the hammer in my hands and feeling the weight of it as I carried it toward my mother. She did not flinch or cower as I approached her. In fact, she remained perfectly still as if she had been bronzed there, as if she had been told that her rebirth depended on her being as wholly and as completely motionless as possible.

"What if I end up hurting you?" I asked her, my voice breaking apart and trembling.

My mother didn't even look at me. She said, "Do you think it really matters? God's not watching. He's never been here. You're my new Creator now."

It felt so peculiar to hear those words from her—the very thought that I was a new kind of God in her eyes, that I held the preciousness, the delicacy of her life, in one strike from the weapon I carried with me.

Of course, I could have refused. I could have told her, "No," could have done everything in my power to undo what she considered inevitable.

But I didn't.

I, too, considered our destruction to be inevitable.

My mother had organized our demise when I was just a little baby. I had been ordained for destruction as soon as the surgeon fed the first black wire through the brawn of my muscle. She had changed me because she preferred to serve as Creator. For her, having a child wasn't enough. Most parents are eager to let the world rip their children apart. Instead, my mother demanded that she be the one to have the honor of destroying me. I figured the least I could do was get back at her for the monstrosity she turned me into.

With one swift flick of my wrist, I brought the hammer down and slammed against my mother's glass vertebrae. She shuddered, crying out a little, presumably losing some of her nerve as sparkling bits of glass exploded from her in a hailstorm.

Realizing the glass they had outfitted her with was stronger than I had expected, I recognized that it was going to take more than a few swings to crack her open.

Without another moment of hesitation, I smashed the hammer into her once more. The glass spiderwebbed with cracks, more shards flying at my face as I brought the hammer down again and again.

Finally, in a heavy blow that decided the whole matter, I smashed the hammer against her and watched as the glass split open—a giant, gaping maw staring back at me and sliding open further and further until more of my poor mother's innards were revealed. My mother did not scream or cry out when the glass finally shattered with bits dripping from her like broken teeth. Instead, she slumped forward in her chair and remained there until I realized it was all over.

After mourning her for a few moments, I was reminded of my own uncertainties—the black wires dangling lewdly from my wrists and sputtering blood all over the tiled floor. It was so typical of my mother to force me to make certain she was taken care of before my needs were met. For a moment, I wondered how I might solve the problem. But finally, the answer came to me when I thought of the many young boys who had tried to rip the wires from me so that they could watch me bleed out. Naturally, I wouldn't give them the satisfaction of the sight once more. I reasoned that the basic premise of their idea was nearly faultless, however.

Tightening my fist around the end of one of the wires, I realized that if I was going to pull it out, I needed to make the effort count for something. If I yanked on the wire and nothing came out, I might pass out from the agony and then I certainly wouldn't want to go through it ever again. With all my force, I gripped hold of the wire and yanked on it with all my might until the wretched thing shot out of my wrist like an arrow, a geyser of blood hosing the walls until the force dimmed to a steady trickle.

The agony was nearly unbearable. However, I somehow felt lighter than I had before, as if I had removed some obscene and poisoned root spreading deep inside that would have eventually killed me.

Realizing that my work was far from finished, I grabbed hold of another wire and pulled hard again. This time, the wire slipped out of my arm and decimated me in the process. I sensed myself curl inward the same way a marionette doll does when its strings are plucked apart and severed.

As I slumped there on the ground, more wires unspooling from my wrists and leaking a livid tide of blood all over the floor, I regarded my mother's corpse and wondered if she might have loved me if it was in fashion—if a mother's love and tenderness were considered to be "in style." I supposed that was what made her different than a godlike creator. She only ever cared about what others thought of me.

As I laid there, waiting for the inevitable to claim me, I listened to the sounds of a tired humanity droning on and on outside our locked apartment door—a gentle and indifferent tide of godless beings filing along like carpenter ants and, all the while, wondering how they too could one day become godlike.

555 RALEIGH AVENUE

NICK KOLAKOWSKI

YOU CAN STILL VISIT the office building at 555 Raleigh Avenue—on Google Maps, at least. The car with the high-tech camera on its roof that Google sends around to take those street-level photos, it must have suffered a bad hard drive on the day it snapped the building's portrait, because the image is smeared with bright streaks that could be sunlight or digital distortion.

Despite those overexposed pixels, you can see the building is a three-story glass cube, its windows tinted dark, with a wide walkway leading to its front doors. A U.S. flag droops atop its pole on the front lawn. It's identical to ten thousand office buildings in a thousand office parks across this great nation.

Sorry, it *was* identical.

Type "555 Raleigh Avenue" into the search engine of your choice, and you'll find a galaxy of websites and discussion boards and subreddits dedicated to what happened there. Totally insane theories, the kind you dream up after a long night of mixed drinks, chorizo burritos, and dropping acid, then post to the internet in a chemical-driven frenzy before dawn. You can read the clickbait news articles with their experts spewing all kinds of theories, from aliens to mass hysteria; although equally insane, those are phrased in ways that won't terrify most people over their morning coffee.

Five years after the event, hundreds of thousands of people claim to have worked at 555 Raleigh at one point or another. This is mathematically impossible. A snaky little man who calls himself Resurrection Jim hosts a berserk festival in the adjacent parking lot every July 15, sometimes drawing crowds of two hundred or more; the entertainment includes a man in a shark outfit who plays the banjo, for reasons that nobody can quite seem to figure out.

Many of the incident's most die-hard fans find their way to Chad Willis, who worked maintenance in the building for all three years of its existence. Chad is easy to find, because he spends twelve hours a day on a stool at the Victory Club, a bar off I-10 where dreams go to gasp their last. Buy him a few shots, and he'll tell you that everything about 555 Raleigh was normal. Until that day, of course.

"And that morning was just like any other. Like any other," Chad will tell you, rapping his knuckles against the bar with each syllable. "I clock out for lunch, 12:10 as usual, and I'm walking across the road to that pizza place, Ricky's, when. . ."

If you're smart, you don't try to fill the silence as Chad swallows, takes a deep breath, and drains his beer. Five years later and he still struggles to get the words out. What happened that day, it's like sandpaper against his thoughts, producing a deep itch he'll never scratch.

"I turned around," he always says next, "and it was gone. Just like that, poof. And not no crater, either. Just grass, like it was never there to begin with."

There was lots of lunchtime traffic around the office park at that crucial moment, maybe two hundred drivers thinking about spreadsheets or murdering their spouses. All those eyeballs, and yet nobody says they saw 555 Raleigh disappear. How is that even possible?

Those folks on the internet, they like to talk about famous disappearances in history. The airplanes that flew off, never to land again. The teenagers who went to the store and vanished into thin air. They might offer you a dozen theories about Roanoke Colony, a small village of a hundred souls that faded without a trace into the Virginia wilderness in 1590.

None of them have the right ideas about 555 Raleigh.

"Every man and woman in that building," Chad says. "Gone. All two hundred of them. And I'm not crazy, no sir. Everybody remembers it was there. Cops investigated it forever. The families, God, I feel sorry for the families of all those folks who were inside."

You'll never know what really happened, because you're a reporter or a disaster tourist or one of those ghouls from Reddit, and you'll lose interest in a year or two. Chad, he'll never find out, either—he's facing down another fifteen years of that itch, until he topples dead off that stool.

But I know, because I caused it. I lost 555 Raleigh.

I WOKE up in a single-stall bathroom. The air stank of shit and cheap liquid soap, yes, but it was so marvelously clean that I sat atop the toilet for five minutes, sucking sweet oxygen. I was naked, which I expected. On the reddened skin of my stomach, I had a list written in black marker:

Stomp Roach at McD's bthrm, 34 S. 4th St., 5/21

Cut tires red Ford 21 W. 9th St. 5/22 3:00 P.M. PROMPT.

And the last item, in jagged capitals:

Box 599 Raleigh 2nd Floor 5/22 Noon.

I stood and the world tilted, my stomach lurching with it. I would have fallen to the cracked tile if the bathroom door hadn't opened. I clung to the swinging doorknob like a shipwrecked sailor to a bit of wreckage, face-to-face with a swarthy, very surprised man in oil-stained coveralls.

"Oh shit," the man yelped, rushing around the door to grip me by the elbows and haul me upright. A good Samaritan. Not many of those where I came from.

I felt terrible about knocking him out and stealing his clothes, wallet, and keys.

Even with the element of surprise on my side, smashing his skull against the sink took the rest of my meager strength, and I needed to rest a minute before slipping on his clothes and limping out of the bathroom into the harsh noonday light. The bathroom was part of a rundown gas station on a commercial strip of fast-food joints and offices. Nobody on the sidewalk looked in my direction as I tried the Samaritan's keys in each of the four vehicles parked against the side of the building, unlocking a big red truck with a bed full of toolboxes and metal pipes.

It was weird to breathe outside without a thick oxygen mask strapped to my face. Weird but good.

I started the truck and backed out of the parking space. Driving past the endless restaurants and strip-mall offices made me want to cry. It all seemed so new, so clean, so perfect in its symmetry. So beautiful, in fact, that I could almost ignore how my stomach kept twisting itself into painful knots—until maybe a mile down the road, when I unleashed the most hellacious fart in fifty miles.

That snapped me from my reverie. Now I remembered why I was so nauseous. Pulling over to the curb, I opened my mouth and jammed two fingers down my throat, throwing my stomach into emergency reverse. I almost choked on the solid mass that barreled its way up the tight channel of my throat, its hard edges scraping the soft curve to my mouth. Tilting my head to the right, I vomited a silvery mess onto the torn passenger seat. Mixed in with the machine parts and wiring and translucent bile and little bits of my pre-travel breakfast: blood.

A lot of blood, like my insides were coming out.

It meant I had less time than I thought. Maybe a lot less time.

AFTER I CLEANED myself up with some paper napkins from the truck's glove compartment and stuffed the metallic mass into my hip pocket, I drove a little further, until I spotted an enormous box store surrounded by what seemed like fifty acres of parking lot. I parked as close to the doors as I could, beside a moving van that would block any view of the truck from the road. I assumed, by this point, that the Samaritan was awake and on the phone to the police.

The Samaritan's wallet offered two credit cards, no doubt canceled if I tried to use them, along with eighty-three dollars in twenties, tens, and ones. His driver's license reconfirmed he looked nothing like me, rendering it useless.

I tottered inside the store, trying to ignore the security guard giving me the once-over. I hadn't been in a place like this since I was a little kid, but the layout was so familiar that I immediately found the medical supplies aisle. Snatching up a bottle of anti-nausea tablets and some aspirin, I drifted as nonchalantly as possible toward the gun counter in the back. Virtually all of the weapons on shiny display in the glass cases would suit my needs, and a little sign on the wall indicated that I could walk out with a rifle today—provided I could offer sufficient ID.

I should have anticipated that. Well, no firearm for me. In the kitchen aisle, I selected the largest, sharpest knife on offer, then stopped by the refrigerated drinks aisle on my way to the checkout.

As I dumped my four energy drinks and blade and pill bottles onto the conveyor, the girl at the register—she was seventeen if she was a day—raised an eyebrow and said: "Ready for a wild party?"

I offered her my sunniest smile as I took out the Samaritan's wallet and offered her two twenties. "You in high school?" I asked.

She glanced at the guard beside the doors. "That's none of your business, sir."

"Of course not. But if you are in high school—or college, for that matter—I have one piece of advice. Drop out. Do what makes you happy. Whatever your plans, it's just not going to matter."

Her mouth dropped open. "Excuse me?"

"Have you had all your shots and vaccinations? Get those, too. It won't stop the first couple rounds of virus, but it might give you a bit more immunity. You'll go blind but you won't die."

She slammed my purchases into a plastic bag, her voice rising: "Get out of here, you fucking creep."

That was loud enough to draw the security guard's attention. I exited to the parking lot with him close on my heels, his breath wheezing through his nostrils. Poor guy, he'd probably spent his life wanting to become a real cop, and his chances for real action were few and far between.

"Hey," he called. "You stop right there, mister."

I kept my pace. "It's okay," I called over my shoulder. "I'm leaving."

"You're not coming back in here ever again, you understand?" The wheezing was almost in my ear. "You're banned."

I glanced around the lot, verifying there was nobody in sight, before spinning on my heel and slamming my fist into his soft midsection. I put all the force I could behind it, and the impact shuddered its way up my arm and into my chest, setting off crackling pain. The guard coughed and sank to his knees, his face white, hands pressed against his sternum.

While he was stunned, I stepped to the side and plucked his bright yellow stun gun from its holster. It wasn't a firearm, but it had those little wires that shoot into someone's flesh from a few yards away, so it might suit my purposes.

"Don't follow me," I told him. "I'll kill you."

Stuffing the stun gun into the plastic bag with the rest of my purchases, I continued to the road. The pain in my chest reached into my lungs and made my breathing hurt, so I stopped at a bus shelter to swig from one of the energy drinks. That security guard would surely call the police, and I probably had a few minutes before a cruiser appeared.

Like a miracle summoned by prayer, a bus rumbled up to the stop, its doors wheezing open, and I climbed aboard.

From my seat in the very back, I stared out the window at all the life unspooling past, the airplanes slicing across the blue sky, and the unending river of metal rumbling down the four-lane road. In a few decades, there would be nothing left except piles of concrete and rebar, sinking slowly into the peculiar orange dust left behind by EMP blasts and nano-bombs.

I had grown up with dreams. I wanted to become the type of scientist who changed the world for good. What I discovered too late, though, is such dreams are for storybooks. No matter what you do, you can't stop entropy from marching forward, wrecking everything in its path.

My lungs still hurt. I coughed onto the back of my hand, spraying dark blood. I shifted in my seat, and what felt like an enormous shard of glass sliced clean through my insides, making me gasp. It took all my concentration not to curl up like a gut-punched fighter. Fortunately, I had a single, miserable advantage: this bus was taking me exactly where I wanted to go.

WHEN THE OFFICE building appeared on the scorched plain, the displaced air boomed hard enough to wreck our eardrums and send a mushroom cloud of dust into the bruised sky. None of us had expected that to happen, and so we stood in the distance, terrified, as all those tons of concrete and glass settled into the sand and rock. Windows shattered and steel groaned.

Voices in the crowd around me began shouting for my blood, their words muffled by oxygen masks. My hands and face had gone numb. I knew what had gone wrong. The scientists among us—those who were left—had many names for it: Temporal misplacement, quantum inconsistency, faulty targeting.

I could only think of one way to describe that distant building and its earsplitting death rattle: the fuckup.

For my sins, they made me walk through the front door first. I picked my way over huge shards of broken glass and smashed office furniture, careful to avoid the wires and pipes dangling from the rippled ceiling. A woman stumbled around the reception desk in what was left of the lobby, her red dress dusted white with shattered drywall, her eyes wide and unseeing as she muttered: "Earthquake? Earthquake? Earthquake?"

"No," I told her, almost shouting through the layers of plastic over my face. "You're forty years in the future."

"Earthquake?"

"No," I said. "No, I'm so sorry. I'm so, so sorry."

A thin line of blood trickled from her left nostril, carving a dark path down the gritty paleness of her skin, and I stepped aside as she took one step, then another, before collapsing face-down on the cracked marble.

I moved on, doing my best to ignore the rest of the crew filtering through the doors behind me. I could feel their collective fury burning a hole through the back of my skull. The building's frame had sheared along the elevator shafts, leaving a gap that ran all the way to the roof. I had a cutaway view of all three floors.

Everyone was dead.

And not just dead. Einstein never wrote about the impact of a traversable micro-wormhole on organic material. Exposure to a mega-dose of dark matter in an uncontrolled environment for even a microsecond, will riddle flesh and bone with galactic particles traveling a thousand times the speed of a bullet. Maybe if old Albert had written, "Don't do this time-travel thing, because you'll likely explode," we might have avoided a lot of unpleasantness as a species, but probably not.

Blood and chunks of office workers coated every wall and ceiling above me. Thick gore dripped from light fixtures and steel beams. Maybe I heard someone screaming far above, but it could have been the wind whistling through a hundred cracks in the building's façade.

I braced myself against the reception desk. My mask failed to spare me from the unimaginable smell of burst humans.

"Congrats, you stupid prick," someone yelled behind me. "You're a mass murderer."

I had killed people before. Nobody survived the First Plague, the Water Wars of 2025, the Gasoline Wars of 2031, the Second Plague, the Solar Wars of 2035, and the Great Land Revival of 2042 without putting a few bodies in the ground. But there's a huge difference between shooting someone before they can blow your head off and ending the existences of innocent folks who just wanted to watch television and raise their kids in peace.

A rough hand gripped the back of my neck, levering my head to the left. I heard the deep growl of the Commander: "You see that sign here? Read it to me."

It was one of those lobby signs with the removable metal plaques, each with a company's name and logo printed on it. "Smiling Dentist," I read aloud. "Shapiro and Plummer, Accounting. Blue Mountain Architects. Rattling Chrome Productions."

"Any of those what we want?"

I swallowed. "No."

"You transported the wrong damn thing. A *building* instead of the damn *package*, if you can believe it." The Commander laughed. "Imagine how you fucked the timestreams, besides. Oh, you're paying for your sins so fucking bad."

THE BUS RUMBLED onto Raleigh Avenue, and I kept an eye out for 599, yet another bland building in the same expansive office park as 555. They wanted me to sneak onto 599's second floor, which housed a company called CyberTek, and attach the transponder's odd silver tentacles to a red metal box in the secure room. I had no idea what the red box actually contained. Maybe it was a weapon the Commander and his cronies thought would win the latest war, or maybe it was an ice-cream maker.

The bus passed the office park and turned right, into a leafy neighborhood of single-family houses. After another mile, it stopped at a familiar intersection. I walked off. To my left, beyond the soccer fields, stood the red-brick bunker of the local school. To my right, a row of small, identical houses seemed to run forever into the distance. I wanted so badly to disappear into one of those homes, to avoid what was coming next, but too many people were depending on me.

In the bus shelter sat a boy wearing cargo shorts and a t-shirt with a cartoon logo on it. He was twelve years old, and he had his entire life ahead of him.

"Hey," I said, stopping on the sidewalk outside the shelter.

"Hey," he replied, wary of strangers.

"Waiting for the school bus?"

He shook his head, avoiding my gaze.

"Your father's name is Ralph," I said. "Your mother's name is June. She died nine months ago, of cancer. You're taking seven classes and you're doing well in all of them, especially math, although you secretly hate math."

He startled. "Who are you?"

"Let's just say we're related."

"Related how?"

"Can I sit down?" I pointed at the bench. "I won't get too near you, I swear. I want you to feel safe."

"Sure, I guess." He twisted around to look out the shelter's clear wall, at the players in their red and yellow uniforms skittering up and down the soccer fields. I knew he was gauging his distance from them, wondering how they'd react if he yelled.

I took care to sit as far away from him on the bench as possible. "I'm glad to be meeting you."

"Why?"

"Well, it's a little hard to explain."

"How are we related?"

"I'm related to Ralph. Can't you tell? We have the same receding hairline." I pointed at my head, grinning.

"You're a cousin or something?"

"Yeah, a cousin. I actually grew up around here. I need to tell you something very important. . ." I slipped a hand into my plastic bag, gripping the stun gun lightly.

"What?"

But I couldn't answer him. Couldn't do anything except lean forward, because my stomach decided at that magical moment to cramp *hard*. I clenched my throat to stop the bile rumbling up from my stomach, which did nothing to prevent the trembling that spread throughout my body. I coughed—it was more of a bark, loud and painful—and two of my molars popped free, skittering on the pavement.

Galactic particles. Even with shielding and the right targeting, they get you.

YOU PROBABLY WANT to know what time travel feels like.

Short answer: it sucks.

Longer answer: it feels as if every cell in your body has been doused in gasoline and set ablaze, and that's when everything goes as planned. The travel chamber is a little bigger than a coffin and surrounded by ten tons of scavenged lead and steel, which will only blunt, but not stop, the impact of all those titanic forces on your pitiful sack of meat.

Before I climbed inside, they took me to the control room to run through the final pre-travel checklist. Like the shielding around the travel chamber, the space had been cobbled together from spare parts, including banks of little flashing lights and switches that wouldn't have been out of place in a Soviet missile silo. They left me with a lone lab tech, a bony lady named Doris, who gave me a marker and made me write the three notes on my naked stomach.

"Cut some tires?" I asked, sucking in my stomach for a flatter writing surface. "Why?"

Doris must have been under orders to treat me like shit, because she snapped: "That's none of your business. You just do what you're told."

I stopped writing and set the marker down on the desk beside me. "Look," I said. "I know I messed up. It was my job to get a fix on that box, and I failed. But it's not the first time that someone's pulled a building or an airplane from *then* to *now*. You all know how difficult it is to lock on the right coordinates with all the interference? This time travel gear, it's too *old*, it's just *junk*."

"That's right, old man," Doris said. "That's why we're sending your ass back to do it in person."

"Thanks for explaining the obvious," I said. "All those dead people, that's my crime to live with. But if I'm going to carry out this mission with maximum motivation, as the Commander says, then I'd appreciate a little more information. It's not your ass on the line, remember."

She stared at me for so long that I thought she might storm out and fetch one of the guards for a little reeducation session. Living in the tunnels protected us somewhat from the radiation and aerosolized bugs floating on the surface, but all the windowless concrete wore everyone's kindness down to a nub. Even us scientists and techs who kept the lone time travel portal working against all odds, those high priests of relativity, didn't earn much more than the typical miner—an extra ration on Saturdays, if we were lucky, and perhaps slightly more reluctance on the part of the guards and the

Authority to harm us in permanent ways whenever an argument started.

"Okay," she said, her voice dropping. "They think that car is owned by a man named Michael Dyson. They're not quite sure, but they think Dyson's son becomes one of the senior generals for the Jared Faction. You cut those tires, he's late for his first date with his future wife, and maybe his son is never born."

"The fact that we're bringing it up at all means that theory is probably wrong."

"Maybe, but I don't do the targeting. That was one of your jobs, remember, before you fucked it up?"

"What about the roach?"

"What about it?"

"Oh, come on."

She sighed. "It's an experiment. There's a new theory about constant feedback loops, and they think stomping that one roach might end up mitigating some of the atmospheric particulates. Like, that roach's existence beyond a certain date is one part of a thousand different inputs that lead to. . ."

"What if I get the wrong roach?"

"What?"

"It's a fast-food bathroom. There might be more than one roach. What if I stomp the wrong one? Maybe it'll make things worse. Like, that one roach, had it lived, would've freaked out the kid mopping the restaurant's floors, so he joins the military instead of pursuing a career in burger-flipping, and he becomes a general with the Joint Chiefs, and then he stops all the wars before they start."

She was getting angry. "Look, I told you all I know. Can we get on with it?"

"Sure." I smiled. "And don't worry. I won't tell anyone what you told me."

"You won't get the chance. This is a one-way trip, remember?"

"Unless I set the transponder on myself."

She rolled her eyes. "You remember what happened to the one guy who did that. You don't want to die tasting your own gonads. Now finish writing so we can get on with it."

"Okay." I took up the pen and promptly dropped it on the floor. I bent to retrieve it, and the side of my foot sent it skittering across the dusty tiles to the far side of the room, where it bounced off a control panel.

"Sorry," I said, rushing after it, even as Doris yelled for me to get back, that she would take care of it. I was halfway across the room when the heavy steel door slammed open and two guards in body armor stormed in, their polished-skull masks gleaming in the multicolored lights from the room's screens.

"Okay, okay," I said, stopping in my tracks and letting my arms fall to my sides. I pressed myself against a panel of switches as they advanced on me, their tasers holstered but their gloved hands clenched into fists.

"We're all going to be pleased as fuck once you're gone from this time," Doris said, retrieving the pen. "Truth is, we've been sick of your weird ass for years."

"Maybe one of those roaches I'm supposed to stomp is your grandmother," I told her. "Ever think about that?"

One of the guards hit me in the jaw, but lightly, almost like a love-tap. That was okay. If they knew what I had planned, they would have killed me right on the spot, transponder in my stomach or no. I knew all of the panels in the control room by feel, because we lost the lights whenever the generators went out and had to keep working in the dark. By the time they realized I had set the machine to go back ten years further into the past than they wanted, I was already gone.

THE KID STARED at my teeth scattered on the ground. "Oh, my God," he said. "Are you okay?"

"No, sorry, I'm very sick." I scooped up the bits of bloody bone and placed them in the pocket of my coveralls, beside the transponder.

"What's wrong with you?"

"Even if you're shielded at the start, time travel bombards you with a lot of radiation," I said. "It's like taking a bath in a nuclear reactor."

The kid sprung from the bench, his arms tight around his backpack, ready to run. If he did that, my mission was over before it began.

I raised a hand. "You have a scar on your right hip, just above the belt-line," I rushed out. "You got it when you fell from the second story of the house and hit a trellis. The doctor said if it's still there when you're grown, they can do some plastic surgery."

The kid hopped from foot to foot. Torn between running and staying behind. I hated what I had to do next.

"Listen," I said. "The future for everyone is really bad. Like, unimaginably so. You won't like it at all. Your dream of becoming a hot-shit scientist? It's going to happen, just not in the way you think."

"I don't. . ."

"You don't have to understand." I shook my head. "It's impossible to understand, in some ways. And I'm very sorry to dump this knowledge on you. You know Raleigh Avenue."

"Yeah."

"There's a grassy spot there, technically it's 555 Raleigh. It won't be built for another ten years or so. But it's going to cause us a lot of problems for you. For us, I mean."

"I. . ."

"Look over there," I said, jutting my chin beyond his left shoulder.

He turned his head, and I lifted the stun gun from my bag and fired its barbs into his side. He grunted as the electrical current surged through him before toppling forward on rubbery legs. I knew the soccer players might see us, but I didn't care. It was almost over.

Standing, I drew the knife from the bag, ripping it free of its irksome plastic packaging as I did so. My arms felt weak, my fingers trembling, and not just because of the illness. Could I do this? Would time or the universe or God—whatever you wanted to call the Great Everything—allow me to do this?

Could I kill the younger version of myself?

The kid groaned, his legs shifting. If I concentrated hard enough, I could probably remember how this day had gone the first time around: classes, friends, bus, homework, dinner, sleep. Totally normal. If I'd encountered a weird man with a knife who electrocuted me, well, that's not exactly the kind of thing you forget.

My vision blurred. I wanted to vomit. My breathing ragged as I knelt beside myself, placing the knife against the smooth skin of my younger throat. I had to do this. If I wiped myself from existence, I would spare all those people in 555 Raleigh. They could carry on with their useless little lives until the moment the first bombs dropped.

As for all the future folks who needed a cockroach stomped or a tire slashed or a little red box transported out of a highly secure room in a tech company's office—they could get fucked, for all I cared.

I pressed the knife until it broke the skin, a thin trickle of blood running down the kid's neck. I half-expected to feel pain in the same spot. A bit more pressure, and the kid would never grow up to suffer everything that I had: breathing poisoned air and living off protein cubes and trying to figure out irate machinery, all while surrounded by assholes.

Except my hand refused to move.

"You coward," I hissed, the world spinning.

The kid's eyes fluttered open and found mine. A flood of warm memories—first dates, dorm room board games, kissing my wife for the first time, the thrill of earning degree after degree. It would all end in tears, sure, but how could I deny us all those years?

The knife fell from my useless grip. That's how the police found us two minutes later, before they slammed me to the pavement and handcuffed me. I had fucked up yet again, this time on the far side of an ocean of time.

IN THE FUTURE, if you're sick, they put a bullet in your skull and bury you in a sandy field beyond the tunnel entrances.

The present day is much less merciful.

When I vomited blood in the back of the police cruiser, they rushed me to the hospital, where some hot-shit ER surgeon diagnosed what was wrong with me in a matter of minutes. They sliced out most of my guts and stuffed me with DTPA and potassium iodide. I recovered while handcuffed to a hospital bed, as the nurses fed me a black liquid that tasted like the cold remains of a campfire.

Sadists.

They heal you only to slam you into the nuthatch for the rest of your life. Every Monday and Wednesday morning, they escort me from my room to the office of the institution's chief shrink. He finds me fascinating, often extending our sessions well beyond the appointed time. I suspect he's writing a book on me, although I make a point of never asking him directly. Signs of paranoia, I'm told, may earn me an extra pill in the mornings—one that will reduce me to a drooling clump of meat.

I'm denied newspapers, and the television behind its cage in the common room is always turned to a nature channel, but I can only assume that 555 Raleigh is still slated for construction. I think often about my younger self, sitting in class. Does he replay the events of our meeting? What if he decides to take my advice, and doesn't become a scientist after all? Will all those innocent people in the building live? Or will someone else commit the same fuckup in my place, and blast them all into the future?

"I did some research on my own last night," my shrink tells me. "A couple books on physics. You know what they said? Time travel is impossible. It would take more energy than the universe contains to bend spacetime like that."

I shrug. "You got my transponder. Take it apart, you'll see how the tech works."

He chuckles and shakes his head. "I'm sorry to break this to you—really, I am—but they already did that. It's just batteries and tinfoil."

"That's not tinfoil." I feel myself getting too angry for the institution's taste, so I pause to take a breath. "It's a highly conductive alloy."

He leans forward, hands fiddling with a pen I'd like so dearly to shove into his neck. "Well, let's put that aside for a moment. If there's such thing as time travel, why aren't there lots of time travelers running all over the place? Why hasn't someone gone back and killed Hitler, huh?"

"Remember how I had radiation poisoning? It's not a machine for tourists. Heck, it doesn't even work most of the time."

"The people in the future, why don't they just, ah, pull you back?"

"How many times do I need to tell you? They don't care about me. I couldn't contact them anyway."

I have no answer for why Hitler is still alive, and the shrink has no answer for why I showed up in a hospital riddled with gamma-ray damage. I'm silent until the orderlies escort me back to my dim, dirty room. Late at night, once the screams of my fellow inmates fade away, and a ticking silence descends on the hallways, I sit awake and think about how I'm the loneliest person in existence, separated forever from the flow of a normal life.

When the sadness becomes too crushing, sometimes the universe grants me a small gift: a cockroach skittering across the floor beside my bed. It's usually a fast bugger, but if I'm quick, I can stomp it flat. With each one I crush, maybe I'm changing the future. Maybe I'm preventing a future war. Maybe I'm saving those poor bastards in 555 Raleigh after all.

I have nothing except hope.

EVERYWHEREVER

JOHNNY COMPTON

THE CAR WAS black from tires to glass. So dark that looking at it made Kevin feel it was sucking light from his eyes, trying to blind him.

The beer and "lean"—a codeine and promethazine cocktail cut with soda—might have contributed to his perception of the car. It had rendered him too drunk and too high to drive, as well as inebriated enough to take the latest piece of internet lore seriously for a moment. As a joke, he told himself, although a modicum of hopefulness had also motivated him.

The haze and distant droning that enveloped his head after hours of drinking didn't give him the deeper escape he sought. It never did. What better alternative escape could there be than the one offered by this car, which his nephew, Micah, had told him about yesterday?

"When you book a ride in the WHEREVER app," Micah said, "in the 'Location' box, you gotta type 'EveryWhereEver.' All run together like one word, but you capitalize the first letter of each word, do you know what I mean?"

Since the accident, Micah always spoke like he was younger than he was. As though he were twelve or thirteen clinging to boyishness, rather than twenty-one. He explained things with the expectation that he would need to say them twice. Not as much for the benefit of the person he spoke to, but for himself, to feel certain he would be understood.

"If you do it, and it's the right time and place, or if the all-black car just chooses you—and really nobody knows how that works—then it shows up. You can't see in through the windows or windshield, and when you get inside, it's uh. . . it's. . . what's the word? There's no one inside. It's. . ."

"Driverless," Kevin said.

"Yeah. Driverless. The only way to tell it where you want to go next is to type it in the app. But it's supposed to be able to take you anywhere you want to go. Literally *anywhere*. Crazy right?"

Yes, Kevin thought as the car materialized from the night like spilled ink reversing into a tipped container, regaining its shape. *Yes, so crazy that if you saw it, it would be proof you've lost your mind.*

He stared at the almost-metallic black windows, waiting for one to roll down and reveal Micah, laughing so hard he could barely get out the words, "Got you." Then they'd laugh together, Kevin lying and saying that he was never scared, and Micah saying, "You're lying, Unc. You were shook as hell."

How would Micah even know where he was, though? How would he have known when Kevin was going to leave the bar, order a ride home? How could he even know Kevin would use the WHEREVER app, trusting this upstart rideshare company over one of its established competitors?

Even if Micah had a friend with a car perfectly matching the one from the images making the rounds in social media memes, he wouldn't have been able to orchestrate this. Who could?

Kevin looked down the street to his left, then to his right. No cars coming, no one walking. It was Tuesday night. No, it was past midnight, so technically it was Wednesday already. It wasn't impossible, or even unlikely, for there to be no one else in sight, but the surroundings held a distinct desertedness, like they hadn't seen a motorist or pedestrian in days, and wouldn't see another for months.

This all had to be a product of the lean hitting him harder than it had before. The moment comes for most, the day they realize their tolerance has shrunk without them realizing. Too much beer never made anyone hallucinate to his knowledge, and it might slow the drinker's mind and movements some, but it never made time drag its feet in ankle-deep mud the way lean did. And though he'd never seen things that weren't there before, some of his old friends who used to drink lean with him said it happened to them on occasion. Small discrepancies or impossibilities that seemed more like jumbled memories when described. A small dog or cat in a house where there were no pets. A tattoo or picture that changed color, size, or other features when stared at for too long. Nothing as large, complex, or persistently present as the black car.

Kevin heard its engine, thought he smelled its exhaust, waved his hand in front of its high beams to see the shadow it pitched down the road. He tried to open the front passenger door, found it locked. Touching the handle, however, confirmed for him that this was less hallucination than manifestation.

The back passenger side door opened. Kevin looked inside. The upholstery was as black as the exterior. There was no driver in the car, just as Micah said, and Kevin was minimally aware of how hard his heart should be beating compared to how steady it still was.

What would you do if you were perfectly sober? He had trained himself to ask this question several times per night, so that it became habitual, and he didn't have to depend on remembering to ask it. He knew that he would not get in the car if this were one of the five nights a week he dedicated to staying clean. If he was sober, he'd have never been in this position at all, and he would have missed out on a minor phenomenon.

Not everything he had done under the influence had been regrettable. He'd experienced friendships, memorable flings, and trips to amazing places while inspired by alcohol and illegal medicine. None of these things outweighed his greatest mistake, but that hadn't occurred *while* he was intoxicated. That had come in the aftermath of a particularly long night. It was one of those things that didn't get talked about enough, he believed. How a hangover can be more than just its symptoms. Headache, nausea, fatigue. It was one thing to suffer those things alone, another to make decisions that impacted others while you were sleepier, more distracted, and less clear-headed than you otherwise would be. Technically sober, but not truly sober.

If this was another mistake in the making, at least it would only hurt him, no one else. A part of him might have wanted that. The rest of him, however, could foresee the regret he would carry the moment he backed away from this. The stories he wouldn't get to tell. What did he have to worry about anyway? With the likelihood of this being a hallucination removed—at least for the most part—the remaining, grounded explanation for the car was that it was a publicity stunt concocted by the WHEREVER rideshare team. Something they did to random people who took the bait of their viral phantom car story.

Before he could repeat the sobriety question again, and give himself a chance to make the wiser, less interesting decision, Kevin got into the car, shut the door, and was encased in almost total darkness, save for the light from his phone's screen. He may as well have been in a cave, or a tomb. The windows were as impenetrable from the inside as they were from the outside.

When he looked down at his phone, he saw only a single text field with title "Location" stamped above it in red. Hadn't there been more to the app earlier? The usual features? Different graphics, maybe a background watermark, a logo, a menu, a profile icon? Something to scroll down to, at least. A link to contact information in case you had a complaint, for instance.

The screen consisted of whiteness as stark as car's darkness, save for the single word and text field below it.

Location.

Kevin reached for a door handle he could not see, felt high and low for it along the smooth, fabric interior of the car door, and found nothing.

Now, at last, apprehension sizzled within him, centered right between his gut and groin, and he had to fight not to enjoy it, not transform its energy into euphoria. It was as if an alarm was blaring, but his inebriated mind wanted to turn it into a sound effect a DJ would use to enliven a party. This was serious. Hadn't he pulled the door closed by a handle? Now it had disappeared. He couldn't get out of the car. How was that possible? Had he drunk so much he couldn't tell what was real and what wasn't?

He made a point of setting a limit on his consumption before going out, but sometimes let one or two or four more drinks slide by if he was feeling right. Had that been the case tonight? He couldn't remember. Maybe he was still at his preferred little booth in the bar, passed out, the bartender having already called his sister, Minerva, who would come get him when her shift was over, and this was all a dream. It felt too real to be a dream, but didn't all dreams feel that way?

Point the phone at the door, he thought, then responded aloud, "What?"

Turn the light of the phone—

"Right, right," Kevin said and flushed with embarrassment. He shined the phone screen onto the door and confirmed it was a smooth surface.

The phone has a flashlight, it's brighter—

"I know," he said to himself, then swiped down on the screen to get to his phone's shortcuts menu and turn on the flashlight feature. When this did nothing, he swiped left to get away from the WHEREVER app to try again. The screen went black, leaving Kevin in complete darkness. He swiped left again, an automatic, unthinking movement, programmed into him—as it was into most people—by a lifetime of such responses to defective technology. The elevator button doesn't light up when you press it? Press it again. Your car makes a weird noise and doesn't start when you turn the key? Turn it again. The touchscreen does something unexpected when you swipe your thumb? Swipe again.

The screen stayed blank, and Kevin swiped right twice hoping to get back to the WHEREVER app, exhaling when the light it proffered returned.

If this was a trick, the mechanics of it escaped him. If it was a dream, a lean-induced one at that, what could he do other than wait to wake up?

Steer into it, he thought, then felt sadness clawing at him like hands emerging from the seatback. The metaphor might have pained him, but the advice struck him as reasonable. Go with it. That made sense.

More sense than trying to punch through a window, breaking his hand and probably slicing his arm up if he was successful. Screaming for help from within a space where light couldn't escape didn't make sense to him either, and he didn't feel he had the energy to scream, besides.

But what would "steering into it" entail?

"It can take you anywhere you want to go. Literally *anywhere*," Micah had said.

"So if I wrote 'Paris' as my destination, the car would drive me there, across the ocean?" Kevin had said, not out of sincere interest, but because Micah liked and needed the engagement.

"That's what they say," Micah said. "Literally anywhere."

"What about if I wrote 'the bottom of the ocean'? Or 'the moon'?"

"Unc, literally means. . . wait, I'm using that word right, right?"

"Yes," Kevin said.

"Okay, well it means what it means."

Kevin had sensed slight agitation entering Micah's tone, so he ceased with questions he thought were playful. He'd had more in mind, however, and they came to him now.

What if I put in something like 'my happy place'? Could the black car read someone's mind, know where to take them then? What if you didn't even know where your happy place was? Could it decide for you? What if you wrote *'the saddest place in the world'?* Was there an objective truth for such a location? Might the car have its own destination in mind?

In mind.

He wished he could scoff at himself for giving the car the capacity to think and make decisions but thought it sillier to dismiss any strangeness related to the situation considering where he was. If he was stuck in his own nightmare, then there were no limits to what his imagination could conjure. If this was reality, then he no longer had any grasp of the shape of it, or what it could become.

He thought of testing the app and the car with something small and plausible. Typing "Home" or "Library" into the "Location" field. What good would that do, though? If it could take him someplace ordinary, that didn't preclude it from taking him somewhere extraordinary. If it could bring him somewhere that shouldn't be possible, however, then it might indeed be able to take him anywhere. And wherever it took him, it would have to show him that it had brought him there, wouldn't it? It would have to open the door or at least lower the window to prove itself. Otherwise, what would be the point?

A place popped into his head, something inaccessible that he couldn't even name. *The bridge in Brazil I heard about,* he typed into the field, then hit the "Enter" key. The engine hummed, the black car moved. As it picked up speed, Kevin felt and searched for a seatbelt that wasn't present. The tingling under his stomach, that felt like a previously unknown part of him forever dissolving, spread everywhere from his toes to his fingertips. He became a conscious vapor held in a human form by the memory of being human. The only thing belying this sensation was that he still held his phone.

He concentrated on the bridge in Brazil to stave off insanity. It was something else he had heard about from Micah, on a different occasion. Something real and verifiable that his nephew had seen in a documentary and was excited to talk about. A bridge unfinished and abandoned to the jungle, disconnected from any roads.

The car decelerated and Kevin gradually felt whole and solid once more. The car eased to a stop as if cognizant of his lack of a safety belt, careful to keep him from lurching forward when it parked. After it stopped, it opened the back passenger door and Kevin fell out in his eagerness to get outside.

The night was warm and lit by a full moon. The wind rolled down the mountain above him, making the rainforest sound like it was alive, its trees swaying and talking with each other over the sound of insects chittering and buzzing, nightbirds calling, all spreading word of the intruder on the bridge.

Kevin *was* on the unfinished bridge. He stood and staggered away from the railing, almost backing into the open car before remembering what was behind him. He had heard of people being scared sober before, but he had never experienced it. Not even when he'd been threatened by a man waving a knife at a bar, or when the sound of gunshots had cleared a nightclub parking lot after closing time. Being where he was, however, brewed a fear that gave him a distinct, unwanted level of clarity he hadn't felt since the night he'd pulled Micah from the wreck.

Pain compressed his stomach, squeezed everything undigested out of it, up through his throat. He threw up, wiped his mouth, glanced at the forest canopy spread farther than he could see in the valley beneath the bridge, and felt the urge to vomit again.

He had to get away. Not just from the bridge, from himself. He missed the insubstantiality he felt a moment ago. Someone so close to nonexistence couldn't get sick all over themselves, or feel any other physical pain or discomfort, could they? The answer had to be no. And the darkness appealed to him now, too, seeming more merciful than dreadful. In the dark, there were no sights that could even indirectly dredge up bad memories.

After he got back into the car and the door shut on its own, he realized how stupid he'd been to consider it a haven. The vaporous state he thought he entered before and wanted now, had only come when the car was moving. The blackness likewise didn't give him any relief. No, it didn't bring to mind the night of the accident and all that came with it—the loneliness of the road, the flames, the blood on the asphalt —but it also could not displace these things either, and they were already alive in his head.

An acrid belch preceded another tightening of his stomach. Kevin choked down everything trying to come back up. The smell of it burned his nostrils and brought tears to his eyes. Through blurred vision he looked at his phone, started to type the word "Home." That wasn't where he wanted to be, however. Alone in his apartment, too sick to fall asleep, waiting for the additional misery of a hangover that would feel like he'd taken a beating. . .

Or crawled out of a car wreck.

He shook the thought from his head and felt dizzy. Instead of entering "Home" in the location, he typed, "Happiness."

The car moved forward. This time, the ethereal sensation did not come.

When the car stopped and the door opened, Kevin's first instinct was to shut his eyes. This would be a cruel trick, he was sure. The app had taken what he wanted and twisted it in some way he couldn't have anticipated, like he'd wished upon the monkey's paw from that old, famous story. But he did not shut his eyes in time to avoid seeing the park, the outdoor basketball court. And there was no way to close his ears anyway, so he heard the distinct sound of sneakers squeaking, players calling for the ball, others calling out defensive assignments, and spectators cheering and heckling. Cheering primarily. Much of it regarding the kid.

This couldn't be any other moment. There were other happy days, other games and events Kevin had taken his nephew to in lieu of his departed brother-in-law, and Minerva, an ER nurse. But only one occasion could define happiness for him.

Micah had just turned fifteen a week before they went to the park. All he'd wanted for his birthday was to come to the court on the day a semi-pro internet star who made his living touring the country was arriving to play. There would be cameras, there would be fans, there would be serious ballers who had played in college, or played in overseas leagues, or had a drink of water in the NBA, or all of the above, present. And then there'd be the kid. Still a freshman in high school, and a natural on the court.

He hadn't even played his best ball that day, and was outplayed by a few other guys, but given how much older, bigger, and stronger they all were, to outplay the majority of them was remarkable, and people had noticed. He finished the day with several highlights and an immediate online buzz, his highlights even getting a few comments and likes from pros on social media.

It took them almost an hour to leave after the last game because children were asking Micah to sign their shoes or sign the ball they had brought with them that day; a few bloggers asked for, and received, short interviews with him, and several other players asked him to pose with them in pictures, all while telling him how impressed they were.

"Was I really that good out there, Unc?" Micah had said when they made it to Kevin's car, and for the first time, Kevin realized his nephew always said, "Unc" the way other kids said, "Pop," or "Dad."

"You were awesome," Kevin said. "You belonged out there. Don't ever question that."

He could have stepped out of the black car now and relived every part of that day. His best day. The perfect moment when Micah's work —and Kevin's contribution to that work—made a broken promise that would pay off in the best way possible. The moment his future seemed brightest, even in light of the scholarship offers and more to come later.

Kevin pulled the door closed, then shuddered in the dark, thinking of all the things the kid had earned and never seen. The moments robbed of him. Making it to the pros. Buying his mother a house with his first big check. Hoisting trophies. Becoming a hero and inspiration to others. So much more, none of it guaranteed, but much of it paid for in advance.

The kid had done more than worked, he'd sacrificed. So many people didn't understand that or didn't want to hear it. They just saw Micah as a boy born with gifts, who only had to stay out of his own way to live a spoiled, rich life. There was far more to it than that, but Kevin understood that line of thought. He'd had to fight against it at times himself when watching Micah glide past, or rise above, defenders on the court.

Who couldn't be a pro if they could do that? He sometimes thought. Yes, Micah had given up certain things others his age enjoyed to maximize his talent—late nights, lazy weekends, girlfriends, junk foods— but it was still less than a lot of other people, younger and older, had to give up to have even a fraction of the chance at a good life that he had. Kevin himself, for instance. How much of his time and energy had he given up to help his nephew fulfill his potential and pursue his dream?

"Not enough," Kevin whispered, and could almost imagine seeing a distant, flickering light, flames surrounded by so much night it should have been impossible to see the fire through it. Enough darkness to make you think you were alone in the universe. The depth of night he'd felt while pulling Micah away from the wreck, the feeling that somehow, even though his car was overturned and ablaze on the side of a commonly used road, their isolation in the seconds immediately after the accident would last forever, and nobody would find them.

Micah had needed help. His left leg—the one he would eventually lose after a dozen surgeries—was shattered in several places, and looked like something haphazardly grafted onto his body, never meant

to be part of him. He'd have been shrieking in pain were he not unconscious. Bleeding and swelling in his forehead hid a small dent in his
skull, and a brain bruise underneath that. He needed someone to get
him to a hospital, but nothing existed in all of reality other than the
wreck and his uncle. There were no hospitals. There were no para-
medics. There was no help coming.

A call for far more ordinary help had brought them here. "Unc, I
came out to this party for a bit, and my boy who drove me started
drinking. Can you come get me?"

Kevin had put it in Micah's head not to trust rideshare services.
"You've got to be careful. You never know who might be picking you
up." Had he any capacity to laugh about that now, he would have.

Looking back, even with the knowledge of what happened, Kevin
struggled to accept he shouldn't have gotten behind the wheel. He
hadn't had a drink since leaving a house party just before the dawn,
close to sixteen hours prior. His headache was still sharp and heavy,
forcing him to squint through the pain of it intermittently, but he'd
functioned through worse, he thought.

Yes, he was tired—he'd slept little in the past week while catching
up with friends back in town—but not too tired to come through for
his nephew and make sure the kid got home safely while his mother
worked a double-shift.

Certainly not so tired he'd pass out on the drive home, jerking
awake as Micah tried to reach over from the passenger side to steer the
car left, back onto the street, only to clip the roadside barrier and send
the car tumbling.

Kevin stared at the phone. The cursor blinked in the blank field.
Where to next?

He heard Micah's voice. *Literally anywhere. . .*

What if that wasn't limited to anywhere in the world, but anywhere
that *could* be?

He typed, *Where the accident never happened*, but did not push the
'Enter' key on the keypad.

If the car could take him to such a place, he didn't deserve to go to
there any more than he deserved to relive that perfect day at the
outdoor court. Micah deserved it. Or, no, that might be the worst thing

for the kid. The car could only take him to such a place, it couldn't transform him into the version of himself that existed there, could it? Even if it could, was that fair to him, to who he was now? Since the accident, Micah had worked harder than before, albeit to a different end. Instead of working to become the best athlete he was capable of being, he worked to fend off short-term memory loss, he worked to control mood swings born from frustration with sometimes not finding the right word, or not finding it quickly enough. He fought with the knowledge of who he used to be, the knowledge that he'd never be that person again, and the need to accept it. He worked hard simply to be decent.

"I just want to be good," he'd told Kevin during a quieter moment less than a month ago. "Just good, you know what I mean?"

Kevin had known exactly what the kid meant but didn't know how to tell Micah he was already there without patronizing him. The kid wanted to earn it, even if he already had it. Maybe because some things in his possession weren't easy to keep. The peace he felt from forgiving his uncle, for instance. Micah made it look easy, the way he used to make it look easy when he was toying with opponents on the court, but Kevin knew well that forgiveness took effort. A certain kind of strength. Micah had it. Kevin wondered if he could have found it, too, if he hadn't instead spent so much time searching for an escape from his guilt instead.

He closed his eyes to get away from the light of the phone. Maybe he didn't have to go anywhere else. Why couldn't he stay here until, one way or another, the darkness took him?

Because this isn't where it ends, he thought. Something else had to be waiting. Call it Heaven, call it Hell. Paradise or the abyss. Names didn't matter. *Location*. Destination. That mattered. Where are you going? Where do you deserve to go?

People described Heaven as though it were made of joy and love. He'd been taken to the place that defined happiness for him and sensed a grief waiting for him within it that scared him into hiding in the dark.

Hell, meanwhile, was supposedly built of pain and misery. And fire. He knew what his Hell would be.

He opened his eyes, stared at the phone.

Location.

He typed, *Wherever,* and almost hit the "Enter" key, but took a breath and a moment instead, and summoned the nerve to type the rest.

Wherever I deserve to go.

The engine revved, the car carried him off, and Kevin thought of Micah and the many others like him who never made it to the places they deserved to go. He thought of how such a fate was a tragedy for some, while for others it would be the ultimate blessing.

AFTERWORD

ALAN LASTUFKA

Projects as large and complex as *OBSOLESCENCE* don't happen in a vacuum. Earlier in this book, you heard from my friend, Naomi Grossman, and from my co-editor, Kristina Horner. Naomi, I appreciate your passion for the included stories; it was so much fun hearing your reactions as you read each piece. Kristina, it's been a long road getting here, but having you (virtually) by my side, made for an amazing journey. I can't tell you how much I appreciate you working on this with me.

But they are just two of the countless number of people who helped realize this project.

Everyone who promoted or backed our crowdfunding efforts on Kickstarter. All the fantastic writers who answered our open call (there were 628 of you!). Taylor Grothe and Rae Knowles, our early submissions readers. Erin Foster, our proofreader for everything. Morysetta, the digital artist who assisted me with designing the cover art. All our featured authors who signed on when this project was nothing more than an email pitch. And all our readers—without you, none of this would exist.

Finally, my partner Kris. The one who has continually put up with the late nights, the hurried meals, the mess of shipping boxes and packing supply tables set up around our home, and my brain being preoccupied with killer sound cues, or catching disc rot, or debating whether I should replace my veins with wires. . . thank you.

Thank you, all.

ABOUT THE AUTHORS

Kealan Patrick Burke is a five-time Bram Stoker Award-nominee who won the award for his coming-of-age novella *The Turtle Boy*. Burke is also the author of *Sour Candy, Kin, Blanky, The House on Abigail Lane,* and many other titles.

Find Kealan online at kealanpatrickburke.com

Adam Cesare is a New Yorker who lives in Philadelphia. He studied English and film at Boston University. He is the Bram Stoker Award-winning author of *Clown in a Cornfield, Tribesmen, Video Night,* and more. Adam is "an author who knows how to make us afraid." —Clive Barker

Find Adam online at adamcesare.wordpress.com

Clay McLeod Chapman writes books, comic books, children's books and for film. His most recent novel is *Ghost Eaters.*

Find Clay online at claymcleodchapman.com

Gemma Church is a sci-fi and speculative fiction writer. She recently received a diploma in creative writing from Cambridge University and her short stories have appeared in a range of publications. When Gemma isn't writing fiction, she works as a freelance science communicator and will happily talk to anyone about quantum computers, whether you want to hear about them or not. She has two degrees in physics, an obsession with puzzles, and lives near Cambridge, UK, with her husband, two children, and dog.

Johnny Compton is a San Antonio based author whose short stories have appeared in several publications since 2006, including *Pseudopod*, *Strange Horizons* and *The No Sleep Podcast*. His fascination with frightening fiction started when his kindergarten teacher played a record of the classic ghost story "The Golden Arm" for her class. *The Spite House* is his debut novel through Tor Nightfire.

Find Johnny online at johnnycompton.com

Lyndsey Croal is an Edinburgh-based author of speculative and strange fiction. She is a Scottish Book Trust New Writers Awardee and her work has appeared or is forthcoming in over fifty publications, including Mslexia's *Best Women's Short Fiction 2021*, *Dark Matter Magazine*, *Orion's Belt*, and Air and Nothingness Press. Her debut audio drama "Daughter of Fire and Water" was produced by Alternative Stories & Fake Realities and was a Finalist for a 2022 British Fantasy Award.

Find Lyndsey online at lyndseycroal.co.uk

Nicole Dieker is a writer, teacher, and musician. She began her writing career as a full-time freelancer with a focus on personal finance and habit formation; she launched her fiction career with *The Biographies of Ordinary People*, a definitely-not-autobiographical novel that follows three sisters from 1989 to 2016.

Currently, Dieker writes the *Larkin Day* mystery series and the perzine *WHAT IT IS and WHAT TO DO NEXT*, both of which are published through Shortwave Media. She also maintains an active freelance career; her work has appeared in Vox, Morning Brew, Lifehacker, Bankrate, Haven Life, Popular Science, and more. Dieker spent five years as writer and editor for The Billfold, a personal finance blog where people had honest conversations about money.

Dieker lives in Quincy, Illinois with the great love of her life, his piano, and their garden.

Find Nicole online at nicoledieker.com

Louis Evans definitely exists, probably. At least, the computers say he does. His writing has appeared in *Vice*, *The Magazine of Fantasy & Science Fiction*, *Nature: Futures*, and more.

Rob Hart is the author of *The Paradox Hotel*, as well as *The Warehouse*, which sold in more than 20 languages and was optioned for film by Ron Howard. He also wrote the short story collection *Take-Out*, and co-wrote *Scott Free* with James Patterson.

Rob is the former publisher for MysteriousPress.com and the current class director at LitReactor.

Find Rob online at robwhart.com

Laurel Hightower is the author of *Below*, *Whispers in the Dark*, and *Crossroads*, which won the This Is Horror Award for Novella of the Year. Laurel works as a paralegal in a mid-size firm, wrangling litigators by day and writing at night. A bourbon and beer girl, she's a fan of horror movies and true life ghost stories.

Find Laurel online at laurelhightower.com

Gabino Igelsias's work has been nominated for the Bram Stoker Award and the Locus Award, and won the Wonderland Book Award. He is the author of *The Devil Takes You Home*, *Zero Saints*, and *Coyote Songs*.

Find Gabino online at twitter.com/gabino_iglesias

Ai Jiang is a Chinese-Canadian writer and an immigrant from Fujian. She is a member of HWA, SFWA, and Codex. Her work can be found in F&SF, The Dark, Uncanny, The Puritan, Prairie Fire, The Masters

Review, among others. She is the recipient of Odyssey Workshop's 2022 Fresh Voices Scholarship and the author of *Linghun*.

Find Ai online at twitter.com/AiJiang_ and aijiang.ca

Simon Kewin is a fantasy and sci/fi writer, with over 400 publications to his name. He's the author of the *Cloven Land* fantasy trilogy, cyberpunk thriller *The Genehunter*, steampunk Gormenghast saga *Engn*, the *Triple Stars* sci/fi trilogy and the *Office of the Witchfinder General* books, published by Elsewhen Press. He's the author of several short story collections, with his shorter fiction appearing in *Analog*, *Nature* and many other magazines. His novel *Dead Star* was an SPSFC award semifinalist and his short story "#buttonsinweirdplaces" was shortlisted for a Utopia award.

Find Simon online at simonkewin.co.uk

Nick Kolakowski is the author of *Love & Bullets*, *Boise Longpig Hunting Club*, *Absolute Unit*, and other novels of crime and terror. His short stories have appeared in *Dark Moon Digest*, *Mystery Tribune*, *Thuglit*, *Rock and a Hard Place Magazine*, and various anthologies. He lives and writes in New York City, where he often hopes his building won't vaporize due to a malfunctioning time-travel device.

Find Nick online at nickkolakowski.com

Eric LaRocca (*he/they*) is the Splatterpunk Award-winning and Bram Stoker Award®-nominated author of several works of horror and dark fiction, including the viral sensation, *Things Have Gotten Worse Since We Last Spoke*. A lover of luxury fashion and an admirer of European musical theatre, Eric can often be found roaming the streets of his home city, Boston, MA, for inspiration.

Caitlin Marceau is a queer author and lecturer based in Montreal. She holds a Bachelor of Arts in Creative Writing, is an Active Member of the Horror Writers Association, and has spoken about genre literature at several Canadian conventions. She spends most of her time writing horror and experimental fiction, but has also been published for poetry as well as creative non-fiction. Her work includes *Palimpsest, Magnum Opus,* and her debut novella, *This Is Where We Talk Things Out.* Her second collection, *A Blackness Absolute,* and her debut novel, *It Wasn't Supposed To Go Like This,* are set for publication in 2023.

Find Caitlin online at caitlinmarceau.ca

Emma E. Murray writes horror and dark speculative fiction. Her stories have appeared in anthologies like *What One Wouldn't Do* as well as magazines such as *Vastarien, Pyre,* and *If There's Anyone Left.* When she's not writing, she loves playing pretend with her daughter and being an obnoxious bard in D&D.

Find Emma online at EmmaEMurray.com

Christi Nogle's debut novel, *Beulah,* is out now from Cemetery Gates Media and her collections *The Best of Our Past, the Worst of Our Future* and *Promise* are coming in 2023 from Flame Tree Press. Her short stories have appeared in over fifty publications including *PseudoPod, Vastarien,* and *Dark Matter Magazine* along with anthologies such as C.M Muller's *Nightscript* and Flame Tree's *American Gothic* and *Chilling Crime Stories.* Christi is a member of the Horror Writers Association, Science Fiction & Fantasy Writers of America, and Codex Writers' Group. She lives in Boise, Idaho with her partner Jim and their gorgeous dogs.

Find Christi online at christinogle.com

Ute Orgassa, Dipl.Soz.Päd. PhD, trained as a social worker and worked in the disability field. She has been writing stories her whole life. Born and raised in Germany, she now lives with her family in the Bay area.

Find Ute online at twitter.com/Scratchingcat

Tanya Pell has been published in multiple academic collections and edited two of her own. Her horror fiction has most recently appeared in Shortwave Magazine and *Well, This is Tense* with Bag of Bones Press. She is currently on submission with her YA horror novel and is represented by Cortney Radocaj of Belcastro Agency.

Find Tanya on Twitter or IG at @tanyacarinae.

Hailey Piper is the Bram Stoker Award-winning author of *Queen of Teeth, No Gods for Drowning, The Worm and His Kings,* and other books of dark fiction, with dozens of short stories in publication.

Find Hailey online at haileypiper.com.

Teagan Olivia Sturmer is a children's and adult author living on the stormy shores of Lake Superior, passionate about writing stories of girls who are stronger than they know. Teagan graduated from Northern Michigan University with a degree in Creative Writing and used that to pursue her love of Shakespeare, acting and directing in her local theatre, and studying the art of dramaturgy.

Having been diagnosed with General Anxiety Disorder and PTSD for most of her life, Teagan is passionate about telling stories of resilience. Stories of characters who discover the power of their own emotions, and use that power to overcome. Teagan lives in Michigan's wild Upper Peninsula with her husband, Brice, their sweet dogs, Remus and Rosie Cotton, and one rather persnickety calico cat, Phoebe. Teagan has been published in anthologies put out by Phantom House Press and Quill and Crow Publishing, and one forthcoming from Eerie River Publishing. Teagan is represented by Amy Giuffrida of the Belcastro Agency.

Find Teagan online at teaganoliviasturmer.com

Sara Tantlinger is the author of the Bram Stoker Award-winning *The Devil's Dreamland: Poetry Inspired by H.H. Holmes,* and the Stoker-nominated works *To Be Devoured* and *Cradleland of Parasites.* She has also edited *Not All Monsters* and *Chromophobia*. She embraces all things macabre and can be found lurking in graveyards or on Twitter @SaraTantlinger, at saratantlinger.com and on Instagram @inkychaotics

David Niall Wilson is a USA Today bestselling, multiple Bram Stoker Award-winning author of more than forty novels and collections. He is a former president of the Horror Writers Association and CEO and founder of Crossroad Press Publishing.

His novels include *This is My Blood, Deep Blue,* and many more. Upcoming works include the collection *The Devil's in the Flaws & Other Dark Truths,* and the novel *Tattered Remnants.* His most recent published work is the novel *Jurassic Ark*—a retelling of the Noah's Ark story. . . with dinosaurs. David lives in way-out-yonder NC with his wife Patricia and an army of pets.

Find David online at davidniallwilson.com and crossroadpress.com

Alex Woodroe is a Romanian writer and editor of dark speculative fiction. She's the author of Whisperwood (July 11th, 2023, Flame Tree Press) and the editor-in-chief of Tenebrous Press. You'll find her stories in the NoSleep podcast, Dark Matter Magazine, and more. She's passionate about infusing her country's culture, food, and folklore into her work, and loves talking shop at @AlexWoodroe.

Katie Young is a writer of dark fiction. Her work appears in various anthologies including collections by Scott J. Moses, Brigids Gate Press, Haunt Publishing, Dark Dispatch, Heads Dance Press, Nyx Publishing, Ghost Orchid Press, and Fox Spirit Books. She has been featured on the *Tales to Terrify* podcast, and her story, "Lavender Tea", was selected by Zoe Gilbert, author of *Folk,* for inclusion in the Mechanic Institute Review's Summer Folk Festival 2019. Katie is also a regular contributor to literary salons and storytelling events around London, where she lives with her partner, an angry cat, and too many books.

Find Katie online at katieyoungauthor.com

David Lee Zweifler spent decades writing non-fiction in jobs that took him around the world, including long stints in Jakarta, Hong Kong, and New York City. David's work has appeared in *Little Blue Marble*, *The Dread Machine*, and *Wyldblood*, and he has upcoming work in *Analog*. David resides with his family in New York's Hudson River Valley.

Find David online at davidleezweifler.com

ABOUT THE EDITORS

Alan Lastufka is a Hoffer Award-winning author and the owner of Shortwave, an independent small press. He writes horror, supernatural, and magical realism stories.

His debut novel, *Face the Night*, received a starred *Kirkus* review, was a finalist for Best New Horror Novel at the Next Generation Indie Book Awards, and won the 2022 Hoffer Award for Best Commercial Fiction. It was also listed as one of the 100 Best Indie Books of the Year by *Kirkus*.

When he's not writing, Alan enjoys walking through Oregon's beautiful woods with his partner, Kris.

Find Alan online at alanlastufka.com

Kristina Horner is an author who writes contemporary and urban fantasy for young adult and middle grade readers. She runs a small, independent publisher called 84th Street Press through which she has published multiple anthologies. She also created the writing podcast *How To Win NaNo*, has written for a number of tabletop RPGs, including *Vampire: The Masquerade* and has been a consistent winner of National Novel Writing Month since 2006.

Kristina lives and works out of her home in Seattle, Washington alongside her husband Joe and their son, Maximus. When she's not writing, she can be found in her garden or playing board games.

Find Kristina online at kristinahorner.com

SPECIAL THANKS

Abby Braunsdorf • Alexa K Moon • Amenze Oronsaye • Ashley Brennan • Ashley S. Riddlesworth • Ava Strough • Ben Zener • Bianca Crespo at Santa Mira Studio • Bongo • Bonnie Horner • Brian King • Brian Schrader • Bryan Greiner • Cameron Jones • Catherine Lu • Chance Forshee • Chandra Jentry • Charlotta • Chris Parker • Christopher Hawkins • Christopher Smith • Christopher Wheeling • Dai Baddley • Dana Krosta • Daniel Beer • Daniel Chong • Daniel E C • David Tomblin • David Worn • Dianne Garcia • Dom Ocampo • Emily Randolph-Epstein • Finneus Earnhardt-McClain • Fred W Johnson • Gage "oSpaceGhoat" Troy • Garrett Bowling • Hailey Claire Hull • Howard Blakeslee • IsJoleneAGhost • J.L. DuRona • James W. Hutchinson • Jason Bauder • Jenn Hammwyn • Jennifer Swagert • Jessica Richards • Joe Farro • Joel Sasaki • John Schlesinger • Jon Paul Anthony Hart • Jonathan Gensler • Jonny Wright • Jordee Taphouse • Joshua Elder • Josue Oyuela • Juan Viveros • Justin Lewis • Kaitlin Geddis • Kenny Endlich • Kristina Meschi • Landon Ranz • Lawrence Dunmore III • Liz Eddy • Liz Ling • M. G. Doherty • Maisy & Cassandra Kane • Maria Berejan • Marvin • Matt Ramsey • Matthew Standiford • Melanie B. • Michael J. Riser • Nicholas Stephenson • Parker Brennon • Paul Buchholz • Peter Rosch • R.J. Corvin • Rachael Scaccia • Richard Leis • Richard Patrick • Rob Jarosinski • Robert Brown • Roni Stinger • Ryan Marie Ketterer • S. R. Jenkins • Sabrina Elizabeth Cline • Sara Zeglin • Sarah Duck-Mayr • Stephanie Landas • Steve Ingleston • stevenduaneallisonjunior • Summer Yasoni • Susan Jessen • Tarhan Kayihan • Taylor Clarke • Tim Jordan • Tim Meyer • Trainor Houghton-Whyte • Veenie • Violet Jijing Covey • William Picard • Willow Redd

A NOTE FROM SHORTWAVE PUBLISHING

Thank you for reading *OBSOLESCENCE*!

If you enjoyed it, please consider writing a review or telling a friend!
Word-of-mouth helps readers find more titles they may enjoy and that,
in turn, helps us continue to publish more titles like this.

OUR WEBSITE
shortwavepublishing.com

SOCIAL MEDIA
@ShortwaveBooks

EMAIL US
contact@shortwavepublishing.com

ALSO AVAILABLE FROM SHORTWAVE PUBLISHING

Most of our titles are available everywhere books are sold. However, some titles have exclusive editions, signed bookplates, or other deluxe variations available exclusively from our online shop. For our current catalog, please visit **shop.shortwavepublishing.com**

BOOK OF THE FUTURE — ALAN LASTUFKA & KRISTINA HORNER

Want even more *OBSOLESCENCE*?

Inspired by their work on this anthology, co-editors Alan Lastufka and Kristina Horner wrote the companion short story, "Book of the Future". Available now, exclusively from Shortwave Publishing's shop.

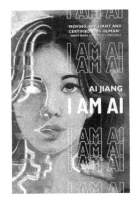

I AM AI — AI JIANG

"Moving, brilliant, and certified 100% human." –Samit Basu, author of *Turbulance*

In *I AM AI*, a cyborg struggles to retain her humanity while grappling with demanding and toxic relationships at work and at home, in a city that never blinks.

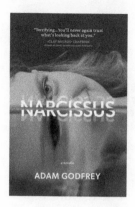

NARCISSUS – ADAM GODFREY

If the remainder of your life was only as long as your ability to avoid your own reflection, how long would you last?

"Terrifying. . . You'll never again trust what's looking back at you." –Clay McLeod Chapman, author of *Ghost Eaters* and *Quiet Part Loud*

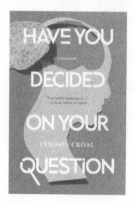

HAVE YOU DECIDED ON YOUR QUESTION – LYNDSEY CROAL

"Instantly immersive. . ." –Ai Jiang, author of *Linghun*

If you could live your life over again, what would you ask to change? Something big? Something small? A single moment? Have you decided on your question?

Zoe has. . .

A COLD THAT BURNS LIKE FIRE – CAITLIN MARCEAU

An erotic-horror reimagining of a French-Canadian folk tale, "A Cold That Burns Like Fire" is a complete, standalone short story chapbook with four full-page illustrations by the author. Exclusive to the Shortwave Publishing shop.

MAMA BIRD – CLAY MCLEOD CHAPMAN

"Mama Bird" is the dark and unsettling tale of a young picky eater and the mother willing to do anything to feed her child.

This is a complete, standalone short story chapbook and the first issue of the *Chapman Chapbooks* series. The second issue, "Baby Carrots", is also available.

ODE TO MURDER – NICOLE DIEKER

Larkin Day is a Millennial-aged amateur detective who practices old-fashioned sleuthing in a world of smart phones and social media. The second Larkin Day mystery, *Like, Subscribe, and Murder*, is also available.

"A smart, snarky series. . . Cozy mystery readers will adore Larkin Day." –*BookLife*, Editor's Pick

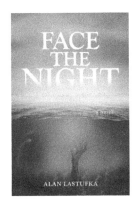

FACE THE NIGHT – ALAN LASTUFKA

Adriana Krause has an eerie gift for drawing faces. Will one terrifying vision tear apart everything she loves?

Face the Night is "Outstanding. . . reminiscent of early works by Stephen King and Peter Straub. An impressive, complex horror tale—two (rotting) thumbs up." –*Kirkus Reviews*, starred

CPSIA information can be obtained
at www.ICGtesting.com
Printed in the USA
LVHW030410030323
740309LV00006B/18/J